Evil Harvest

Evil Harvest

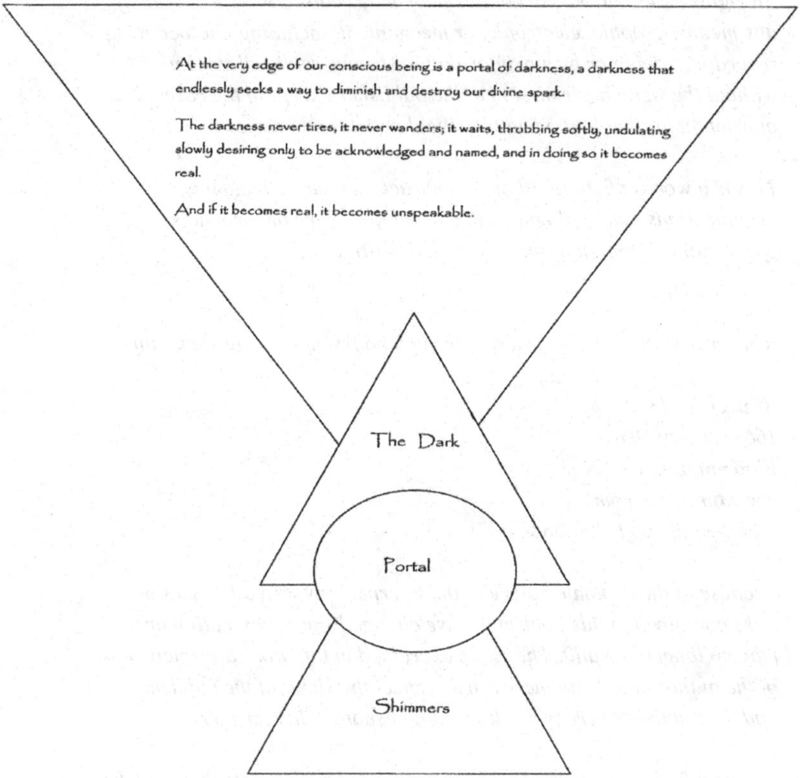
At the very edge of our conscious being is a portal of darkness, a darkness that endlessly seeks a way to diminish and destroy our divine spark.
The darkness never tires, it never wanders; it waits, throbbing softly, undulating slowly desiring only to be acknowledged and named, and in doing so it becomes real.
And if it becomes real, it becomes unspeakable.
The Dark
Portal
Shimmers

WENDY RITCHIE

iUniverse LLC
Bloomington

Evil Harvest

iUniverse books may be ordered through booksellers or by contacting:

iUniverse LLC
1663 Liberty Drive
Bloomington, IN 47403
www.iuniverse.com
1-800-Authors (1-800-288-4677)

ISBN: 978-1-4917-1077-7 (sc)
ISBN: 978-1-4917-1079-1 (hc)
ISBN: 978-1-4917-1078-4 (e)

Library of Congress Control Number: 2013918801

Printed in the United States of America.

iUniverse rev. date: 11/25/2013

This book is dedicated with love to my mother Margery, for her lipstick kisses and afternoons of childhood bliss sitting in the red recliner, listening to her heartbeat and the sound of her voice reading from the Children's Golden Book of Poems. To my beloved Christy for reaching out to capture me in her gently waiting hand, and to Anthony, who read with me by candlelight and the light from the Man in the Moon.

PROLOGUE: 1875

The raising of the barn had been the event of the year, bringing every farmer and craftsman in a twenty-five mile radius for the construction. Brandon Grimmer, the property owner, was been a successful merchant in nearby Lamont, and his purchase of this prime piece of property caused much talk among the neighbors and town inhabitants.

Local gossip came to a head when Brandon returned from a trip to Cambridge, Massachusetts and brought a young bride with him. He had always good naturedly spoken of his confirmed bachelorhood as set in stone, so when he returned with his bride, Annaleah, a collective gasp was heard around the county. Several eligible young women, once companions of Brandon, cried more than a few tears and were anxious to see what Annaleah had that they did not.

Brandon found in Annaleah the peaceful grace and gentle beauty that he so craved. Her bangs, cut to the middle of her forehead, framed her willowy, soft and startlingly green eyes like a picture. Another cause for whispers was that she shied away from long sleeves and high collars that smothered other women. Being a good seamstress, she instead made dresses for herself that had some sleeves above her elbow and collars cut to the base of her neck that were considered quite scandalous. The fact that they seemed natural for her kept the whispers relatively short-lived. Had these same people seen her sundresses, which she wore only in the privacy of their back yard and garden, the whispers may have continued unabated.

Her olive colored skin, inherited from her original Italian bloodline, was the secrete envy of the pale, milk colored skinned ladies of the day, and husbands, brothers and sons spoke among themselves of how healthy and robust she looked compared to the majority of the local women. Brandon did not listen to the foolish prattle of jealous women; rather he reveled in the unusual beauty and grace Annaleah brought not only to their home, but to their town.

The house he built for his beloved Annaleah was impressive but not grandiose. It was a home of gatherings and festivities, a magical place with rooms of books where in quiet solitude you could step through a portal of time through words.

The people of Lamont soon came to love Annaleah, and strangely enough, several former companions of Brandon, once jealous of him choosing Annaleah over them, came to be friends with her. She won them over with the same thing that had ignited Brandon's adoration of her, kindness, grace and unassuming humility.

It was no wonder then, that the actual construction in 1874 provided a considerable amount of anticipation and fanfare. Once the barn's planning and design were complete and materials arrived, the raising began the first week of September. Annaleah organized a picnic, which included breakfast, lunch and dinner over a two-day period. Brandon's workers erected in the shade of several silver maples, two large tents; cooking pits were stationed in the area for roasting several whole pigs whose cavities were stuffed with fresh chickens, sage, rosemary and apples, then trussed and put to the spit over a fire of hickory wood logs that caused the fat and skin to sizzle and crackle. Eager young boys volunteered to turn the spit slowly, the scent, mingled with the aroma of a side of beef roast with a caramelized crust, filled the air for what seemed miles around. When the workers finally sat to table for dinner the first day, it was truly a table of plenty.

After the completion of the barn, Brandon bought five horses; a butternut bay, two quarter horses for him and Annaleah to ride their property, and two Arabians with which he hoped to start a breeding program. Fresh hay filled the lofts above the stables. It smelled of sunshine and warmth and the aroma mingled with the sweet scent of molasses-dressed grain and the dusty golden sawdust that covered the stable floor. They painted the barn a beautiful deep red with white trim around the peak, windows and the cross hatch on the sliding door. The shingles were of black locust, abundant from Pennsylvania to Northern Georgia, the color and texture complementing the color of the barn.

The couple so loved the barn that Brandon enhanced a ten by twelve foot area in the middle of the east wall for reading and relaxing. They did not furnish the area with chairs, rugs, or household items, but with soft foams of hay and blankets on which they could recline. They would retire to that special place, which was warm from sunlight cascading through the panes of glass in the cupola, and there they would read aloud to one another, the sound of their voices serene and peaceful.

But by far the best time was sunset with the big double doors pulled wide so they could watch the sun begin its decent towards night, emblazing the sky with colors no artist could capture; yellow, red, gold, amber and deep purple. As they lay side by side on those evenings, watching the magic of the world saying its last sultry goodbye of the day, it seemed nothing could dampen or dispel their happiness.

In February of 1875, Annaleah had taken Brandon into her arms and whispered what he longed to hear, that she was with child. For Brandon it was his moment in time of perfect contentment and love; a celebration that would make the circle of life complete. And so, it was with unbridled joy that they planned the baby's room in anticipation of the birth that was expected at the end of October.

On the morning of the last Saturday of October, Brandon had kissed Annaleah goodbye as he and Shawn, his farm manager, made ready to ride the property to plan spring planting. Annaleah, now heavy with child and due any day, could no longer ride with them.

It was quiet in the house. Sarah their housekeeper had sent the two young girls that helped clean to Lamont for supplies.

Sarah herself was going for a quick visit to her cousin that day, with plans to return by early evening.

It seemed to Annaleah a good day to spend in the reading room or the 'quiet room' as she called it, because it was far away from the rest of the house and afforded a sanctuary for reading in the high comfortable chair with a footstool that Brandon had built for her. Now, at the end of her pregnancy, when she reached the reading room she remained for quite some time because she tired easily. Sarah had made a pot of hot chamomile tea and a plate of fresh oatmeal cookies, Annaleah's favorites, and confirmed all was in order before leaving for her visit.

By late morning, Annaleah was dozing on and off, floating in that golden place before sleep where relaxation is complete and all consuming. The faint smell of smoke was not alarming to her because she knew that Sara had banked the oven after her baking and was sure the fireplace grate in the living room was in place. Sarah never forgot because she knew well of Annaleah's fear of a log rolling off onto her favorite rug.

Annaleah drifted between wakefulness and dreams, thinking that when Brandon came home they should go to the barn for a while, to watch the sun go down during this beautiful time of year. She smiled to herself thinking how he would fuss that there was now a chill in the air, but she knew she would win the discussion with the promise of a warm shawl and warmer kisses. The golden place closed around her and she gave herself over to peaceful sleep.

Meanwhile, Brandon and Shawn were resting their horses and taking lunch under the fat oak tree that reminded anyone looking at it of a ladies opened fan; a tree with a wide trunk that turned into a 'V' of branches so perfected by nature that no gardener, no matter how good their pruning skills, could hope to replicate. Sarah had packed sliced roast chicken on hearty homemade bread with the last of the lettuce that she kept warm under a blanket of straw in the garden, along with corn salad and crisp apples, while the icy clear creek nearby offered cool drinks that quenched their thirst.

The horses were grazing contentedly nearby, and as Brandon and Shawn stood, brushing away a few crumbs from their pants and preparing to pack up the saddlebag, it began.

The horses suddenly snapped their heads simultaneously, and began pacing and whinnying, their nostrils flared wide, their eyes glassy with fear.

As Brandon and Shawn rushed over to grab the reins and steady their horses, wondering what in the world could have spooked them, they both saw at the same time black billowing smoke in the northeast, a hideous hot orange glow lighting the sky.

No words in any language could explain the terror, dread and pain that coursed through Brandon's body like a jolt of lightning.

"No," he breathed, "dear God, *no*!" He swung into his saddle in one fluid motion slapping his horse's reins so hard they cracked like a whip.

A mind-numbing pain overcame him . . . he could not think—he could not reason—he could not imagine. He could only ride. Ride towards the billowing smoke, a man possessed. He could hear Shawn thundering behind him. He was vaguely aware of Shawn calling out something, but his mind could not process the words, his body could not stop the punishing beating of the reins against the flanks of his horse, whose eyes were now bulging, and corded muscles strained to the point of snapping

Nothing ever imagined, no book he had ever read, could prepare Brandon for what he saw as he crested the last hill. Never in his darkest nightmare had a glimmer of this hell been formed into thought or word.

His house was engulfed in flames. Flames vomited from every window, from every door, and blasted out of the crumbling chimneys as mortar exploded, driven by a hurricane force that screamed and keened in a high-pitched inferno. Dante's madness come to fruition.

The roof caved in like an inverted pyramid, and then like well placed dominos, the entire structure began to fold in upon itself. Sparks shot into the sky to pour down like searing rain, a shower of death; fire so hot that leaves on nearby trees smoldered and ignited in one section after another, small novas of blinding light and heat.

As if in slow motion, Brandon realized his horse was falling. Somehow, within his frozen thoughts he knew the terrified animal had died beneath him, and as it fell, he wondered if his heart would explode too. Somehow, he rolled to the side and felt more than heard something inside him break. He felt arms pulling him free, and he saw a dark form above him, a square chin he knew, something familiar—but a voice so twisted with emotion, grating and raw that he could not be sure it was Shawn.

Brandon lay limply on his right side as the last of the burning inferno collapsed. In that moment the light in his eyes went out. The husband that he was, the father he would have been, stopped like a forgotten clock, his heart never to be wound again by the love that gave him life.

Four days later the ashes of Annaleah and her unborn child were laid to rest under a cobalt blue sky in the high, sweet grass outside their barn. Brandon, disheveled and drawn, fell to his knees, his hands clawing the loose dirt covering his wife and child, the scream tearing from him was more terrible than anything those attending had ever heard. They turned away, faces ashen, eyes blank in sorrow and disbelief.

Shawn found Brandon later that day, on foam of hay along the east wall of the barn, the double doors open, awaiting the setting sun. He sat with Brandon's body, watching the last light of day quiet into the night sky, watching until he saw a shooting star . . . and he knew beyond the wisdom of reason or the explanation of words that they were together again.

Somewhere a clock chimed softly one last time, *Annaleah.*

CHAPTER 1

Early May 2011

Army and Danni Petrucci wanted to raise their son outside of the city, and spent six months looking for a property they could call home. After inquiring with realtors, responding to ads in the paper and internet searches, as fate would have it, on a sunny Saturday during a drive they had stumbled across the perfect piece of property. They had fallen in love with the view and solitude and that even though they were not too far from the city of Lamont they technically lived in the country.

The Grimmer Property was devoid of a house but the surrounding rolling hills and the beautiful barn had gotten their interest. The property had long been vacant and much of the acreage sold from a trust that had been in the family of one Shawn O'Farrell since late 1876.

Army and Danni wanted their twelve-year-old son, Anthony, to grow up somewhere that he could lay back and watch the clouds go by; the Grimmer property was the perfect place. Army and Danni had a few small investments and by tightening their belts, changing their life style from eating out three nights a week, renting the latest movie releases and trips to the mall, they had discovered another 10% of available money.

The bank appraisal and subsequent loan had gone through slowly because of the housing collapse but finally the split-level house plans were approved and the builder had completed construction several days early, which gave them some extra time to move.

On the last Saturday of April, after they had been in their new home for two full weeks, Danni and Army were getting ready to run some errands in town. Anthony, tired of the constant back and forth trips, had asked if he could stay at the house and play in the barn until they returned.

After discussing the request for a moment, Army and Danni had agreed, with the stern admonition from Danni that he was not to be jumping from the loft while they were not there.

Anthony rolled his eyes up at the sky in a half-moon sweep as though he were watching for a winged alien lizard to drop from the clouds and save him from having to agree with his mom.

"Anthony I mean it," Danni said, her voice rising on the first syllable of his name as if she were affirming that his hearing had not suddenly been shut off like a cheap set of headphones.

"I won't Mom, I'm just gonna swing on the rope Dad put up."

Danni turned to look at Army, whose head appeared connected to an invisible line that pulled it in the opposite direction of her gaze, and he dropped the car keys stooping to pick them up hoping to end this particular line of conversation.

"Ok bye, see ya!" said Anthony as he galloped away full speed toward the barn, reaching the double doors at the same time he heard the crunch of the car's tires turning out of the driveway.

He did not know what it was about the barn, but for him, it seemed to have a voice of its own, a voice that whispered softly to him and made him feel welcome. He could not put it into words, he only knew being here made him feel something special.

The doors creaked softly when Anthony slid them open, and as always, it almost sounded like a name that he could not quite hear or make sense of, so as most twelve year-old boys would do, he absently pushed the thought aside as sunlight streamed through into the interior.

The swing that Army had put up several days before was a wondrous thing indeed. Army had purchased 65 feet of rope from Kaller's Hardware; 2 inches in diameter double twined reinforced, it looked as though you could tie off the Titanic. His mom had picked it out.

"Danni," Army had said at the time of the purchase, "how am I going to tie this off at the top? It's so thick I don't know if I can loop it!"

Danni, her eyebrows raised and a slight smile on her lips had said, "Well hon, if you *really* want Anthony to be able to swing forty feet across the barn jumping from a stack of hay, I'm sure you'll figure it out."

Hanging the rope had turned out to be more hazardous than the actual swing itself. Army and Anthony had spent an entire morning standing in the barn looking up until their necks hurt trying to figure out just how Army was going to get up there.

The fact that the wood beams were solid oak was the cause of the issue of how to tie off the rope at the top of the beam. Army remembered an old Boy Scout knot called a round turn with two half hitches that was excellent for securing rope to a post or ring. They practiced on one of the beams across an old stall until Army was positive he remembered it and that it would work. Problem solved.

The two-story aluminum ladder had been pulled all the way out allowing Army just barely enough room to climb onto the load-bearing beam. Once there, he tied himself off with another rope just in case he lost his balance, and shimmied side to side to until he finally reached the middle where the rope was intended to hang. The fact that the rope was tied around his mid-section did not ring a danger bell with two individuals of the male species whose minds were focused like laser beams on being the first to 'fly' across the barn and drop into the huge pile of hay on the other side.

On that unusually warm spring afternoon, under cover of Danni's grocery shopping, Anthony and his dad had accomplished just that feat and Army had finished tying the mammoth knot at the bottom of the rope on which they would sit, wrap their legs around and hold on for dear life.

"Dad," asked Anthony, "could we pile a couple bales of hay up and jump off?"

When Army looked at the height of it, he knew Danni would not approve, but then he thought they were probably in deep enough trouble as it was and a couple more bales of hay would not change the outcome of the tongue-lashing they were both destined to receive.

"Yep," said Army, "I think that would be a good launch point son."

The day was hot, and as they sweated, hay dust was sticking to their exposed skin and forearms, and soon their faces began to turn a light sooty gray. When the pile of hay bales was ready they both stood back to admire their work.

"Who goes first?" asked Anthony, his eyes wide in anticipation. Beads of sweat formed on his upper lip along with dirt that looked slightly like a ridiculous pencil mustache

The father-turned-boy-again struggled with wanting to be the first one to grab the rope, climb up the stack of hay and jump, sure that he would feel the adrenalin coursing through him like a test pilot before takeoff.

Instead he said, "You first kiddo, let's see if you can fly!"

Army climbed up the bales with his son and steadied the rope while Anthony figured out how to hold and jump onto the knot for the first time. Anthony looked at his dad, who winked at him and said, "Better get this over with before your mom gets home."

As Anthony launched himself onto the rope, it was with such a feeling of fear mingled with wild expectation that later he did not remember the actual jump itself. What he remembered was the sensation of sailing across the barn as everything flew by in a blur, coming to the apex of his forward momentum and starting back, turning his body slightly so that he could see his dad's face covered in one huge smile rushing towards him with what seemed incredible speed.

As his body came up to the stacked bales of hay he heard his dad shout out, "Drop into the hay on the other side!"

The pendulum of the swing began its rush back toward the far side of the barn. Anthony had a split second to think, *I have to let go,* and he realized how hard he had been gripping the rope with his hands and legs. Let go he did, and that momentary freefall was a dizzying experience, floating through the air to come down in the soft pungent hay. When he landed, hay motes flew upward like a tornado above him, millions of them, caught in the shaft of light razoring through the cracks in the barn siding and looking to Anthony like fairy dust from a magical land.

"Whhooooo!" Army heard his son yelling in glee. "Come on Dad, its great!"

The rope hadn't come all the way back when Army half hopped half slid down the bales to grab it and make a dash back up to the jumping point. When he launched, his legs locked around the knot and he felt himself flying and, for the most fleeting of moments, he was twelve again. Blood pounding through him in an intoxicating rush he pushed off the opposite wall, his added body weigh taking him even further, and at the height of the swing the exhilaration of letting go. WHOOSH! He hit the deep pile of hay, and he heard the sweet sound of his son's giddy laughter.

"Let's go again!" said Anthony in a high, excited voice. "Come on Dad, c*ome on!*"

"Wait!" another voice said.

It was Danni.

"Oh boy, here it comes," Army said softly to Anthony, and they stood waiting for the storm to rain down on them.

"Wait," she said again, urgency in her voice, "I have to run and get the camera!"

It was such a good day, one of the best. Anthony and his dad actually got Danni to swing on the rope several times. Once, when they were all laying in the hay laughing and talking, Anthony thought he heard that soft voice again coming from somewhere in the barn. He cocked his head slightly for a moment, listening, and felt a stirring deep within him, something that he could not name or touch.

"Anthony?" his mom asked, "Are you ok—just tired?"

He thought for a moment and said, "Just hungry I think."

"Come on then you two," said Army, "let's rinse off and I'll light the grill." He turned to Danni. "Did you get the hotdogs and burgers hon?"

"No," replied Danni, watching the disappointed looks on both their faces. A smile turned up the corners of her mouth as she said, "I upgraded to steak!"

With a loud whoop, the father and son did what they later called the 'steak dance' and the three made their way back towards the house to shower. Later they grilled steak, charbroiled potatoes, and had a crisp fresh salad. They finished off the meal by eating warm peach cobbler topped with a brown sugar cinnamon crust that Danni had brought home from the store.

When Anthony crawled into bed that night scrubbed and full, he glanced at the barn in the light of the waning moon. *It was a good day*, he heard somewhere in his mind. The voice was soft and gentle, a woman's voice, but not his moms. *That's weird,* he thought as he drifted off to sleep.

The feather soft brush of lips upon his brow went unnoticed.

It was the third Friday in May and Anthony was off from school because of parent/teacher conferences. Danni and Army had elected to have him finish out the school year at his original school and today was the last meeting they would have with his teacher. After they arrived back home Anthony had hurried down the hill behind their house to wade in the icy water of the creek at the bottom of a ravine overlooked by a beautiful ancient oak tree. His feet ached with the cold, but oh, how wonderful it felt, as they sunk ever so slightly into the soft and silky mud.

He was bent over with both arms up to their elbows in the clear cold water, one hand moving ever so slowly to remove a small rock where he saw a crawfish hiding, his other hand was cupped at the top of the stone where he thought it may jet to in its effort to escape. Slowly he moved the rock and as the crawfish jetted towards his awaiting hand, an unexpected voice right next to him surprised him.

"Hey, who are *you*?"

Startled, Anthony pitched forward splashing down into the cold water his knees sinking into that same soft mud were his feet had just been. His shorts wicked up the icy water to his groin, causing him to draw a quick breath through his teeth, as the crawfish escaped.

Anthony started to stand up, staggered, lost his balance and ended up sitting down hard on the bank behind him. A pair of yellow tennis shoes, brown knees, and ragged shorts now joined the voice he had heard, and as his eyes moved up they came to rest on a crop of reddish brown hair and a face covered in freckles.

"Who the heck *are* you?" the boy asked again.

"Who the hell are *you*?" said Anthony, feeling that a good swear word or two was now in order.

"I'm Sammy, I live over that way," said the boy pointing with his thumb over his shoulder. "You need a hand up?"

"Yeah, sure," said Anthony. As he reached up to grasp the hand Sammy offered, he found himself abruptly yanked to his feet.

"So what's your name?" asked Sammy again.

"Anthony," he said, as the two boys locked eyes for the first time.

"Ok. Well, hate to tell you this Tony," said Sammy as he sat down on a rock "but . . ."

"It's not Tony. It's Anthony."

"Oh. Ok. An-tho-ny, said Sammy drawing out the o. "Well anyhow, you're not going catch those mud-bugs without a net, and," he said with a slightly smug smile, "I just happen to have one."

Anthony chuckled as a grin stole across his face pulling the left side of his mouth slightly higher. "Hate to tell you this Sam-u-el, but I already caught five." He pointed to a plastic bucket a few feet away.

A heartbeat of silence passed between them, and then the freckled face boy said, "It's Sammy, not Sam-u-el. So, show me what ya got."

The boys spent the remainder of the day becoming acquainted. They waded in the creek catching several more crawfish that they eventually let go, and they walked through a field finding and eating some wild blackberries both ending up with darkly stained lips and fingers from the sweet, sticky juice. They learned some very important things about each other, as important things between two boys go. Anthony could burp louder and longer than anyone Sammy had ever heard before and Sammy could make a louder arm-fart than Anthony could. At one point Anthony pulled his shorts up to his chest and did an impression of Jethro from the '60's *Beverly Hillbillies* sitcom, making Sammy laugh so hard he really did fart.

From that afternoon on, they spent every moment possible hanging out together. Each morning, after gulping down their breakfast, (Reese's Puffs being Anthony's favorite and Toaster Strudel Sammy's) they would sprint out their respective doors with an admonition from their mother's to 'be careful' and meet somewhere in between their houses.

Everything interested the two boys and they never ran out of things to talk about, pick up, crawl over, wade through, or read.

It turned out both boys were voracious readers. They shared books about outer space and books about inner space, books about deep-sea exploration, and books about bugs, dragons, magic, and monsters.

Sammy was the bigger daredevil of the two, and one day he decided to launch himself at Anthony off a low branch. "I vont to darink your blooood!" he yelled in his best Transylvanian accent, his every intent being to land on Anthony and roll him to the ground thus claiming victory. However, much to his lament, his shorts caught on a small stub of branch, which not only abruptly stopped his planned fall but also yanked his underwear into the worst most painful wedgie in the annals of recorded history. Sammy's eyes bulged as he struggled to unhook himself from the branch and then jumped around trying desperately to pull his underwear from the dark recess of his rear end. Anthony had laughed so hard he cried.

Galloping through the fields or swinging from the rope inside the barn they could be *Frankenstein* or *Dracula*, the *Mummy* or *Wolfman*; they took off to Mars, they explored the ocean bottom and found Black Beard's treasure chest and took turns riding the dragon of their dreams, emerald green with red tipped wings and golden oval eyes. Who was the hero and who was the victim changed daily and life could not be any better.

Each day seemed to be a kaleidoscope of new adventures for the two friends. It was no surprise to the parents of either boy that one of their favorite places was the barn, and the now famous swing. Early on Anthony and Sammy found it difficult to fly on the swing together so they lost no time in rigging a double knot. The extra weight caused them to swing much higher which of course made for longer hang time when they let go and free fell into the awaiting pile of hay.

Bologna sandwiches with lots of horseradish mustard, or peanut butter with sliced bananas and honey on soft white bread washed down with an ice cold root beer made life all the sweeter.

They found the east wall, which was the back of the barn, their favorite place to have lunch and read. That area seemed almost out of place in the barn, it felt more designed and separate. It was a place of peace and quiet as odd as that sounded, and often they would take a nap there because the built in chests were perfect to sleep on with a rolled up shirt.

On the nights they slept out in the barn, they found that sunset was spectacular from that particular vantage point. It was there that they discovered their affinity for telling their own stories, the scarier the better. If it had fangs dripping with blood or carried a chain saw and wore a hockey mask, it really rocked. As the cool light green of spring turned into the emerald green of July and then the hard military green of August, they ran across the crisp, dry grass and breathed in the dusty aroma of late summer forming a bond that forever change their destiny.

Nothing they could have imagined in their wildest flights of fantasy could have prepared them for what was soon to come to life by the light of dozens candles in a house not 10 minutes away.

He was a strange, unsettling man who kept mostly to himself. When he came to town, he would smile and talk to himself, and people went out of their way to cross the street or go into a store if they saw him coming their way. If anyone had taken the time to look closely at that smile, they would have seen something darkly evil and predatory. A twisted smile that appeared like a slash made with a hunting knife across a piece of leather pulled too tight, much like the mouth of a shark ready to feed, all teeth, eyes rolled back in its head.

He felt no mercy, he had no remorse, for he had no soul; it already belonged to the Dark One.

What he craved and desired was insatiable. He existed to gorge himself on death, inhale the coppery intoxicating smell of blood, and revel in the delicious horror in the eyes of the chosen one.

It was always . . . exquisite.

CHAPTER 2

Kaller's Hardware was located at the corner of West Park Ave. and Main St. and been in the same location since 1915. Tim Kaller had started the business and sold everything from tools, to bolts of cloth, hats, and even shoes. It still had the same oak floorboards burnished smooth by the thousands of steps taken by the town's inhabitants while looking for their plumber's putty, Fells Naphtha soap and orange shellac. The perimeter wood floor outside of the traffic areas was dark from years of cleaning with Bob's Wheelbarrow Soap. The floorboards creaked deliciously, and no matter where you were in the store, Tim would know exactly in which aisle you where shopping. Bob and Tim Jr., TJ for short, took over ownership of the store when their father died unexpectedly, choking on a pickle plucked from the briny, salty barrel kept to the right of the register.

No one was in the store when it happened so the townsfolk could only try to surmise the circumstances surrounding Tim's death. In piecing together the evidence, it looked as though while eating a pickle he had choked on it, and while choking, he staggered about the floor bumping into a display of hammers. As he fell, a 3lb short handled sledge had fallen and cracked his skull.

Only one person in town knew that Lamont had experienced its first murder. That in reality, someone had grabbed Tim's head as he stood near the pickle barrel and in one fluid motion snatched up a jumbo green pickle and shoved it down a surprised Tim's throat. That same person stood for a minute finding pleasure in the gurgling wet sound coming from poor, wild-eyed Tim. He had taken Tim, who was now blue faced and clawing at his own throat, by his shirt and yanked him across the floor, picked up a nice big shiny new hammer and slammed it into the back of poor Timmy's head, pleased with the crunching sound accompanying the blow. As Tim fell forward, his right arm swept a half dozen other hammers onto the floor as he slumped glassy eyed against the shelf.

At the funeral, Tim's wife and two sons stood in mute shock. The boys flanked either side of their mother and protectively put their arms around her helping to support her in her grief. Neither of them took notice of the man to their right with a slight smile on his face, a smile that each of them had seen before when working at their father's store. If they had noticed Jigs, they would have only remembered that his attempts to joke with them had always made them uncomfortable.

It was unlikely they would have remembered that he always bought a pickle.

The people of Lamont did not like James Ivan Garvin Seederly, known around town as 'Jigs,' he was simply tolerated. There wasn't any one specific thing they could pinpoint about him that they disliked or mistrusted, he just gave most people an unsettled feeling, or the 'creeps' as some called it. Usually it made you look over your shoulder at him when he passed, just to make sure he had not stopped and turned around to smile at you with an unsettling expression on his face, one that lifted the left corner of his lip much like a rabid dog might do before it attacked. It was almost as if he knew something about you that you did not want anyone else to know, personal things done in the privacy of your home with the curtains drawn and the lights out.

Jigs always made it his business to go to every funeral in town whether he knew the deceased or not. In reality, even if he had known the dearly departed, they still would not want him at the services, but there was no way to keep him out without causing a scene, and he knew that.

Jigs would wait in line with the mourners; standing silently, hands folded that odd, feral smile on his face. He always wore a gray suit that appeared covered with little fuzz balls, a shirt that at one time was probably white but was now gray, and a black tie with small yellow dots and its share of food stains.

He would spend a lot of time standing by the coffin gazing down at the dearly departed with a look that feigned sadness. However, in actuality Jigs lingered overly long near the coffin, lost in dark thoughts of evil deeds and horrific acts, and he so liked the underlying smell of a corpse.

After the service, he always made his way to the church basement for the usual bereavement meal. Prepared by the Women's Guild, it was the customary Rotini in marinara sauce, iceberg lettuce salad with Thousand Island dressing, rolls, 2 types of pie, and hot coffee. He always sat alone, and if anyone was looking for a seat and the only one was next to Jigs, well, they would just stand along the block wall to eat their food.

"I'm glad I came," he would say, seemingly more to himself than anyone nearby. Never, *I'm sorry about your loss.* He was not sorry; he liked death, he liked suffering that was why he attended. He knew no one wanted him there, but again, that is why he went to the trouble of putting on his gray suit. The more suffering he could feel around him the better *he* felt—it was a thrumming feeling, like a battery charging. He would say to himself, *Jigs is getting jazzed up!* By the end of the church luncheon, he was literally humming like a warm motor.

When it was time to leave he always headed straight home where he hurriedly changed from his suit into old, dirty, gray sweatpants with a matching sweatshirt that was equally as grimy, grab a set of keys from a hook inside a cupboard door and make a beeline to his shed, or what he called the *Hell Hole*.

The 12x14 foot shed looked normal on the outside, unless you looked closely and saw the triple core lock, the hardened steel latch, clasp and hinges. The inside had one single shop light overhead and an assortment of gardening tools all still shiny and clean, except for a misshapen shovel that sported a badly bent tip.

Besides murder, Jigs seemed to have an aptitude for woodworking, and over the years, he had collected, stolen and bought an assortment of tools, (many from Kaller's hardware store where poor Tim had met his demise at the end of that pickle). In the middle of the back wall under the never used grill was a cleverly hidden hatch that led to a 24 x 14 foot underground room that he had giddily named the *Hell Hole*. Jigs had ever so patiently fashioned the boards for the floor so that they perfectly mirrored each other. Instead of plywood or particle wood, Jigs had milled poplar wood into individual floorboards. They had a tighter seal and he thought they would be the most trouble to remove if someone ever came snooping around. The tongue and groove had been extremely labor intensive but it was what he wanted. The individual boards were first glued to the floor joists, nailed and finally from beneath he had used metal strapping to cris-cross the boards creating a webbing effect. A hatch had been cleverly devised around two wooden 'keys' and there were floorboards fit on either side of the hatch. Each had three countersunk nails and the point of each nail had been carefully filed back, then ¼ inch of the tip bent so it looked like a 'L.' To work, each nail had to be rotated to match a slot cut in the hole. He accomplished this ingenious feat, by using a magnet that he had hidden in the handle end of a screwdriver that hung on a peg-hook on a wall with many other tools. The nails were, in essence, the deadbolt to the keys. Once the nails were removed, the pieces of floorboard could be lifted. The key on the left had to be lifted from right to left; the one on the right had to be lifted left to right. It was the only thing that allowed the hatch to open. Additionally, cleverly built into the wall was a small manual winch. To mask his real intent, Jigs had reinforced some of the 2x4 studding with an additional 2x4 and had also doubled up on some of the cross members. If anyone had looked inside the shed, (and that was extremely unlikely,) they would think it was done to reinforce the area for shelves around the inside, shelves which were jammed full of weed killer, old gallons of paint, a box of oil soaked rags, anti-freeze for his car and an old box of heavy nails, all of it junk. All but one reinforced 2x4, that one was special.

Oh how Jigs sometimes clapped his hands with glee when he used it! He had cut out one four-foot section and drilled three holes in each end. He hammered into those holes, a six-inch piece of quarter-inch rebar allowing three-inches to stick out of each end. Those ends were then set into their sister holes drilled into the pieces of 2x4 still attached to the wall. The horizontal cross members, which appeared to be support beams between the 2x4s, were in actuality a lift beam for his manual crane. Hidden in the end was a pulley. Oh yes, Jigs thought himself, so very clever. Hanging on one of the shelves was a coil of rope attached to a leather harness of sorts. It was sooooo much easier to strap that on the *invisible* and lower them into the *Hell Hole* instead of trying to carry them down. Wondrously, it all folded so neatly back into the wall where he had put above it, a final coiled fifty-foot garden hose on a hook looped down to hide his clever, clever winch.

The substructure was beam reinforced with culled lumber from a local box store set into the heavy clay that made up much of Western Pennsylvania. Three wooden posts down the center reinforced the roof to the *Hell Hole*, its twin being the floor of the shanty. Jigs had tapped into an outlet in the above shed hiding it behind the clapboard siding. He had pulled the cord along the three support posts, and at each was a light bulb adapter with a bare bulb for light. Underneath the roof overhang of the shed on each side was a small vent that ran down inside the walls via a four-inch PVC pipe, which connected to two small intake fans. The fans provided enough fresh air when needed, but equally important, it could be sealed off to prevent sound from escaping from the *Hell Hole* to the outside world. Black plastic was stapled to the studs pounded into the dirt to form walls, the extra bonus of that black plastic was it drew moisture from the dirt behind it, and moisture in conjunction with the normal state of darkness drew the 'crawlies' as Jigs called them. Huge hunter spiders, with black fat bodies bristling with coarse hairs, lived there en masse because of the myriad of worms, centipedes, millipedes and plump white slugs.

Jigs liked to catch the slugs between his thumb and index finger and *squeeezzee* until they swelled and popped. What a good laugh that gave him! *Oh what fun!* He would think happily. Usually he would throw the slug near one of the hunter spider nests, but sometimes he ate them, licking his thumb and finger as if the remains were some type of grotesque sweet-treat.

The black wall of the *Hell Hole* was adorned top to bottom with symbols that embodied the Dark One, many of them ancient and imbued with old and powerful evil, which he had never been able to tap because he had no knowledge of their particular malevolent adornments. Some he had bought, and two, the ones he had been most drawn to, he acquired by torturing and murdering the owners and then taking possession of the unique talisman. The ones obtained by pain were by far his favorite and the most coveted by the Dark One that he served, and therefore the most powerful. Guiding his hand was an iniquitous force to position these symbols into a pattern, a pattern that formed a circle, a circle that had a center that at times seemed to roil in a black and menacing mass. What he did not know, what the Master kept from his eager dedicated minion, was that after all these years, it was nearing completion.

Though he was not a handsome man by any stretch of the imagination, Jigs had still found it relatively easy to pick up girls. They were usually skinny and hungry looking with bad complexions and dark circles under slightly unfocused eyes. He called these girls the *invisibles* because no one cared if they went missing; it was as though they never really existed.

Jigs had learned the nifty trick of cutting a stack of paper the same size as a twenty-dollar bill. He would put a real $20 on the top and bottom of the bogus stack, wrap it with a rubber band, and badda-bing! It looked as if he was the proverbial trick, flush with money.

The *invisibles* became easy marks then. Whether it was drugs or booze, they were always willing to party with Jigs. Surreptitiously, he drew out his 'badda-bing' money, and without question, they would get into the piece of junk he called a car. His 1972 Pinto, originally lime green, was mostly rust and the ever-popular furnace tape, but in the dark, with those areas spray-painted with cheap paint, the *invisibles* climbed right in.

Jigs kept a pair of meat cutter's chain mail gloves that had been fitted into a plain brown pair of work gloves under the front seat of the 'Pinta'(as he lovingly referred to it). He had deliberately taken out the interior light and left junk on the passenger seat; coffee cups, fast food containers, magazines and the like that bought him the extra moments he needed while the *invisible* swept the garbage onto the floor and got into the car. In those extra moments he had time to slip the glove onto his right hand and as the *invisible* finally settled into the passenger seat, KA-WHAP he landed a chain mail backhand to the left temple of the *invisible's* head. As their head lolled forward and their body slumped, out came that same versatile furnace tape for a quick trussing and then it was time to take the last ride of her life down the highway to Hell.

Jigs himself had installed the little cassette player in the Pinta, and it had never, ever played any other tape except *Don't Stand Still* by AC/DC with the cut 'Highway to Hell' obviously being Jigs favorite. The tape had broken once and Jigs had lovingly spent several hours ever so carefully prying apart the case, splicing the tape, slowly rewinding so he left no prints on it to distort the sound. Then he replaced the springs, holding the case in place while he fused the two pieces back together with a small round wood file that he heated and placed against the halves slightly melting the plastic. No wonder of modern brain surgery or heart transplant had ever been more meticulous or lovingly performed.

Only once did an *invisible* have the audacity to regain consciousness in route to the *Hell Hole*. She interrupted him she did, in the middle of his air guitar, with his thighs jammed under the steering wheel guiding it down the back road. The second back-hand he gave her with the meat cutter's glove was hard enough to turn her temple spongy and blood dripped off her chin into her hands which were flared like flower petals. Oh my yes, plastic seat covers were such a blessing. She died long before they arrived at the *Hell Hole*, but no matter, his plans were still the same.

Jigs had sneaked through life drawing scant attention to his existence while effectively taking advantage of the government 'crazy check' program for being unable to work. Actually, it was not that he could not work; rather it was that no one would hire him because no one wanted him to work *for* him or her, and no one wanted to work *with* him. The Social Security caseworkers who had reviewed his case over the years had referred Jigs to many different doctors. Had those doctors ever come together and discussed his case as a group, one common thread would have stunned them; they were all, every last one, afraid of him. Afraid of his reptilian eyes, his unnerving smile, and the way he constantly licked his lips and rubbed them together while he stared, unblinking, at the unfortunate doctor currently examining him. At one such appointment he had sent a female doctor, fleeing the examining room when he took from his coat pocket a small gray mouse rolled up in a paper towel. Then while quite obviously staring at the doctor's ample breasts, he proceeded to squeeze the unfortunate creatures until its eyes popped out of its sockets while Jigs quiet obviously sported an erection.

When he was thirteen, while at a neighborhood garage sale he found two items that forever changed his life—a Ouija board and book titled *Journey to the Dark Lord* buried at the bottom of a box. He bought the Ouija board for 75 cents and shoved the book down the back his pants.

Anyone else would have asked himself or herself why the book and the Ouija board, with instructions, were in absolute pristine condition; never opened, never touched, no breath ever crossed the pages or ruffled an edge. They had in fact been waiting for him, longing for him, hungering for *him* like a lean hungry snake; wanting to devour his mind and ingest his soul.

He had sat night after night for almost two weeks, fingers lightly placed on the planchette, believing it would move of its own volition, willing it to be possessed wanting to *be* possessed by the power he could feel radiating from it. Looking down through the clear plastic orb in the center, a jewel to the underworld, he was certain it could show him his way, his future, his destiny. It remained though, a cloudy piece of cheap third world plastic. *It* was nothing, like *he* was nothing, and his fury was enormous.

Crazed that no extraordinary events were taking place as he had envisioned, doubt began creeping into his mind, and he pushed away the board and the planchette haphazardly shoving them to the bottom of his unkempt, dirty bed. In his eagerness to communicate with the Ouija he had forgotten about the book, now he sought to retrieve it and look again at the pictures that he had seen that day at the yard sale.

Jigs had never been a good reader. His alcoholic, single mother, who drank containers of Listerine when she didn't have the money for anything else, could not have cared less if her teenage son could read or not. She did not care if he attended school or stayed in his room hours on end, she did not care that he felt abandoned, she did not care if he ate, if he slept, if he hurt, if he cried, if he lived or died. At a time when CYS didn't exist, abandoned, abused children were in essence left to fend for themselves, so, without lifting a hand, she created the perfect environment for evil, the pliable clay that could be molded and shaped into what the Dark One needed.

When he finally dug the book out from under the pile of dirty laundry that smelled of body sweat and urine, he slowly read aloud *Journey to the Dark Lord*. As he began to read, trying to sound out words, his head began to throb, but as his head throbbed, he began to read more clearly. The boy who did not know a noun from a verb began to form words that should have been impossible for him to understand. However, his dark teacher had him marked for a special purpose and had branded him to perform unique biddings. As Jigs read, he would come across words in italics that strangely seemed to whisper to him in each breath. They imbedded pernicious images in his mind that made him sit staring, unblinking, glassy eyed, while depraved visions played in a loop repeatedly, until he was panting and bathed in sweat his soul abandoned to a squirming sinister perversion that promised fruition of the fiendish dreams. He did not understand the ancient words, vile and mesmerizing, but as he continued to speak them aloud as his teacher, evil incarnate, celebrated. He retrieved the Ouija board and very soon the planchette began to move and spell words and have conversations with him and what he was empowered to do was horrific beyond the comprehension of any but Jigs.

Oh, how they filled him with wild anticipation.

The first day of September, Jigs woke up late after having spent the night in the *Hell Hole*; not with an *invisible*; he was getting too old for that and had to depend instead upon his memories and his large cache of home movies. Instead, he had spent the night practicing the summoning as he had done on so many other nights. The right words in the right combination, that was all he needed, it was everything he craved and now it was all he lived to perform. The Dark One had taken his life in many different directions, sating many of his appetites, but igniting his hunger for other, even more perverted desires.

Tonight, Jigs thought, *tonight I will look into the eyes of the Dark One and at last, he will give me my reward.*

"Tonight," he breathed hoarsely.

Jigs spent the day resting, reviewing in his mind each step of that evenings ultimate summoning. After everything he had given to the Dark One, all the *invisibles* he had procured, would it finally now be his turn. Would his reward be as rich and dark as all the blood he had spilled?

The light was waning as Jigs, feeling recuperated, attended to the final preparations in the room. The Dark One permitted his childish décor, which included costumes and weapons, but masks were his favorite. He had them on the walls between dark fantasy posters. He had them on mannequins he had collected from department stores. He had them in corners held up by thin dowel rods glued into the heads and pushed through holes in the plaster so they looked suspended, and in large glass jars filled with water so they floated like a specimen awaiting the final animation. He stuffed some of the masks to form their features to grotesque life-like dimensions using anything and everything from crumpled newspaper to the shredded/fluffed blue jean material that was a form of insulation that had the ability to be easily molded when mixed with glue slightly thinned with water. That way he had more time while molding and filling the voids of the masks to truly make them his own and embellish the monstrous features that he so adored. He found that placing his masks on spikes afforded him the opportunity to plant his garden of horror and lovingly watch it grow.

It was here, that he would conduct tonight's ritual, for which he had been preparing longer than he could remember. It had been hard to find all the items he needed; but he was guided to special locations for the herbs; asafetida's, betel nut, henbane and wormwood. He had anointed the black candles with dressing oil, using the index finger of his strong hand, carefully moving from the center up and around, then down and around the circumference while focusing on the intent given to him to empower them for the rite. Finally, the previous evening he had made the required sacrifices. Sneaking like a shadow around three neighborhoods he had cased weeks ago, he had delighted in catching the cat first, binding its head in shrink-wrap and skinning it alive. The dog had been so easy to entice away from the yard, but slightly harder to contain. As he had hoisted it up by its back feet to hang on a low tree branch, the dog had continued to struggle, its eyes wild and milky through the plastic. As Jigs had sliced through its throat, the coppery aroma of blood surrounded him and he had watched in ecstasy its final pitiful struggle. Cutting through a field on the way to his car, he happened upon a chicken coop not far from a red barn. It was more risky, because he could see the outline of a house not far away, but he knew he was the master of death when the chickens made no sound as he gutted them.

All was prepared . . . the candles were now lit around the room, the intricate sigils on the floor that had required long agonizing hours on his knees copying line for line from one of his special grimories glowed with an unnatural light.

He was ready. It was time.

From his point of view, Jigs could not have planned for a better night. Throughout the day, the sky had been clear and as the sun had set, the air became cool and silken. He needed a dark moon, but oh, it could not have been a more perfect velvet sky, brimming with stars, brimming and full of promise.

Jigs believed this was finally his time. All the long years of waiting, living only for the moments of the *invisibles* final cry of pain and anguish as they passed into the darker realm he created for them. Sometimes, when he had chosen correctly and converted them in those last agonizing moments of their absolute despair and terror, he knew something infinitely more insidious was waiting for them.

An hour before the rite was to begin, Jigs had jogged in place and stretched, feeling the blood pumping through his veins as it had on those hot nights full of humid dark desires. The entire time he had continued repeating, *No mistakes, no mistakes, no mistakes.*

He had brought forward his favorite masks and pushed the poles into large pots filled with loose sand. The faces on the spiked masks had gleamed with a surreal sheen of sweat as though in their last moment, a climax of ecstasy had sealed their features.

He rang the silver bowl on the altar running his finger along the edge to bring forth the song it held, and finally he knelt within the ring of sigils as candle light danced in odd slashing patterns across the walls and floor. Jigs began the complicated incantations slowly, pronouncing each word precisely as he had practiced. The walls of the room began to move counter clockwise ever so slowly while the ring remained in place and the sigils glowed, throbbing heatedly.

Jigs knew the finality of anticipation of all that he had planned for, wished for, and had prayed for to his black and writhing lord. He kneeled at the edge of the sigils his right hand resting on the pole that held his most prized and beloved mask. The grotesque face was tipped back as though braying to the moon, eyes gleaming with demonic light, a large twisted mouth opened wide its lips and teeth stained with real blood that had been savaged from some of the *invisibles*. Jigs had worn the mask during many of his sessions with the *invisibles* and he had slurped their thick, coppery, hot blood through those lips, his heart pounding in his ears as the *invisibles* had passed into the abyss of the tortured.

He did not notice that the mouth of the mask was pulled up in an obscene smirk, nor did he see the yellow light glowing behind the reptilian-like eyes as the cheek-bones became pronounced and harshly cut as though by some darkly depraved sculptor.

"Now! Now!" Jigs screamed, all his energies, all his attention focused on the sigils.

Then it took him.

Razor edged claws clamped around his throat and cut off what would have been his final "NOW!" as his voice erupted into a wet, gurgling babble of pain and powerlessness.

Blood bubbled out of his nose and flooded his eyes, becoming droplets of red bloody tears on his face while a river of red flowed from each ear canal.

Jig's heart stuttered to a stop, and his body slacked in the grip of death his master had planned for him all along. As he tumbled and plunged down the slide into Acheron, he began to hear laughter and the voices sounded strangely familiar.

"*We're waiting for you! We're not invisible anymore!*"

It was not the consummation of which he had imagined and dreamed. Instead, it was the same frenzied nightmare he had initiated on so many *invisibles* over the years. His brain seared in agony, a supernova of heat as his blood boiled in his veins exploding every organ in his body and the Dark One made sure he felt each moment of indescribable pain.

The mask tilted back on its pole, mouth opened as though to the portals of hell, and with the horrid breath of sulfur, death, and pure malevolence, it began to laugh.

It was unspeakable.

Jigs body was not found for five days and then only because of a gas leak that placed an Alliance Gas worker at his door as they evacuated the block. When repeated knocks brought no response, he tried the door and found it open. A mailbox full of ads and bills along with a car in the driveway signaled a problem, so he elected to enter the house. As he stepped inside the door, before a *Hello* could pass his lips the ripe, wet smell of death, unlike anything he had ever encountered, assaulted his sense of smell causing him to cover his nose and mouth quickly. He back-pedaled out the door in a jerky motion, his mind numb to any thought or emotion except getting away from the stench. He stumbled over the threshold, his arms cart wheeling like a crazy lawn ornament in a high wind. He made it to the curb gasping for clean air before he gagged and vomited. As he wiped his mouth with the back of a shaking hand, he fumbled for his cell phone and called his supervisor.

CHAPTER 3

Sammy woke slowly on that early September Saturday morning. He was trying to remember a dream from last night, it had been so peaceful, but he could not quite recapture the details. It was about a woman, not his mother, but he knew she *was* a mother. He could recall the feeling that she was warmly holding his hand. Her voice was comforting and serene, she had kissed his forehead and murmured visions of sweet dreams, and he had felt so safe. As he came more fully awake hay dust filled his lungs, and he began sneezing. Sammy managed to take a deep breath as he rubbed his arm across his forehead and scrubbed the back of his hand across his face. Rolling over to block the early morning light, Sammy felt the familiar pad of hay under his back, cradling him in a manger of comfort.

Out of nowhere, Anthony's arm came crashing over hitting Sammy on his temple bringing to an abrupt halt the peaceful moment.

"Hey!" cried Sammy, "watch it, that hurt!"

As Anthony left the golden place of a good sleep, the first thing he was aware of was the warm rays of sun on his arm and he realized it was beginning to get hot in the barn even now. The late summer/early autumn mornings were deceptive in their heat, but he liked the way it felt hot and smelled like bread all at the same time.

"Sorry bud," Anthony murmured as he turned to sit up.

Sammy reached out and gave Anthony a quick snap to his ribs, not to hurt him; it was just the 'don't piss me off' reminder of most boys that age.

"You're dead meat!" Anthony shot back as he started to unwind himself from the sleeping bag he had again managed to wrap around his torso like a tornado funnel.

Thus began their morning ritual of a quick wrestling match. Whoever won the fight was the winner of the first piece of crisp, pan fried, smoky bacon that would soon be sizzling in the cast iron skillet over the still hot coals that were the remnants of last night's fire.

Sammy claimed victory that day. His backward summersault caught Anthony on the head making his vision slightly blur for a brief moment, just long enough for Sammy to land on him with his knees pinning him to the ground. Sammy then turned his body and began to tickle the exposed flesh of Anthony's stomach. No matter how hard Anthony tried, he could not buck Sammy off, his legs burned with effort, and his stomach muscles ached from laughing.

"All right, all right, you win!" cried Anthony. As Sammy relinquished his winning hold Anthony said, "You can have the first bacon, I'll go check for eggs."

Sammy began digging in the cooler, and with a satisfied 'Ah-ha' he pulled out a rasher of bacon and put six pieces in the cast iron skillet that Army had found at a yard sale.

The skillet, perfectly seasoned to a deep black, made the best bacon and eggs ever in the history of the world in the minds of two boys who loved to cook, sleep, and live outside. He also pulled out the potatoes Danni had diced and put in water with a little lemon to keep them from going brown overnight.

Army had taught the boys the fine art of frying potatoes in bacon fat with garlic and onions and scrambling eggs in the same pan to pull up all the 'good stuff'. The toast could be challenging, but oh, it was good with soft, salty butter, the bread a little more than toast and a little less than a crouton, which they used to soak up smoky bacon grease and soft eggs.

"I'll cook extra so you can have some," called Sammy and Anthony started toward the chicken coop. Sammy had such a sweet nature that it did not occur to him that he was doing all the work—banking the fire, keeping the bacon from burning, placing the toast against the hard stones to brown. All the while Anthony was only hiking a hundred yards or so to grab six fresh eggs. It was such a pretty morning that Anthony stood looking around at the fields and trees and the blue sky, thinking about how much he liked this time of year. Suddenly on the morning air he could smell the cooking bacon and thought he'd better get a move on, still, he lingered a moment longer, drinking in the day then finally started again towards the chicken coop.

The downside was that early morning in a chicken coop usually smelled bad, like a deep sharp breath of ammonia. He filled his lungs with a last clean breath of air, opened the door to the coop for their breakfast eggs . . . and stopped dead in his tracks.

No chickens clucked at him, they could not. All six chickens, seven including the rooster, were hanging from their feet with their bodies slit from top to bottom and their guts hanging in odd, bloody ropes. There had been no quick death for these birds, but a true slaughter that left even their bird eyes glazed with terror.

Anthony backed out on instinct, his held breath expelled in a huffing sound. Unfortunately, between shock and terror he took a deep breath before falling out of the coop. That breath would never leave him, never. It was a breath of putrefying blood, and the oppressive smell of rotting entrails.

Anthony stumbled backwards and fell hard on his back driving the last little bit of breath out of him. For the briefest moment, he blacked out and woke up to Sammy standing over him looking back and forth between him and the coop, while a half chewed piece of bacon in his hand fell to the ground.

"What . . . what the hell happened?" Sammy asked. Then a froth of vomit bubbled at the corner of his lips and spewed out of his mouth as he doubled over and expelled chunks of his hard won bacon, splattering the ground in a brown greasy mess.

Anthony started to sit up, mostly to get out of the way of Sammy's stream of puke, but as he crabbed-crawled away from the chicken coop, he realized he just wanted to *get away*. It was not as if he had not seen dead chickens before, but this was different. They were butchered to cause pain and suffering, and for no other reason.

"Anthony! Sammy! Hey guys, where are you?" Danni called. Anthony could tell from her voice that she was by the fire pit.

He bolted up grabbing Sammy by the shirt, rubbing his hand across his friend's mouth to remove the last vestiges of bacon vomit, and ran toward where his mother was standing. Their commotion caused Danni to look in the direction from which they were running.

"Mom, we're here!" he shouted running forward, hoping to keep his mom away from the chicken coop.

"What are you boys up to? asked Danni suspiciously seeing the pale and obviously weak Sammy being dragged by Anthony. "Sammy?" she asked, and as the boys stared wide eyed at her, she turned her head towards Anthony expecting an answer.

"It's my fault mom, I made Sammy run uphill and back down to see who would win breakfast," as Danni continued to stare at her son, he added, "I wanted the bacon.

Danni looked between the two boys and said, "Go put that fire out and pick up your things. I'll see you both back at the house in ten minutes, and," she said in a deadly quiet voice, "I want the truth, not that BS you just gave me."

By the time the boys got back to the Petrucci house, they had a story together, but it had enough holes to drive a truck through and neither were good liars. Anthony tended to embellish too much because he felt so guilty about telling a lie, and then he would forget his embellishments. Sammy, on the other hand, was a dead giveaway immediately. He could not make eye contact, tended to shift nervously, and definitely looked guilty.

As they approached the house, it immediately struck Anthony that his dad was home. That meant something was wrong because his dad never missed work.

The boys hesitated outside the kitchen door when they heard a heated conversation between Army and Danni. Thinking it may give them another moment before having to face Danni, they slid to a stop outside the screen door.

"I know he was weird Danni, I've heard all the stories just like you, but that's probably all they are . . . stories, and I might find a lot of stuff we still need for the house," argued Army.

Danni's eyes widened in disbelief and her lips pressed together in a thin line. "More like you have heard he has lots of tools, and let's see, huumm, maybe some Halloween decorations?" she replied her voice sounding angry.

As Army was about to respond, he noticed two small shadows on the porch behind Danni. Leaning left, he saw the boys standing wide-eyed on the porch.

"What are you two doing out there?" he snapped.

"You two get in here right now," Danni ordered. She swung around at Army and said, "You stay put too."

Danni and Army had called the police immediately, and the on duty officer arrived within fifteen minutes. Under the scrutiny of Danni's laser-beam stare, the boys' recounted exactly what had happened, determining there was no need to make anything up. The officer took notes and asked questions, his head bobbing up and down slowly, looking between his notebook and the boys, all the while Army's jaw tightened and flexed in an angry rhythm.

"Are you *positive* you didn't hear anything?" the officer asked for the final time.

They both shook their heads in unison.

"Why don't you guys go sit under the tree there while I talk to your parents?" the officer said. It was not a request, but a directive.

They had been sitting under a tree for the last half-hour, pulling out tuffs of grass and picking them apart, straining to hear any of the conversation.

"Shit Anth, what do ya think *did* that?" Sammy said finally.

"I don't know. I can't quit thinking that whatever it was must have known we were sleeping out in the barn," Anthony responded in quite voice.

"Yea, especially the way you snore!" said Sammy trying to change the mood.

"What a stupid thing to say!" Anthony replied angrily. Sammy stuck out his tongue, Anthony threw a handful of his shredded grass at Sammy, the wad hitting him square in the mouth causing Sammy to choke and sputter.

Suddenly they realized that the police officer was on his way to the patrol car and Danni and Army were walking toward the tree where they sat.

"You two ok?" Danni asked in a quiet voice as she knelt down.

"Yea," said Anthony looking at Sammy, "we're ok."

"What did the police say?" Sammy asked.

Army and Danni looked at each other, and something in their hesitation caused a sudden small jolt of fear to rocket through Anthony.

"What?" he asked anxiously.

Army took a deep breath, "He couldn't give us a lot of detail, but apparently last night there were several other incidents of animal mutilation."

Anthony and Sammy sat there, staring at Danni and Army trying to make sense of what they had heard, their eyes blinking quickly, darting between the two parents.

"Like what?" Anthony asked.

"You mean like the x-files?" Sammy said blinking rapidly.

Army squatted down next to his wife in front of the two boys and said, "A cat was found skinned, and a dog hung upside down from a tree with its throat cut."

All the color drained out of Sammy's face, and Anthony leaned back bumping into the tree. Both Danni and Army moved to the boys and put their arms around them.

"Officer Dunbar said they were pretty sure it was a cult group that moved through the area," Danni told them. "The police do not feel they are a threat to any of us, but we should be alert to any strangers."

"Just the same," Army said looking at the boys, "no more sleeping out for a while and you will be home before dark until we say different."

"Come on Sammy," said Danni as she motioned with her outstretched hand, it's time for you to go home. We need to talk to your mom and dad."

Under the circumstances, neither of the boys complained.

For the next ten days, the animal mutilations were front and center to almost every conversation in and around Lamont. Homes in the area sported new motion sensor lights, dead bolts, and home security systems. Neighbors were watching out for each other and cell phone sales at the local wireless company hit a new high with parents wanting their kids to have a quick reliable way to reach either them, or 911.

By the end of September though, the mutilation cases had moved to the back burner with no further information or evidence of the suspected cult members uncovered. It was as if the city took a deep breath and issued a collective sigh of relief.

As life eased back to a relatively normal pace, Army's thoughts had returned to the estate sale of Jigs Seederly's home and belongings . . . the issue that had caused the quarrel between him and his wife the day the of the slaughtered chickens. A newspaper ad listed items that would be for sale and the list had been half a page long. It was the tools Army said he wanted, and he justified attending the sale in his mind and in his conversations with Danni by telling her he would use them to make a little extra money refinishing furniture. Finally worn out, Danni had relented.

The day of the sale was the last Saturday of September. An autumn day when the sky was cobalt blue and clear, and the air had a slight chill that made a long sleeve shirt and a cup of coffee comfortable companions.

A hunter green van with the name *Benson Brothers Auctions* in tan script gracing its sides sat parked on the left of the garage, and cars were beginning to line up and down the street. Army had arrived early and was anxious to be the first to look through the tools once the sale began. He always kept his eyes open for any antique tools, usually found at a neighborhood garage sale. Often the people selling them only knew they were dad or grandpa's tools, they did not know they were potential collector's items. Occasionally you could find rare pieces and the fun was figuring out what they were originally intended to do. Army was sure that was not going to happen at this sale though, because professional auctioneers organized it.

Army had another quirk. He loved Halloween. He remembered vividly the first time he saw the original *Frankenstein* in glorious black and white. He had realized years later, that the make-up artists' had been way ahead of their time with make-up applied to actor Boris Karloff. Much to Boris Karloff's lament, the fame that role brought him seemed to pigeonhole him into horror films for the remainder of his career. That never mattered to young Armando he never looked back. His creative side led him to fashion costumes that rivaled any others in his neighborhood. His father, from who Army had inherited imagination, had helped him build 'theme sets' as they called them. One year their theme had been 'Dracula's Lair' and with plywood, 2x4s and hinges they had built a three sided back drop that housed a sturdy cardboard coffin set atop straw surrounded by cut logs. It sported tiki torches attached to the walls, plastic skeletons, strobe lights, dry ice in an old lard kettle used as a witch's cauldron and of course, a glass vase with a single blood red rose. Army's cousin Skip had dressed like the Grim Reaper that year, and had hidden behind the backdrop. Army of course, had played the staring roll of Dracula, and if the kids coming down the driveway were old enough, Army tapped twice on the wall. Skip would then fire up an old chain saw that had the chain removed and race out from behind the backdrop chasing the screeching children up the drive way. That alone had brought the neighborhood kids and parents out in droves.

Each year it seemed to get a little bigger. Army's mom took to cooking a big pot of homemade Sloppy Joes that they would serve with kettle chips, pickles and cheese. Ice cold soda for the kids, coffee, and cheesecake for the adults. It was memories laced with the musky, intoxicating smell of leaves, wood smoke and ripe apples still on the trees.

It became a lifelong passion for Army to collect Halloween memorabilia (junk Danni called it), and he had, in his own mind of course, some unique pieces. Costumes, music, lights, voice shifters, hang-up cutouts, faux tombstones and his ever popular, ever evolving Ax-Man were a large part of his treasures. He had taken a pair of old coveralls and stuffed them with dry leaves originally, but later they were re-stuffed with hay and most recently plastic bags, which held their shape better. The legs ended in an old pair of steel-toed work boots donated by a friend, and he had found some horrific huge rubber hands with long black fingernails, warts and horrible looking cuts. The mask that had adorned it sported grotesque pallid skin, black hair, empty eyes and enormous fangs. Ax-Man had been held together with a huge tomato stake driven down through its back that Army could pound into the ground wherever he wanted Ax Man to be displayed. He had also found an ingenious way of using willow branches to prop up Ax-Man's hands. Once, he positioned Ax-Man to hold a blow-up skeleton with a blond wig and a flowing nightgown. His princess wife. Another year he had Ax-Man holding another mask by its hair in his right hand, a plastic ax in the left and a bale of hay draped with an old pair of sweat pants complete with discarded tennis shoes and a tattered t-shirt simulating, to the horror of his mother, that Ax-Man had chased a jogger down and decapitated him.

The best though, was the year he staged Ax-Man as though he was sitting on the front porch in a rocking chair reading a Marvel Comic book. *Ho-hum,* the neighborhood kids thought, *how boring, Petrucci must be losing his losing his touch.* Little did they know that Halloween night before Trick-or-Treat while the kids were getting dressed to go out, Army dressed *himself* in Ax-Man's clothes and sat down in the chair with the comic book waiting for the first kids to arrive. When the first crew of four came up on the porch, whispering, giggling and getting their bags ready, Army waited until they knocked on the door, and then . . . he simply stood up. The effect was incredible. It scared the neighborhood kids so bad each group would stick around hiding until the next group got their scare. It was still a legend in his hometown and he smiled every time he thought about it.

Army's enthusiasm for Halloween had imprinted itself on the DNA of Anthony, and the two looked forward to the Halloween event every year. Since this would be the first year in their new house, Army and Anthony, with the addition of Sammy, had planned a big decorating gig with neighbors invited. Because of the recent cult scare, it had been on the back burner, but now it took a new, deep breath of life.

Therein lay the last leg of Army's trip to the estate sale of James Ivan Garvin Seederly. Scuttlebutt had it that he not only was a half-bubble off center, but it was rumored he had a huge collection of Halloween masks. Danni got wind of that part of the Jigs story and that was the cause of the recent argument. She voiced her very real concern that maybe this 'Jigs' did more than collect masks, that he had possibly been involved in darker practices, but Army had laughed and hugged his wife assuring her that Lamont wasn't a hotbed of supernatural occurrences.

Fate has a funny way of positioning you in the exact place you are supposed to be at the most relevant time. On that exquisitely beautiful day at the end of September, fate was dealing Army a Texas Hold 'em big slick hand.

It was 9:55a.m. The sale was about to begin.

CHAPTER 4

Since the Alliance Gas company worker had stumbled upon the corpse of Jigs, Jon Wendels felt in his gut there was more here than just a man who had possibly experienced a massive aneurism. He had been the detective called to the scene, and the bizarre death site had been unlike any he had ever previously investigated. The putrefied body was so badly decomposed it looked as if it had been in a swamp for the better part of a month rather than 5 days in a house. He had been able to confirm through several receipts found at the residence, that Jigs had indeed made purchases the day before his death. Detective Wendels established this preliminary timeline by the five days worth of ads and mail in his mailbox, and one days worth of mail on his kitchen counter. He felt certain that the decay of the body was so excessive that none of the tests would accurately establish a time of death.

When the body of Jigs Seederly arrived at the morgue, no one thought much of it except for the two dieneras' who had to prepare what remained of Jigs for autopsy. They had probably bagged hundreds of bodies between them, this one though had left them nauseated and wanting a shower. They posted their completed paperwork and the usually good-natured co-workers had parted silently, heads down, making their way through the parking lot to their cars.

Dr. Scott Champion, Chief Coroner for the county, had opened the body bag in the morgue with Jon Wendels present. With the usual cameras filming, he took one look at Jigs and narrowed his eyes as he glanced at Wendels.

"What the hell is this about Jon?" Scott asked.

Wendels took a tube of Vicks out of his pocket and applied a small glob under his nose, an old trick used during autopsies on badly decomposed bodies. It deceived the brain from processing what the nose actually smelled and usually kept the person in attendance from blowing their cookies while witnessing the autopsy. Usually.

"Finding out how this guy ended up like this doc, that's what the hell this is about," said Wendels while taking a breath of Vicks and motioning towards the bag in which Jigs now resided.

Dr. Champion pulled open the side of the body bag and glanced up. "Jon, I can't autopsy something that is basically . . . soup," he said sarcastically.

"I need answers Scott. If that's really Jigs Seederly, a well known half-whack, whatever happened to him is nothing I've ever seen, read about or even heard an old urban legend that explains this . . . have you?"

Champion stared unblinking and silent for several moments then finally said, "Jon, I just might be able to write a paper on this for the coroner's Newsmax page. Who knows, maybe I'll win an award if I can put this guy back together for you."

"That's what I want to hear doc," Wendels said as he pulled another deep breath of Vicks up his nostrils. "Ok then, I'll get a strainer and you start spooning."

Scott Champion had finished the autopsy on the individual that Jon Wendels suspected was Jigs Seederly. Champion's gut instinct was that indeed, it was Jigs, but it was the most remarkable, yet disturbing, autopsy he had ever performed. It appeared that the internal organs had literally exploded inside the victim's body; what was left of the organs looked *cooked*, as if a microwave inside of him had been turned on high. Equally bizarre was the accelerated decomposition of the body. Champion ordered every test available including exotic strains of flesh eating bacteria, but even that did not add up. Detective Wendels had left before the end of the examination and Champion was surprised, (and frankly impressed) that the detective had stayed as long as he did.

Scott stepped into the clean zone outside of the autopsy room to remove his examination jacket, mask and gloves. Even with the air scrubber on full blast, he felt like his clothes reeked of death and putrid stink. He wanted to scrub down in a cool shower and have an even cooler Scotch on the rocks. Maybe he had not been far off the mark when he told Wendels that he would write a dissertation on this one. It was playing out to be one for the books.

Wendels had stayed well back from the examination table at the county morgue, but he had felt that weird sensation in your jaw and salivary glands just before you puke. He had not asked questions or prompted Dr. Champion, he had listened and observed as the examination had progressed. He held out from the smell and the gruesome vision of Champion lifting dripping globs from the bag, but finally the wet sloppy sound of body pieces being picked up and placed on the stainless trays and scales became more than he could endure.

"Doc, I gotta take off," he had quietly said, "I still have to try and determine what the hell *sand* was doing scattered all over the house."

Champion had merely grunted his understanding that Wendels was leaving as he continued his examination.

Walking through the office area, Wendels had grabbed a tissue from a box on the secretary's desk and wiped the Vicks from his nose. As he pushed the heavy steel door open to the outside, he did not think fresh air had ever felt or tasted so good. He inhaled huge gulps of that air, filling his lungs and blowing it back out of his mouth each time in a big *whoosh*.

As he settled in his car placing his cell phone on the seat next to him, he began thinking about the condition of Jigs house when he had done his original walk through.

After the initial shock of the body, the house had seemed strangely organized for someone with supposedly such a messed up brain. Pillows neatly placed on the sofa with a coffee table at each end. The kitchen immaculate with just a dishtowel folded and lying on the counter. There were no dishes in the sink, no overflowing trash in the can. The bathroom had no soap-scum in the shower or ring in the toilet and it even looked as though a new bar of soap was in the dish. Across the neatly made bed, lay a pair of folded sweatpants. Oddly, though, all through the house he had found fine gritty sand. It was as though someone had stood in each room and thrown handfuls in front of a fan and let it fly through the air to land in every nook and cranny. Sand everywhere, except for what appeared to be a den adjacent to the kitchen where the body had resided. That room appeared to have not one grain of sand; instead, it appeared littered with at least a dozen strange, disturbing Halloween type masks. Tipped over were two empty containers, close to the masks, and twelve candleholders on the wall with obviously burned candles. The middle of the floor had the appearance of a blackboard hastily wiped with an eraser, leaving white powdery streaks in a circle.

Jon had finished his surface tour of the scene and thought it was time to start opening doors, drawers and closets. That was when everything radically changed. Each closet, drawer and cupboard was jammed with every type of item you could imagine. Strange statues in glass, ceramic, wood and what appeared to be coal; food, clothes, plastic bags, boxes, cards, and candles; lots of candles of every shape and size all in either red or black.

In all the hidden dysfunctional mess, he spotted the most disturbing thing of all. Purses . . . women's' purses. Every size, shape and color, and each one looked to be stuffed with something.

He had called out to Joe Kingston who was the police photographer on site. "Joe! Get your ass over here now."

When Joe moved up behind Wendels, after a moment he had said softly, "Jesus."

"Jesus doesn't have anything to do with this Joe. Shoot it. I want to pick-up that first purse in the front, see it?"

"Yep, I see it," he said as his wrist turned back and forth on the lens to bring the scene into focus. Snap . . . snap . . . snap. "Ok, I've got it Jon," said Joe moving away.

Jon Wendels had reached in his back pocket, pulled out a pair of latex gloves, and put them on. He picked up the purse closest to him, pulling it down, and feeling the weight of it. Placing the purse on the nearby table, he slowly pulled open the zipper, the noise of the teeth disengaging soundly oddly threatening.

Inside, neatly folded, were a woman's underpants and a bra. Seeing that there was something underneath, he motioned for Joe to come and take more pictures as he held open the purse. Snap . . . snap . . . snap. This time Joe did not move back but stayed standing next to Wendels.

Jon reached inside and gently pulled out the undergarments and saw the stack of pictures at the bottom of the purse. His stomach tightened and he felt that odd, cold feeling you sometimes get when you know something ugly is about to happen and you're positive you can't stop it.

As he looked through the twenty-four pictures of a woman who was more than likely the owner of the purse and the undergarments, he saw scenes of depravity unlike anything he could have imagined even in his most dreadful nightmares. Jigs had captured not just what he had done to them, as hideous as that was, but he had zoned in on their fear, the fright and the horror that was reflected in their eyes; eyes hysterical with fright, eyes pleading for death and release from pain, eyes glazed in imminent madness. Eyes that were vacant, and mercifully, finally, eyes that were devoid of the spark of light as their soul was released.

Wendels placed the photos back in the purse and let his hands fall to his sides as he looked up. Joe's face was ashen and he was swallowing rapidly. Wordlessly, he took a step back, turned and walked out of the room with his head down.

Jon Wendels felt the most completely overwhelming, devastating sorrow he had ever known, not only because of the pictures but because he realized the cupboards were full of purses.

CHAPTER 5

It was just after one, and though the sale at Jigs Seederly's house was still going on, Army was on his way home, happy and excited with the items he had purchased. The drivers' window was down in his Honda and the autumn air blowing in, the radio turned up playing one of his favorite songs by Bon Jovi, as Army belted out the lyrics, *Shot through the heart and you're to blame, you give love a bad name!*

In his trunk were some of the best wood working tools he had come across at any sale and they were in outstanding condition, clean, sharp and now part of his collection. He had found a twelve piece set of wood chisels in a banded leather carry case; an antique wood plane with four different blades along with two beautiful hand miter saws that accompanied an oak miter box with stabilizer wedges. He had spied an odd hand tool that looked like two skis side by side with blades along the bottom and adjustable to about eight inches. He did not know exactly what it was, but it would be fun to do the research with Anthony and find out all the particulars. The tool sale had been exciting; dickering with other men, some collectors only, others, like Army, not only wanting unusual items but also planning to put most of them to use. They were all vying for tools for their own personal reasons, but they had one thing in common . . . owning tools was part of a secrete brotherhood, like the Free Masons or the Illuminati. Instead of a secrete handshake or code words, they recognized one another by their faded, frayed jeans that always had a darker area at the waistband where they carried their tape measure and usually wood stain under their fingernails.

Army had one more purchase, but it was not lying in the box with the newly acquired tools in the trunk, nor was it on the back seat, or even the floor. What Army had hidden in the spare tire well in his trunk was the most remarkable Halloween mask he had ever come across. It was a full head mask, not just a frontal mask. The rubber was unusually pliable and had seemed to adhere to his skin when he had placed his hand inside of it. It looked as though it had been recently washed or rinsed, but still had some old stains around the lips and down the chin that gave it an added effect of menace. There was also a strange picture inside, possibly a symbol of some type, but he paid little attention assuming it was something from the manufacture of the item, probably in Taiwan.

The skin had an unusual bluish tint to it, and the elongated ears appeared *forked* for lack of a better word. Remarkably the hair, instead of rubber, was some type of thick wig pulled back into one large plait that someone had put a good deal of work into because it was intricately done. The eyes were blood red with an eerie yellow pupil that seemed unusually realistic and cold and had the unsettling characteristic of appearing to follow you. The best attribute in Army's mind though, was the effect of the head being slightly tilted back with the mouth opened in a simulated howl revealing enormous canine teeth, both top and bottom, in an impressive display of gruesome finality. *What a terrific find!* Army had thought.

He already had an idea about how he was going to use the mask, but he would run it past Anthony and Sammy to include their ideas and thoughts so they would feel like major players in the new Halloween extravaganza. Ax-Man was about to get a new face and a new identity. He just needed to find a way to get it into the house unseen by Danni, and then get her to believe the mask had been a part of his Halloween collection for a long time, and that he just had not used it in the last couple of years. Right . . . Danni was on to him and his Halloween infatuation so it was not going to be easy.

As he turned left onto Brandywine Street, he heard a loud *thump* that sounded as if came from the back of his car, possibly the trunk. Thinking that he had run over something he pulled over to the side of the road and put on his flashers. Leaving the key in the accessory mode so he could continue listening to the radio, he checked the side mirror to make sure there was no traffic behind him and opened the door. As he made his way around the car on the driver's side, he looked at the tires, which appeared, undamaged, then continued around the back of the car to the passenger's side. He decided to look under the car to see if the muffler had come loose from it hangers or if anything had caught under the chassis. Nothing appeared to be wrong, nothing hanging, nothing caught. Army stood up, walked around the front of the car and leaned in the open driver's side window. He reached down between the door and the seat grasping the trunk latch which he pulled until he heard the familiar *plunk* as the latch released; he smiled when he realized another of his favorite songs, Billy Squire's 'In the Dark' was now playing.

As he began to walk to the trunk and open it, Army was thinking what a great day he was having. He slid his hand down to the bottom of the trunk lid, and as he lifted it up, he noticed the sky was still cobalt blue and warm, and he felt lucky that he had purchased some great tools at the estate sale. He let his mind wander to how a cold beer would hit the spot when he got home, that first icy sip that almost stung your throat and bubbled lightly on your lips . . .

The revolting stench exploded from the trunk engulfing him like a poisonous cloud and he staggered back a step as the lid to the trunk snapped the rest of the way up to the open position. Army immediately felt himself break out in a clammy sweat as an incredible wave of nausea washed over him in a nanosecond. His vision slightly blurred, but at the same time, he felt his eyes bulge as he stared into the trunk fully expecting to see some repulsive manifestation from his worst nightmare. Rotting, putrid, rank, stinking, moldering fetid, rancid, revolting, decaying—a frenzied hysteria of smells and sensations more gruesome than any author of graphic horror could possibly hope to describe using any verbiage known to man. It was so overwhelming that time simply seemed to *stop.*

Then it was gone. Army found himself staring into the trunk of his car at the tools purchased not two hours before at the estate sale. He looked around; unable to believe what had just happened and without thinking, he quickly slammed shut the lid to his trunk and started to walk towards the car door. His legs felt as though strings manipulated them or wires, jerky like a marionette, as if he was a puppet to some dark foreboding puppeteer.

He opened the car door and slid into his seat and in the same motion grabbed for the keys to start the motor. He fully expected the engine not to start, for the terrifying delusion go on and on, spinning him out until he was pulled so thin that he simply snapped and fluttered away in the wind. Fortunately, it fired up without hesitation and as he put the car into drive and pulled sharply away from the curb he realized the impossible, Billy Squire was *still* singing . . .

You never listen to the voices inside,

They fill your ears as you run to a place to hide . . .

Army drove like a man possessed toward the brightest light he knew existed, the love of his family.

As Army was buying tools and a peculiar Halloween mask, Sammy and Anthony early in the afternoon on that beautiful autumn day, were sailing across the barn on the rope swing pushing the limit like most boys of their age, never thinking that the rope could break and they could fall and be seriously hurt. It was a spectacular day, and as they flew through the air on their way to rescue a warrior brother stranded on a precipice of rock (to anyone else it looked to be stacks of hay), Sammy and Anthony let go of the rope in perfect practiced unison. They rolled on the top tier of hay bales, coming effortlessly to their feet. 'The Lord of the Rings' style swords they had cajoled their parents into buying, slashed and parried at imaginary invaders as they moved shoulder to shoulder around the top edge of the bales of hay. Sammy kicked the ghost adversary from the rock ledge and they slumped down in an exhausted heap all smiles and sweat.

"Wow that was sweet," gasped Sammy sticking the plastic sword into the bail crown.

Anthony huffed breath in and out of his mouth inflating his cheeks like small balloons feeling the burn in his lungs begin to lessen. He hocked up a glob of mucus and spit it over the edge. "Whew, that feels better."

"Watch this!" Sammy chimed in. He tried his own hawker and let fly, but the blob only went about three inches out of his mouth then plopped on the straw where it stuck like gelatin.

"God all mighty Sam, get it over the side at least!" Anthony said sarcastically. "Hey, is there any cold root-beer in the cooler?"

"Yep. Want me to get a couple brewskies?"

"I'll go, you went last time," Anthony said.

"Na, your hawker was a winner and all I can do is spit like a baby, I'll go." Sammy began sliding down the hay and when he made it to the bottom, Anthony laid back feeling the coarse hay stick him in a hundred places on the bare skin between his shorts and t-shirt and hay dust stuck to his damp flesh like so much gaudy theatrical makeup.

The barn had turned out to be to be the boys favorite location to play and they had become best friends within the walls of that special place. Unspoken between the two boys was the fact that they felt a calming presence while there. It was not something they could put into words, it just *was.* When they slept out in the barn, once they had settled down and the fire outside had burned low, just before sleep, they would feel a protective peacefulness. Anthony was sure he had felt the soft breath of *goodnight* on his cheek many times in that golden place just before sleep that seems to cradle the soul. It was never anything he could put into words and because of that, neither friend told the other what they felt. In Sammy's mind, he thought of it as the sleep angel while Anthony thought it was what his mom called a guardian angel.

The boys' mothers had also formed a special relationship together because of the connection between their sons. Danni, and Mindy, (Sammy's mom) had talked often over cups of coffee and day-old glazed doughnuts warmed in the oven until crusty on the outside and creamy on the inside, about how life brought people together at specific, significant times. Mindy and Dan provided a sound, stable environment for Sammy and shared the same values as Danni and Army. The only thing Mindy and Dan lacked what a barn. Through the summer, the four parents had played cards together on the deck at Danni and Army's house, the men sharing cold beers and ranch chips while the women had enjoyed chilled glasses of wine and strangely enough, the chocolate, crispy delight of Kit Kats. Always in the background, they could hear their sons on their latest adventure in the barn; whether it was playing C*ombat,* (an old 60's rerun they loved), diving in the straw and hay and building forts, or swinging across the barn saving a life, rescuing a warrior brother or lately, coming to the aid of a damsel in distress. Recently the parents noticed girls had morphed from icky to *hot* much to the lament of Danni and Mindy and the delight of Dan and Army. However, nothing could dispel the sweet enchantment and happiness the parents experienced hearing the laughter of their boys on those balmy summer nights. They always discretely made their way to the barn once the boys had gotten the evening fire going, watching them hone their cooking skills. Overcooked hotdogs and burned potatoes had morphed into grilled cheese burgers cooked on a grate the boys bought at a yard sale for 50 cents; potatoes were now wrapped in foil with butter, salt and pepper to become crunchy on the outside *mostly* cooked on the inside and kissed by the smoky flavor from the fire. Danni and Mindy more often than not wished they could wipe the boy's sweaty faces with a cool washcloth; but Army and Dan always said to leave them alone, it was a boy's rite of passage to sweat and be dirty when saving the world. The barn had become a haven for the boys and a sounding point for the adults.

Sammy made his way to the bottom of the haystacks and opened the cooler Danni had packed up for them to take to the barn that day. Sammy thought again, what a cool mom Danni was. She always made sure they had water, she was after all, a MOM; but she always included some special stuff too. Root beer, their *brewskies* as the boys called them and always some sandwiches (not the usual Pb&j either), turkey and cheese, fried egg and bacon, possibly burgers with thin slices of red onion and always salty peanuts. Of course, she was a mom and so a piece of fruit each, apples, pears or grapes were in there too.

"Hey Anth!" Sammy called up.

Anthony looked over the side of the bale just as Sammy heaved a can just missing his friends head. Anthony performed a little juggling act before actually catching the can.

"Nice catch, bro, tap the top!" Sammy shot back with a smart-ass grin on his face. The trick was to tap the top of the tab with your index finger for about thirty seconds. The urban legend claimed that it would calm down the soda so it would not blow a volcano out the top when opened. It did not always work and the boys knew it was a risky roll of the dice, but that was what made it fun.

"What'd mom pack us?" Anthony asked his stomach growling loudly. "I'm starved."

"I'm lookin' now."

"Hurry up or I'll chuck another hocker over the side and land it on your frickin' head!" Anthony had pulled himself on his stomach to the edge of the haystacks to stare over at the feast.

Sammy had found the first two sandwiches wrapped in wax paper. He loved the sound of opening wax paper, it sounded crispy. He whooped like an Indian when he realized what the sandwiches were and at the same time, spotted the two small bags of kettle chips.

"What! What?" yelled Anthony his body from the waist up dangerously hanging over the hay.

"OnmyGOD" breathed Sammy as he pulled back a piece of the bread to make sure what he smelled was really in the sandwich. "Pepperoni!"

"With cheeesse?" Anthony drawled softly as his stomach grumbled all the louder in anticipation.

"Oh yea man, with cheese *and* sauce . . . and Anth, she toasted the bread."

Anthony had let his body fall too far forward trying to look at the sandwiches and he slid down the side of the haystack with boneless ease, like someone deliberately throwing himself down a slip and slide. He landed in a heap, his head just grazing the side of the red cooler.

Sammy was already chewing a mouthful of sandwich, pushing a small piece of pepperoni hanging from his bottom lip into his mouth with his right thumb, his lip glossy with the pepperoni grease; he made a small sucking sound as red juice languidly ran down the inside of his forearm and he hurried to stop the run-away sauce. Sammy's crooked smile met Anthony's hungry gaze as he leaned over the cooler for his sandwich,

"How ya doin' bud?" he drawled as he picked-up another root beer and tapped his finger on the top of the ice cold can in a ritual that they felt made them *real* men.

"Gimmie," said Anthony with his hand out, anxious to taste the salty pepperoni, silky cheese and spicy sauce.

At that first bite, his teeth moving through bread that was slightly crunchy on the outside from grilling, then soft and lightly wet with sauce, his stomach felt that first sensation of a magnificent feast on that bright and sunny day. He reached for another root beer having left the one thrown to him on top of the hay bale, and Sammy laughed because he knew what was coming. Anthony had an unusual way of drinking soda from a can. When he first opened it, he slurped three sips from the can, but only those first few sips. A habit which annoyed Danni to no end, and made Sammy laugh every time. *Slurp . . . slurp . . . slurp*

"I love your mom," murmured Sammy as he pulled open the bag of kettle chips and tasted the salty snap that made a small vein on his right temple throb.

The smile between the two boys cemented the perfect memory on that golden afternoon. They would soon have occasion to remember longingly the innocence of that day.

CHAPTER 6

It was a relief when the alarm clock went off. It woke Jon Wendels from the reoccurring dream plaguing him since leaving the crime scene at Jigs Seederly's house.

The dream always started with the muffled cries of a woman and Wendels was trying to get to her, to help, to save her from what he knew was going to be her fate. He was always lost in an underground maze that seemed small yet complex, black walls covered in odd, yet disturbing symbols he could not understand. He was always clawing his way through what felt like thick spider webs, cocoons almost. They clung to him, sticky on his face, and he could feel the panic raise in him with every step. In his dream, wet, heavy bugs dropped on him from above, he could feel them in his hair, or hitting his shoulders and worst of all, sliding down the collar of his shirt onto his back. As the woman's cries became more hysterical, he struggled harder to find his way through the dark maze. Then came the naked light bulbs hanging from above swaying and blinking off and on off and on like strobe lights making his movement's robot like and surreal.

Today's high will be 66 degrees with sunny skies. Tonight's low will be 42 with a chance of rain. This is Rita Terrence for WPGH news on your morning commute.

Wendels hit the off button instead of snooze, he did not want to take a chance of drifting back to sleep and repeating any portion of the dream terrorizing his sleep of late.

As he sat up in bed intending to swing his legs out, he realized it was Saturday, and he had the day off. He experienced the momentary euphoria everyone enjoys when they think they have to go to work, then realize suddenly, they do not.

Oh, thank God. Jon let his body fall back into the warm sheets. He pulled the blanket across him rolling to his right side and throwing his left leg out and across the covers pulling the linen tightly between his legs into his groin, briefly feeling that sweet pleasure that makes sense to only men.

He remained like that for several minutes with his eyes closed, then rolled onto his back lifting his right hand to his face, his thumb massaging his temple in a circular motion then rubbed the 'v' between his nose and forehead with his index finger and thumb trying to quiet the jumble of thoughts that lately never seemed to stop.

What the hell is wrong with me? Wendels thought as he flung his arms above his head his fingers nails tattooing on the wood of the headboard. Something about the whole Jigs Seederly case was haunting him. He was missing something, he knew it, he felt it, but he could not put his finger on exactly what *it* was or decide his next move. Maybe it was the overwhelming volume of the lives apparently taken; thirty-two purses recovered to date and hopefully the final count. God, he hoped so, he did not think he could look at any more pictures of women being tortured and murdered. Although the Homicide Team for this investigation had grown expedientially by bringing in detectives from other municipalities, what they had found were *purses*, not bodies, and nowhere within the house was any evidence that the murders had occurred at that location. After the forensics team had finished with the house, they moved onto Jigs car, which had provided at least a small amount of evidence, although strange. Both front seats had plastic seat coverings. A chain glove, the type a meat cutter would use, right hand only, that also had the right hand of a plain brown work glove inside of it, had been located under the driver's seat. The interior light had been deliberately removed and the passenger's seat was loaded with junk, and very old junk at that . . . fast food containers, magazines which turned out to be a bizarre mixture of S&M and wood working publications, and within the pile of trash they had recovered several hairs. Luminol testing had identified blood splatters on the cloth ceiling and right front dash and door panel, but nothing close to the unrelenting, horrific pictures that were lovingly placed into those purses by the deranged murdering enigma named Jigs.

They had been able to type two spatters of blood, but had no bodies to connect them too, the same with the hair samples. Now began the long process of trying to put the few Humpty Dumpty pieces together.

He and the other detectives didn't think Jigs could have pulled off crimes of this magnitude by himself, he must have had someone else helping, planning, or possibly another location where the actual murders took place, so Wendels had attended the recent estate sale to watch the crowd. No one had *looked* suspicious but that did not rule anyone out. At the end of that day, no one had purchased the house. Oh yes, many curious individuals had done a walk through, looking he knew, for the room in which 'Jelly Jigs' (word of his autopsy condition had introduced a whole new cottage industry of morbid humor) had been found by the unfortunate utility worker. However, you could tell even a walk through gave them the willies. Jokes, jibes, laughter and smiles seemed to turn off like a switch.

In addition, no matter what *Benson Brothers Auctions* tried, including planting a multitude of *scrubbers,* containers of absorbent crystals intended specifically to remove the smell of corpses from a house, there unfortunately remained a peculiar odor. Like apples and onions left in a dark basement too long, or old vinegar mixed with the rank raw smell of bacon gone bad, left opened on a counter under a brown piece of butcher paper to discover its own insidious destiny, that of rancid meat and fat that smelled salty, bloated and *green.* You would know deep down that something obscene lay hidden under that grease soaked brown paper, and yet the voyeur side of your brain wants to *see* just what that putrescent little sweet treat looks like. Usually the rational side of that very same brain recoils and fights to turn off such thoughts with a self-protecting shutdown of sorts . . . usually. It made people entering the house pull their lips down in a thin line unconsciously drawing their nostrils into a purposeful closed position. Somewhere, deep in their brains, their ancestral DNA told them something was terribly *wrong* in this house.

The property more than likely would eventually go to the sheriff sale and the hope of the *Benson Brothers* was that someone outside of the local area would spot the ad on the internet and consider it a seductive properly to flip.

All this whirled around in his mind as he got up and put on coffee. He got in the shower, scrubbed down and shaved since it was easier and less irritating once his face warmed up from the steam. Besides, there currently wasn't a woman he wanted to impress with perfect hair and sideburns and a nick here and there amounted to nothing more than a momentary sting and a piece of toilet paper on the cut once he was out of the shower.

God he wished he had a delete key to his brain. He felt contaminated by an evil virus Jigs had spewed and the ghastly rank miasma threatened to envelop him.

CHAPTER 7

By mid afternoon, the boys had exhausted their muscles with play and sated their appetites on the banquet from Danni's excellent picnic cooler.

Laying flat on their backs, head to head like two inverted clothespins, they had floated off to that glorious space between wakefulness and sleep, adrift, quite comfortably on a sea of hay. When sleep blissfully took them, it was complete and profound. Their breaths came measured and even, the deep reverie of spirits immersed in a very relaxed state.

"Anthony! Sammy! Hey guys, where are you?"

Anthony felt himself nudged awake by his father's voice. It sounded distant and close at the same time, like listening to someone speak through a long cardboard tube. He sat up, hay sticking out of his hair like a human porcupine and stuck to his back as if he had been rolled in toasted coconut, he was pulled reluctantly from blissful sleep, his brain resisting returning to reality.

"Boys come on! I've got something to show you."

Two things occurred simultaneously flipping the switch in his brain to full power.

He realized he had to pee like 60 (a term his granddad used, though he did not know why) and that his father's voice was incredibly animated which could mean only one thing . . . *Something* was up. Something *really cool.*

He reached out giving the still sleeping Sammy a push that elicited a double snort that sounded horse like in the quiet of the barn.

"Huh? What is it? What's wrong?" Sammy began to sit up but overcompensated in his sleep-saturated state and rolled onto his left side like an overstuffed rag doll.

Anthony snagged the top of Sammy's t-shirt pulling him forward with the hopeful intent to get him off his fanny. Sammy now totally off kilter just rolled the other way.

"Come on bro, it sounds like dad has something to show us and I've gotta pee so bad. Come on!" Anthony swiveled to his knees and directly to his feet in one fluid motion, a movement reserved for the young and incredibly limber.

Sammy struggled to stand, stumbled, and by the time he got his legs under him, Anthony was already sliding down the haystacks like a sled on new snow.

"Hang on! Wait up! Don't start anything without me!" He begged making his way to the edge of the hay and, giving up any sense of safety, he dove over.

As Anthony made it through the double barn doors, to his absolute astonishment, Sammy shot past him legs sticking out of his green shorts pumping as if they were two pistons stoked on high-octane fuel. Sammy's mad rush to catch Anthony had soaked his muscles with so much adrenaline that his sprint seemed inhumanely fast. As Sammy realized he had not only caught up to, but also passed Anthony, his eyes rounded in disbelief.

Inertia has a way of mating with gravity and bringing seemingly amazing feats to fruition, and so it happened with Sammy. His forward motion downhill had far exceeded the ability of his pumping legs to keep up. His body's protective response was to send his arms pin wheeling in huge circles to try to slow his momentum and thereby avoid disaster.

Maybe it was because only moments ago Sammy had flopped in the hay like the preverbal rag doll appearing ungainly and slow, but as his body pitched forward in what should have been skinned knees and a bloody nose event, Sammy redeemed his self-esteem with magnificent luck and heretofore-unknown skill. He put both arms out in front of him bending them skillfully and with seemingly perfect timing, tucked his head in and let his body tumble into a seamless summersault for which any gymnast would have been awarded a perfect '10' in any competition. The icing on the cake was, he came up on both his feet and somehow remarkably was still running. He glanced back at Anthony for a split second with a look on his face indicative of someone saying, *how the hell did that happen?* Then realized he was in the lead and whooped with unbridled delight. Anthony, so taken aback by this turn of events that he pulled up, stopped, bent over and resting his forearms on his thighs began a belly-whopping laugh. He sat back on his haunches and laughed, he plopped on his butt and laughed, he rolled on his back with his feet up still laughing and fighting the overwhelming urge to pee his pants all at the same time. Under these circumstances, a few drops of pee did not count.

Wiping his eyes with the palms of both hands, Anthony looked toward the garage and saw the victorious Sammy hi-fiving Army who had a huge grin on his face. It was then Anthony realized that he may be the one missing the *prize* that his dad was about to unveil and he found himself the one now shouting up to the garage, "Wait for meee!"

As he got to his feet and loped towards the garage, he heard Sammy rumble up a good hocker and saw him let fly a great wad of spit. Sammy looked at Anthony in delighted vindication and mopped the back of his hand across his mouth. It was of course, the manly thing to do.

Army was waving him on with a *hurry up* gesture and as the driveway gravel crunched beneath his feet as he approached the Honda, the excitement between the trios crackled like a bright halo of static.

"What is it dad, what'd you find?" he panted.

Army looked around, up at the house and at both boys. "Your moms aren't here right?"

Sammy and Anthony nodded in solemn unison and stood transfixed as Army pressed the trunk open button on his keychain. As the trunk swung up the boys saw . . .

"Tools?" queried Anthony. "Umm, wow cool beans dad. What are they for?"

"Yea, cool Mr. Petrucci," chimed in Sammy glancing sideways at Anthony for confirmation of the shared confusion.

"I'll tell you about them in a minute," said Army moving them to the far left side of the trunk compartment and peeling back the carpet held in place by Velcro to reveal the spare tire well. He picked up a paper grocery bag with the top folded down three times like a huge lunch bag.

"Think Halloween Extravaganza boys, Ax-Man's got a brand new face!" exclaimed Army as he looked back and forth between Anthony and Sammy.

As Army began to roll open the flaps, Anthony had an overwhelming emotion to reach out and stop him and say, *"wait dad, don't."* However, the sensation passed as quickly as it had occurred and he found himself riveted beside Sammy as his father extracted his latest *keeper* from the unassuming grocery bag.

"Holy crow," whispered Sammy in wonder.

"It's a beauty isn't it?" beamed Army.

"Here comes mom," warned Anthony.

Had they practiced for weeks on individual assignments and timing, the three of them could not have worked in a more synchronized harmony than they did in the next thirty seconds. Army dropped the mask into the bag and swept the bag back into the spare tire well. Anthony picked up the oak miter box pushing the carpet back over the trunk floor.

"Ouch! A bee stung me! Oooohhhh!" yelled Sammy as he threw himself on the ground to the left of the Honda.

It all happened with such organized fluidity that Danni did not wonder if they were hiding something. She knew it.

"Hey guys, I've got pepperoni pizza and chocolate cake in the car, will you help me carry everything in the house?" she crooned deceptively.

Sammy shoved Anthony out of the way, the phantom bee sting forgotten. Anthony managed to trip Sammy sending him sprawling in the grass and causing more pain than the phantom bee sting while the compassionate ringleader, Army put his arm around his wife and turned her skillfully away from the car.

"Thanks babe, I'm starved."

"Welcome," she said giving him a peck on the side of his cheek. "How was the sale?"

"Good, good. It was really good." He felt as if the infamous Spanish Inquisition was about to string him to the rack.

"Oh, that's nice honey. Did you find what you wanted?" she asked ever so sweetly.

"I did and then some!" his defenses cleverly and totally wiped out by her charming disposition.

It was a relatively easy motion really, turning her body out and away from the arm he had put leisurely around her hips, and in one unconstrained movement, she was before the open Honda trunk.

"Show me what you have sweetheart," her voice now held a dangerous combination of sugar and spice tones as she reached in the still open trunk of the Honda. Army's 'fight or flight' mode engaged and he moved to intercept his wife before she took anything out of the trunk. He had the right side of the trunk lid, she had the left, he was pulling down, and she was pushing up. Their eyes locked, and as hers tightened in the corners, an eyebrow arched warningly while her smile never wavered.

Army's reaction was immediate and decisive. He gave up.

Danni's eyebrow relaxed, her eyes returned to normal and the dark circle of death swimming around Army's vision cleared.

Be a man, do what you always tell your son to do—tell the truth and face the music, he thought. He took a deep breath and prepared to tell the truth, sure it would not be just music he was about to face, but a head banging punk band.

"Well, I bought some tools," he said sweeping his hand in an exaggerated Vanna White gesture.

"Oh I see the tools, and they are lovely," said Danni, her laser beam gaze never leaving his face. "I'm most curious though, about what is in the bag in the tire well." Her hand moved to pull back the carpet.

Army stayed his wife's hand and maneuvered the tools out of the way. Without a word, he pulled back the carpet, extracted the paper bag and set it on the ledge of the trunk between the bumper and the inside.

He waited one last second in hopes of a miracle, resigned himself to his coming fate and opened the bag.

Oblivious to the drama unfolding at the trunk of the Honda, the boys had made it to Danni's car (shoving and pushing at one another the whole way), and were untying the handles of the half dozen plastic bags in the back seat of Danni's Saturn. Among the fruit, veggies (yuck, broccoli thought Anthony as his stomach churned), bath soap, ground beef, brown rice and toilet paper they found a *frozen* pizza and a *boxed* cake with directions that promised it could be ready to bake in just minutes.

Anthony and Sammy, each halfway in opposite rear car doors, looked at one other and then back towards Army and Danni.

"We sure fell for that one," said Sammy.

"God, she trapped him," replied Anthony, pity in his voice and he watched his father set the bag on the edge of the car trunk.

The recently famous sprinter, tumbler and hocker, Sammy Brogan said, "We might as well go see what the mask looks like close up before your mom tosses it."

"Your right bro. I didn't get a good look at it and knowing mom, it won't last long. Besides, we should probably support my dad."

The boys backed out of the car and stood up slamming the two doors closed.

No one would ever have guessed the two best friends had just minutes before run like Achilles, as they trudged with heavy limbs and leaden feet towards the Honda.

CHAPTER 8

As Danni peered cautiously into the bag where Army had stashed his latest Halloween prize, she realized that the boys were on their way back up the driveway. They had the most disheartened look on their faces and her husband was standing with his hands in his front pockets, his head tilted down in a dejected stance. His posture one of defeat.

It was another mask, an exceptionally ugly one. She knew Army to be a warm, caring man, it was one of the reasons she fell in love with him. It was also, why she could not understand his attraction to Halloween horror masks. Granted, the guys had a great time planning, building and decorating each year for Halloween, and she must admit it was fun dressing up in different consumes every year. She hated just those horrid masks. Maybe it was because when she was eight, her older brother Andy, had donned a Wolman mask their mother had gotten him as part of a costume, and typical older brother that he was, he had waited for her in the dark at the top of the stairs. Danni had always been afraid of the stairwell in the first place; she had hated that there was only one bare bulb in a socket at the bottom of the steps. That single bulb cast shadows that seemed to pulse and swell and she had this feeling that the shadows could swallow her if they wanted. She always made her way up the stairs on the right side along the handrail. She would hold onto the railing with her right shoulder pressed along wall. If any of those shadows tried to swallow her, she intended to put up a fight. Her parents' bedroom was at the top of the stairs on that same side and Danni knew if she could make it that far the danger, for the time being, was over. Her bedroom was at the opposite end along the long portion of the hall. When she was seven, she had awakened from a bad dream and wanted only to find safety and comfort next to her mother. She made a dash down the hallway, but when she came to the short side of the hall, the side where the hated stairwell descended into the dark, she came to a screeching halt. Her dilemma was that she must find the courage to pass that seeming portal to hell to find sanctuary in bed with her mother. After several agonizing moments of indecision, a creak in the wood floor behind her sealed her resolve. Her legs unwound like a tightly coiled spring and propelled her past the stairwell into the safety of her parents' room. The moment she saw her mother's side of the bed Danni had launched herself into the air to come down with her elbow smack in the middle of her mom's left eye. That woke the whole house up and fueled a firestorm of yelling from her dad. Her mother's subsequent black eye left her feeling ashamed and silly for weeks afterwards.

Andy had played on that fear and had hidden at the top of the stairs. The unsuspecting Danni had made it to the top, to what she considered safety, when out from the dark came her brother wearing the Wolfman's mask, a horrible growl erupting from the rubber lips. Paralyzed in fear, her immediate reaction was to wet her pants much to her brother's delighted laughter.

Think this through don't just react . . . think.

"So guys, just exactly what is the plan for this. Let me guess, the ax guy is getting a new face?"

Army's head came up for a wide-eyed glance at his wife and as he turned his head to the right where the boys were standing (also with dumbfounded incredulous expressions); a smile began to form from the middle of his lips and worked its way in both directions. By the time he was looking at the boys it had become a full, sparkling, joyous grin.

They all began to talk at once.

Danni had the oven preheating on 375° and the pizza was in a pan ready for toppings. Army was cutting up the extras for her as she was famous for the way she 'doctored up' a frozen pizza and made it their own with olives, onions, fresh tomatoes or extra cheese, whatever she might have on hand. She looked at her husband and thought again, about what she was seeing; Army was cutting up the extras. *What the heck, if that is all it takes to make him this happy, be grateful!* She chided herself as Army continued chattering away.

"I'm pretty sure we have enough good left over lumber in the garage that we can really build a cool back-drop, and I was thinking this year of doing a collage of Halloween favorites, you know, instead of just one theme like I've done in the past, this year get as many of them together as we have stuff for, Dracula, Mummy, Frankenstein, Swamp Thing, Jason and Ax-Man, maybe they could all be chasing each other or fighting or something and Sammy is going have a blast 'cause this will be his first one with us and Mindy and Dan can come over and . . ."

"Honey, take a breath!" Danni laughed. "You're going to pass out for God's sake!" She slid the pizza into the oven, wiped her hands on the tea towel thrown over her shoulder, looked again at Army's animated face, and began to laugh again.

Army walked to his wife and put his arms around her pulling her body close to his. He always marveled at how perfectly her head fit under his chin and the feel of her hand stroking the back of his neck; it made him strong and vulnerable at the same time. When he looked into her eyes, sometimes he felt as if he were being drawn right into her soul to float peacefully on the beautiful flowing river that was Danni.

"I love you Danniella," he breathed softly in her ear.

She leaned more fully against his body and he felt that delicious all consuming jolt roll through him as he shifted his weight slightly to more fully enjoy the sensation.

"Hey Mom," came Anthony's voice from the bottom of the basement steps, "is the pizza done yet? We're starved!"

Danni patted Army on the chest and stepped away looking at the oven timer.

"About eight more minutes' honey," she called down glancing at Army with a smile on her lips.

Sammy's disembodied voice laced with excitement drifted next up the stairs. "Mr. Petrucci, are you coming down? You gotta see this!"

"You goof ball, he knows about it, he built it!"

Both Army and Danni barked out a laugh when they heard their son's reply.

Meanwhile, Anthony was holding the new mask and laughing at Sammy's antics. He lifted the mask with the intention to put it on his face and go after Sammy. As he brought it up to his face, he noticed that on the inside left, was a very odd drawing. He partially turned that area inside out in his attempt to see it more closely. A star within two circles and the star appeared to have a horned face within it

Anthony felt frozen in place.

"Sammy, come and look at this."

"Look at what?" Sammy asked as he twirled with a black cape on that billowed out like a bell around him. "Watch this!" he yelled attempting a cartwheel towards Anthony and ended up flipping over an old chair and falling on an upturned leg landing right on his nuts. "AAAuuuggghhhh," he groaned.

Anthony slid to the floor laughing so hard he was sure he was going to pee his pants for the second time in one day. The mask fell away from him onto the floor forgotten as Sammy's cries of anguish and Anthony's howling laughter drifted up the basement stairs.

"Your loyal fans await you my dear," said Danni as she chuckled listening to the boys downstairs.

As he passed his wife, Army stopped and ran his fingers along his wife's face and kissed her gently on the lips.

"Thanks for not being mad about the mask," he said sincerely.

Danni was quick to pull the towel off her shoulder and snap him on the backside as he turned to go down the steps.

"Just watch it buster, Halloween is still 4 weeks away."

As he looked at the boys laughing, he began to laugh too, stooping to pick up his new mask and put it back in the bag.

Five minutes later the timer went off and all three boys, Sammy, Anthony and Army stampeded up the stairs yelling "PIZZA!"

They ate on the deck in the early evening on that cool autumn day. Pizza and chocolate cake with ice-cold glasses of milk was a feast they all enjoyed as the sun's rays lengthened along the ground as the Earth turned its head towards winter. The sound of bright, happy voices filled the autumn air as they joyously made plans for the new Halloween display.

At the bottom of the basement steps the brown bag from the trunk crinkled as something moved insidiously within. The ominous laughter that spilled from it like jagged shards of glass would have frozen the blood of the most soulless serial killer.

*

At the coroners' office, Scott Champion had finally received all the tissue and blood sample analysis he had requested on the Seederly case. Since foul play was low on the cause of the death ladder in this instance, any other analysis on other samples from other cases were elevated a higher priority.

Champion's interest though, had not waned. In fact, he had continued research on his own time because of his interest due to the unusual circumstances surrounding this particular death.

Since a conventional medical explanation was not plausible in this instance, and because he really did want to write a paper, he had been researching unusual, unconventional and yes, bizarre possibilities.

If nothing else, he had learned there were opinions and speculations that were not only interesting but also that boggled one's mind. For instance, TLDM signals (Targeted Long Distance Microwave) that it was rumored the Defense Department was working on at a secrete facility; Spontaneous Human Combustion, Paroxysmal Metabolic Syndrome, were a few, and with the condition Jigs body had been in, hell he had not ruled out voodoo. Thank God for the internet and laptops. They allowed him to conduct much of his research in a pair of sweatpants and t-shirt. It sure beat the days in medical school 30 years ago. Hours on end at a long wooden table with the finish worn off at the edges all the way around from the thousands and thousands of hours people had leaned on laid across and propped books against; sitting in a equally worn, horribly uncomfortable chair until his skinny ass ached. Now though, his posterior was a tad more ample, and probably would more comfortably pad any extended visit to a library 'chair of pain.' In addition, he had serious doubts about keeping a bowl of Fritos at hand to munch on at the library as he did at home—Fritos, his favorite, and a major cause of his now larger posterior.

What the heck, he thought has he popped another salty, greasy, crunchy delicious Frito into his mouth and clicked his mouse pad on another website.

He lost track of time when he realized he had clicked his way into a bizarre search string. The list contained choices as: Wicken/Moon Spells/Shamanisms/Goth Craft/High Magic/

Black Magic/Satanism. He realized his eyes were watering, the result of too much time staring at the monitor and not blinking. He had uncovered a multitude of unusual and at times gruesome information concerning types of magic, spells and curses. There were spells to make you rich or to make you appear desirable to another person, spells to make you successful or even famous. And then there were the curses; curses to make a person fall out of love with your rival, curses to bring misfortune to their finances or curses that would make that rival become unattractive to the person you desired. Curses now, they could be tricky, for, if done incorrectly, each could bring disaster for the intended recipient or the caster.

Scott continued a while longer perusing the internet, then paused and stood to stretch and decided to refill his corn chip bowl. As he put a clean paper towel in the basket he used for corn chips and a blue 'chip clip' on the bag to seal it he glanced at the clock . . . 9:30 p.m. He thought about going to bed but decided to give his research another 30 minutes and then call it a night. He wiped up the counter with a damp dishcloth where some stray corn chip crumbs had fallen, brushing them into his left hand and tossing the crumbs into the wastebasket. For a moment he considered putting the corn chips back in the bag then decided, *I'll put back what I don't eat. Ha! Fat chance of that*. As he made his way back to the double recliner, he popped two corn chips into his mouth and sat the basket on the fold down table that was part of the double recliner. He brushed off his hands on his sweatpants, sat down settled into his research position.

A small pillow to set the computer on.☑.

Bottle of cold water.☑.

Reading glasses.☑.

Basket of corn chips.☑

He moved his finger across the mouse pad again and back to the last search string he had been reading. He clicked and read, clicked and read, clicked and read. Several times, he sent interesting articles to the printer for review later or saved them to his favorite's toolbar. The quite of the house was interrupted only by the soft tap, tap, tap of his fingers on the keys, and an occasional crunch.

He began reading from a site called, *Serving the Prince of Darkness*, which was under the subtitle of Satanism. In the back of his mind he thought, *what in the world draws people to this kind of thing? Well, I'm reading it. Maybe this is how they are hooked. Maybe, while looking for something entirely different you came across this type of information, and it snags you.*

All this whirled through his mind as he picked up another chip and considered it was time to go to bed. As he popped the last corn chip (literally the last, so much for putting back the ones he didn't eat), and his index finger swirled across the black mouse pad of the laptop and his thumb clicked on the final site of the evening, his jaw stopped in mid chew. The picture at which he was looking canceled out the last command sent by his brain.

Impossible . . . Impossible. It's a twisted trick of some kind.

What appeared on his laptop monitor in full color appeared to be a body. Or, more accurately, what was left of a body. He leaned forward for a closer look at what eerily appeared to be the twin of Jelly Jigs in all his bloated, decomposing glory. Beneath it the caption read:

Wrath of the Master

CHAPTER 9

Sammy could not keep from repeatedly glancing at the wall clock with the agonizingly slow second hand. It felt like English class would never be over. He did not like English class, but he did like his teacher Mrs. Bowman. A short, petite woman with a kind disposition and a good sense of humor, she related well to the students and controlled her class with strength and respect. At this moment though, she was at the blackboard explaining in animated tones and facial expressions the finer points of sentence diagramming along with the proper use of past participles and adjectives in the English language, thank you very much.

Yuck thought Sammy as his right leg bobbed up and down on the ball of his foot at the same time he was tapping the eraser of his pencil in synchronized rhythm to the clocks second hand.

All he wanted to think about was getting out of school, getting his homework done, wolf down some dinner and rush over to Anthony's house to work on the Halloween backdrop. Mr. Petrucci wanted to complete all the painting so they could get set up by the weekend and have three full weeks to tweak it and enjoy the effects. The boys had painted the three pieces of 4x8 plywood light brown to simulate large stones and were beginning the process of painting in the mortar a lighter color with chip brushes. The result was time consuming but effective at simulating the dark foreboding walls of an underground labyrinth. They had found and end-of-season stash of tike lights at one of the box stores and offered the store manager a good price to take the last eight out of inventory. They had then taken rags from Army's workshop, rubbed them with brown and black shoe polish and wrapped the bamboo lights with the rags to make them look old and used. Then they had drilled four one-inch holes in the wood back drop at an angle so they could slip the tike lights in and drilled a hole through each bamboo pole to put a screw through that would hold the light in place. When lit, it would be awesome and eerie, which was perfect. After many discussions about the Halloween theme, they deemed Army's idea best. A collage of some of the most famous monsters would grace their backdrop—Frankenstein, Dracula, Freddie Kruger and the new improved Ax-Man. Brunhilda the Witch would be standing next to the old lard kettle under which they stacked wood, and Halloween night would see it lined with candles and filled with dry ice. They had a faux cemetery planned with wood tombstones sprayed with stone texture to make it look like cement.

A huge spider web had been hand tied between two of the porch posts, a great hairy spider graced the middle and angel hair (usually popular at Christmas) was used to imitate the spider's webbed victims. Danni looked at the spider web production and dubbed it GROSS so they knew it was very cool. Once the backdrop was complete, they would begin to put up the 'players' as Mr. Petrucci called them, and Sammy could hardly wait. It was all he and Anthony talked about and . . .

Sammy stopped suddenly in the middle of his delightful reverie realizing that the classroom was utterly quiet. When his eyes focused, he realized two things. 1) Every student in the classroom was swiveled in his direction and 2) Mrs. Bowman was standing not more than ten feet away watching him with unblinking eyes.

"Welcome back Mr. Brogan. Would you kindly share with the rest of the class where you've been while they have been studying sentence diagramming?"

Sammy continued to stare at Mrs. Bowman, rapidly blinking his eyes, realizing he had nowhere to run and nowhere to hide.

"Class dismissed," said Mrs. Bowman in a quiet, deadly voice.

Sam got up to run.

"Except for you Mr. Brogan."

He hung his head as the rest of the students gathered their books to go to their lockers and catch the rumbling busses waiting outside. Even after everyone had left, the silence from Mrs. Bowman continued to draw out for what seemed an eternity.

He did not squirm, and he did not look up, he just waited for the preverbal ax to fall.

Finally, she said, "So, Samuel. Follow me to the chalkboard and let's see if you can diagram the sentence we worked on this period. That way I'll know how much you absorbed and how much homework to give you."

Sammy shoulders slumped in abject defeat, not so much worried about what his parents would say about not paying attention in class and having to stay late, but rather that he would be forced to miss tonights painting in preparation for Halloween.

Two days after the incident at school, Sammy had permission to return to Anthony's house . . . with restrictions of course. First, his homework must be done, then his chores (of which there were many more now) and he must eat dinner with the family. Then and only then if there was time left before eight o'clock his mom would drive him to the Petrucci house for a few minutes of work on the Halloween display.

Sammy's dad, Dan, had intervened on his son's behalf, making a case of vindication for his lack of attention in this instance. On this particular evening, Sammy had gone to great lengths to position himself so that he could overhear their discussion of him. In his thick socks he had stealthily made his way ever so slowly, sliding his cushioned feet along the wood floor to avoid detection, picking his moments to move when the discussion became more animated. Finally, he made it to the second entrance into the kitchen, furthest from the hallway.

He settled slowly to his knees with his fingers planted on the floor like a sprinter in the last final seconds before the starting pistol went off, ready to dart away if they should suspect him eavesdropping on their conversation. He did not notice the small tendrils of sweat slowing coursing down each temple to converge at his chin and drip onto his t-shirt.

His heart was pounding as he listened to his father reading part of the note from Mrs. Bowman, which said, *I am concerned with Samuel's un-attentative behavior and lack of interest in sentence structure. It is worrisome to me as it pertains to Samuel's overall academic growth at this point of his development.*

"For crying out loud Mindy, I had to read her note twice before I got the gist of what she was trying to tell us," said Dan as Sammy held his breath and thought, *thanks dad* . . .

"I understand that Dan, but you have to remember she's a good teacher with good intentions and she sincerely cares about Sammy. Don't you remember she told us at the last parent teacher meeting that she feels Sammy has good potential for writing?"

"Humph, come on Mindy, give the kid a break it's *sentence diagramming*! That has got to absolutely be the most boring subject in school. Did you like it?"

"Dan, that's not the point and you know it. I'm worried that he is spending too much time and is too involved with this whole Halloween thing. Maybe we should consider not letting him go until after Halloween and have him concentrate on his school work," Mindy said as she continued scrubbing the same pan repeatedly at the kitchen sink.

Sammy held his breath when he heard his mom put verbiage to what in his mind, would be his worst punishment. *No mom, please not that, anything but that* . . .

"Mindy, you know the Petrucci's better than that. How many nights have we played cards with them and talked about the kids? You know their values as well as I do and that is the reason we have become close friends. You know Army is a good person, you've said that yourself. Ok, so he goes a little bug shit over Halloween. It's his once a year outlet and he goes all out. Think about how you like collecting New Age music; don't shake your head Mindy, you know what I mean. There isn't a CD spinner you walk past in any store that you don't check for Yanni, or David Arkenstone or anything Feng Shui, and you know it. Has Sammy been a little carried away? Ok, well maybe. However, this is the first time he has been involved in a project like this, and when I say *like this* I mean all the planning, job assignments, timelines and work. Yeah I get it, it's only Halloween but he is learning about commitment and teamwork and at the same time having fun. Would it bother you if he was into Santa Clause and snow angels with this much enthusiasm?"

Mindy blew out a frustrated breath from her nose and turned from the sink picking up the kitchen towel on the counter to wipe her hands. "That's an unfair comparison and you know it Dan. Santa Clause and snow angels don't have the reputation of slashing your throat and drinking your blood, chasing you through the woods to crush your head or slicing your body to ribbons with razor sharp steel fingers, now do they? And the music I collect is supposed to be inspiring and relaxing. Freddie Kruger, he inspires . . . what?"

"Come on Mindy, you know what I mean. Why don't we make a point of stopping over to see what is going? We'll tell Sammy in very clear terms that we are going to be watching him *closely* and that any drop in his grades or any more serious incidents of not paying attention, even in boring sentence diagram class, and he's shut off from the Halloween display. He may have some hidden talent here that we could be suppressing, you know set design or something."

He looked at Mindy and realized how lame that last statement had been, and tried another tactic.

"Try to remember how you felt about, well about . . . hey wait a minute. What about those stories you told me when you and your sister spent hours and hours building that Barbie castle. Didn't you say you blew off your chores and did as little homework as possible during that phase? Weren't you supposed to wash dishes and you both took the pots and pans and stuck them in the oven so you could get back to your *castle?* Didn't you forget those pots and pans were there and went to bed, and when your unsuspecting mom turned on the oven the next day, it was to discover the unwashed stuff when they started smoking up the house. Huummm?"

Mindy never took her eyes off Dan. She folded the towel very precisely into quarters and quietly laid it on the counter letting her hand rest on top of it, unconsciously running her fingers across the fringe.

"Ok Dan, I trust your judgment on this one. I want us to both talk to Sam tonight and lay down the law on this though. I will call Danni later and ask her if we can stop over tomorrow night. And for your information, there were only three pans and they didn't catch on fire, they set off the smoke alarm."

Dan smiled at his wife and said, "Well, some things haven't changed. Sometimes you still set the smoke alarm off when you cook!"

Mindy let out a yelped and took off after Dan who by the grace of God made a mad dash down the hallway in the opposite direction of where their son rigidly sat. She was hot on his heels, and got a two-hand hold on the back of his pants, yanking up as hard as she could to give him a giant wedgie.

"Oohhh!" he cried as his momentum dragged them both into the bedroom laughing.

In his little section of the opposite hallway, Sammy released the breath he seemed to have held for an eternity and filled his lungs with new, wonderfully cool air. He took the bottom of his t-shirt in both hands and wiped off his sweat soaked face. He heard his parents laughing in the bedroom and knew he had a reprieve and intended not to screw it up.

He quickly headed back to his room sliding noiselessly into the door on the same soft socks he had just used for his stealth mission. He flung open his English book and his notebook and began diagramming like a boy possessed; wanting to understand everything a diagramed sentence could teach him. He put the Halloween display in another compartment of his mind running it side by side with his homework, just as a computer runs two programs at once, primary and secondary. Primary was the Halloween display. Secondary was the sentence diagramming he was so studiously working on when both parents knocked softly on the door jamb to his bedroom and stuck their heads in, glancing at him and then at each other with a relieved smiles on their faces.

It was a talent Sammy would soon be glad he had honed, a skill, which under the right circumstances, could be the cause and effect of a life-altering event.

CHAPTER 10

Saturday—late afternoon.

It was cold for the third week of October and Detective Wendels wished he had picked up his coat before heading out to the Seederly property. The 'For Sale' sign was still in the front yard, though it appeared a neighborhood kid had been double-dared by one of his friends to give it a good whack.

It was near dusk and he had walked the property again looking for something, he did not know what, just *something* that his gut told him he had missed. Whatever that something was, it was important enough that it was keeping him awake at night, invading his sleep, nagging at his mind. It was an unsettling feeling, as if being so close he should only have to reach out to touch it, the sensation of almost understanding how to put all the pieces together. So close, but he couldn't quite touch that tangible part of whatever he was looking for, or maybe, whatever was looking for him. It left him confused and angry and strangely, empty, like a man dying of thirst, his throat dry as fine sand, his belly hollow and shriveled, and the water, ice cold and sweet was there in a clear glass, droplets of cool liquid salvation running seductively down the frosted side. Yet no matter how far he stretched, he could not quite grasp the glass and sate his maddening thirst.

As he walked the rear portion of the property, he noticed again, how odd the tree line seemed at the back of the battered shed. Stringy brambles wove around it and seemed to cling like wicked claws around the side. The woods were shadowed with little light shining through to the ground. Usually Wendels liked the woods in deep autumn, the way light would splay dappled through limbs and leaves, nature creating places you wanted to sit and watch the flurry of leaves rain down from the canopy of branches above. He liked those kinds of days.

This place though, felt different. It felt altered and angry. It felt like something grievous had happened here in the dead of the night or in the solitude of being just outside the range of any neighbors who would have been able to hear a cry for help or an angry retort.

He stood with his hands funneled deep in his pockets, the wind buffeting at his back his unzipped coat blowing like a cape behind him. It was then he realized a simple fact that had escaped him the other half dozen times he had been to this place. The trees and undergrowth, except for the sharp brambles, stopped within twenty feet of the backyard shanty. It was not a mowed area; it was more like a dead zone where nothing *wanted* to grow. The tree boughs draped sullenly near the shed, like a dark umbrella, and he was struck by the thought that it was not as if those branches were surrounding the shed in protection, but instead, in shame, as if they had seen or heard or *felt* unbearable sorrow and sadness and pain. The feeling of some old evil shimmering like waves of heat you see but don't see on a blistering hot summer day when looking across the school yard black-top, when the heat drafts up making you feel enveloped by invisible strings that some other entity is plucking.

Here thought Jon, *the answer is here, I can feel it.* He pulled his hands out of his pockets and walked towards the shed, and though he could see the padlock still securely attached, he grabbed and yanked at it thinking it would by magic, break off into his hands in two perfect pieces. It did not.

He walked back towards his car resolute in his actions. Opening the trunk, he pulled out the bolt cutters he had placed there some weeks ago. He did not know why, yet he felt this was the reason he had put the cutters in his trunk. He made his way back across the yard and when he reached the front of the shed, oddly he thought about how spongy the grass felt.

Probably from the moisture and constant shaded effect of the trees his mind thought numbly. An essence deep within him felt a foreboding, a warning that thrummed through him like low volt electricity, propelling him forward then pulling him back. It was almost as though two opposite poles of a magnet wanted so badly to come together, yet the invisible waves of magnetic energy kept pushing them left, then right, up then down. Always apart never quite together, so close, so very close.

As he walked toward the shed with the bolt cutters held out in front of him like the mandibles of a giant beetle snapping menacingly, something seemed to push him in his chest and he stumbled back a step. He struggled to move forward. *Two steps forward, one-step back. This must be what a dog feels like chasing its tail.*

Now he was not thinking, he was just reacting; then he was not reacting, he was only thinking. His mind was awash with tumultuous thoughts, vague and confusing then suddenly sharp and painful. His back arched as though a bolt of lightning was coursing hot through his veins. The bolt cutters fell out of his hands as he stumbled forward, catching the toe of his left shoe in the spongy ground. He tried to break his fall with his hands but he landed hard against the double doors on the shed. Going down, he jammed his right knee excruciatingly on the ledge of the shed. He cried out in pain and then felt both knees sink into the soft earth as his pant legs wicked up the cold wetness.

The door shuttered hard, as though someone had put a shoulder into it, and then the latch simply fell off. The lock remained on the latch, no damage appeared done to it; nothing broken or dented rusted or cracked, the latch simply seemed to have fallen out of the wood.

Watch for The Hand of God, blazed a voice somewhere, his mind folded, creasing common sense and fear together into some new altered state . . . like paper folded into an origami form. This form however, took flight within him as a folded horror, and then suddenly it bloomed like a supernova. The aura around him, his life force dimmed and almost winked out. The Hand of God though, watched over him, and He held His flame to the aura of Jon Wendels, capturing his light, cradling his life. Jon knew for that instant that he was destined to be a catalyst to some unknown life-changing event. It was a blessing that he lost consciousness at that moment; it was a blessing his aura was held high and burned strong. For what flew out of those now unrestrained doors surrounded him, keening in evil rage, pummeling his back and head in uncontained ferocity with sharp leathery wings.

The lair was violated.

ঌ৽ ঌ৽ ঌ৽ ঌ৽ ঌ৽ ঌ৽ ঌ৽ ঌ৽ ঌ৽ ঌ৽ ঌ৽ ঌ৽ ঌ৽ ঌ৽ ঌ৽ ঌ৽

He tumbled down, swirling in a nightmare of eddies and undercurrents. He felt as though he was fighting a current of sludge, and strength flowed out of his arms and legs making them feel like so much limp and useless dough. His eyes felt glued shut and he became overwhelmed by the horrifying sensation of something cold and dead pressing against his lips—pushing like the insistent tongue of a demanding unwanted lover. His brain screamed to his legs and arms to move . . . move! Still the sludge encased him weighing him down until even taking a breath had the sensation of a constrictor encircling his chest. With every breath he let out, it left less space for him to inhale. Claustrophobia threatened to complete the ever-tightening circle of madness inside his head, until suddenly he felt a great push from behind him, as though the weight of the sludge was propelling him forward, his body forced into a thick and gelatinous membrane, pressing hard against his nose causing indescribable panic. Little sparkling points of light rolled behind his closed eyes as his oxygen starved brain fought to keep him conscious. His mind processed only one thought *I'm dead* . . . and suddenly the mucus textured plug seemed to burst and he felt himself forced through the membrane with the sludge pouring out behind him like some noxious afterbirth.

The weight rolled from him like a wheel completing a tight turn and suddenly he was able to suck in a deep ragged breath.

Oxygen flooded his lungs and exploded in his brain like a hit from a junkie's crack pipe, but he was able to move then, and his limbs unwound like a garden hose rolling down a slope. Wendels tried to pull himself up but could get no further than his elbows. As he opened his eyes, he discerned a shadow, which meant a light source from somewhere. He remained perfectly still, though rapidly blinking his eyes, his ears pulled back like a dog listening intently, trying desperately to get his bearings. In the near darkness, he heard a noise that stretched his face into a hideous, silent mask of absolute terror for he recognized it . . . he was in his nightmare.

He was back in the tunnel.

Wendels pulled himself up from his elbows onto his feet, and in the dim light, he had his hands outstretched in front of him afraid of what he might touch or run into. He could hear their cries, he could feel their pain; the agony seemed to be a part of him. Women's' faces appeared around him a brief flashes in the near darkness, the effect like a strobe light, unearthly and disorienting.

He stumbled forward his body moving jerkily to the flashing faces, struggling to maintain his balance with his waning strength. A pair of disembodied hands seemed to reach out to him in supplication. Light and shadow ebbed and flowed around him, its movement seemed alive and cunning. He could not stop thinking, *I must find my way out, I cannot save their lives but I can save their souls. Think . . . think* he tried to command his mind. He heard a voice calling him back, softly at first, then calling more and more incessantly. Suddenly the heaviness dropped away like the shell of a cracked egg allowing him to flow back to . . .

"Jon? Jon! For God's sake, wake up!"

Wendels thought he recognized the voice but could not put a face to it yet. Hands were shaking him gently at first, and then suddenly he felt the sharp sting of a slap on his face. He felt the rest of his soul mercifully yanked out of the stench-filled horror of the tunnels.

"What?" he heard a voice, his but not his, a croaking sound to his ears.

His tongue stuck to the roof of his mouth like some ghastly sweet treat. He felt the slap again and dimly realized that he was drooling and that someone was trying to force him awake.

"Come on Jon, come on buddy, *wake up!*"

He recognized the voice now it was Scott Champion. Wendels found himself in a half sitting position leaning against the shed looking into Scott's concerned face.

He grabbed Champion by both his shoulders unable to understand what had just happened to him. He felt a sob escape him as he pulled himself into the safe haven of the of the medical examiners embrace.

"God help me," he wept.

Saturday—5:30 p.m.

Angela, Dan and Danni were following Army, Anthony and Sammy around the yard listening to their voices that were a cornucopia of excitement and pride.

The front yard was alive with the Halloween set and decorations both from years past and created especially for this monumental year. The 'set' or backdrop of the main characters were the 4'x8' sheets of plywood the boys had painted, laboring on so diligently every opportunity they had in the past couple of weeks. Mindy was thinking *he should work so hard on his schoolwork!* She kept quiet though, not wanting to diminish their accomplishment and enthusiasm. After all, Dan was right in regards to the fact that Sammy had not faltered in this commitment and it was a good lesson and opportunity to learn the value of teamwork. He had also kept his promise of maintaining his grades and Mindy had made a call to his

English, teacher Mrs. Bowman, who had reported he had been very attentative and completed all his homework.

As they walked about the yard, Mindy was struck by the detail of their work. The main characters, Frankenstein, Dracula, Freddie Krueger and their very own Ax-Man, were displayed in intimate detail. Frankenstein was grappling with Dracula, one of his huge blue veined scarred hands holding a spiked club that was positioned in a downward arc, his other hand clutching Dracula's shoulder to hold him still until he could club him. The simulated bolts that were holding Frank's head to his shoulders glowed red from the lights Army had deduced a way to hook up. Dracula was attached to the backdrop in such a way that made him look as if he was floating. His claw-like hands outstretched hands reached towards Frankenstein's throat and extra large fangs had been added to his famous mask. Sammy had come up with the idea to squirt several large drips of latex caulk onto wax paper, let them dry, and then paint them red and attach them to the oversized fangs.

The other half of the set had Freddie Krueger and Army's very own creation, Ax-Man.

Freddie of course had his signature metal glove with the four-finger knives, tattered hat, red and black striped shirt and scared face. The boys had positioned him in a crouching position his head looking up cocked to the left. His right hand was sweeping the wicked looking metal glove towards Ax-Man. His left hand was holding a garbage can lid as a shield. Ax-Man was dressed in his blue overalls an old pair of Army's work boots on his feet. Army over the years had adorned the rubber hands with wood hole plugs painted brown to look like warts and glued clumps of hair from an old mask to the palms of the hands then trimmed the hair short giving it a stiff bristling appearance. Ax-Man was positioned stepping forward toward Freddie, his left arm upraised and holding an ax that had been expertly painted to appear covered in blood. The new mask that Army had picked up at the Jigs Seederly estate sale sat atop the blue coveralls. Army had come up with a way to take individual mini Christmas lights and wire just as many as he needed for his displays and attach them to a battery pack that he hid under the clothes. The boys had used two, taping one behind each eye, which gave them an eerie, disturbing glow.

The lit tiki torches, candles and glowing pumpkins, enhanced all this. The cemetery had the headstones the boys had worked so hard on with the texture spray. They had put names like Wolfman, The Fly and Jason on some of the faux tombstones. Then they took one of the many rubber hands they had, partially stuffed it with plastic bags and put it in the ground so that it looked like it had clawed its way to the surface and grabbed a jogger. The jogger was portrayed by an old pair of Army's sweatpants and shirt that was finished off with a beat up pair of tennis shoes.

As Army, Anthony and Sammy ushered Danni, Dan, and Mindy around, it was hard to tell who was more excited, the boys or Army. They were all talking at once, each pointing out something different and explaining the smallest minutia. What they had done was quite amazing, and now six days from Halloween they could do two things, fine tune it and enjoy the results.

"Better buy lots of candy Danni," Dan said with a huge smile on his face.

"Since it's the first year at this house, I'm hoping that not *too* many kids know about it yet," replied Danni.

Mindy turned to Danni with an uneasy look on her face and said, "Danni, I hate to tell you this but Sammy informed me that he has told absolutely *everyone* at school what they have been doing." She looked back at the boys and at Danni again. "I'll start baking cookies tomorrow. I can have the freezer pretty full by Halloween."

Dan let out a whoop and started laughing as he took in the guilty look on his wife's face.

"Honey, if Sammy has been telling everyone at school, not only all the kids will be here but all their parents too. We're going to have to find another freezer to hold all the cookies you're going need!"

"Oh dear God, I'd better double up on the Sloppy Joes!" Danni said with a laugh.

Dan took one look at Mindy and put his arm around her shoulders pulling her close to him.

"I have a feeling that this could be the most eventful Halloween we ever hosted," said Danni as she reached out and took Mindy's hand as they watched the three mad scientists rushing around the yard.

Danni looked again at the backdrop and her eyes swept over Frankenstein, Dracula, Freddie and Ax-Man. It was so imaginative and her husband and the boys had worked hard on their creations, yet she could not help but feel a deep anxious dread each time she looked at Ax-Man's new face. Of all the masks she had ever laid eyes on, that mask chilled her soul and left her wishing that Halloween was over and all the decorations packed up and put away. She looked again at the masks and had a strange unsettling vision of a field of masks swaying ever so slowly to a deadly malevolent breeze that smelled of rot and decay.

What she saw in her mind was not a meadow or pasture from which a nourishing crop would be gathered, but rather to her growing alarm, in her vision she saw a dry, dead field of twisted masks and knew in her soul that the only thing that could come from it would be an evil harvest.

As Anthony and Sammy darted around the yard, their excited voices ringing like music on that beautiful night, the first weekend in October, Anthony noticed that the right arm of Ax-Man kept moving down and his body was leaning slightly further forward than when they originally set him.

"Hey Sammy, look at Ax-Man," said Anthony in a curious voice.

"Ok, I'm lookin' but what am I lookin' for Anth?" responded Sammy absently.

"I've fixed his hands three times and now his body position has changed . . . what's up with that?"

"I dunno." Sammy shrugged his shoulders. "Why don't we go get your dad and see what he thinks?"

"Nope. I think I'll try to figure it out tomorrow. It's gotta be that we don't have the support stake in the ground far enough to hold the body weight, and the dowel must be in the wrong place for his arm to keep moving like that. It just seems weird though, you know?"

"Yeah, ok," said Sammy as he turned his nose as he often did, toward the wind like a hound sniffing the air, paying little attention to what Anthony had actually said.

"Oh man," Sammy groaned, "let's go get a Sloppy Joe sandwich. I heard your mom say she had a pot on with cold brewskies and chips."

"Yep she does, and chocolate chunk cookies," Anthony laughed. "And Sammy," he said in a soft voice, "She *toasts* the buns and puts cheddar cheese on 'em too."

Anthony got the reaction he wanted. Sammy's eyes opened wide and he licked his lips. Anthony struck during Sammy's moment of weakness and darted toward the house. Sammy let out a yelp and tore after Anthony, slipping on the wet leaves and falling. His growling stomach and vision of Sloppy Joes on toasted buns with sharp cheddar cheese injected him with a spurt of speed. As was the norm with the two friends, once they started running, it quickly turned into shoving, pushing and tripping each trying to prevent the other from getting to the food first.

It was unusual that the athletic Anthony tripped going up the steps to the front door, but he did, and it allowed Sammy to claim victory by making it to the door first. S*weet* as Sammy would say, using his new favorite word.

"First dibs!" cried the jubilant Sammy as he shot through the door.

"That's ok Sam, I get *all* the leftovers!" called Anthony as he watched Sammy vanish inside his house.

As he made his way to the top of the stairs and onto the porch in the wake of the front door closing, he could smell the tomatoes, spices and browned beef that made up his mom's excellent Sloppy Joes. As he put his hand on the doorknob to go inside the house, he turned and looked out in jubilant wonder at their new and improved Halloween decorations.

He stopped in his tracks; his hand remained motionless on the door handle as he noticed with a sick kind of alarm that Ax-Man looked like he had *moved.* Not just a sagging body or twisted arm on an improperly placed piece of wood, but literally moved. Anthony stared hard at the spot double-checking what he saw.

Geez, it really looks like it moved. How could that happen? I'd better let dad know.

Then he was in the house and the smell of toasting buns, Sloppy Joes and homemade chocolate chunk cookies called his name. Amid all the warmth of the conversation and the crackling of logs in the fireplace, he forgot all about the strange movement on the right side of one of the 4'x8' wood backdrops.

Outside by the Ax-Man/Freddie display a low rumbling growl bubbled from the lips of the twisted, jagged grin on the mask that was Ax-Man's face.

"At last master, it has begun!" It hissed, the noise sounding venomous.

No one inside the warm and cozy house heard anything.

Later, much later, they would each remember a moment of indescribable doom that had passed through them on that golden autumn night.

CHAPTER 11

Saturday—6:00 p.m.

Champion still did not know what had prompted him to take a detour past the Seederly residence Saturday evening. Like a magnet however, he had been inexplicably drawn there. As he had turned onto one street and then another on his way to the secluded Ellison Drive, his common sense voice kept repeating *what are you doing.* Yet some stronger force kept him moving toward Jigs former residence.

As he rounded the curve on Ellison Drive he had immediately noticed, Jon Wendels unmarked police issue car parked close to the house. He pulled in the driveway directly behind Wendels vehicle and put his car in park. Gazing at the house, he did not detect any movement inside. The blinds and curtains were still drawn, no lights, no open door or windows that he could see, from this side at least.

As he had stepped out of his van closing the door, he walked past Wendels car, letting his hand slide along the hood on the driver's side. It did not feel warm to the touch, which meant it had been sitting for quite some time for the engine to be cool, and as he continued to walk towards the front porch all his senses switched into high alert mode. His ears picked up the soft crunch of gavel under the soles of his shoes, his eyes narrowed slightly as he surveyed the house with a raptors gaze. His muscles tensed in unconscious anticipation of possibly having to react quickly. His breathing slowed and his nose picked up the damp, slightly musty smell of the leaves on the ground.

Trying the handle, he found it locked and called out, "Jon, its Scott Champion, you in there?"

As he looked around, he rapped with a closed fist on the wood front door and called out again, "Jon! Are you in there? It's Scott."

When there was still no reply, he cupped his hands around his eyes and tried to see through the dirty window glass. He saw no movement inside and did not believe that Wendels was or had been in the house.

He dropped his arms down from the window and straightened up. *He has to be here somewhere* he thought as he made his way down the three steps and started around the front of the house to the right. The day was overcast and dreary, but here, in this place that felt and smelled like the evil that pursued you in your very worst nightmare, it felt ten times worse.

As he rounded the right side of the house and walked into the back yard, two things hit him at the same time. Utter, complete and deadly silence, and at the back of the yard in front of the shed lay the form of a man. Recognizing the form on the ground as Jon Wendels, Scott had gone several steps forward when he felt an odd wave of heat blow past him, momentarily stopping him in his tracks. His brain, trying to process what he was seeing, was attempting to ascertain if it was a corpse, or a live though obviously unconscious man. The hot wind smelled sulfurous and sick, much like you might imagine a city in the grip of death during the black plague and oddly, enough even though it was hot, it made him break out in goose bumps and shiver involuntarily. He rushed toward the slumped body on the ground and indeed found Jon Wendels. He was on his left side in a fetal position with his right arm covering his face. The part of Wendels neck that he could see was covered in deep slashes that were oozing blood and discoloring in deep purple bruises. His coat was twisted and muddy and looked as though it had been shredded. He could see the blood and mud soaked shirt was also in tatters. At that same instant, he became aware that the only noise he heard was that of Wendels whimpering in unrestrained fear.

Scott's knees sank into the soft muddy ground next to Jon as he pulled his arm away from his face.

"Jon" he said gently, his voice catching in his throat. Wendels face contorted in fear, his chest heaved and he thrust both hands in front of him, warding off some invisible daemon. His breathing seemed to stop and a thread of spittle bubbled on his lips.

"Come on Jon!" He almost shouted as he pulled his friend into a sitting position and tried to lean him against the shed.

"Come on buddy, wake up!"

Wendels eyes flutter open and what Scott Champion saw in those eyes caused him to pull the full grown, tough as nails detective into a protective embrace.

BEWARE THE BEAST

*

Saturday—6:45 p.m.

The van marked *County Coroner* was idling by the curb, a plume of steam coming from the tailpipe. When they had gotten back to the van the first order of business for now Doctor Champion was to clean and dress the deep slashes the detective had on his back, neck and to a lesser degree, arms. They had the look of claw marks, ugly, deep and inflamed. Wendels had almost passed out from the pain as Champion had wadded up a large piece of gauze, soaked it in alcohol and used the texture of the gauze to scrub the wounded areas. He had used every packet of Neosporin he could scrounge up from his med bag and dressed the worst injuries with clean gauze strips. What he found on his back though, was beyond description and he had initially recoiled in horror, but luckily, Jon did not notice the coroner's reaction. Scott knew Wendels needed further medical attention and antibiotics and he had already phoned in a prescription to the local Rite Aid.

Inside the van, the heater was on high and heat poured from the defroster. Scott was starting to sweat, but beside him Jon Wendels, wrapped in a blanket that Champion always kept in the back, was trembling. His wet, torn shirt and coat had been removed and he had on a gray sweatshirt from the gym bag in the van. Scott knew that the chill that racked his body was caused by the shock of whatever had just happened to him. The injuries to his body were nothing in comparison to what his soul had just endured, and Scott was trying to unravel the events and make sense of what Wendels and recounted to him. The part of his brain that did not believe in UFOs or Big Foot could not accept the premise of fighting a daemon. Yet all evidence pointed to that reality and Jon Wendels was no nut, he was not a half bubble off level or one bottle shy of a six-pack.

Jon was rubbing his temples in slow circles, his bandage arms and back making the sweatshirt look bulky and Popeye like.

"Scott," he said in a low weary voice, "I know we've had the cadaver dogs out here twice now with no result, but I am positive there is a grave site here."

Champion took in a slow deep breath through his nose and then blew the air out of his mouth in a whooshing sound. He raked his hands along both sides of his head joining his fingers at the back and tilted his head back trying to stretch out the tension in his neck.

"Jon, I can try and requisition the dogs back for another cadaver pass, but I doubt the chief will approve it again." He looked at Wendels pale, strained face, as he silently clenched and unclenched his jaw. "I'll call him if you promise to let me take you to the emergency room and have those puncture and claw wounds cleaned thoroughly. A friend of mine is the doctor on duty tonight and will keep everything discrete."

Wendels slowly turned his head towards the coroner lost deep in thought; his eyes seemed to blink in slow motion, a 'V' appearing on his forehead between his eyes.

Long moments seemed to pass and just as Champion was about to break the silence, Jon Wendels said, "Ok Scott, I'll go, or let you take me or whatever. I'll let you come up with the story of what attacked me, fill out the report for a dangerous animal at large and come up with a bogus reason that you just happened to stop by when you saw my car parked. You know they are going to ask all that and more. Jesus, the way things are now they could be thinking you and I are lovers and this happened during a domestic dispute. You know the routine better than I do . . . are you willing to file and sign a false report?"

The silence hung heavily between them.

"Are you?"

"I am."

"OK, just don't say it was at the Seederly house; tell them it was along the road near the entrance to Shailer Park."

Wendels became quite again and Champion could see that the detective was struggling to control his shuddering.

When he reached down to pull the gearshift into the drive position, Wendels grabbed his wrist with a cold quivering hand.

"Scott, please don't leave me alone," Wendels voice held the jerky cadence of a woman just raped.

"I won't."

He pulled the car into drive and eased slowly away from the house, made a tight 'U' turn on the road and aimed his vehicle toward St. Margret-Mary Hospital.

What the hell happened to him?

The normally cocky detective sat rigidly next to him in the car. Champion kept glancing at Wendels out of the corner of his eye, checking on him. When he realized that the wet sheen on Wendels face was not sweat but tears, he felt a shiver of real tangible fear snake its way down his spine. All the old stories of things that go bump in the night became real. The childhood stories he had heard during the camp-outs on moonlit nights; dark formed shadow people, and hag attacks. Daemons clinging spider like to the top of cars, waiting patiently on a teenager to exit the car after a heavy make out session, the daemon grinning as it wrenched the head from the shoulders of the hapless teenager and drank the hot spurting blood in orgasmic, gasping gulps. The old folk tales, the age-old reality clicked, clicked, clicked in his head like the frames of an old movie as it spun around the reel.

Scott Champion had thought he had seen the face of evil before in some of the thousands of people frozen in death that moved in and out of his morgue in the last 30 years.

He was wrong.

The malevolence he felt here, now, in this car leaving Jigs Seederly's former residence washed over him in a tidal wave, rolling his soul tightly in a knot and freezing his limbs to inaction.

His eyes shot to the right as something moved into his field of vision, seemingly dark, powerful and fiendish.

It was as if in slow motion he moved his foot to slam on the break of his car, and at the same time threw out his right arm in a protective gesture towards Wendels. The air bags inflated, and for a moment, he smelled the powdery residue that spewed into the air.

The grotesque face of an otherworldly entity swam before him outside his driver's window, and for a crazy moment, he hoped it was some smart-ass kid in a Halloween mask pulling a stupid and dangerous prank. Then when a darkly forked tongue studded with thick bristly hairs slowly licked the window where his face rested against the glass, he knew it was not a hoax.

He vaguely heard the sound of Wendels moaning in the background and felt a gauntlet of panic tighten painfully around his mind. He heard a rasping voice, dark and malevolent, chortle in glee. The palm of a monstrous hand, mottled red with long fingers tapering into black sharp claws, pressed against the window, then suddenly curled into a fist and struck the side window glass with such vicious force it caused the glass to spider-web into a thousand tiny fragments, glued together only by tempered film.

Scott had always thought of himself as pragmatic and meticulous, never jumping to conclusions, but rather hunting for answers, solving mysteries or finding a logical thread to resolve issues. Yet here, now, in this hellish nightmare, his mind transported him into another reality. One of gargoyles and devils and daemons; logic fluttered and tried to wink out in place of madness.

A blinding light suddenly enveloped the car seeming to pierce his skin with a million white-hot needles causing him to close his eyes against the brilliance. Though he felt his body roil in agony it was an agony of purging, much as a drug addict must feel as his body releases the poison that keeps him a prisoner. He could feel his friend beside him suffering the same, he could not stop it, nor did he want to.

He did not know if the screeching sound was his or Jon's, or the thing outside the car; he only knew dimly that they passed out of darkness into light.

THE BEAST IS HERE

Saturday—8:00 p.m.

The fact that he was the County Corner and he was with one of the top city detectives did not hold any water when they got to the hospital.

"Why didn't you call for backup?" Officer Timmerman had asked him half a dozen times.

"I'm not an officer Craig; I can't call for back-up. My main concern was to get Detective Wendels here for treatment." He was lying, and he knew they knew he was lying, but Timmerman kept digging. He was young and he wanted to play good cop and save the world.

"You don't have any idea what you hit?"

"I didn't hit anything, something hit me."

"Was it big or small? Was it a deer? Could it have been a person?"

"That's enough!" snapped Champion. "You know as much as I do. I saw what I believed was Detective Wendels vehicle and thought he might need some type of assistance. Don't ask me again what it was because as I told you, I don't know."

"This just doesn't make sense."

"I know. Give it a rest for a while, will you?"

Scott's cell phone rang and as he moved to answer it, Officer Timmerman moved closer and partially extended his hand as if to receive the phone.

"It's personal Craig; get the hell away from me," Champion snapped.

It was a stroke of luck that Mike Catsmill, the attending physician, who knew Scott from med school, came from behind the portioned curtain and firmly took the officer by the arm.

"Let's go son."

"Excuse me doctor but, I'm the responding officer to the call and I need to get all the facts together," Timmerman said irritation now apparent in his voice.

"And I'm the emergency room director and you are going to move your ass now or I will throw you out. This is my patient and medical doctrine overrides your questions at this time."

The officer narrowed his eyes at the coroner, and took a deep breath, puffing out his chest in an attempt to intimidate both the doctor and the coroner. It did not work.

"I said move your ass," Dr. Catsmill said in a deadly quiet voice.

Officer Timmerman reluctantly took his leave with the doctor tight on his heels. Catsmill turned and gave a brief nod to Champion as they pushed past the curtain.

Scott flipped open his cell phone one ring before it would have bumped into voice mail. He had recognized the number and wanted to take the call.

"Hello?"

The voice at the other end, surprising feminine said, "Done deal. Vehicle in question is located at the south entrance of Schenley Park."

"Do you think it will pass investigation?"

"Yep, Deputy Dawg could have easily overlooked the car the way I placed it. Trust me, it's a dead end."

"I owe you big time."

"Yeah, you do. Gotta go, the drag show is about to start."

The line went dead and County Coroner Doctor Scott Champion felt his blood pressure drop 50 points.

Two down and one to go, he thought.

He got ready to go and file his first false report. What it could possibly do to his career was secondary on his mind. What was he going to say attacked them. A rabid dog . . . a bear . . . Big Foot? Hey, how about that crazy ass Punxsutawney Phil who decreed it was six more weeks of winter or spring when he poked his fat nose out of his hole and some half-drunk man wearing a raggedy top hat declared. *He Saw His Shadow.*

What did it matter anyway? It was all going to be a lie so he might as well make it a good one.

Saturday—8:15 p.m.

Dan, Mindy and Sammy were on their way home after a relaxing afternoon and evening at the Petrucci's house. Dan was thinking that Army was probably one of his closest friends even though he was slightly jealous of Army's workshop. Dan had decided he had the perfect place at the back of the yard for a new 12x12' shed that would make an ideal workshop for him and the sheds with the skylights were on sale at the local Home Depot. He had been working on rationalizing to Mindy that he could get his stuff out of the basement and that she would finally have room for the craft area she had been wanting. At least that was how he was pitching it to his wife. He would have to work on her for some new tools, and as his train of thought played out; his first project would be to build her a new crafting table. As he continued thinking, he realized that it would be so nice if he and Sammy could start some projects together. He liked the way that Army and Anthony had traditions and he felt they shared a special bond because of those traditions; he truly did want that same type of bond with his son.

He heard soft breathing from the back seat and knew his son was asleep. Glancing over at Mindy, he could see her eyes closed and her head just barely nodding forward. It was a wonderful sensation, that feeling of having your family around you drifting off into the safety of sleep. As Dan brought his full attention back to the road a small smile played across his lips as a picture came into his mind of how gangly and disoriented

Sammy would be when he woke him to go into the house. He knew he would have to keep an arm around him so that he would not stumble and fall, as all kids his age were apt to do when they were drunk with sleep. It was always like that, and he loved it.

The soft snoring of Sammy turned into a hiccup then a snort as Sammy woke himself up. Dan chuckled quietly and looking in the rear-view mirror said softly to his son, "Woke yourself up, huh, kiddo?"

Sammy scrubbed his hand across his face and realized he must have been drooling too when he found spit on his chin. "Was I snoring?"

"Yep, but just a little, you weren't rocking the car or anything," Dan joked.

"You know Dad, I think maybe I snore when I'm hungry," said Sammy.

"Hungry?" Dan said incredulously, "You've got to be kidding Sammy! You were wiping up your plate with the last bun and ready for dessert before the rest of us were halfway through our sandwiches!" Dan glanced back at his son who had a wide grin on his face.

"Gotcha didn't I dad!" said Sammy in quiet glee, not wanting to wake his mom.

In a split second, the peacefulness of that moment disintegrated as Dan saw a huge form standing on the passenger side of the road. It crouched down and as their car came abreast of it, whatever *it* was, it sprang like a panther deliberately hitting the hood of the car violently rocking the vehicle and leaving a deep dent in the hood. Somehow, it rolled across sliding back off the driver's side then sprinted into the darkness. For a brief moment, Dan had a glimpse of what looked to be work boots and maybe coveralls as he instinctively hit the brakes and swerved to the left trying to avoid hitting what appeared to be a man.

"Jesus!" he cried out.

He heard Mindy's startled cry of, "Oh my God!"

As he struggled to keep the car on the road, he felt the weight of his son's knees push suddenly against the back of his seat and heard his frightened voice say, "Dad!" as his shoulder harness locked forcing air suddenly out of his lungs.

Dan steered the car back into his lane and brought the car to a halt about 100 yards from the incident. Mindy had already turned back to Sammy to make sure he was not hurt.

His voice tense he said, "You guys all ok?"

"We're ok," said Mindy as she put her hand on Sammy's shoulder and ran it down his arm in a comforting gesture.

Sammy's eyes were wide and glassy as he scooted further to the front of his seat to be as near as possible to his mom.

"What was that dad, what did you hit, what was it?" Sammy asked the edge of fear in his voice jagged.

"I'm not sure. All of a sudden, there was this huge form, this . . . *thing* on the side of the road. Whatever it was, it deliberately jumped onto the car." He rubbed his eyes with his thumb and forefinger pulling his hand down to the bottom of his face, then looked at his wife. "I heard a loud *bang* when it hit and all I saw was something rolling across the hood and saw what looked like a man land on the other side and take off into the woods. Whatever it was, it didn't look hurt the way it ran."

Mindy looked at Dan then back at her son. "Should we call the police?"

"I don't know," Dan said. He was trying to put his jumbled thoughts in order, to make some kind of sense of what had just happened. "Yeah, I think we should, at least for insurance purposes," he said reaching down on the passenger's side floor for his cell phone that had popped out of the middle console when he had hit the brakes. "You know we'll probably be here a couple of hours while they look around and ask us questions."

"No. Please dad, no," begged Sammy. This time the fear in his voice was raw. "I don't want to be out here any longer, can't we just go home?"

The panic in his voice was heart wrenching to both Dan and Mindy and as they looked at each other, the answer passed between them.

"I'll take you guys home and then come back out and call the police. I can come back to this same spot, give them a call and explain what happened."

"Are you sure hon?" Mindy asked anxiously.

"Yeah, it'll be ok babe," he said squeezing his wife's hand. "Sammy, you ready buddy?"

He turned to look at his son. An expression of utter relief flooded the boy's face and he nodded his head, his eyes shifting left to right looking out the windows on either side as the darkness seemed to close in on them. Sammy had seen exactly what his father had seen, and the realization of what had just happened was causing fear to roar through him like a tidal wave of lava, making him hot, then cold. Goose bumps came up on his arms and he felt them making their way down his body.

Dan turned and slipped the car into drive accelerating more quickly than he had intended, kicking up loose gravel under his tires that sounded like a quick blast from a machine gun on the underside of the car, ping, ping, ping, ping.

He felt it too, what he was sure his son was feeling. As if something or someone was just at the edge of the woods behind the curtain of darkness getting ready to pounce again on them, toying with them like a cat with its prey. He felt an odd, cold feeling in the pit of his stomach, the hairs on his neck stood up, and the eons old human emotion of *fight or flee* bore down on him.

For now, he chose flee.

THE PORTAL IS OPEN

CHAPTER 12

River Ridge Hill was a small borough outside of the city of Lamont. The name was meant to imply beauty and grace, and for many years, it had been a peaceful community of neatly mowed lawns and late evening baseball games. That was indeed its history, but not the current state of affairs. State and local imposed high taxes had driven out most of the good employers in the area and as the city had fallen on hard times, the downturn forced the stable citizens into finding jobs elsewhere, generally out of state.

Those who had been part of the past were few and fewer still each year. The area was rife now with seedy bars, drug dealers, miscreants and those who could inhabit a house that except for the millipedes, spiders and termites, had lain empty for years.

Charles now, he was an old timer who had done his duty in Korea and loved to tell anyone who would pay any amount of attention, about his adventures with his service buddy 'Saltpeter' and the time they spent in Japan on R&R with the Geishas.

"We were sore for a week after we left there, those Geishas worked us 'til we were wore out 'cause they knew we had money," he would reminisce even if no one was really listening just to hear himself talk.

Charles had come home, found a sweet girl named Jillian he had known for exactly two weeks, and married her because he wanted to settle down . . . well at least that was what he thought he was supposed to do. Jillian thought she was getting a good man who wanted to make a home, have some kids and cook hot dogs and hamburgers on Memorial Day and Fourth of July.

She did not know that Charles had a dark and moldering secrete that was ever so slowly eating him alive from the inside out.

Now, Charles liked his beer, but my how he loved his wine, loved it even more than the soft skin or tender embrace of his young wife. Soon after coming back to the states, he became friends with a man named Carl whose job it was to distribute communion wine to local churches. Charles dubbed him *Chalkjaw* for no other reason that he liked the sound of the name and Carl seemed to like it. Every other week Chalkjaw would sell Charles two cases of wine, each bottle one gallon, and out of those eight bottles, Charles would drink four all by himself and share the remainder with some buddies from work who would stop over for no other reason than to get drunk.

For the first six months Jillian thought it her duty to feed the boys and when they were there visiting. She would fry up rashers of bacon until crisp then cut thick wedges of potatoes' and onions and put them to sizzle in the bacon fat until they were dark brown and crunchy on the outside and then she would take orders for sunny-side-up or over easy eggs. All served up with a pile of toast and butter. All washed down with glasses of red communion wine that by evenings end was running down the chins of most of the boys.

By the second six months, Jillian was looking for any opportunity to find a way out and finally was able to jump a ride (yes there is a paradox here) with of all things, the preverbal 'Fuller Brush Man'—what a kick in the balls that was to Charles, what a kick in the old hairy gonads.

Behind his back, the guys at the mill made remarks like; *maybe he should have buffed her brush a little harder!* Then laugh their asses off at his expense. He was not ignorant of their comments, he heard them and a time or two even laughed along with them when there was nothing else he could do, but it hurt in a place that never showed to anyone.

Charles never did remarry; oh, he had the occasional girlfriend, worn out hookers mostly, who would spend an evening or two, but Charles was usually too drunk by the end of the evening to complete his copulation. He paid up front to make sure that his lady friends would not talk about him too much, but of course word got around and Charles could continue to count on being the brunt of cruel jokes.

Regan may have been blamed for the mills shutting down, even though history got it right and could truthfully place the blame on high taxes and regulations put in place during the years of the peanut farmer, Jimmy Carter. Yet as others moved away, Charles stayed and worked at his part time job where he sold tools, cut keys and shot the shit with the locals who were left.

His meager salary was mostly eaten up by his communion wine habit, and his soul was being eaten up by his dark festering secrete. Eventually, unable to pay taxes on his property, Charles had to move into one of the abandoned habitat houses, one that no one would inhabit but a worn out, broke and tired drunk.

Now Charles had an abundance of time on his hands, time to think, time to remember, and time for regret . . . so very much time for regret.

He had not meant for it to turn ugly that night in Tokyo, but Saki, Saki and more Saki he had soaked up like a sponge. Everything was spinning that night, the room, his head and the floor was occasionally rising up against him in a sickening flow. Saltpeter had just stuck his head in the door with his trademark-crooked grin on his face and his arm around yet another Geisha. She stood beside him, all pale and powder, not an emotion on her face, resolute in her station in Japanese society. A whore in America, an esteemed Geisha in Japan treated like so much trash by the service men.

"Come on Chuckles, ain't you done yet?" taunted Saltpeter from the doorway. "Come on man, they're $2.00 a hump, shoot your load and let's go!"

Not only was Charles unable shoot his load, he could not even get a round up to fire. Suddenly Saltpeter realized the problem and started laughing, bent double, laughing at Charles, the Saki sodden Charles whose pickled peter could not raise a flea.

Charles suddenly felt a madness wash over him, cold and calculating, deadly and deep. He put his hands around the throat of the submissive, innocent non-resisting woman beneath him, and his hands tightened, squeezing the life and breath out of her.

Suddenly her small sparrow like arms came up and beat a tattoo against his body, raining blows against his face and chest with no more strength than that of a child. As her face turned purple, Saltpeter realized what was going on and grabbed Charles by the shoulder. The thoroughly Saki soaked Charles grabbed his service pistol from the holster hanging on the hook beside the bed and pressed it against the sweat streaked cheek of Saltpeter. Time stopped.

Charles did not know that his eyes narrowed to lethal slits and through his clenched teeth, a deadly snarl came from him.

"Back off."

Saltpeter's Geisha stood still as a statue, nothing in her demeanor revealing whatever horror she may be feeling at the helpless, hopeless struggles of the purple faced girl beneath Charles, her resistance almost at an end.

"I'm movin' back man, I'm movin' back. Put that down and let's go, let's go before anything more happens."

"Back off and close the door."

"Let her go Charlie, just let her go and we'll go back to base. Come on, let's go."

"Close the door," said Charles, his voice cold and lethal.

Saltpeter put his hands up and backed away the Geisha trailing with him, and for the first time emotion showed in her eyes saying more than any words could ever express.

The door closed like a tomb, and for Charles, a door to his soul closed forever.

Saturday—10:00 p.m.

Charles awoke with a start, pulling himself out of the nightmare that had seemed to plague him more often lately and the answer to that was another glass of wine. He half sat up scrubbing his hand across his face, which made a dry sound like sandpaper against the stubble of his unkempt beard.

He half rolled, half fell off the dilapidated couch and realized he had to take a piss; in fact, he realized he had to piss like a racehorse. Wobbly, he began to push himself up, and in the attempt stubbed his toe hard.

"Son of a bitch! Son of a BITCH!" he said. His foot, painful already from arthritis, now burned like a white-hot poker.

Suddenly he heard what he thought was the back door close and what sounded like a stealthy footstep. He stopped his rant to listen and his full bladder ached painfully. He mentally shook himself more fully awake and heard it again . . . a sliding shuffle.

What briefly passed through his mind was probably some punk kid was trying to invade his habitat or give him a scare for the fun of it. Maybe they thought he had something to steal, well, Charlie was in no mood to have any of it.

"Get the hell out of here you asshole, before I put a hole through your god damned stupid head!" he said in what he thought was an authoritative voice, but in reality was the wavering thin voice of an old used up man. He was trying to remember where he had laid his gun down, which he kept loaded, but he was usually to loaded himself to remember where it was and it was a miracle he had never accidentally shot himself.

"I said get the fuck OUT punk!" he yelled again in a thin reed like voice.

He stood still for a moment listening, not realizing his old waxy ears had actually drawn back in an attempt to more accurately hear any sound. No more shuffling. *Ok maybe I just imagined it.* Suddenly he heard booted footsteps coming his way and something in those boot steps made what little color he had in his face drain away.

Then within the half-light that filled the room like a sinister mist, an iniquitous face suddenly took shape in the doorway, illuminated just enough for Charles to see it, mottled and lumpy. The lumpy things seeming to throb under the gray cadaver like skin where what appeared to be blue veins squirmed like maggots trying to get out. Demonic fire burned within the feline shaped yellow eyes, the red slit in the center, a gateway to all things loathsome and beastly. Large lobed, elongated ears came to two points and lay tightly against that garish, hideous head as the dark, rope like *things* twisted and writhed.

It was worse than a movie, it was worse than his worst hangover, it was worse than anything he had ever dreamed or imagined. It was oh so much worse than the final pitiful thrashes of the Geisha beneath him all those years ago, worse even than when he had awaken of top of the dead girl he had killed and then had felt her stiff cold flesh beneath him. All these long years he had thought there could be nothing worse than that damnation of him, that there could be nothing that could terrify him more deeply.

He was so very, very wrong.

The mouth of the thing in front of him opened, huge, as though the bottom jaw came unhinged like some immense snake, while large canine teeth unfolded and slid into view, and a stench of everything rotting in hell poured forth from that terrible maw.

Charles painful bladder hurt no more as urine poured down his legs in a river staining his dirty and wrinkled pants black.

His baldhead disappeared into that gaping, hungry mouth, and as the jaws snapped with a sound like a walnut cracking open, Charles at last was expunged of the black deed that had haunted him his entire adult life.

Sunday—8:00 a.m.

Anthony woke up slowly, feeling warm and cocoon like in bed, *snuggled up,* as his mom called it. He tightened his legs down pointing his toes and felt that delightful sensation of stretching. *Why does it feel so good to stretch?* he wondered. He pulled his arms out from under the covers and putting them above his head, making the universal sound of, *uuuummmmmmm, aaahhh*!

He could smell bacon. He could smell coffee. He could hear the voices of his mom and dad in conversation. Safe, warm and protected, that was how he felt, and it was wonderful.

Sunday morning was one of his favorite days. They all had breakfast together and then got ready for church. (That seemed like the longest hour of the week but he loved everything leading up to and after that). When they came home, depending on the time of year, his mom would cook.

Anthony was sure his mom could make more types of hamburgers than anyone he knew. Sometimes she would make two thin patties and put a slice of sharp cheddar cheese in the middle, seal them up and grill them. She was known to stuff them with and onions, olives and feta cheese, even sauerkraut, which though it sounded weird, was *good.* Toasted buns, toasted sour dough bread, toasted bagels. Her imagination truly had no end. He loved the corn she would soak in their husks for a couple hours, and then put them on the grill until the husks began to blacken. When the husks were removed, they would smear the corn with butter that Danni had spiced up with fresh chives or lime juice. The snap of the corn, the crunch of the bun and juicy surprises in the burgers, it was all incredibly good.

Today though, was post roast day. Little slits cut in the meat would be stuffed with slivers of garlic, then it would be salted generously, dusted it with flour and seared to a dark caramelized brown in a hot cast iron skillet. Water, kitchen bouquet, bay leaves, Worchester sauce Dijon mustard, liquid smoke, all baked at 350° for a couple of hours and the last 90 minutes she would pile in potatoes, carrots, onions and celery. The meat would fall apart and the vegetables would be sweet. He always had one or two thick slices of bread slathered with butter and washed down with a tall extra cold glass of milk.

Anthony sprang out of bed because the smell of bacon was calling his name, and calling it quite loudly, thank you very much. He was thinking about yesterday and the great time they all enjoyed. Sammy's mom and dad had seemed impressed with the Halloween decorations and he and Sammy had been so proud of their work. Of course, his dad was the driving force, but as Anthony got older, he was contributing more and more to the finished product. Just six more days until Halloween!

It had been such a perfect fall day the way the trees were colored; he loved the way the sun shifted in the sky making the shadows longer and everything seem just a little more golden.

As Anthony washed his hands at the bathroom sink, he glanced in the mirror to check his hair, which never seemed to be messed up. Looking in the mirror, he could see the reflection of the three Halloween backdrops. He squinted as he looked, then turned around and walked to the window.

That can't be right, he thought as he stared out the window. He closed his eyes and shook his head to make sure he was seeing correctly. *That's **not** right* his mind told him. He hurried back to his room, shucking off his pj's as he went. He pulled on his sweat pants and shirt, shoved his feet into his slippers and started downstairs.

"Morning honey," said his mom and she spotted him at the bottom of the steps, "how do scrambled eggs sound this . . ." she broke off in mid sentence as she watched her son bolt toward the door. "Anthony, where are you going?" she said as his hand reached for the back doorknob. "Don't you dare go out there in your slippers, the grass is wet!"

Initially puzzled by his behavior and then by the fact that he had not answered, her puzzlement turned to concern.

"Army . . . Army come here! Something is wrong with Anthony!"

Army had been sitting in his recliner reading the Sunday paper and she heard the recliner close and the sound of her husband's padded footsteps coming quickly toward in her.

"What's wrong Danni?" he said, his eyes following her gaze out the back door.

"I'm not sure. He just took off outside and didn't say anything when I asked where he was going. I think we'd better see what's wrong."

Army was already getting on his skipper shoes. Danni followed suite and slipped on the pair of crocks she kept by the back door. As they started down the back steps, she never took her eyes off her son and something in his face scared her deeply causing her to call out to him.

"Anthony! Honey are you ok?" she said as they both jogged toward him. Army was in his t-shirt and sleeping shorts, Mindy in her nightgown with a short robe that she was pulling around her as they approached their son.

Army got there first. "Son, what's wrong?"

"Dad," said Anthony in a hollow voice, "look at Ax-Man."

Army followed his son's gaze toward Ax-Man. It appeared as if some kids had played a joke on them, that was obvious. Freddie was knocked down and Ax-Man was bent over him with something gooey and dark dripping out of his mouth.

"Dad?"

"Army?"

"It' just a prank, I'll get dressed and fix it," he looked at Anthony, it'll all be ok son, honest."

"I don't think so dad, I think he can move."

"No Anth, that's impossible," Army said as he felt an apprehensive tingle wash down his spine.

After ten o'clock. Mass, Army had come home, changed his clothes then worked on moving Ax-Man back to his original position and fixing Freddie. He decided to get sturdier stakes to attach Ax-Mans arms to and a longer, much longer, stake to drive down his back into the dirt. It would make it a lot harder for whoever did this to try to do it again. Oddly, Anthony had said he felt tired and did not want to help. What was really honking Army off was the fact that this had scared his son and his wife.

He also wanted to know what rotten gunk they had shoved in Ax-Mans mouth. God all mighty, it had stunk like really bad road kill. It reminded him of that weird day coming back from the Seederly estate sale when he thought he had hit something and then imagined that revolting stench coming from the trunk. *How could those smells be the same?* He thought as he drove down highway 910 toward the home improvement store. *One more week until Halloween and I hope the dirt bags that trashed that backdrop will show up.*

It was good he did not look in the rear view mirror; he would not have recognized the reflection it captured.

Sunday—11:35 a.m.

While Army had been working outside, Anthony had been brooding inside and finally decided to call Sammy and get his take on what happened.

The phone rang just once and Mindy answered. "Hello?" her voice sounded strained.

"Hi Mrs. Brogan, its Anthony, is Sammy there?"

"He is, but he isn't feeling very well just now he's taking a nap. I'll have him call you back, ok?"

"Sure Mrs. Brogan. I'll talk to him later."

"Thanks Anth, I'll have him call you. Bye."

"Ok, bye," was his reply as he heard the phone connection drop.

He really needed to talk to Sammy, but he guessed it would have to wait.

He put his hands behind his head and on that innocent day of October during the autumn that would change his life forever, he closed his eyes.

Sunday—2:10 p.m.

Anthony was still lying on his bed when a soft knock came on the door. It pulled him out of the half slumber he had been in, the place between sleep and wakefulness; his mom called it the golden space. He loved that place it felt safe and wonderful.

"Anthony is it ok if I come in?" said his mom from the other side.

"Yeah sure," he said trying to sound the tuff guy that he was not. He could not let his mom know that there was a strange fear in him that he could not touch or explain.

Danni came in and went over to the bed where Anthony was laying and sat down next to him. She put her hand under his chin and looked in his eyes.

"Do you feel ok?" she asked softly.

"Nothing's wrong mom, I'm ok, just thinking."

"What are you thinking about?"

"Nothing."

"Well, if you're thinking, you have to be thinking about something honey, what is it?"

He hesitated for a moment and said, "It was really weird mom. Last night while everyone was here, just before Sammy and I came in I noticed that it looked like Ax-Man had moved," he quickly checked the look on his moms face to see if he should say anything more.

"How do you mean *moved*?" asked Danni quizzically her left eyebrow arching up as it always did when she was puzzled.

"His right arm kept changing. Not much but enough that I could notice and his body seemed to lean forward. I fixed it, but later it had changed again," he shifted so that he was looking fully into his mom's eyes. "I said something to Sammy but he blew me off. He was too busy thinking about something to eat," he sighed as his mom laughed and reached out to ruffle his hair.

"Anth, you know Sammy. He was born with a growling stomach. He didn't mean anything by it, that's just the way he is. You must admit it *did* smell awesome, didn't it?" she laughed as Anthony rolled his eyes and nodded his head. "You can get pretty focused yourself. Just think about you, your dad, and the whole crazy Halloween thing you have. If I didn't remind you, sometimes you guys' would forget to eat!" she said in an attempt to lighten her son's mood.

"That's different," Anthony said defensively.

"Oh, it is, is it? And how would that be?" inquired Danni affectionately.

"Well, it's like our tradition. Eating is something you *have* to do," as soon as he said that, he realized how lame it sounded.

Danni tilted her head back and laughed gleefully making Anthony smile and he began to laugh at too.

Laughter is good medicine and Anthony began to feel the tight spring that was in him unwind. Danni put her arms around him and rocked him back and for a minute.

"Hey," she said, "you know I love you?"

"I know," he replied," I love you too."

Danni stood up and looked out the window. "It's only a little after noon. Try Sammy again and see if he can come over. Tell him my world famous roast is in the oven that should do the trick. You guys can just hang out, get a fire going in the pit and I'll get some potatoes ready for you. Maybe some homemade cocoa how does that sound?"

"It sounds great! Thanks mom."

"You're welcome Anthony. Just let me know if he's coming over, ok?"

"You're the best."

"Huumm, you know what, your right!" they both laughed as she turned to leave his room.

Anthony leaned over and picked up the receiver from the phone by his bed. He dialed Sammy's number and he answered on the second ring.

"Hello?" It was Sammy's voice, but he sounded somewhat weird.

"Hey, it's me, how are you doin'?"

"I'm ok."

"When I called earlier your mom said you weren't feeling too good. Do you feel any better?"

"Yeah, I do. I was just tired."

"Why don't you come over for a while? I thought we could make a fire in the pit and mom said she'll get some spuds ready for us."

There was a moment's hesitation where Anthony thought he was going to say no, but Sammy replied, "That sounds good, let me ask my mom."

He laid the phone down and Anthony could hear him walking across the floor and yell, "Hey mom, is it ok if I go to Anthony's house for a while?"

Anthony could not hear Mrs. Brogan very clearly in the background but he thought she asked him if he wanted a ride. He could however hear Sammy's quick answer, "No, I don't want to ride in that car."

What is up with that? It sounds like he's afraid to get in his own car.

He could hear Sammy's feet coming back toward the phone.

"I can come over. Mom just said I have to be home before dark."

"Ok, I'll see you in about a half hour?"

"Yeah, umm, Anth, what is your mom cooking?"

Anthony started to laugh and laugh hard.

It got Sammy going until finally Sammy said, "What's so funny? What are we laughing about?"

That set Anthony off on another gut wrenching round of laughter. As soon as he could talk he said, "Get your butt over here and I'll tell you then."

"I'm on my way!"

Sunday—2:00 p.m.

The boys had a good fire going and while it burned down, so they could pop on the potatoes, they decided to play in the barn. After a while of climbing, swinging and tumbling, the fire had burned down sufficiently enough that they put six large butter and salted foil wrapped potatoes in the hot coals. They added a little more wood and went back to the barn, to the back alcove where they stayed on sleep outs.

As Anthony lay on his back with his head cushioned in his folded arms, chewing on a piece of straw he said to Sammy, "Are you ok?"

"Yeah, I'm ok, just a little tired," he shifted onto his stomach and slowly traced a finger through the powdery soil and hay on the floor, "I didn't sleep very well last night," he said casting a sidelong look at Anthony.

"Why not, did something happen?" asked Anthony turning on his side so that he was facing Sammy.

Haltingly at first, Sammy told him about the incident in the car, and the look on his face told Anthony everything he needed to know.

"Geez Sammy, what do you think it was?"

"I don't know for sure, but, well, this is *really* going to sound crazy, it reminded me . . ." he paused causing Anthony to look over at him.

"Reminded you of what?"

"Well, it reminded me of Ax-Man," said Sammy looking quickly at Anthony to gauge his reaction.

Anthony felt his blood run cold and the hairs on the back of his neck and forearms stood up.

"Sammy, tell me exactly what you saw," Anthony said quietly.

"I know it sounds crazy, but it looked like Ax-Man, I'm tellin' you. I know what I saw," he said defensively, expecting Anthony to begin laughing any second.

He did not laugh. He looked at Sammy and said, "I believe you."

"Wha . . . what?" Sammy stammered, "You do?"

"Yeah, because I'm pretty sure he moved last night."

For the next fifteen minutes, Anthony proceeded to tell Sammy about what he found that morning.

"Wow, said Sammy, I wish I had paid attention to you last night and looked when you told me to."

"I wish you had too," Anthony responded.

The sun was golden that afternoon, moving through the cracks in the wood siding sheathing the barn. They were both vaguely aware of the crackle of the fire and the smell of wood smoke as they stared at each other and talked about what they had seen and felt.

Suddenly they heard the vicious barking of a dog and voices shouting somewhere over by the Halloween backdrop.

They looked at each other, neither knowing their age of innocence was over, and as usual the two best friends fought for who was going to be first to see what was going on.

Anthony and Sammy made a beeline for the door and ran full tilt toward the house determined to face whatever was going on, together.

Sunday—3:00 p.m.

Anthony slid in the damp grass and tried to pull up before he went head-over-heels-ass-end-up, but the sudden termination of his forward inertia caused a domino effect. Sammy did a summersault in an attempt to miss Anthony's legs and succeeded only in running up Anthony's left shin bending his ankle painfully back.

"Shit Sam, get off me!" howled Anthony grabbing his ankle and rolling to his right trying to get up on his left leg.

In one fluid motion Sammy, the un-athlete, grabbed Anthony's right arm and yanked him to his feet allowing his forward momentum to propel them around the corner of the house and into view of the front yard where the Halloween set was located.

There are those times in life, when what you see just does not make sense, and does not compute. This was one of those times.

The barking dog was Ebony. A big black female Heinz 57 variety that belonged to the Russelton kids who lived about a mile down the road further out of town. Ebony was normally a docile dog who loved to have her soft nose rubbed and if you messaged behind her ears with your index finger and thumb, well, she practically fell down on the ground in a doggy coma of happiness with her soft pink tongue lolling crazily out of one side of her mouth. In her constant state of happiness, her large furry tail would wag so hard and so fast that she could knock you off your feet. That was part of what did not make sense. This normally loving, gentle dog was crouched back on her haunches facing Ax-Man; her were lips pulled back in a vicious snarl, fang teeth bared, eyes wild with those soft ears pulled back in a look that screamed *attack.*

Still more amazing, she seemed to be blocking, or shielding Christine, Justin and Freddy from getting any closer to either the backdrop or, it seemed more specifically, Ax-Man. Ebony was displaying no such behavior towards any of the other characters, only Ax-Man. As Justin, the middle child and the same age as Sammy and Anthony, tried to push her aside to get a closer look, she literally launched her body at him, causing him to stumble and fall hard on his butt.

"Ebby what is *wrong* with you?" he yelled at her.

Ebony had already turned again her jaws snapping at Ax-Man, a growl rumbling deep in her throat. Freddy, the youngest at eight, was hiding behind his sister, his head poking around from behind the arm she had protectively put behind her to comfort her brother.

It seemed everyone arrived at this same spot at about the same time, just in different ways. Sammy and Anthony stumbling and tripping over each other, Danni and Army in full gallop with hastily pulled on jackets and boots. For a moment, everyone seemed frozen in time as Ebony continued her tirade aimed at Ax-Man.

Christine broke the spell. She moved over with Justin and grabbed the dog by the collar. "Ebby! Stop! Stop right now!" she commanded as she tried to pull the dog away from the Ax-Man figure.

Ebony struggled with her, but as Justin backed up with Freddy, she started to calm down, but continued to keep herself between Ax-Man and the children.

She began barking again as Danni came past the Halloween display on her way towards the children, but Christine kept a tight hold of her collar. As Danni moved closer to the children, the dog quit barking, and remarkably sat down and began to wag her tail, not in her usual knock-you-over mode, but in little leaf raking swirls.

"Kids, are you ok? Danni asked anxiously, "did something happen, did something scare you?"

Army had walked over to meet up with the boys about twenty yards from the backdrop, Anthony leaning on Sammy holding up his left leg and obviously favoring his ankle.

"Anthony, what happened?"

"We didn't see anything, just heard a dog barking while we were out by the barn. We took off to see what was going on. I fell and twisted my ankle, Sam grabbed me, and we finished running here. I dunno what's up with Ebony; she was barking her head off at Ax-Man, geez with those fangs showing she looked like a devil-dog!"

"Is you ankle ok?"

"I'm ok. Let's go see what is going on." He started to hop on his left leg pulling Sam along, and as the two friends made their way towards where the ruckus took place, Army strode ahead, glancing back over his shoulder once to make sure the boys were ok.

When he got up to Danni he said to the other kids, "What happened? Did something fall and scare Ebony?" He looked at the backdrop, particularity Ax-Man, and with a start realized that the damn thing had shifted again.

They had all moved further away, and Ebony was again her usual wagging silly self and was all over Justin, apparently trying to make up for dumping him on his ass.

Christine spoke up first, the tone in her own voice questioning, "I don't know exactly Mr. Petrucci. Justin had been telling us how great your Halloween decorations are, and since it was so nice outside mom said we could walk down with Freddy. Everything seemed ok. Ebony was fine running along beside us until we got to your yard. The closer we got to here, she seemed to get . . . I don't know, defensive or something. Then she started running in some kind of crazy loop around us, almost as if she didn't want us going any closer. Freddy and I stopped but Justin kept going and that seemed to make her go crazy."

Ebony now loped lazily around them, oblivious to what had just happened; that was the beauty of dogs, they lived in the moment.

Danni turned to at look at Army, her eyes narrowing slightly. She bent down in front of Freddy.

"Hey kiddo, would you like some hot chocolate?" He started to nod his head and then looked up at his sister for the go-ahead.

"We don't want to intrude Mrs. Petrucci, I'm sorry if coming over caused any trouble or anything."

"Nonsense honey you haven't done anything wrong. Come on everyone, I've got some oatmeal cookies in the kitchen."

Umm, Mrs. P?" said Sammy letting go of Anthony and allowing his to sway precariously on one leg.

"Yes Sam?"

"Are there any of those chocolate-chunk cookies left?"

Danni burst out laughing shaking her head back and forth in wonder. "No Sam, you polished those off last night."

"Oh yeah, right, sorry."

"Nothing to be sorry about, Sam, but if you guys left those potatoes on the fire, they are probably charcoal by now."

"Crapola!" cried Anthony hopping around on one foot to turn and look back up at the barn, the pungent aroma of wood smoke permeating the air. "Come on Sam, give me a hand and we'll go look at 'em."

"I'll go Anth, you take a load off your ankle and I'll meet you back at the house."

"Wow. Well, ok, bud, thanks," Anthony said.

Sammy trotted off in the direction of the barn, as the Russelton kids started toward the house with Danni. Justin lent his shoulder to Anthony.

"Go on guys, I'll meet you there in a minute," said Danni in a bright voice.

She turned back towards her husband who had started to tag along behind them, stopping him dead in his tracks and said, "Army, I told you I didn't like that thing . . . your Ax-Man. Something's not right and you know it, I can see it in your eyes."

"Come on Danni! It's a stuffed suit with pieces of wood and poles holding it in place!" he exclaimed defensively.

"Army I don't like it," she said, punctuating each word.

Ebony was now baking happily on the front porch, almost knocking Anthony off his good leg.

"I know you don't Danni, but it's just a prop." He looked at his wife pleadingly. "I won't use it again next year, or I'll get rid of the mask or something. I promise. Next year I'll get rid of it."

Danni spun around and stalked toward the porch. "Go ahead in kids, I'm on my way!" she called out to them.

"Mrs. P!" called Sammy excitedly, "It smells freakin' fantastic up here, what's for dinner?"

"Sam, don't use that word, please." she replied trying to suppress a smile. "I thought you were on your way up to check those potatoes?"

"I am, well, I was but I didn't want to miss anything," said Sammy happily. "They're already charcoal so what's the hurry?" he said innocently.

Danni surrendered to the logic of Samuel Brogan and decided to simply enjoy the moment. "Kids, why don't you call your parents and see if you can all stay for dinner? There is plenty to eat, that is if you can get to it before Sammy, and we'll drive you home.

"Sam stop shoving and open the door for Christine," she grabbed the back of his shirt and pulled him up short.

"Yes Mrs. P," said Sammy opening the door for Christine. Danni gave his shirt a little tug of appreciation as Christine, Freddie, Justin and Ebony went inside.

Danni turned to gaze back to where Army stood looking at Ax-Man with a perplexed look on his face, and thought, *if that thing can move, I wish it would run out of our yard.*

Eerily, her next thought was an old saying.

Be careful what you wish for.

Sunday—6:15 p.m.

Dinner with a house full of kids had been an adventure. Danni had decided she had better make sure she could stretch the roast far enough, so she had supplemented with a big bowl of egg noodles tossed with butter and fresh parsley. Since Army and the boys' loved crescent rolls, she always had at least two extra tins in the fridge and Army had heated some fresh cider with a couple of cinnamon sticks and an apple studded with cloves.

It was a noisy, laughter filled food fest that seemed to be just what Sammy and Anthony needed to pull them all the way out of their pensive moods. By six o'clock that evening, everyone was loaded in the car. Freddie on Christine's lap, Justin and Sammy had Ebony between them, while Anthony was up front with his mom and dad. Everyone started to laugh when Ebony passed gas, probably from the scrambled eggs and cereal Justin, Anthony and Sammy had decided would be a fitting meal for their Ebby dog.

"Oh God!" coughed Sammy, "why did I have to get her butt end on my lap? The fumes are all on my side!"

Army hit the buttons to put down all of the windows in the car and Ebony happily hung her head out the window in typical doggy fashion with her ears blowing back in wild abandon. The fumes cleared and their eyes quit watering about the same time they pulled into the Russelton driveway. The kids poured out of the car while Ebony ran in circles barking and jumping as though she was trying to say, *this is my house, this is my house!* She threw herself on the ground at every chance, legs akimbo, bearing her soft underbelly to all and begging for a tummy rub.

Everyone was talking at once as Kelley and Jim Russelton came onto the porch already laughing at the antics transpiring in the yard. By the time, everyone had finished telling his or her stories and Kelley had given Danni a fresh apple pie, from which Sammy attempted to snitch a large chunk of homemade crust, it was full dark.

"Thanks again for letting the kids stay for dinner Danni." Kelley said as they walked toward the car.

"They're great kids Kel, Christine looks *so* grown up, and she is such a sweet girl."

"Oh Lord, tell me about it. All those boys that were yucky two years ago are now hot and the phone never seems to stop ringing. Jim calls them 'those damn boys' and has selective memory about the way *he* behaved. Somehow, that was different!"

Danni let out a squeak of laughter, and with her thumb, pointed over her shoulder to Sammy and Anthony behind her. "Yeah, those two have just hit that strip of land too. You, Mindy and I should get together and compare notes."

As they reached the car, the boys' fist bumped Justin, jumped in the back seat and yelled their good byes' to Christine and Freddie. It was that beautiful point of sunset in fall, just before full dark, when everything turns golden and the light is soft and magical. The boys looked back as Army made the turn onto the road, and they saw that Ebony had perched herself as a sentry at the top of the hill, eyes sharp and bright as she gazed down the knoll, her ears billowing in the slight autumn breeze, her beautiful feathery tail thumping slowly in the leaves on the ground.

They did not know then it was the last time they would see Ebony before the beast found her and enacted its revenge.

CHAPTER 13

Sunday—8:30 a.m.

He became aware he was waking up when he realized that his body hurt all over. Not just a little, but a lot. Nothing like the times he had played tag football as an adult, or the couple of years of Tae Kwon Do he took where he had to warm up and stretch before he could put on pads and pound the hell out of someone. No, this really hurt.

As his eyelids fluttered open, his eyes feeling grainy and hot, his right hand gingerly explored the left side of his rib cage, which seemed to be taped. A painful probe caused him to take in a sudden breath, which ignited an electric jolt of pain that stitched along his entire left rib cage. He took in short shallow breaths until the pain subsided, trying to make sense of what had happened. And, by the way, where the hell was he?

He continued to explore his body, and realized he had bandages all the way around his neck and down his back. It's funny how your mind will block out traumatic events to protect your psyche from collapsing from the weight of a reality that could possibly crush all that you believe to be real.

Jon was trying to piece all that together as he attempted to push himself up on his right side to get a better sense of his immediate surroundings. Suddenly, he realized the smell of coffee and bacon was permeating the air around him, and someone was softly knocking on the door. His initial reaction was a gripping fear that seemed to bubble deep within his gut.

His voice was shaky as he called out, "Come in."

The door gave a soft *click* as it opened, and Jon tensed involuntarily still not sure where he was. The face of Scott

Champion appeared in the opening and then the rest of his body followed through in a flowing motion. As he saw Scott's face, Wendels painfully let out the breath he had not realized he was holding. Again, a paralyzing point of pain stabbed his ribs and he clamped his teeth together for a moment until it passed.

Scott came to the side of the bed and placed a practiced hand on Wendels forehead. The look of concern in his eyes was evident and at that moment, Jon realized with certainty that last night had been real.

"That's a good sign," declared Scott as he removed his hand and let his arm fall to his side.

"What is?"

"You don't seem to have a residual fever. Are you able to sit up? I want to take a look at those gashes in your neck."

As Jon struggled to sit up, Scott leaned over and gently helped him get into a sitting position. Jon felt as though all the strength he had, and it was tenuous at best, seeped out of him and he felt his battered body slump against Scott's legs.

"Just a minute more Jon, I promise," said Scott quietly.

Wendels could feel him pull away some of the dressing around his neck, and he felt a slight prickling pain as small parts of the gauze stuck to the gashes. He bit his lip and clenched his fist around a small portion of bed sheet.

"Their clean looking, redness which is to be expected. I should disinfect the area again later and re-dress them," silence followed, "Jon? Come on, I'll help you lay back down."

"No," said Wendels, "I want to sit up and I want us to talk. In fact, I want you to help me get out of bed. The coffee smells good."

Scott Champion looked down at Detective Wendels. "Ok. I think it would be best if you let me bend down and you put your other arm around my neck. If I try and pull you, it's going hurt like hell."

"It already hurts like hell," replied Wendels. "Let's get it over with. Once I'm up I'll be ok."

As Scott bent over Jon put his right arm across Scott's neck locking it at the elbow. Scott stood up slowly and Jon began to push up with his legs. It was excruciating, but he pushed through it and was on his feet. Sweat had beaded on his forehead and temples and his legs shook with the pain and Scott held onto him another minute.

"Can you stand on your own?"

"Yeah . . . let me try. The worst I can do is fall back on the bed, right?"

"Don't do that," said Scott, "that'll feel like a grenade going off in your rib cage if you do. If you feel like you can't stand, tell me and I'll help you down. Got it?

"Got it."

"Ready?"

"Let's go."

Jon unhinged his arm and elbow from around Scott's neck and Scott watched him sway ever so slightly, catch his balance and smile.

"Let's get some of that coffee. Do I smell bacon burning?"

"Holy shit!" said Scott and shot out the door, "come to the kitchen!" he called back.

Wendels realized that once he was upright, the raging pain in his side subsided somewhat. He moved gingerly the first few steps thinking, *Ok, all right I'm good.* Then he lost his balance and the small adjustment he made caused a supernova of pain that this time encompassed all of his left side and he felt as though his back had been horse whipped. He vaguely wondered how bad his back could be to hurt this much.

"Bacon's not burned. It's extra crispy though, that ok?" Champion called from the kitchen. "What do you want, scrambled or fried?"

"Scrambled," said Jon as loudly as he could without inducing another round of ungodly pain. *Scrambled, yeah, that's what I feel like,* he thought; *I might as well stay consistent.*

Sunday—10:30 a.m.

In the bright kitchen of Scott Champion's house, both men had eaten in relative silence, but strangely, they had eaten ravenously. They had eaten all the cooked eggs. One dozen. Jon had eaten his with bright puddles of Buffalo's Original Wing Sauce on each helping. They had devoured an entire package of Heritage Farms real (yes real) smoked bacon, not all of it extra crispy, but all of it good. They had eaten three slices of toast each slathered with black currant jam and consumed an entire pot of coffee, black no cream or fufu creamers. In the light of day as they drank the last of the coffee, Jon finally made the first real conversation since sitting down.

"God that almost seems indecent after what we went through last night."

"Humm," said Scott as he tipped his head back finishing off his cup. "Kind of like your last request before they swab your arm and inject you with pentobarbital."

"Yeah, just like that."

"I made a couple of phone calls early this morning and we can get the cadaver dogs again."

Wendels perked up immediately leaning his elbows forward on the table. "When, today?"

"No. I won't know when they're available until Monday."

"What the hell, we need them now!" said Jon heatedly.

"It doesn't matter detective. They're on another assignment in Massachusetts and their handler, who by the way has agreed to keep this off the books and out of sight, said that it was absolutely the earliest he could get me an answer." He watched Jon's eyes moving rapidly back and forth, considering, thinking and finally coming to terms.

"Ok, yeah, that's best. It's just that it will be five days before Halloween. What a pisser that is, looking for tortured, dead women just before Hallow-Fuckin-ween," Jon ran his tongue along the front of his top teeth and swallowed, "Christ I sound ungrateful, don't I?"

"Not really, just anxious. I would assume anxious for the truth, not anxious to return to Jigs old shed?"

The shudder that rippled through Wendels body reminded Scott of a wet dog shedding water. His face went momentarily rigid, his cheekbones paled and fear flashed in his eyes.

"Do you want to talk about it now, in the light of day?"

Jon ran his hands back through his hair where they linked at the back of his head clasping just below the base of his skull. He began to pull his elbows towards each other and arch his neck to ease the tightness in his back when the pain hit again. He winced and looked at Scott. "Tell me about what my neck and back look like."

"Not good," said Scott simply.

"Don't avoid the question, what does *it* look like?" prodded Jon.

"What does *it* look like? What a curious choice of words. Your back looks like it was shredded with a cat'o'nine tails," Scott took a deep breath through his nose and blew it out of his mouth, "Jon, in thirty years as a doctor and coroner, I've never seen anything remotely like what your neck and back look like. Not ever."

Jon looked at him unblinking and said, "I think it's time you changed my dressings."

"Not yet," said Scott firmly.

"Yes now, so I can see it. I'll need a mirror."

Scott put the palms of his hands flat on the kitchen tabletop, hesitated and pushed himself up.

"If you have a problem with that Scott, tell me now."

"No, I don't have a problem showing you your back. It just seems a shame to have you puke up all the good food we just enjoyed. I'm out of eggs now, you know."

Little did Jon realize then that the only thing that could hurt worse right now, other than breathing, was puking.

Sunday—11:45 a.m.

Scott left the bathroom quietly, closing the door on Jon Wendels to give his some privacy. He had not been positive about his friend's reaction to the actual state of his neck and back, but as it turned out, he was not far off. As he had pulled the gauze bandages away, he was again stunned by what was on Jon Wendels back. The gauze stuck to the seeping wounds, causing Jon to winced time and again, the muscle in his jaw flexing in and out like a rhythmic heartbeat.

"Is that everything?"

"That's everything."

"Where's your mirror? Do you have a big mirror?"

Scott sighed, and said, "I'll be right back."

He came back with an large mirror with beveled edges and a small-embossed conch shell design in the upper left hand corner.

"Wow, that's some mirror," Jon commented as he reached out to take the glass.

"A gift from a doting Grandmother."

"Why a mirror?"

"It's a shell mirror. To display unusual shells; I used to collect them."

"What, like reloads, you mean like that?"

"No you idiot, sea shells. Here, let me hold that for you," He took the mirror back from Wendels and opened the linen closet door in the bathroom, which had a full-length mirror on it.

"Turn around."

Jon faced Scott as he held up the mirror.

The change to his face was immediate.

The change to his face was one of disbelief.

The change to his face was horrific.

"Jon," said Scott quietly, using every ounce of self-control he possessed to fight the fear raging through him, "in my life I have seen things done to people that I believed were evil, but never anything even remotely like this."

He tilted the mirror so that Jon had a better view. Deep claw marks, four on each side, running down from the outside of each shoulder to the small of his back made a wide V.

Crimson and puffy, yet gaping, like an old steel plow just cutting through virgin dirt; and then, in the middle between his shoulders, was something awful and beastly, more loathsome by day than it had been by night.

An eye.

The outside looked like the swirling mass of a hurricane from a satellite view. Wispy ends churning into a tight mass, the color of blood, interspersed with dark purple patches showing through the badly damaged skin and muscle. In the center, the horrible, ghastly center, laid the eye. The white of the eye was Jon's own pale skin, the iris an unnatural blood red. The black pupil was shaped like an upside down cross.

"Sweet Jesus in Heaven," whispered Jon.

"This doesn't have anything at all to do with Heaven my friend," Scott said softly.

Jon's hands shot to his mouth as if to stifle a scream, his eyes became hollow orbs of disbelief. As vomit bubbled from between his fingers, he stumbled towards the toilet.

Scott Champion reached for a washcloth and thought, *I have a feeling before this is over, and we are all going to be calling out to Jesus.*

ঙ৹ ঙ৹ ঙ৹ ঙ৹ ঙ৹ ঙ৹ ঙ৹ ঙ৹ ঙ৹ ঙ৹ ঙ৹ ঙ৹ ঙ৹ ঙ৹

Sunday—1:00 p.m.

After putting fresh bandages on Jon's back and giving him another injection of Amoxicillin, Scott had gone back to the kitchen to brew some tea, and Jon to the bedroom to put on fresh clothes that Scott had provided, thankfully with a loose fitting shirt.

Jon walked slowly to the small kitchen table and sat down across from Scott. "What happened to me? What could have done that?" he asked in a voice tight with fear. He paused for a moment watching Scott run his finger in a slow circle around what appeared to be a water ring on the table.

"Jon," said Scott slowly, "as bad as your back looks now, it was a lot worse when I first treated it last night . . . a lot worse."

"What do you mean worse? How could it be worse than whatever . . . whatever, *thing* is my back? It's almost as if something branded me. Do you know what I wish, what right now I want more than anything? To be able to unzip my skin and step out of it. Get it away from me. What could be worse than that, Scott, tell me?" his voice had raised and had a slight hysterical tone to it.

Scott stopped tracing the white watermark on his kitchen table and reached forward to grasp both of Jon's forearms tightly, as he fought to control his own rising fear at what they potentially might be facing.

"When I first found you by the shed, you were in bad shape. Something, and I mean some*thing* tried to stop you from leaving; some*thing* tried very hard to kill you. I think when it couldn't kill you, it left you a message, and that message on your back is that you are being watched," Scott released his grip on Jon's arms and slid his hands back to his side of the table. "You and I have known each other for a long time now, but last night I realized there are some important things I don't know about you."

"Like what?" asked Jon, looking fully into Scotts face, his eyes hollow and anxious.

"Like do you believe in a higher power, a life force, a creator? Do you believe there is a God?" Scott inquired cautiously.

"Yes," replied Jon without hesitation.

"Then maybe we have a chance, because so do I."

"You mean the light, the white light don't you?"

"So you do remember it. That's good."

"Actually, until you asked me that question, I thought I hallucinated that part of it."

"Jon, we have to face the fact that there is an evil force around you, trying to stop you I believe, from digging any deeper into who actually was Jigs Seederly."

"He was pure evil Scott, that's what I believe now. I believe he has been murdering woman, torturing and murdering them for years and it has something to do with that shed and the ground out back. That's why I want those cadaver dogs again. I also want a court order now to move the shed and dig around it."

Scott slowly tapped his thumb against his pursed lips, his eyes unblinking.

Jon interrupted his train of thought as he asked in a quiet voice, "What did you mean my back was a lot worse last night?"

Scott stopped tapping his lips and looked up, his eyes meeting his friends. "I was so adamant about you going to the hospital because those wounds where worse when we were sitting in my car. I couldn't believe you were conscious much less coherent."

Jon straightened his back, arching his shoulders, panic washing through him in a hot wave.

"Something intervened last night, you know that don't you?"

Jon remained still and quite as Scott continued. "Let's get this out; I think we will both feel better. We aren't crazy, either of us. There is an evil force at work here, a force of darkness, we both agree . . . Yes?" he looked quizzically at Wendels.

"Yes."

"If we can believe there is evil, and you and I have seen enough of it, then we must believe there is good. There is darkness and there is light. Jon, I believe the white light was sent to save us, so we might get to the bottom of this together." Scott leaned forward again, his eyes searching the eyes of Jon Wendels. "Tell me then. Tell me what happened before I found you outside the shed."

Jon took a deep breath and blew it out from between his lips. He told Scott of his terrible journey, of the voices crying out, pleading for help, the torment and helplessness that he believed belonged to the faceless victims who had suffered at the hands of Jigs Seederly; hands guided by a dark force to feed a vile, demonic hunger.

When he finished recounting his experience, a silence hung between them. Jon struggling to accept what had happened, not doubting, never doubting himself, for he knew it was real, but falling into the oh so human trap of *why me?* Scott on the other hand, was trying to solve a puzzle to which they did not have all the pieces, but he was trying to place the pieces they did have available into some order. Old stories about Jigs Seederly, the condition of his corpse, the links to the dark arts found in his house, the dead woman he remembered performing an autopsy on at ten years ago who had had strange symbols cut into her back. All the little bits and pieces that might have the information available to turn the puzzle into a picture . . . a picture that could provide the answers to what had already transpired and possibly reveal what was to come. So deep were they in their respective thoughts, that when the phone abruptly rang, it jarred both of them and they jumped in their chairs as young boys caught lighting up pilfered cigarettes.

Scott pushed back his chair, the legs making a low thudding noise as they stuttered across the linoleum. His landline phone was just around the corner in a niche he had turned into a message station complete with a corkboard full of pushpins and scraps of paper and post-it-notes stuck on top of the scraps of paper.

"Hello?" said Scott tentatively.

"Good morning Dr. Champion, it's Jess Givens from south-central. Have you heard from Jon Wendels?" Jess Givens held the rank of Sergeant and therefore Wendels supervisor and was a very astute woman; in fact the only woman who held rank in the detective division. It made her somewhat of a barracuda when it came to digging for facts.

"Why," he asked, his voice sounding cautious, "is something wrong?"

"That's the reason I'm asking you, doctor. He was scheduled to pull a mid and he hasn't shown up or called in," she waited for a response and when she got none, continued, "word is Craig Timmerman saw the two of you together in Lamont Hospital emergency room last night. Is that information correct?"

The silence from Scott's end of the phone was deafening.

"Doctor Champion, are you still there?"

"Yes, I'm here Jess," he replied thinking furiously of how to proceed with the conversation and keep both their asses out of a meat grinder.

"OK, so what's the deal with Wendels?" Jess Givens asked again. She was searching, inquiring, probing. Scott could hear it all in her voice and she was *very* good at getting answers one way or another. "Craig said Jon was allegedly . . . ," Scott could hear papers being shuffled in the background ". . . allegedly attacked by a pack of feral dogs?"

Scott groaned inwardly and thought *here it comes.*

"Feral dogs," he repeated.

"You tell me Scott. I'm reading from a report you filed and I want to find out if Wendels is all right." The silence dragged out another moment and Jess repeated, "Scott, what is going on? Is he all right? For that matter, are *you* all right? What the hell is going on Scott?"

He realized that the longer he remained mute, the worse this was going to get. "Well Jess, the best thing I can say is that he will be ok, he just needs some rest. He's resting now or I would let him talk to you personally."

"He's resting, that's good. That's excellent. Ok then, well, anything else you want to let me in on. Like when he may be back to work? Why he's staying with you instead of at home? Or why your van looked like a professional had swept it when I did the inspection. I need some type of answers to pass along to the Lieutenant."

"He should be much better in a couple of days. His back is badly bitten. Thank God he remembered to roll on his stomach and protect his neck, or it could have been a lot worse," said Scott lamely.

"Mmmhumm. You have him call me tomorrow. No excuses, no delays. I'm here at 10:00 a.m.—I want my phone to ring at 10:01 a.m. and I want the voice at the other end to be Jon Wendels . . . understood Doctor Champion?"

"Understood."

"There's something else Scott, call your office immediately."

"It's my day off Jess, I'm not AWOL, so whatever it is can wait until tomorrow. Unless it's an emergency of some type?" he asked with a note of sarcasm in his voice, which he hoped would conclude this conversation.

Jess could be heard taking a deep breath in the background of the phone, her voice had changed; it was now softer, with a note of compassion. "I'm reading from a report I received earlier this morning Scott, and I have some bad news for you." She hesitated just a moment, and then began to read. "The mutilated body of one William Champion, aka Fancy Mei, noted drag queen at the *Leather n' Lace* gay bar was found in the grass behind the parking lot. The door to his car was open which caught the manager's eye when he was leaving. Fancy's cell phone was on the passenger's seat. Jess's voice hesitated, and then continued, "The last call on his phone was to you."

Scott's body had gone numb. "Thank you," he said his voice trembling with emotion.

Suddenly he realized that Jon was beside him, hanging up the phone.

"What's wrong Scott? What happened?" said Jon. Immediately he was afraid for his friend, not understanding the look on his face.

Scott turned slowly to Jon, his face taunt with sorrow and something else that was unreadable, "Jess just told me my brother has been murdered."

Sunday—1:45 p.m.

Scott Champion got ready to go to his office. He had had a brief conversation with his assistant Phyllis Johnson who was on call when the body of his brother had been delivered.

"Scott, I think you'd better sit this one out," said Phyllis Johnson, "I'll do the workup myself and you'll be the first one to get the report, just sit this one out, ok?"

"I appreciate your concern Phyllis, but I want to be there. I'll let you do the actual autopsy, I'll just oversee," he sighed deeply, "give me 30 minutes to get there."

"OK boss, if you insist. See you in a bit then," replied Phyllis her voice giving away the fact that she did not agree with his decision.

Scott hung up the phone and turned to Jon Wendels. "Will you be ok here for a couple of hours?"

Jon stared unblinking for several long moments at Scott then said, "I don't think you should go on this one Scott, I really don't."

"I've made my decision on that and I'm asking that you respect that decision. Now, will you be ok here for a while?" Scott again asked.

"Yes, I'll be ok. I think I'll make some more coffee, and if it is ok with you, do some research on the internet if you'll let me use your laptop," replied Jon.

Scott picked up a piece of paper, pulled a pen out of his jacket pocket, and wrote down a series of letters and numbers.

"That's my login and password," he said. "It's case sensitive, so it has to be put in exactly as I printed it." He handed the paper to Scott, who took it and sat it on the small kitchen table placing the saltshaker on it. "Jon, I think it might be a good idea if you spend the night with me again. It would be best if I redressed your back later this evening, and to be honest with you, I don't want to spend the night alone in this house." He glanced at Jon for a confirmation.

“And here I was wondering how I could get around to asking you if I could stay,” Jon replied quietly.

“You have my cell number if anything comes up, right?” Scott asked Jon.

“Yep, I’ve got it and you can bet I’ll call if I need you.

“I’ll call you when I am on my way back to the house.” Scott picked up his car keys and went to the door. As he turned the handle, he flicked the lock back to the on position. “There’s no one coming to visit or see me, so don’t answer the door if the bell rings.”

“I won’t,” Jon said simply.

As Scott closed the door behind him, Jon heard him test the handle to make sure it was locked. The sudden silence throughout the house made Jon uneasy so he went to the small radio and turned it on. He found it ironic that the song playing was Blue Oyster Cult,

I’m living for giving the devil his due
And I’m burning, I’m burning, I’m burning for you

Jon switched the radio off, and stood for a moment while the lyrics ran back through his head. Something *was* burning for them, and he intended to find what it was before their time ran out.

Scott pulled into his assigned parking slot at the coroner’s office, switched off the motor and just sat still. He was steeling himself for what was to come next; he did not want Phyllis Johnson throwing him out of the examination room because he broke down. No, he wanted to see firsthand the condition of the body and be present when they opened up his brother. He breathed in through his nose and out of his mouth several times to calm himself, opened the car door and stepped out pocketing his keys.

There were two other cars in the lot. One would belong the coroner rigger, who was usually a student, whose job it was to get the bodies into the cooler, and when the coroner requested a body for inspection and dissection, they would do the set up, get the trays, surgical instruments, check the saws, assure the drains were open and make sure the scale was calibrated correctly.

Scott punched in his code on the keypad to enter the building, and as the door swung open, the familiar smell of death assailed him. He made his way to his office, took off his coat and hung it on the hook behind the door. He could see the light on in examination room two and made his way in that direction. Just inside the room was a small alcove that had a closet for supplies and a small desk area. He reached inside the closet and took out a clean jump-suite, worn during an autopsy, slid his shoes into the covers that came with each jump suit and snapped on a pair of gloves. When he pushed the round button on the panel, the doors of the autopsy room opened with a loud swoosh.

Phyllis looked up when he came in. She reached over and clicked the switch that turned off the microphone they used to record their findings during an examination. Scott was grateful for her thoughtfulness not knowing what his reaction might be. As the door closed behind him, he remained motionless. He could see a body on the table. Or, more precisely, what was left of a body. His brother's arms were along the side of his torso and he saw the bright red acrylic nails, of which his brother was usually so proud, looked ragged and torn. He realized with a jolt that his brother's head was not connected to his torso, but lay near the left shoulder.

Scott's vision seemed to have an explosion of swirling sparkling points of light, and he heard a voice calling his name, "Scott . . . . Scott? S*tay right there!* Suddenly Phyllis was next to him holding onto his arm. "I don't think this is a good idea, why don't you wait in your office while I finish?" she said quietly.

"No," he replied his lips feeling numb, "no, I want to be here and I need to see what happened to my brother," he said in a voice that did not sound like his own. He could feel Phyllis's eyes on him, watching him closely. He turned to look at her and said, "I need to see my brother Phyllis. Please?"

She released the pressure on his arm and dropped her hands to her sides. "Do you want me to wait here?" she asked.

"No, come with me, I think. Yes . . . please come with me?" his voice was quiet and full of pain.

As they stepped closer to the waist high stainless steel autopsy table on which his brother laid, he could hear the water running that washed away the blood that would be released during the procedure. It was then that he realized that she had not made the 'Y' incision that would extend from each shoulder to the bottom of the breastbone with the tail extending from the sternum to the pubic bone. She could not, because the front of his torso was ripped open and it looked as though his heart, lungs, liver and stomach were torn out. As he looked up to his brother's ruined head, what was left of his face was a flap of skin that had what appeared to be triangle teeth marks in two rows on each side. Scott reached out to roll the flap of skin back that was his brother's face and saw the remainder of the stage makeup he wore at the club. It was smeared with blood, the garish rouge and lipstick were in stark contrast to the pallid white skin, but were identifiable; a false eyelash hung on to the corner of one mangled eyelid. As he moved what was left of his brother's head to the left, what Scott saw caused him to suck in a stuttering breath. There was a large ragged hole in the back of his brother's head. It looked as though it had been punched hard enough to splinter the bone into feathery outcroppings around the perimeter. Scott turned slowly toward Phyllis.

"Is this how he came in?" said a voice that must be Scotts but did not sound like him.

"Yes," replied Phyllis, "this is exactly how he came in. I've only started the verbal overview."

There was no brain inside the cranium; it looked like an empty shell. It reminded him of an egg that had had the insides sucked out.

"It ate him," he said in a strangled voice, "it ate my brother."

"What are you talking about Scott? *What* ate your brother? You need to tell me if you know what is going on, if you know what or who did this," Phyllis said sternly.

Scott stepped away from what was left of his brother and continued to back up. He rolled the rubber gloves off his hands and threw them into the nearby wastebasket.

"Scott," said Phyllis again. "Scott, what is going on?" she demanded.

"I don't know what it is, but I do know my brother was murdered by something . . . some*thing* very evil that was brought here on purpose." Moments drew out as he stared at the table across the room.

Finally, he said, "I have to leave Phyllis. I have some arrangements to make," he turned and looked at her, eyes red rimmed and wet with tears, "I'd appreciate if you'd finish the autopsy the best that you can; and Phyllis, let's keep this between us for now, ok?"

Phyllis looked at Scott for a long moment, her stare like a laser. "Ok Scott. I'll call you with the results, and have him funeral home ready in three hours. And Scott, what do you want me to tell the police?" she asked cautiously.

"Call me when you're done, I'll handle them."

He took off the jump suit, put it in the hamper, threw away the booties and did not say another word as he grabbed his coat and started for his car. He and Jon Wendels had a lot of work to do, and they had to do it quickly before anyone else was eaten alive.

While Scott was gone, Wendels had set himself up at the kitchen table for some serious research. He had made another pot of coffee, dug out a yellow legal pad, found a pen and a pencil and was logged onto the internet.

He had been surfing the net trying to find information on how evil objects or entities transition into the world of humans, and had printed off several articles to show Scott. He was about to log out when he came across a site titled *Opening and Closing Portals of Evil.* As he scanned the article, his heart started to pound and he felt a light sheen of sweat on his forehead . . . he had found something quite significant.

Portals can be caused by people dabbling in the occult and opening a portal by accident, but more often, it is a deliberate effort by an individual or a group of individuals wanting to bring evil into their realm.

. . . smelling rotting flesh . . . receiving bodily scratches . . . hearing screaming or other voices . . . disturbing visions . . . nausea . . . feeling like you are underwater or in a wave of heaviness.

Wendels sent the document to print as he continued to read, and saw on the last page: *'How to Close a Portal' Find the offending item, the trigger, whether it is a room in the house or an object. Holy water is essential. It must be totally destroyed so no one else can ever use it. It is by the name of Christ that you can cast the demons out and close the portal forever.*

He knew. He knew where the place was. He had been there. It was the shed, the shanty of Jigs Seederly. He knew they had to go back there, he knew he had to find the *trigger.* First, though, he had to talk to Scott; they had to go to a Church and get holy water, and they would have to have anointed oil and holy candles. As he sat riveted to the computer screen with all these thoughts swirling around his head, he suddenly realized someone was standing behind him. He felt his body tense and the thread of fear bloomed into full terror. As he began to turn around, coldness washed over him as a hand came down on his shoulder.

Sunday—5:15 p.m.

When Jon felt the hand on his shoulder, he jerked around scraping his back along the wood slats on the chair. A white-hot pain shot up to his brain paralyzing his movement for a split second, enough time for the owner of the hand to step in front of him.

"Jesus Scott, why didn't you say something when you came in?" shot Jon acidly. He then took a good look at Scott's face and came to his feet. "Sorry man, I'm really sorry. Do you want a cup of coffee or something?" said John sympathetically.

"I'll have a shot of something," said Scott as he sat down heavily across from where the computer was parked on the table.

"Point me in the right direction," responded Jon.

"Around the corner under my corkboard office, cupboard on the right."

Jon was back in a second with a bottle of Jim Beam and a water glass. He sat back down across from Scott and poured the tumbler half full. He slid the glass towards his friend who turned the glass in a half circle for a moment, considering the amber liquid, then picked it up and downed the half glass in several noisy gulps. When he set the glass down, his face was flushed and his eyes bulged for just a moment.

"Want a water chaser?"

"No. I want that booze to hit me like molten lava and numb me for just a while."

Jon nodded his head in acknowledgement watching Scott sit with his eyes closed for several minutes.

"What were you able to find?" Scott asked suddenly with his eyes still closed. He was taking deep quiet breaths in through his nose and blowing it out of his mouth in soft puffs. The puffs smelled like the JB he had just downed.

"I think I hit on something," Jon said shuffling the papers around him into a neat pile and laying them in front of Scott.

"The problem may be getting a priest who will cooperate in helping us find what we need in a timely manner."

Scott opened his eyes, pinched the bridge of his nose with is thumb and forefinger then picked up the sheets of paper and began reading. As he scanned the last page, he said to Jon, "Let's make a list of what we need. We really don't know the quantity of each item do we?" he asked looking up at Jon for the first time in several minutes.

"No, I don't yet. When we locate a priest maybe he can give us guidelines or something," he paused for a moment and continued in an ironic tone, "Yea, right. We need to find a priest that can give us *guidelines* on how to kill an unknown evil entity. Location? Well Father, we're not sure yet, but we think in may be in a shanty on the property of a former serial killer," said Jon sarcastically.

The comment brought a sardonic smile to Scott's face. His eyes were slightly blood shot, either from the Jim Beam, the stress of his brother's autopsy or both.

"I forgot to tell you I got a call from Jerry White about the cadaver dogs on my way home," he said.

"And?" asked Jon anxiously as he leaned forward toward Scott.

"We can have one dog one hour . . . ,"

"One hour?" Jon interrupted angrily.

". . . and not until Friday afternoon," finished Scott.

"Shit," said Jon raising his voice, "one friggin' hour on Friday afternoon. What's the point?"

"The point is," replied Scott calmly the whiskey blunting his sorrow, anger and fear, "Jerry pulled a lot of strings for us to have the dog that long. We need to put our heads together and come up with the best way to utilize our time and appreciate that we have that hour."

Jon stared at Scott a moment, the anger draining away.

"I didn't mean to be an ungrateful asshole, I'm just anxious to get back there. We've got to find the portal and I'm positive it's there." Jon stopped talking, looked at Scott and continued,

"Do you believe there's an evil portal Scott, or do you think I'm half a bubble off level?"

"Oh, you're a half bubble of level all right, maybe even a sandwich short of a picnic," a slight smile came to Scotts face then left just as quickly, "but I also believe there is an evil portal that, for whatever reason, we have been chosen to close." He laid the papers back in a neat stack between the two men. "It just so happens I know a padre that I'm pretty sure will help us. Let's get some of this info together and we can go see him tomorrow afternoon," Scott pushed the chair back from the table and stood up, swaying slightly in acknowledgement of the Jim Beam coursing through his veins, "I stopped and got some groceries, the bags are still in the car, I'm going to get them."

"I'll help you carry them in," Jon offered.

"No, I can get them. Your job is to get us both another drink. I'll have the same as you just poured me, just add some ice if you would."

"I don't know if my doctor will allow me to drink right now. I'm on medication," Jon said to Scott.

"Your doctor says it's a.o.k. to have a couple of drinks with him, in fact it will do you a bit of good yourself," Scott replied.

Jon stood and picked up the tumbler Scott had been drinking from earlier. "I'll clear my mess off the table and open the bar." He closed the laptop and began picking up the papers as Scott started for the door to the garage. "So what's on the menu?" he called over his shoulder. "I just hope it has nothing to do with eggs."

Scott looked back at him and said, "Why drunken chicken, of course."

CHAPTER 14

Monday—10:00 a.m.

The two families had decided to take a mid-week vacation for several of reasons; one being that the rates were cheaper and also Dan and Army had a couple of vacation days to use. Two, the boys had a couple of school days with not much going on so they could afford to miss with permission from the principal. Last but certainly not least, Danni and Mindy had decided they needed a break from their daily routine.

While cruising on the internet, Mindy had come across a delightful, rustic looking inn named *Gateway Lodge*. It was located in Cooks Forest, which lies just below the much larger Allegheny National Forest in western Pennsylvania. It appeared to have the serenity the adults were looking for along with some great opportunities for the boys. In particular, horseback riding, hiking and a survival course that Anthony and Sammy were very excited about.

The lodge itself housed a highly rated restaurant, a small spa that the women intended to indulge in, and a billiard room for the guys. It also had a wonderful long porch with wicker chairs and a table sliced from one long log, polished and gleaming. In one corner of the porch hung a swing with a warm inviting checkered afghan draped across it in which you could wrap yourself, with a cup of tea or a glass of award winning wine.

Danni was most looking forward to the huge raised fireplace that was surrounded by three large leather couches, perfect to nestle in and read. An afternoon teatime with fruit, cheese and crackers was on the agenda, and she was anxious to just sit and do nothing. Nothing that is, but relax. The guys were going to hang together and the girls were going to savor some spa time.

The trip up was breathtaking. The rolling hills moved seamlessly into mountains laced with rivers. A vista of colors and texture seemed to dance a slow rhythm and invited you to immerse yourself in healing reflection. The aroma of autumn, loamy with the richness of residual heat and rain from summer, was mind calming. It smelled full of the goodness of insects, birds, squirrels and all the lovely small creatures that paint a living picture. Deep and rich, silky and soft, quite and bright, red, gold, orange and brown leaves and every earth tone in between, leaves veined with swirls of color and light, leaves maturing and lovingly falling to the ground to give their life to the sweet, supple earth.

All could pass by unnoticed unless you gave yourself to that moment in time. A moment to allow your soul to emerge and adapt and immerse itself in the great gift that flows like a river, like time, never stopping but bringing us an unveiled joy, a treasure to adore and cherish.

That is what Danni felt on that bright autumn day, the Envoy full of friends and kids, packed with sandwiches and cold cans of root beer and small bags of salty chips and sweet peanut butter cups. Danni's iPod housed her favorite kind of music, quiet and serene, and at that moment, it was softly playing *The Song of the Seahorse*, one of her favorites. The sun felt so surreal and warm on her face. Drowsy and intoxicated with serenity, she and Mindy sat in the back, Danni with her right side against the door, Mindy leaning sleepily against her. In the background, the husbands talked about the Steelers while their sons whispered together dreamily about Colleen and Megan, their very own dream team.

Mindy squeezed Danni's hand and in that dreamy moment, alive with warmth and whispers and dappled light, life was perfect.

Since they were going to arrive earlier than check-in time, they planned to drive a little further to a small town called

Sheffield, where there was supposed to be a fall festival complete with a lumberjack competition and horse team pulling. It was such a beautiful day to drive, no one minded. While Mindy and Danni drowsed, the boys had been having their own quiet conversation lying down in the cargo compartment behind the back seat. Since the suitcases were on the luggage rack on top of the car, there was ample room for them to lie down. The down side was that they had both grown enough through the summer they could not stretch out completely, but they were comfortable enough with their heads towards the driver's side wheel-well with their knees up. The upside was they were near the food, and Sammy had pounded his way through one bag of chips and was now thirsty.

As Anthony rummaged through the cooler for a bottle of water, Sammy said quietly, "So, do we tell our dads' what we think is going on with Ax-Man? I don't want to tell my mom, it would just freak her out."

"I'm thinking it would freak out our dads' too," he handed him the bottle of cold water and Sammy twisted off the top. "My dad just thinks he hasn't staked him into the ground tight enough and that maybe he overstuffed the coveralls this year and that is why the arms keep moving."

"What about the feet being different Anth, doesn't he think that's weird?"

"Na, he just thinks it's some jealous neighbor kids. Which ones," he lifted his shoulders up in a shrug, "you know as well as me that we don't *have* any neighbor kids except for you and the Russelton's." Anthony looked at their mothers to make sure they were still napping. Their slow, steady breathing continued, so he turned back to Sammy. "I was looking up some stuff on the net about spirits and zombies and Halloween, junk like that. I found one really weird site that talked about the *dark one* and how *he* could use evil spells and stuff, rites I think it said too, to animate objects and things to do his bidding. Imbue, that was the word they used. Anyhow, it said how these things . . ."

Sammy interrupted his eyes wide, the water bottle still in his hand not a sip taken from it. "You mean like that freaky movie *Pet Cemetery* where dead people and pets come back to get you?"

"Yeah, kinda like that, but it said *objects* too. Wouldn't Ax-Man be considered an object?"

"Umhumm, I think so. What do you mean in-brew? What does that mean? Anth, you're weirding me out."

"No, *imbue*. I had to look that one up, it means like, fill up, drench, saturate, like that."

Sammy finally took a swig of water and, for some reason, Anthony watched closely as his throat moved up and down when he swallowed.

"I know it weirded me out too, reading that stuff," continued Anthony. "It also showed some kind of evil symbols. One was called the *Third Circle of Satan* and it's used to call spirits to make them obey the commands of the dark one."

"Jesus," said Sammy quietly, some of the blood looked like it had drained out of his face.

Anthony noticed, but he continued because he felt he needed to get this out. "Yeah, you're right because I'm almost positive that I saw that same symbol *inside* Ax-Man's mask that day dad brought it home and you and I were screwing around in the basement, remember?"

"I remember smashing my nuts but not seeing a picture," said Sammy, his brow furrowed in thought.

"That's when I saw the picture. Then I started laughing at you and I guess I laid it down or something. I hadn't thought about it again 'til last night."

"What are we supposed to do?" We don't know anything about this junk," said Sammy in a hushed tone.

"Well, I did find something about a grimorie, which is a magical text book of some kind, and it's supposed to tell you how to make a *Devil's Trap*," Anthony dug down in his pocket and pulled out a piece of paper folded into a small square. He began to unfold it, looking up several times at Danni and Mindy to make sure they were not listening.

He handed it to Sammy. It was a printed page from the website Anthony had been on last night and it said:

Devil's Trap: a symbol to immobilize and control demons and prevent them from entering a place or gaining access to something.

Grimorie: A textbook containing rituals and spells for invoking and controlling demons.

Below that was a picture titled: *The Grand Pentacle* and one called *The Fifth Pentacle of Mars.*

The Grand Pentacle

The Fifth Pentacle of Mars

"What are they?" asked Sammy. The paper was shaking as he trembled.

Anthony took the paper back from Sammy and read from it in a whisper, "'The *Grand Pentacle* serves to convene all sprits, when shown to them they will bow and obey you. *The Fifth Pentacle of Mars* is a symbol, a seal that *protects its bearer from demons and dark forces.*'" Anthony looked up at Sammy and they stared at each other in silence for a long minute.

"That's it? What's this *Devil's Trap* look like?" asked Sammy.

"No, there was more but I heard mom coming down the hall to tell me it was time for bed. I had to get off the site before she got there. I didn't have time to find a picture of a *Devil's Trap*. I'll tell you Sam, I didn't want to turn the light off after some of the stuff I read and saw."

"What do we do now?"

"I don't know, I really don't know. I think we have to find a way to learn more about this before we go to our dads. We have to have something they will believe. Until we get back home and check out that mask, we'd better keep quiet."

"This is some scary shit Anth."

"You've got that right Sam-man, some seriously scary shit."

From inside the Envoy, the trees continued to buzz past them in a cornucopia of color, but the boys sat in the back, thinking quietly, feeling a dark foreboding storm close by, and wondering who the storm would strike first.

CHAPTER 15

Monday—noon.

Jim Russelton's cell phone rang just as he was leaving work to go to lunch. He reached for his phone on the holder clipped to his belt, saw it was his wife, Kelley, and answered.

"Hi babe, any sign of her yet?"

"No Jim, and I am really worried, I think I'll call the police."

"I think that's a good idea. Look, I'm going to leave work early and drive a couple of the back roads. I pray to God I don't find her laying on the road somewhere."

Kelley sucked in a sob, "Please Jim, don't even say that, I couldn't bear it. That would devastate the kids . . . it would devastate me!"

"Me too honey," said Jim somberly. "You didn't hear her bark; just that yelp you thought was her, right?"

"Yes, and I feel awful. I got busy with some laundry and forgot all about her being outside. You know how she usually barks to come back in. But if she did, I didn't hear her. Then that yelp, like she was in pain," this time Kelley did start to cry.

"It'll be ok Kells, we'll find her."

"Are you coming home now?"

"Yep. Let me run back in and tell Tom I need to take the afternoon off. I'm pretty much caught up on work, it shouldn't be a problem."

"Ok. I'll call the police and see if they are willing to look around the house.

"Ok. Love you, bye."

"Love you too, hurry home."

Jim started back toward his office, and then saw that his boss Tom must have already left for lunch also, because his car was not in his parking slot. Jim decided to call him on his cell phone on his way home. Jim had an understanding boss and worked for a good company that understood that sometimes you have family issues to take care of and they do not always happen when you are not at work.

He called Tom, and explained the situation.

"You go ahead Jim, your family comes first. Anything we need to follow up on for you?" asked Tom.

"No, I'm in good shape actually. Hey, thanks Tom."

"No problem. See you tomorrow."

"Yeah, see you tomorrow."

Jim Russelton had been driving back roads around their house for the last forty-five minutes and had not seen any sign of their dog Ebony. It was a blessing and curse. A blessing because he did not want to find her lying along the road, a curse because, one way or another, he needed to find her.

His phone rang and he snatched it up hoping for good news from his wife. "Hey babe, any news?" he asked.

"Nothing yet Jim, the police just pulled in. How far away from home are you?" asked Kelley anxiously.

"Only about five minutes," he responded, "hang in there, I'll be right home."

"I'll fill him in on what has happened so far."

"Ok, bye," Jim hung up and pressed the accelerator kicking up some gravel under his tires. Fortunately, the back roads around his neighborhood had little traffic and he could get away with rolling stops through the signs. He made it home in six minutes, and as he turned in the drive, he saw his wife and the police officer standing on their front porch. The police car was pulled into their turn-around so he was able to pull up near the garage door. As he got out and began walking to the porch, the police officer turned and looked at him.

"Hi, you must be Mr. Russelton? I'm Officer Craig Timmerman," he put out his hand and Jim shook it.

"Thanks for coming out. Has my wife brought you up to speed as to what's happened?" Jim inquired.

"Yes sir, she has. Normally the police department doesn't get involved in missing pets, but when the call came in, I was nearby, radioed that I could stop in and look around. How about if we walk the property and you can show me any places that your dog would frequent."

"Sure," said Jim and Kelley almost in unison.

As they made their way down the front steps, Officer Timmerman noticed, four large crows circling in the high grass about one-hundred yards north of the house.

"Anything specific over there?" he asked as he pointed in that direction.

Jim and Kelley both looked toward where he was pointing.

"No, not really, said Jim, "the kids will play over there sometimes and Ebony has been there probably thousands of times. Do you want to go there now?"

"No, let's just continue the way we started, we'll make it to that side soon enough."

Walking the property, Officer Timmerman was looking closely at the ground. It had not rained for several weeks, but the nights had been cool and he knew it was unlikely that any paw prints could have been left. What he noticed though, as they made their way to the back yard, caused him to stop about twenty feet from the basement door.

"Mr. Russelton, do you wear work boots?"

"No," said Jim, "I have some hiking boots but I don't wear them often and I know I haven't had them on for a couple of weeks. Why?"

"Have you had anyone here doing work for you recently?" Officer Timmerman continued.

"No," it was Kelley who answered.

Officer Timmerman stooped down and said to them, "Take a look at this."

Both Jim and Kelley bent down beside side him and as they did, the police officer took a pen out of his shirt pocket and traced what appeared to be the impression of a boot of some sort.

"Someone has been here recently with work boots on. Here . . . ," he turned to his right and pointed again, ". . . here and here."

Kelley and Jim looked at the footprints, and then Kelley turned to Jim and said, "When Army and Danni were here yesterday did he have on work boots?"

"No," said Jim, "and we didn't even come out back."

Timmerman stood up and motioned ahead of him. "They seem to go in that direction, let's take a look over there to where the tall grass is." Jim and Kelley followed slightly behind Timmerman as he continued pointing at what appeared to be boot prints.

"Do you see any paw prints?" asked Kelley

"No, but your dog probably doesn't weigh enough to leave any markings, the ground isn't soft enough for that. Who ever made these footprints must have been fairly heavy I'm thinking."

As they approached the tall grass, Jim could see where it had been trampled. "Look at that," he said pointing toward the grass.

"I see," said Timmerman.

"What Jim? I don't see anything," said Kelley her voice reflecting the anxiety she was feeling.

Jim put his hand on his wife's shoulder and pointed to the trampled grass. "There Kells, do you see it?"

They were close enough now that they could see a path of trampled grass and Timmerman put up his hand in a 'halt' gesture.

"Why don't you wait here while I go further in?" he suggested.

"No," Jim said pointedly, "we'll go with you.

As they waded through the grass, it rustled dryly, the sound for some reason seemed ominous to Kelley.

Jim said to Timmerman ahead of him, "Officer, there should be a clearing just ahead. We have a small fire pit there and sometimes have cookouts in the summer."

"Ok, yeah, I see it," Officer Timmerman said over his shoulder.

It took them approximately thirty more seconds to get to the edge of the clearing, Timmerman slowed down and then stopped. "Let me go in first, please," he requested. "If there are more footprints I don't want them stepped on. Just give me a minute or so, ok?"

"Ok," said Jim as he looked toward Kelley for confirmation and she nodded.

Officer Timmerman went forward into the clearing. Jim and Kelley could see his head and that he was walking around the perimeter, then suddenly he was out of sight.

"Officer?" called Jim, "Officer Timmerman?" he called when there was no immediate reply.

As he began to step forward, they heard Timmerman's voice say, "Just give me a second, I'll be right there."

Jim was first to see his head come up again and said to his wife, "I see him, here he comes."

As Craig Timmerman came back to them, both Jim and Kelley could tell that something was wrong by the look on his face.

"What is it?" asked Jim

"Mr. Russelton, would you come with me please?

"I'm coming with you too," said Kelley to both men.

"With all due respect, it may be best if you wait here," Timmerman said quietly.

Kelley looked between the two men, and walked forward without another word.

"Wait, let me go ahead of you then," said Timmerman to Kelley.

As they crossed into the clearing, they both noticed something odd lying on the other side of the fire pit. Getting closer they could make out something billowing in the slight breeze. As they reached the fire pit, Timmerman heard the sharp intake of breath from Kelley Russelton

"Oh please God, no, no," said Jim in a strangled voice.

The grass was badly trampled and the large footprints they had been following were everywhere. There was a dark, wet looking spot and right next to it was all that appeared to be left of their dog Ebony.

The stump of her once beautiful, flowing wagging tail.

CHAPTER 16

It was just past noon and Mindy had been quietly enjoying the scenery after waking up from her brief nap when suddenly she spied a billboard partially hidden behind some crimson colored trees. If she had not seen the billboard just then, they would have missed the small festival. They decided to take a detour from the planned stop in Sheffield since this looked intriguing. It was located on a back road in the middle of nowhere. *Willow 'N the Wind* was an eclectic gathering of some buildings that had spirals of smoke coming out of their stone fireplaces, but mostly small tented booths chock full of everything autumn. Hot salted peanuts cooked over a wood fire in lard and seasoned with sea salt, beeswax candles smelling of pine; pumpkin, and carrot cake; honey, laced with lavender and lemon and finally the intoxicating aroma of fresh doughnuts sprinkled with cinnamon and sugar.

There was a light breeze, making it cooler under the trees, and the boys had put on their jackets before leaving the car. Now each was eating a baked apple wrapped in crispy dough topped with cold vanilla ice cream. It was nutmeg, sweet, hot and cold all at the same time. Danni and Mindy had found a booth that had quilts, throws and comforters and the boys had heard them *oohhh* and *aahhh* over what they were seeing. Army and Dan had headed off in the direction of a blacksmith and antique tools where *oohhh* and *aahhh* were replaced by *look at this baby!*

Sammy was busy running his spoon around the plastic bowl determined to get every drop of yummy goodness. As he lifted the bowl to his mouth to lick it, (something which his mother would most certainly not approve of him doing), Anthony spied a booth off the beaten path, hidden under two oak trees, and poked Sammy in the ribs.

"Hey, let's go check that out."

Sammy grunted rubbing his ribs where the bony elbow of Anthony had made a direct hit, "Check what out?" Why did you hit me in the ribs?"

"So you wouldn't lick that bowl anymore. I'm pretty sure Selena Gomez would think that so un-cool and she is your dream goddess now isn't she?" Anthony's gaze had moved to a shady area under a couple of trees. "Check out that old guy over there. I think he is carving stuff. Let's go see, I love carving."

Sammy dropped his bowl and spoon into the fifty-gallon barrel next to him that was already halfway full of wrappers, bowls and other trash. He wiped his face with the napkin and dropped into the trashcan too.

"That old guy doesn't look anything like Selena," he said with a smart-ass grin on his face. "He must be your type."

He was just barely able to duck under the blow Anthony sent whizzing past the back of his head. They both were laughing as they set off towards the trees and the tented booth, leaves crunching beneath their feet, wood smoke drifting, incense like, in the cool air.

The old man had his back turned away from them as they approached, and he appeared to be shaving a piece of wood he was working on with a small, 'U' shaped tool that made long curling pieces of very thin wood spiral out and away from the carving. The first thing Anthony noticed in the display pieces on the table was a carving that looked like a breaking wave in the ocean that progressively turned into a Pegasus. It was fascinating how the carver had captured the birth of the magical creature in sea spray. Sammy meanwhile, moved to a group of five rings all carved from a single piece of wood, smooth and highly polished.

The old man turned around and said, "Can I help you find anything?"

As Anthony's fingers caressed the wood of the Pegasus, he looked up into the old man's eyes. The smile that had started to form on his mouth never quite made it; his fingers became motionless on the carving. The old man's face was weathered and a scarf around his neck thrown over each shoulder. He had high chiseled temples and just a hint of soft wispy hair on his head; and his eyes, his eyes were an unsettling shade of blue, like the eyes of an Alaskan husky, and Anthony couldn't help but feel he was being pulled into a place he had never imagine existed.

"Can I help you find anything my young friend?" the old man repeated.

Sammy looked up at Anthony then back and forth between him and the old man. "Anth?" Sammy's voice held a note of worry in it.

"Ah, no . . . well, I like carving and just wanted to see what you have," Anthony stammered.

"And you like Pegasus?" quizzed the carver.

"Um, yeah, I like magical things I guess," replied Anthony, sounding unsure.

The old carver stood up and put out his hand towards Anthony. "My name is Jebadye and you must be . . . ," he looked at Sammy then back, ". . . Anthony?"

"How'd you know that?"

"Your friend here called you Anth and I assume that is a shortened version of the full moniker given to you by your parents."

Jebadye's hand remained extended and Anthony slowly reached up to shake it. The old carver's hand was warm and firm and something seemed to pass between them in that moment they first touched. Jebadye looked deeply into Anthony's eyes and continued to shake his hand.

"I think that I have items you may be more interested in. Come around the side here, and back to my workbench, he turned and said to Sammy, "you too young man."

As Sammy hesitated, Jebadye said, "Come along with me now please."

Anthony had walked behind the tables and back to the old worn work bench and Sammy snaked his way to stand beside his friend.

The old carver reached down and swept up a wooden disk approximately the size of a fifty-cent piece. He handed it to Anthony and said, "Does that look familiar to you?"

Anthony looked up at Jebadye and said in a quiet voice, "Yes."

"What is it Anth, let me see," said Sammy urgently.

As Anthony held out his hand to show Sammy what was in it, he looked at the carver and said, "Why are you showing me this? Why me?"

"Ah yes," replied Jebadye, his eyes never leaving Anthony's, "well you see, we all have a special talent, and mine is reading people, reading their needs, and your eyes tell me you . . . ," and he turned to Sammy, ". . . and you young man," he returned his attention back to Anthony, "*need* this. You each *need* one. It's called *King Solomon's Silver Seal the . . .*"

"The Fifth Pentacle of Mars," Anthony interrupted as Jebadye began to hold out a small piece of wood.

"Very good indeed, that is exactly what it is," the old carver replied.

"Anthony," said Sammy with a trace of fear edging into his voice, "what is it?"

Anthony dug into his front pocket and took out the folded paper he had showed Sammy earlier in the back of the Envoy. He handed it to Sammy who unfolded it and looked up as Anthony said, "I saw the *Third Circle of Satan* . . . it's inside a mask my dad found at a yard sale."

"Yes, I am aware. It is a great danger, that which you have seen." He put his hand out toward Sammy, who without a word turned it over to him.

After glancing at the paper, he looked again at Anthony, "I see you have been researching your *need,*" said Jebadye. "Does that piece of paper tell you that this seal protects its bearer from demons and dark forces and it must be worn close to the body?"

Anthony took a closer look at the piece, noted the incredible detail in the scorpion's body, and realized that the barb at the end of the tail and the claws were inlaid with something.

"Sterling silver," he heard Jebadye say. "The chain too is sterling silver and the wood is olive wood from Bethlehem. Both are very rare and very powerful."

He picked up the medallion and placed the chain around Anthony's neck, "Keep it close to your body."

Anthony touched the piece, which felt warm and tucked it down inside his shirt.

Sammy had not said a word, but as the old carver picked up another medallion and stepped toward him, he took a half a step back.

"Sam, don't be afraid, let him put it on," Anthony said strangely calm.

Sammy's eyes darted back and forth between Jebadye and Anthony and he moved forward to meet the carver and dropped his hands to his sides while the medallion he placed around his neck also. He too, felt the warmth, and tucked it safely beneath his t-shirt where it seemed to radiate across his chest.

Next Jebadye handed Anthony a small cloth sack that felt light but Anthony could see it was full of something.

"The rarest of Bethlehem olive wood; branch clippings are slowly heated in a clay oven until they become hardened pieces of charcoal; charcoal with which you can write or draw a picture," he said.

"I don't understand what am I drawing? What is it you want me to draw?" asked Anthony.

"It's not what I want you to draw. It is what you will *have* to draw, what you *must* draw," the carver quietly replied. He then pulled out a much larger piece of carved wood. It appeared to be three inches in diameter.

It was a *Devil's Trap.* Exquisitely carved into the same wood as their medallions, it showed *The Fifth Pentacle of Mars* carved within center of *The Grand Pentacle.*

"You know the place you will confront it. You will use the holy charcoal to draw this symbol to trap and hold the entity and another of your kind will close the portal," Jebadye said in a soft, hypnotic voice as he put his hands on Anthony's shoulders. "It is a great burden you carry, but you and your friend," he looked up and nodded at Sammy, "will have to do this."

"I don't have any money to pay for these Jebadye," said Anthony as he put his hand to his chest where his medallion rested and clutched the bag with the holy charcoal against his leg. "And I don't know this place you are talking about," he continued, "or who the other is . . . I . . . we . . . ," he turned and motioned to Sammy, ". . . only think that maybe one of our Halloween dummies might be moving."

"A form of payment is not necessary young master, and your Halloween creation is actually the abomination of a dark one, born from greed, lust and evil. He sought out and deceived the one who would unknowingly complete his caustic plan."

"But how do you know? How do you know all this? We only just met."

"Because I know what you *need.* It gives me a picture of what will be and you and your friend must put a stop to what is unfolding."

Suddenly in the background, the boys heard Mindy and Danni calling their names. They looked at each other, then at the old carver.

He stared long and hard at Sammy, then handed him the *Devil's Trap* and said, "Guard this with your soul. Now, go to your parents. They are anxious about you and their *need* is to see you immediately."

As the boys turned away, they realized that much time must have passed without them realizing it.

Danni and Mindy spotted them when they came out from under the oak trees.

"Where have you boys been? We've been looking all over for you and calling for the last five minutes," said Danni in that voice parents have that hinged between anger and fear when they imagine something bad has happened to their child.

"Back there, at the wood carvers," Sammy volunteered hopeful to avoid any trouble.

"What wood carver?" asked Mindy looking over to where Sammy had motioned with his head.

He unconsciously put his hand into his jacket pocket with the *Devil's Trap* so neither mother would see it and ask any questions. At the same time, Anthony slipped the bag of holy charcoal into his jacket pocket, paying attention not to break any pieces.

"What are you two talking about?" Danni demanded.

The boys turned following her gaze and saw the two beautiful oak trees swaying slowly to the whim of the autumn breeze.

The tent was gone. No sign of the old carver remained. The grass and leaves were undisturbed and on that breeze they both thought they heard his voice whispering, *I know what you need, trust in me, I know what you need.*

CHAPTER 17

Monday—11:30 a.m.

Jon had been the first one up that morning. Two things woke him; the ache in his bladder from having to piss like a racehorse, and a pounding headache. Make that three things . . . he was thirsty from dehydration. As he rolled out of bed, a hot jolt shot up his back. He could not stand to think about it, about the *face*, the *thing* on his back, so he blocked it out. Light poured in through the window on the east side of the room, light that caused Jon to squint against the slivers of piercing pain it caused. He saw the clock and was surprised to see it said 10:22 a.m. *What the hell time did we go to bed?* He thought as he ran his tongue around the outside of his top teeth, the sour slightly burnt taste making him want to rinse his mouth ASAP.

When he opened the door into the hallway and started toward the bathroom, he not only tasted something burned, but smelled it too. *What the hell? Oh, that's right, we burned the chicken*, he thought. He flipped on the bathroom light which sent another round of pain deep into his gray matter.

After emptying his painfully full bladder, he rinsed his face with cold water, brushed his teeth twice and ran a comb through his hair. Leaving the bathroom, he found the house was still and silent. Making his way to the kitchen, he had to pass the dining room table. The remnants of last night's festivities lay waste on the table. A platter with one remaining pitiful chicken leg, which had shrunken as it cooled. Mash potatoes that looked like a small misshapen soccer ball in a blue bowl, gravy that had congealed to the consistency of glue, and one lone crescent roll left in a small wicker basket that was probably so hard by now it could be shot from a cannon. Last but not least, a few final, wilted lettuce leaves and there in the middle of the table, the crowning glory. A completely drained bottle of JB flanked by two tall tumblers from which they had imbibed the golden brew. He found himself gagging slightly at the smell of everything and moved off quickly towards the kitchen.

As he stood in the doorway, he thought, *not too bad, it only looks like a very small nuclear explosion went off.* He went to the sink and cleared out the dirty dishes piled in a heap, then started to clean off the dining room table. He began to methodically scrape the hardened food into a plastic bag in the wastebasket and rinse the dishes with hot water before stacking them in the dishwasher. He uncovered an empty bottle of Marsala wine and a charred pan, a dishtowel burned beyond redemption and a partially melted plastic spatula. *Scott did try to deglaze the pan with the chicken in it . . . that was quite a fire.* He noticed on the floor in the corner was the smoke alarm and batteries that Scott had pulled down in the midst of their fine dining experience.

When he was nearly done wiping up the counter Jon heard Scotts bedroom door open and a moment later the bathroom door close. He went back to the kitchen and found the antique percolator, apparently the only coffee pot Scott owned, and put on a pot of coffee. When it finished brewing Scott still had not come out of the bathroom so Jon poured himself a cup with a heavy dose of milk and sat down at the dining room table. He sipped it slowly, the warm liquid soothing his churning stomach. He was almost halfway through his cup when he heard the bathroom door open and slow footsteps coming towards the kitchen. Scott stepped through the doorway his unshaven face pale with dark circles under his eyes. He had on an old pair of black sweat pants and a gray sweatshirt that was wet at the sleeves, most likely from the water with which he had undoubtedly rinsed his face.

"I thought it would be worse," he said looking at the table and then at Jon, his eyes bloodshot.

"Oh, it was. Much worse," replied Jon, a small smile finding its way to his mouth. He took another sip of coffee. "Fresh pot, would you like a cup?"

"Isn't it better to have a 'hair of the dog' as they say to help get rid of a hangover?" asked Scott, his voice raspy from the whiskey.

"That dog is D-E-A-D my friend. The empty shell that housed bow-wow is currently residing in your recycle bin under the sink."

Scott pulled out a chair, the legs squealing slightly as they dragged across the floor and sat down heavily. "A cup of coffee then, extra milk," Scott replied.

"That's the same medicine in my cup—one more coming right up."

He stood and started into the kitchen. As he passed Scott, he patted him on the shoulder.

Scott winced and groaned, "My head feels like it's going to explode."

'Not surprising considering you had a two-tumbler head start on me," Jon smirked.

"Did I?" Scott raked his fingers through his still damp hair. "Why did you let me do that?" he said attempting to inject his own form of humor.

"Just following doctors orders my friend."

Scott sat for a moment with his elbows on the table, the heels of his hands pressed lightly against his eye sockets.

Jon nudged him on the arm, set the coffee in front of him and said, "Here, drink this," and he laid down two aspirin, "and you might want to swallow those up too." He took a sip of coffee and then dry swallowed the aspirin.

"Why didn't you take the aspirin with the sips of coffee?" Jon asked, his eyebrows drawn together in question.

"I can't take pills with hot liquid," said Scott simply.

"Why the hell didn't you say so? I would have brought you a glass of water," Jon said.

Scott waved his hand in dismissal, “I like the taste,” he said in response.

The jarring ring of the phone caused them both to jump slightly in their seats. Scott stood up; momentarily unsteady because of the residue Jim Beam his body was still processing, in addition to the pounding headache. He steadied himself and went around the corner to the phone.

“Hello?” Jon heard him say. It felt like a full thirty seconds before Jon heard Scott reply, “I’ll tell him. We’ll both be right down.”

Jon heard Scott hang up the phone and looked up questioningly as he came back around the corner.

“We both forgot you were supposed to call Jess Givens no later than 10:01 this morning,” they both glanced up at the clock, which read 1:45p.m.

“Whoops,” said Jon.

“Yea, whoops is right,” replied Scott sourly, “she just chewed a hole in my ass big enough to drive a Mac Truck through since I was the one who promised you’d call. How’s your back feeling?”

“I had some intense pain when I first woke up, but it’s backed off now. It bothers me more that I have that *face* on my back to be honest with you.”

As Scott stood, he picked up his coffee cup and drained it. “We’d better get dressed. You ok with clothes, I’ve got another pair of pants if you need.”

“A clean shirt I think, thanks,” said Jon.

“Ok then, let’s get dressed. I’ll get you a shirt. Oh, there’s a blue coat you can wear in the hall closet. It should be loose enough not to irritate your back much.”

They both took their cups to the sink. Scott looked around at the cleaned stove, sink and counter. He sniffed the air, “Smells like somebody caught something on fire in here,” he looked around the kitchen and gave Jon a sideway glance. “Wow, the cleaning crew did a good job I’ll have to recommend them.”

“Don’t bother, they’re booked already,” Jon responded.

Scott started down the hall towards his bedroom, coming back out with a soft beige long sleeved button-down shirt, and handed it to Jon.

"Here, wear this."

Jon took the shirt and started towards his room. He changed and then went out to the hallway and took out the blue jacket. He was deep in thought remembering all the different myths, stories and legends regarding Hell and wondering if he was about to find out which ones were true.

"You ready?" Scott's voice jolted Jon out of his thoughts.

"Yeah, let's go," said Jon zipping up the jacket. He looked up at Scott as he slipped on his own coat and slid a small notebook into his inside pocket.

"What's that?"

"I thought we would stop by and visit the Padre I was telling you about after we finish our business down at the station." He patted the pocket into which he had just put the notebook. "This is just a small incentive in case we have to prod the padre a little to provide the assistance we need," answered Scott with a tiny lopsided grin. He opened the door for Jon and said, "You first my friend."

Jon quipped, "Your kindness is exceeded only by your cooking skills."

"Why, thank you. Now move your ass before Jess Givens calls again."

Lost in thought, the two men had passed the majority of their trip in silence.

At a stop light about one mile from the station, Scott turned to Jon and said, "So what are you going to tell Givens?"

"That I need a leave of absence for personal reasons," said Jon.

"You know she's going to ask what the personal reasons are considering what's been going on, don't you," replied Scott as the light changed from red to green.

"Yep."

"Well, what are you going to tell her?" Scott prodded impatiently.

"That by law I don't have to tell her, that's why it's called *personal time*," said Jon in a calm voice.

"Oh boy, this should be some shoot-out," added Scott in a voice dripping with sarcasm.

"Yep," said Jon again, "but I'm a better aim."

Scott directed his van into the parking lot and pulled into a restricted slot. "Who do you want to be, Butch Cassidy or the Sundance Kid?" asked Scott as he put the van into park.

"I want to be the one who gets the girl in the end."

"Neither of them gets the girl in the end," said Scott.

"Sundance then, I like that name," replied Jon

"Can you swim?" asked Scott

"No, why?"

"Just wondering. Ok, let's go."

Ninety minutes later, Scott found Jon down in the locker room cleaning out his locker. His first thought was *ah-oh, this doesn't look good.* He stood for a moment in the doorway watching Jon take out his extra clothes, a pair of sweat pants, some papers and a picture of Doris Day off the inside of his door.

"So, if you're taking Doris down there must be trouble in paradise," said Scott not moving from the doorway.

"No, not at all," said Jon. "In fact I have a new one, color actually, that will be taking the place of this one." He signed and looked over at Scott. "I have FMLA, that's what Givens agreed to."

"Ok," said Scott slowly. "Well then, I guess I'd better call in my chips too. I'll get a week of bereavement for my brother. I have a ton of vacation and sick time I've never used and I'm pretty sure I can get one of my colleagues to write me a get out of jail free card."

"Get out of jail free?" grinned Wendels suddenly.

"In the words of a dear friend . . . Yep," said Scott returning the smile. "Say, what are you going to do with that picture of Doris?"

"Why? You interested?"

"Well, I was thinking, since you have had it in this seedy, testosterone dripping off the walls place, maybe I could give that classic beauty a real home," replied Scott.

"In the morgue?" said Jon with feigned sarcasm.

"No, on my *shell* mirror, you know? The one that you thought I did reload's on?"

He watched as Jon rolled his eyes in mock surprise, and then handed the picture to Scott.

"Take care of her, ok?"

"Yep," said Scott.

St. Mary Di Rosa Church on Middlefield Avenue in Sarvin, Pennsylvania, was a big church but a small parish. In the last few years, churches were consolidating, parishes disappearing and many dioceses were in deep trouble financially. An amazing issue if you considered the wealth housed in the Vatican.

Occasionally, those were the thoughts of Father Kaylan, the priest at St. Mary Di Rosa Church. His church was no exception to the cutbacks, but he was extremely talented at squeezing everything out of a quarter—*until the buffalo farts,* as his father had been fond of saying. That had usually earned his dad a sharp retort from his mother if she was anywhere in the vicinity when he made the remark. Nevertheless, it was not only a valuable lesson taught by a kind and loving father, it was a good laugh for Richard and his brother Nicholas. He could close his eyes and still hear his father saying, *why you are throwing that piece of paper away, you can still write on the back of it! Gather up those little pieces of soap and soak them in some warm water, all those little pieces will melt into one big piece you can wash with for a week! Son, that piece of foil can be used again, just smooth it out and save it, no shame in that. Take those potato skins and give 'em a good douse of salt and bacon fat, that oven is still hot, roast 'em until they're crispy!* There was never a day that went by Richard did not think of his father and thank God for him.

Those simple lessons had proved to be more valuable than any graded class in any school. The Lesson: *God gives us all we need. Open your eyes and it will be shown to you.* Those examples had given Richard Kaylan a base that he had grown into a garden of plenty. Was his church in need of help? Yes, but they found a way to continue their traditions and their vision of service. Yard sales, garage sales, bake sales and the good hearts of good people inspired by a faithful and good man who had found his calling as a priest, buttered their bread. It was not enough to make anyone fat, but no one starved either.

Father Kaylan was trimming back the candles in the sanctuary when he heard the double doors open. The light that flooded in briefly blinded him as he squinted against the glare. He saw two figures enter surrounded by a halo of light, his optic nerve not yet ready to accept the amount of stimulation suddenly imposed upon it. Something about the two men caused him to stop, his hands motionless at the crown of the candle, wick untrimmed. Then his hands fell to his sides, the thumb and index finger of his left hand black with carbon from the wicks, his right hand still held the small scissors seasoned with two decades of wax and wear, sharpened so many times that the metal was thin.

"Hello? How can I help you?" he called out to his unknown visitors.

"Father," he heard a familiar voice say, "we need your help."

Father Kaylan sighed as he disengaged his fingers from the scissors and wiped them on a cloth secured in his belt. He had a case, much like a small glasses case, that he had found at one of his yard sales in which he kept the scissors. He pulled it from the deep pocket stitched into his robe and placed the scissors carefully on the felt inside. He then wiped his hands on the soft cloth that he would later polish the brass holders with, the residue of wax establishing a protective film that would add luster and shine to the holders.

"Ah, Dr. Champion. It's been a long time since I have seen you during service," said Father Kaylan simply.

"It's good to see you too," said Scott in a reply that seemed to be slightly sarcastic.

Father Kaylan did not miss a beat. "I see you have brought a friend. A new addition to our church perhaps?"

Scott moved further into the church interior and from a distance appeared gently to pull the other man with him. "Father, we need your help," he repeated, his request echoing softly in the cool, dim interior of the church. The smell of linseed oil and incense mingled to produce an almost mesmerizing effect that soothed the turmoil roiling within them. "Please?" it was a quiet plea.

"You need only ask my son," was the reply the two men in the back of the church heard, and something in that voice pulled them forward, quietly up the aisle, their footsteps soft, their purpose urgent, their mission immediate, their success—questionable.

Between Jon and Scott, it took about thirty minutes to layout what had recently transpired in an order that made a modicum sense. While they were talking, Father Kaylan had looked over their list. He was watching the two men, but mostly Jon Wendels.

When they finished, Scott said, "So, now you see why we've come to you for help.

"Scott, have you found the trigger to the portal?" asked Father Kaylan.

Both Jon and Scott looked at each other, Jon shrugging his shoulders.

"We're not sure what you mean by a *trigger* Father, we read about it, but what is it?" said Scott. He had a confused look on his face, as did Wendels.

"For a portal to be opened there is an offending item, a trigger so to speak. It could be a room in a house or an item in a room of a house. It would have been used to open the portal. If you can't find the trigger, it will be much more difficult and dangerous to close the portal. When you find the portal, you must be willing to face it. Prayer is essential, for this is a war you are fighting, and you must cleanse the area by the authority and confidence you have by faith."

Jon interrupted Father Kaylan. "Father, I believe I have been in the portal, or at least been pulled to it. We think we know where it is but we have to find a way in. That's why we want to take the holy candles and holy water with us, because when we find the entrance to the hidden room, we think things will happen very quickly."

"Yes, Jon, you're right, you will need those items but what you need more importantly is your faith and belief in God, His Holy Angels and His Son, Jesus Christ. It is only by the name of Christ that you can cast the demons out and close the portal," said Father Kaylan quietly. "Do you believe, either of you? Do you *truly* believe?"

"Yes, we do believe. That's why we're here Father," said Scott.

Father Kaylan looked at John Wendels, "And you?"

"I believe with all my heart Father," he said quietly.

"Very well then," Father Kaylan moved behind the men to the door they had just come through. He firmly closed it and engaged the dead bolt. He then walked to the other door that lead to the church offices, closed, and locked it. Near the door was a phone which he picked up and pushed a square green button. When no one seemed to pick-up, he hung up the phone and walked back to the two men.

"Fortunately, our volunteer staff has left for the day. Follow me, both of you," he walked past them his robes stirring up a small breeze as he moved.

As they reached the front of the church, he stopped and bowed to the cross. He then turned and looked at both men. "It is a sign of respect and grateful adulation." He swept his hand to the spot next to him. Both Jon and Scott moved to the spot and bowed toward the cross.

Then Father Kaylan said to Jon, "Please, remove your coat and shirt; I need to see your back."

Scott looked at Jon and nodded. Jon unzipped the coat, took it off and laid it on the pew behind them. As he began to unbutton his shirt, a strange stirring rippled through the church, and Jon winced in pain.

Immediately Scott moved to his side, "What is it Jon?" he asked anxiously.

Small droplets of perspiration appeared on Jon's forehead and he clenched his hands into fists. "The burning pain on my back is unbelievable, it just started up again."

Father Kaylan turned to his left where there was a rectangular shaped pool. It was the baptismal pool.

"Scott, give me a hand with this," he said. "It folds here . . . here . . . and here," he motioned toward the cover. They reached down, folding the rigid cover at the three locations and set it to the side. The pool appeared to be ten feet long by five feet wide and three feet deep. There were three shallow steps down into the pool and a long bench in the middle.

Father Kaylan moved towards Jon and took his arm. "Come with me. Come now Jon and trust me. You must trust in what I am about to do." Jon, unable to speak because of the pain, nodded in acknowledgement

"Scott," said Father Kaylan, "please go into the sacristy. On the right side of the door are two shelves. On them you will find fresh baptismal robes, bring one to me. Hurry please."

As Scott started to run, Father Kaylan turned back to Jon.

"Move forward with me Jon."

"Father," he whispered, "the pain, I can't bear the pain!"

They both heard the sound of a door banging closed, and in another moment, Scott was back with the white robe.

"Kick off your shoes Jon, you'll need to take off your socks and pants first, leave your shirt until last," said Father Kaylan.

Jon had begun to tremble from the pain, and Scott said, "Sit on the pew; I'll get your shoes and socks off." Jon did not reply, he simply sat down, hands clenched, the color draining from his face.

"You must hurry now Scott," whispered Father Kaylan urgently, "his possessor knows what we are about and our window of time to save this man grows short."

Both men stood up grasping Jon under his arms pulling him into a standing position. Wendels skin had grown cold and clammy. Scott fumbled with the buttons on Jon's shirt, his hands shaking as Father Kaylan picked up the gown gathering it to put over Jon's head. As Scott pulled back the shirt, tugging it down over Jon's arms, Father Kaylan moved to put the robe over his head. It was then he saw for the first time, the insidious horrific picture clawed into Jon Wendels back.

"Mother of God," he breathed, "save us all."

The eye, the fiendish bloody eye, the centerpiece of the vile artwork on Jon's back looked up at Father Kaylan and he felt his blood run cold and his resolve waver. A force pulled his gaze from the baleful carving back to the cross above the altar, and he felt the rush of glowing hot strength wash through him. He quickly pulled the robe over Jon's head and let it fall to his feet.

"Quickly Jon, follow me." He took his arm as they moved to the top of the steps of the baptismal pool.

"Listen to me now, and respond with 'I do'." Jon's face had become vacant, and Father Kaylan hurried on.

"Scott, come here and stand on his other side. When I finish and say *now* we are going to lower him quickly, face up into the water. Get him to the bench in the middle; the water won't completely cover him. Whatever happens, do not let go of him. Do you understand me?" Scott nodded.

Father Kaylan made the sign of the cross in front of Jon and said, "Blessed be God, The Father, Son and Holy Spirit." A low rumble began around them, but he continued.

"Repeat what I say Jon," who managed to nod woodenly.

"I confess Jesus Christ to be my personal savior. I confess and renounce every inequity transgression and sin that I may have committed."

In a voice ripe with pain, Jon repeated what Father Kaylan said, and at each intermission, the rumble grew.

"Do you renounce satin and all his spiritual forces of wickedness that rebel against God?"

"I do," said Jon, teeth gritted.

"Do you renounce the evil powers of this world which corrupt and destroy the creatures of God?"

"I do."

"Do you renounce all sinful desires that draw you from the love of God?

"I do," Jon's voice was getting weaker now, and Father Kaylan spoke more quickly.

"Do you turn to Jesus Christ and accept him as your savior?"

"I do."

"Do you put your whole trust in his grace and love?"

"I do."

"Do you promise to follow and obey him as your Lord?"

"I do," A gasp of pain escaped his trembling lips.

"Do you renew your commitment to Jesus Christ?"

"I do."

"Scott, get ready," said Father Kaylan. He stood very close to Jon and said in a strong voice.

"Now, in the name of Jesus Christ I bind every evil spirit in or around this man and command them out! In the name of Jesus Christ, these doorways to his soul and flesh are now closed. Go! In the name of Jesus Christ, I claim for this man the release and freedom promised by our Lord and Savior!"

Father Kaylan said to Scott, "Now! Move him into the water. Don't let him out no matter what happens until I tell you!"

They both started down the steps of the baptismal pool pulling Jon with them. As soon as Jon's feet hit the water, he began to scream, a hideous gurgling sound. He began to fight them, and at the same time, Scott and Father Kaylan plunged him down face up into the water.

Instantaneously the water around them began to roil and seethe and a stench born from all things corrupt and pernicious enveloped them like a miasma. Jon's body went rigid, and then began to buck and fight, twisting in a manic macabre attempt to get out of the pool. His legs were kicking in a drumming motion on the water, splashing and churning it foamy white. Gargoyle features flickered, pulsing strobe like across his face, changing it into something demonic and violent.

"Hold him! Hold him!" commanded Father Kaylan as Jon fought feverishly to get out of the water.

"I'm trying!" barked Scott, "his body feels like a bag of snakes! I can't get a good grip on him!"

The sound around them was like the roar of a tornado, piercing their ears, almost paralyzing in its power. A cacophony of howling and screaming enveloped them, sharp, stabbing and deadly. God against Satan, Good against Evil, Heaven against Hell.

From Jon came an unholy noise, a mixture between a shriek and a wail. It was the sound of a man fighting for his very soul. Both men struggled to hold his body in the holy water as the world around them heaved.

Suddenly Jon's body became fixed and heavy, his struggling ceased, complete silence blanketed them and the previously churning, boiling water went dead calm in a nanosecond. Scott looked up at Father Kaylan, his hold on Jon easing, droplets of water running down his face like sweat.

Bearing down hard on Jon, pushing him against the submerged bench, Father Kaylan yelled, "No, "don't let go, not yet!"

As Scott's muscles tightened and he let his weight press onto Jon, a tsunami like force detonated up around them, carrying the water up in a curtain surrounding the pool. Something exploded out of the water and away from the men. It careened and bounced off the walls like a dark malignant pinball, shattering lights, cracking plaster, shredding banners, all of which fluttered down around the men in the pool. In less than ten seconds, it hit a skylight, which burst into so much glass snow at the same time the water washed back into the pool as though poured from a pitcher. Just that suddenly the nightmare was gone. Scott had collapsed across Jon's chest, and inertia had somehow moved Father Kaylan to the second step of the baptismal pool.

In the silence that followed, the sounds of labored breathing and fluttering confetti like debris filtered around them. Jon groaned and Father Kaylan rose shakily to his feet as Scott stood up straight, his hands on Jon's chest.

"Jon, can you hear me?" said Father softly. Jon's head lolled back and forth for a moment, his eyelashes fluttering moth like in the muted light. He opened his eyes, slowly, ever so slowly. Scott was busy taking his pulse and checking his breathing.

"Father, are you ok?" asked Scott.

"Yes, I'm ok," he replied. "Do you think we can sit him up?"

"In a minute, let me see if I can get him to respond to my voice," said Scott. He put both hands on Jon's shoulders, "Wake up Jon, come on back to the party."

Slowly his eyes opened, glassy and dazed at first, but as he focused on the worried faces around him, a crooked grin touched his lips.

"Scott," he said in a hushed rasping voice, "this is the last time I come to church with you until you go to confession."

"Shut up, smart ass," Scott grinned.

"That will be four Hail Mary's and three Our Father's," said Father Kaylan, and as he looked around at his damaged church he finished, "and a generous donation to the church treasury. We take checks."

* * *

The three men had made their way to the in-house parish apartment. Each had a towel around their shoulders and a clean dry baptismal robe with them. Jon had not wanted to put on the pants or shirt in which he had arrived.

As Father Kaylan held the door open, he motioned with his head, "Straight ahead are two spare bedrooms, each of you take one and get into those dry robes, I'm going to change in the bathroom."

"I'd rather use the bathroom if you don't mind," said Jon.

A look passed between Scott and Father Kaylan, "Yes, certainly," said the vicar. "Do you need anything specific?"

"A mirror, do you have a large mirror?"

"Yes, why?" replied Father.

"I need to see it first," said Jon. "My back, I need to be the first one to see it."

"Yes, of course, of course. There is one in the vanity under the sink. Will you be all right?"

"I think so. If anything comes up, I'm sure there will be some kind of commotion."

"Let's hope not," interjected Scott.

They each went to change. The apartment was very quiet, the only sounds were the swish of the pendulum on the clock in the hallway and its ticking.

A few minutes later, both Scott and Father Kaylan stood outside the bathroom door both swathed in the white robes. Ralph had on a pair of pale blue slippers. Scott's black socks stuck out in stark contrast to the robe. They waited and listened. A moment later the knob on the bathroom door turned and a soft *click* sounded. The light went out as the door opened, and as Jon came through the door, he let out a startled yelp when he saw the two figures hovering near the door, waiting on him.

"Jesus!" said Jon.

"Truly so," Father Kaylan replied.

"Well?" Scott asked impatiently.

"Well what?

"Let's see your back."

Jon turned around and shrugged the loose fitting robe off his shoulders revealing his back to the two men.

"Precious Lord," Ralph Kaylan said in awe.

Scott stood mutely for a moment, unable to speak, then said, "How do you feel Jon?" as he continued to stare at the unblemished, perfect back of Detective Jon Wendels.

"I feel clean," said Jon joyously.

At 5:30 p.m. on Monday night, the local network news, KDKA had carried a story about concern by parents in Lamont and surrounding areas regarding the disappearance of pets, the majority being dogs—four missing, several cats, though harder to count but two reported missing and in one instance a pet pig. A neighbor of the family owning the pig was under suspicion because he had recently had an altercation with the 'pig family' as he called them, because he was tired of them letting their pig wander the neighborhood rooting, oinking and shitting all along the way. The news anchor told cyber audience,

"Earlier this summer there was a string of animal mutilations that local authorities had determined was an occult group thought to be passing through the area at that time. They are confident that these were isolated incidents and the public can rest assured the disappearances of the pets are still under investigation. The chief of police has stated in an interview, "'Cats are transitory in nature and may very well have found a warm bowl of milk at a neighbor's house. Dogs however, tend

to be more family oriented, though there are occasions they will wander away, usually lured by another dog in heat.' "The chief of police also stated that if anyone has information regarding the disappearance of the pet pig or any other missing pets to call the number that you see at the bottom your screen." The story also made page B4 of the local news paper, *The Village Vindicator* but was, for all intents and purposes buried in the 'nobody reads' section.

It was an unusual sight, three grown men sitting around a large mahogany oval table with three unmatched chairs, all wearing white robes. Father Ralph's parish was a wonderful mixture of Italian and Polish inhabitants, so he always had on hand a good supply of homemade food provided to him by his kind and loving flock. When the men had finished examining in wonderment, the pristine, unblemished back of Jon Wendels they had all been hungry. Like three monks, they had traveled single file down the hall toward his spacious kitchen/dining room, their white robes swirling around them. After rummaging in the refrigerator, Father Ralph had pulled out a container of homemade pirogues coated with lots of butter and onions. He had then produced a big cast iron skillet and slid in about sixteen of the lovelies, and set them on the stove to reheat. Also housed within the haven of food in his refrigerator was some homemade kielbasa. Father Ralph liked grilling so he had searched for a range top unit that he could use throughout the year. One day among some of their donated items he had come across a very nice version that had not caught the attention of anyone else, so he blessed it and took it to his humble abode where it now was loaded with the Kielbasa along with a large white onion cut in half and set in the corner to caramelize. Next from his amazing larder, Father took out a large bottle of homemade wine donated by an Italian household who bottled their own. So, while Jon had sliced large pieces of bread from a crusty loaf, Scott had set the table, poured the wine and Father Ralph put platters of hot food on the table before them.

Scott had been first to reach across for the bowl of pirogues when Father Ralph had cleared his throat and said, "Let us give thanks to our Lord for this bountiful table, shall we?"

"Oh, yes, sorry Father," mumbled Scott as Jon nodded his head.

"Scott, you do remember how to fold your hands?

"Of course Father," was the somewhat annoyed reply from Scott.

"Ah, good, good, then let us bow our heads."

It was a simple prayer, by a truly grateful man of the cloth, and had he looked up he would have noticed two equally grateful men alongside him.

The dishes clinked for several minutes until all their plates were full and the first few bites taken when Jon interrupted, a fork of crispy kielbasa hovering midway between his plate and his mouth.

"Father, you told us about a *trigger* earlier. If we don't know what the trigger is but we find the portal, can it still be closed?"

Father Ralph cut another bite of Kielbasa and skewered a piece of pirogue together on his fork before he looked up at Jon. "Please understand, I have never faced an entity such as this personally, but in my reading and studies I have amassed a great deal of knowledge that I am confident will be useful."

"Would that be like a pilot that had read all the books but has never flown a real plane?" Scott asked as he took a bite of bread slathered with butter.

"God will forgive you my son," said Father Ralph locking a stare on Scott. Jon looked at the two men realizing there was some unspoken history between them.

"Please continue Father, I'm listening," said Jon

"We live in a world where what is seen with our eyes and heard with our ears is hardly as much as the eyes and ears that see and hear us. What does that mean? It means there is a vast invisible world of good and evil around us every moment of every day. Obviously, an evil entity has entered your realm, which means now you must invoke Christ and the Holy Angels. You see, our free will is a shield that can, so to speak, get holes in it, which in turn leaves us considerably more vulnerable. A portal is a place an invitation has been made through use of a material object, which becomes a channel through which the unholy can move. The offending item could be given or sold to an unsuspecting person, thus passing the connection along with it. Whether the person knows about it or not, they have just made a binding contract with the demon by agreeing to accept the gift.

"But the trigger Father, how do we find out what the trigger is?" asked Jon again.

"I'm getting there Jon, be patient. God allows *touchstones* of good to be utilized as aids to help. Crucifixes, pictures of Jesus, holy water, holy candles, all are aids in closing a portal. When you find the portal, you must pour a thick line of holy salt in front of it, and then surround yourself in a circle of holy candles and holy salt that will keep the demon from you. You will need to move very quickly, you understand. You must invoke the name of Jesus Christ, prayer is essential. Also, you must be specific in your wording, stating that you have the authority as a child of God through the name of Jesus Christ to close the portal, and you must, and this is important, you must find a way to get holy water on it. Splash, spray or somehow douse the portal. It will all depend on the portal. Now, if you are able to find the trigger, it must be totally destroyed, broken, buried, or burned. In any event, this is no time for fear, you must believe. Your conscience must be clean," Father looked pointedly at Scott, "and you must make confession."

"But I'm not Catholic, can I do that?" asked Jon.

"Yes, you can. It's not the words, but the lifting of your heart to God that truly matters. If you're sincerely sorry for your sins, God will forgive without the sacrament of penance."

They continued eating in silence for several long moments until Father Ralph said, "Scott, I'm aware of your brother's death, I'm deeply sorry. Is there anything I can do? Anything you need?"

Scott studied his plate for a moment, swirling a piece of onion round and round in a small pool of butter on his plate. "Thank you Father. I can think of one right now, in fact," he looked up, "tomorrow morning I'm going to make the funeral arrangements. Because of the circumstance, I've decided to have him cremated, and on Thursday a small memorial service." Time ticked on for several moments before he continued, "Father, there is something you could do, not for me, but for Bill. Could we . . . could you do a small service for him here at the church?"

"Of course Scott, who's handling the cremation?"

"Mason/Winters Funeral Home. I'll call them later today and ask them to contact you. Thank you Father." There was a humble tone to his voice, and sincere gratitude.

"Shall we consider the slate wiped clean then Scott?

"Yes, the slate is clean."

They looked at each other for several long heartbeats, Scott looking away first. Jon could feel much of the tension leave the room.

After they had finished all the pirogues and kielbasa, mopped up their plates with bread, cleared the table and uncorked another bottle of wine, the three men sat around the table discussing what came next.

Scott poured himself another glass of wine and said, "I've become quite a lush in the last few days."

"Me too," said Jon, "I don't think I'm over yesterdays binge yet."

"Who did you go on this binge with?" asked Father Ralph.

"Jim Beam," Jon answered.

"Mmmm, Jim Beam, I know him well. I have had occasion to also suffer under that tutelage."

"How many candles do you think we'll need?" inquired Scott, switching back to the subject at hand.

"Ten I think . . . yes ten. You will need them to surround yourselves to keep any entity from trying to enter either of you and use you as a host," Father Kaylan responded.

"As a . . . host?" said Jon looking at Scott.

"Yes, exactly. Now, since we don't know where the portal is or how close you will be able to get to it, you have to figure out, for lack of a better term, a 'delivery' system."

"What do you mean?" Scott asked as he pushed his plate away.

"You'll need a way to deliver the holy water onto the portal."

"We could fill a couple of balloons with holy water and chuck 'em at the portal," offered Jon in jest.

Scott considered the information for a moment and said, "How about one of those pump-up water sprayers? We could cover a pretty good area with one of those I think."

"Not practical. It would be too cumbersome to carry a sprayer. I do think what would work though, is one of the churches' Aspergillums."

"What is that? What does it do?" inquired Scott.

"During baptismal reaffirmation it is what the priest uses to disperse holy water to the congregation. Some have to be dipped into an Aspersorium or pail and then shaken. We have three at this church of the type that have internal reservoirs that dispense the holy water when shaken. We could fill up one for each of you. They would be easy for you to carry as long as you carry them upright. I could sew a small flap inside each of your jackets that would hold it in place I think."

"You can sew?" Scott said with a smirk in his tone.

"I can sew, yes. Is that some kind of an issue?"

"No, I just didn't realize you were a man of so many talents."

"I can box too, or have you forgotten?"

Scott became immediately quiet, and after a moment, Father Kaylan continued.

"Do either of you have a small bag?" Jon nodded in affirmation. "Good. Don't forget you'll need a good lighter.

Take two to be on the safe side. When are you going to the portal?"

"We aren't positive where it is yet," Scott replied.

"*I'm* positive," said Jon. "We just have to find our way in. We'll have access to cadaver dogs . . ."

"Cadaver *dog,*" interrupted Scott.

". . . dog then, on Friday. Depending on the outcome, I would say possibly Friday, Saturday for sure."

"Saturday? You do know what Saturday is?" asked Father Kaylan.

"Halloween," said Jon.

"Hmmm, divine intervention possibly."

Scott stood and picked up the glass from which he had been drinking. "Jon, we need to change and get back to my place. I have some phone calls to make regarding my brother and to be honest with you, I'm tired and I'm starting to get drunk again."

"Father," said Jon as he pushed back his chair, "do you have a shirt I could borrow?"

"Certainly, I'll lay one on the bed for you. Are you ok with the pants?"

"Yeah, I just don't want that shirt against my skin again, you know, the back part and all. I'll get it back to you tomorrow."

"Don't believe him," said Scott, "that's my shirt he's dumping on you. I lent that to him and he's not returning it to me."

"I'll clean it for you Scott," said Father Ralph.

"No Father, actually I'd prefer if you would burn it instead."

"Consider it done then."

While Jon went to change, Father Ralph and Scott finished picking up the glasses; Scott poured the remainder of the wine from the bottle into a decanter Father Ralph had indicated. Scott rinsed the wine bottle for return to the maker for a probable refill, then went over to where his coat lay and picked it up, fishing inside for something. He pulled out the small notebook that he had picked up from his house, turned and extended it to Father Ralph. "This is for you, he said.

Father Ralph looked questioningly at Scott, and then accepted the small book. He opened it, flipped slowly through several pages, closed the book and said simply, "Thank you."

"Don't thank me, I don't deserve it. I should have given it to you long ago. In fact, my point in bringing it with me was to use it as leverage if you were unwilling to help us. I'm glad I didn't do that Ralph."

They looked at each other for along moment, and then hearing the bedroom door open, they watched Jon walking towards them.

"All yours," he said signaling back towards the bedroom with his thumb; he could sense he had interrupted something.

Scott started down the hall and Jon turned to Father Ralph and said, "Is he ok? Is something wrong?"

"Scott," said Father Ralph Kaylan, vicar of St. Mary Di Rosa in a voice full of emotion, "is in danger of becoming a good man."

CHAPTER 18

After leaving the *Willow 'N the Wind* on Monday the Petrucci/Brogan clan had made their way to the Gateway Lodge by four o'clock and after getting settled in their rooms on the second floor, they had gone down to the Great Room for afternoon tea, coffee, fruit and cheese.

The adults settled into the comfortable leather couches that surrounded the fireplace to enjoy the fragrant, warm hearth with their savory snacks. The boys took their plates of fruit and cheese to the other end of the Great Room where several comfortable huge stuffed chairs and a pair of double doors that opened onto a log deck that had rustic wood chairs, a swing and a fire-pit. Both had noticed there was no one currently out there and realized it would give them a chance to talk privately. They set their plates on the wide railing, and leaning their elbows on each side of their plates leaned forward to look over the edge. Both boys pulled the carved medallions of *The Fifth Pentacle of Mars* out of their shirts, each silent for several minutes as they examined and touched the beautiful carvings.

Anthony was the first one to speak on that late autumn day, the sun streaming dappled through the leaves. "Where did you put the *Devil's Trap?*" he asked quietly.

"In one of my socks rolled up with my underwear."

"When we get changed for dinner we'll be sure we're ready first, then while our parents are getting ready, we can sneak it out to the car and hide it in one of those little compartments in the back that way we're positive we won't forget it, ok?"

"Yeah, that sounds like a plan. I keep thinking we must have dreamed the whole thing. Then I feel the medallion under my shirt and know it was real."

"Shit, I forgot to tell you, I didn't know until we unpacked that Dad brought his net book with him. Somehow, tonight we'll have to find a way to do so more research. We should be able to get a connection here; I know they have wireless internet service, I saw it posted at the front desk when we checked in."

"Where can we go?"

"Dunno yet, we'll figure it out though."

"What do you think Jebadye meant when he said, *you know the place you will confront it*?"

"Dunno that either Sam-man. He said we'll use that charcoal to draw the trap and another of our kind will close the portal. What does it mean? Where is it?" he sighed and chewed on a piece of cheese.

Anthony saw Sammy's hand snaking toward his plate and realized he had already cleaned his own. As he made a move to protect his food, their hands collided and knocked the empty plate off the railing into the bushes below.

They looked at each other and said in unison, "Ah-oh."

"We'd better go get it," said Anthony

"You think anyone will really miss it?" said Sammy as he grabbed the last piece of cheese off Anthony's plate.

"Nope."

"Then?"

"Maybe just because we should, like it's the right thing to do, you know?

Sammy swallowed and nodded his head in agreement. "Yeah, I guess you're right. You know if we don't, something bad will happen.

"Let's go now, ok?"

"Sounds like a plan. On the way past the buffet, I'll get some more cheese and crackers."

Anthony just laughed and shook his head in wonder. "I don't where you put it all Sammy."

"What, you you know? We have different compartments in our stomach. One for junk food, that one takes a long time to fill up. The vegetable compartment is *always* full, that why

I can't eat any vegetables. The dessert compartment is *never ever* full, always empty, always ready for more."

They had come back into the great room and as Sammy was finishing his dissertation on stomach compartments, he was busily filling a paper napkin with cheese and crackers.

"Samuel, that's enough now, you'll ruin your dinner," said Mindy. Both men along with Anthony looked at each other and burst out laughing.

"Never happen," said Dan.

As the adults continued their friendly banter, the boys made a quick getaway toward the door they thought would lead them out back to rescue the plate before it became a casualty of their recent bad luck.

They found the plate, unaffected by its fall, and went back inside to look for the dining room. They found it just to the right of the front desk. There was no one in the dining room at the moment, so they decided to leave it in the small bar.

When they arrived back at the great room, another log had been added to the fire and the crackle and pop sound of wood burning filled the air. To the right of one of the leather couches were two big soft chairs, each with large footstools. There were bookcases on either side, and in one of the bookshelves, they found a chessboard and a box of chess pieces. The boys sat down and opened up the board.

"Antony," said Sammy quietly

"What?"

"Are we allowed down here anytime?"

"Yeah, as far as I know. One of the things mom liked was that they keep the woodpile full and I guess you can add wood whenever you want. Why?"

"Well, if we can get the net book out without your Dad knowing, we can tell them we are coming down here to play chess," he looked up at their parents, "set up some pieces now so they can see us playing," he whispered. Anthony picked up the black pieces while Sammy picked up the white. They began to set the board.

"And?" whispered Anthony

"We can tell 'em we're coming down here to play chess and sit by the fire, but really use the time to surf some information on the net. We don't need to have it plugged in do we?"

"No, the battery lasts for about four hours."

"They probably won't care because it'll give 'em time to soak in the Jacuzzi without us there."

"Sammy, you're not just an empty stomach, you're a genius."

"I was wondering when you'd figure that out," said Sammy smiling.

They made a few pretend moves on the board and listened to the conversation of their parents before changing for dinner.

As the four adults made their way up the steps to their respective rooms, Anthony and Sammy looked at each other.

"Even better," said Sammy.

"What do you mean?"

"If they come down to check on us while we're doing our research, we'll see them coming down the steps and have time to hide the net book."

"Are we really playing to win death by chocolate dessert?" asked Anthony.

"Why?

"Cause if so, I intend to win."

"Show me your best, brother."

The families had been able to take their time that afternoon. After tea, everyone had returned to their rooms to clean up and get ready for their dinner reservation at six o'clock. Mindy and Dan had spent some time on the deck enjoying the cool air and warm sunshine while Sammy had taken a short nap on the couch in front of the small fireplace each suite had. Danni and Army on the other hand had sat together on the couch in front of their fireplace while Antony had stood on the deck looking out into the beautiful vista of fall, all the while his mind was running a million miles an hour on what had happened earlier that day.

One of the unique things about Gateway was their upscale dining that did not require a suite or tie. You could come to the dining room dressed to the nine's and not be out of place or you could just come for dinner in a pair of Dockers which was what the Petrucci/Brogan clan had decided. It was a testament to the moms that their boys would eat other food besides burgers or pizza, so they had ordered from the seasonal menu that Gateway Lodge offered. They had all shared a wheel of brie topped with apricot jam baked in filo dough that they served with sliced apples and cinnamon, homemade bread sticks with toasted sesame seeds along with a complementary bottle of white wine. The boys had ginger ale with a twist of lemon in wine glasses which made them feel special and grown up. Anthony had chosen the fillet mignon with gorgonzola sauce and blue cheese crumbles a baked potato with *tons* of butter and asparagus that he had tried and actually liked. Sammy on the other hand, had opted for a poached shrimp dish. Shrimp poached in aromatic broth with saffron risotto and baked fennel. No potato. No vegetables. He was saving it all for the dessert round

There was always an element of surprise and disaster involved with the boys. This occasion was no exception. Sammy, in an attempt to spoon up all the broth that his shrimp were delightfully swimming in, had perched his last bountiful, beautiful shrimp on his fork, sitting on an angle across his plate. As he had scooped up the broth, he had somehow managed to plop some portion of his arm on the fork handle. Much like a child's seesaw, that wonderful, beautiful, succulent shrimp had become airborne and landed in the breadbasket of the couple sitting at the table behind them. Many apologies and much laughter later they had taken their dessert to the great room and sat together, Sammy wondering what the big deal was, his dad shrugging his shoulders in a o*h well, that's Sammy,* and his mom running through the available options of what she would do to him when they got home. Their host, Dustin, had brought them hot mugs of coffee with sweet cream and the boy's ice-cold glasses of milk. The fire crackled, laughter was like music in the air and life for this beautiful moment in time, seemed simple and serene.

When they had gathered up their dishes and made their way upstairs, Danni, Mindy, Army and Dan had gone out to the deck off the Petrucci's room. Army had asked Dustin if it would be possible to send a bottle of wine up for the adults with four glasses. Dustin made it a point to get four frosted glasses, a bottle of a Zinfandel wine and two bottles of very cold ginger ale for the boys. The fireplace in their room provided a flickering glow against the walls that reflected through the sliding glass doors. Citronella candles were lighted along the railings in amber colored glass holders giving the deck a golden hue. Sammy and Anthony were hanging over the end railing with their cold glasses of ginger ale listening to their parents' laughter, which was soft as the moonlight.

Anthony tipped his head back finishing off his drink and looked at Sammy.

He said loud enough for all to hear, "Hey Sammy, how about a chess rematch?"

Sammy blinked his eyes for a second and then got it, "Oh yeah, a rematch. OK, let's go. You're dead meat Anth," he added in an attempt to be dramatic.

"Mom can we go down to the great room and play chess?" asked Anthony.

"Me too?" piped in Sammy.

The grown-ups all looked at each other.

"The great room only," said Danni. She looked at both boys and said sternly, "got it?"

"Got it," both boys said in unison.

As they stepped through the sliding door and pulled the screen closed, the adults turned their attention back to their conversation and the ambiance of the deck. Anthony had been hoping for that and made a quick stop by the couch picking up the small net book, then holding it in front of his body.

Sammy had stopped with him and Anthony whispered, "Keep moving! Open the door."

Sammy took a couple of long steps to reach the door. He opened it and let Anthony go through first, effectively blocking anyone from seeing him with the net book. As he closed the door behind them, Anthony took the lead going down the steps. He noticed there was only one person, a woman, sitting on the middle couch at the end that would be furthest from them. She had her head leaned back, eyes closed, and appeared to be asleep.

"Get the chess set," Anthony said quietly to Sammy as he pushed the two large footstools together.

Sammy retrieved the chess set from the nearby bookshelf, and opened up the chessboard on the stools. "Do you want me to put pieces out?"

"Yeah, put them kinda all over, you know, like we're in the middle of a game."

"Gotcha."

As Sammy set up the board, Anthony settled back into one of the huge chairs, flipped up the screen of the net book and pressed the *on* button. As the net book powered up and ran through its startup menu, Sammy came around and sat on the wide arm of the chair.

"What are we looking for?" he said quietly, glancing over at the apparently still sleeping woman.

"That site I told you about, the one explaining what a *Devil's Trap* is and how it's used," Anthony replied.

"Do you remember where it was?"

"I remember the search string I used, it should be pretty easy to find. I hope. I don't want to spend much time looking for it, I want to use the time we have reading what it says."

He was typing as he talked, and as he hit *enter,* a log of websites became available.

"Wow," said Sammy, "which one do ya pick?"

"I think I can remember," said Anthony as he scrolled down the list. In the silence that followed, he clicked page two, three and then four. "I think this is it," his voice had an edge to it. It was as though he knew he was about to enter something forbidden and dangerous.

As he hesitated, Sammy said calmly, quietly, "Let's see it Anth."

Anthony looked up into Sammy's eyes briefly, as though he knew in that moment the age of innocence was over, and then he swirled his finger across the touch pad and left clicked to open the site. It was what he had found before, what he had briefly looked at and read.

"Where do we start?" asked Sammy anxiously.

"I remember reading parts of this; I think I can find what I was telling you about. Hold on," his thumb continued to move incessantly, down the page, following the line of information he was looking for.

"Here, see, this is it," he double clicked on the site and it opened to reveal a table of contents covering everything from the Angel of Death to Charms to Ouija boards and Wendigo's; half way down was a site titled, the *Devil's Trap*. He doubled-clicked to open it, and all was quiet for several minutes as he and Sammy read, the only sound the crackling fire and the slow, sleepy breathing of the unknown woman on the couch.

"Holy shit Anth," Sammy's voice was quiet, hushed.

After a minute Anthony said, "Ok, what are we going to take from this? What can we use?"

"It's possessed Anth, that's what we're going take from this, it's possessed."

"What's possessed Sammy? What do you think is possessed? "I've seen some stuff, you've seen some stuff. We need to put it together somehow. Something is going on."

"I think it's Ax-Man," said Sammy so very quietly, his body never shifting from the arm of the chair, his breathing the only movement.

"I do too."

"How do we prove it?

"When we get back, we'll go up with our necklaces," he reached under his shirt and pulled out the medallion, "we'll see what happens.""

"Then what, what'll we do?"

"We need some kinda plan," Anthony looked up at Sammy. "Keep reading, maybe we can figure it out. We have to figure it out now, before our parents come looking for and we have to go back, read Sammy, just read. Hey, do we have any paper or pencil or anything?"

"No."

"Go down to the desk in front and see if you can find anything to write on, anything Sammy. Got it?"

Sammy slid off the arm of the chair and stood up. "What am I? Your gofur?" he said in an attempt to inject some humor.

"You're such a good gofur."

Then Anthony's voice took on a deeply serious tone. "We don't have much time Sammy. I don't know why, but I can feel it."

The fire crackled and popped, the light illuminated fans and spirals of shadow and light into the space, moving, rhythmic and changing. Yet the dark around them felt chill and foreboding.

He moved like liquid, Samuel did, past the fire. He seemed different, more grown up. He stopped for just a second then turned back and looked at Anthony. Time stood still for just a slow poignant moment. He left without a word and came back shortly with a paper and pen. Wordlessly he handed them to Anthony.

"We have to lure it in Sammy, that's what it says."

"Lure what in?"

"An evil spirit I think; the devil."

One . . . two . . . three . . . four. The seconds ticked by.

"I don't want to Anth; I don't want to go there."

"Me neither."

Five . . . six . . . seven . . . eight. Time ticked by so very slowly.

At last Anthony said, "It all depends on what we find when we get home. The mask is the key I think."

"I'm scared."

"Me too. Really scared."

Sammy stood up straight, "Well, do you remember when we first met, you had wet pants?"

"Yeah, I was feelin' for crawfish and you scared me. You had wet pants too from wading."

"I told you I knew how to catch' em and you said *watch this*?

"Yeah?"

Nine . . . ten . . . eleven . . . twelve—the dye was cast.

"Ok wet pants, let's go then," said Sammy with resolve.

It was odd how things worked out. After all the boys had read, you would have thought they might have a rough time sleeping, but they did not. Actually, when they got back to the Petrucci's room both boys felt exhausted. Their parents were still on the deck and had cracked into the second bottle of wine. The fire still painted dancing shapes on the walls inside the room, the candles still danced and swayed outside where the low sound of their voices and laughter ebbed and flowed. As they entered the room with the key entrusted to them, Danni was closest to the sliding screen and saw them first.

"Hey boys, who won?"

"Won what?" said Sammy. He got his second shot to the ribs that day from Anthony.

"Oh, you mean the chess game? It was a draw."

"A draw? Who had the most pieces left?" asked Danni.

"Me!" they said in unison.

By that time, the other three parents had moved to the open door and had a good wine enhanced laugh at the response. The boys sat down on the couch leaning their heads back much the same as the woman who was probably still snug in front of the fire in the great room.

The conversation droned on outside and Anthony felt his eyes growing heavy. Sammy was out, a soft snore escaping his parted lips. Slowly his relaxed body slid toward Anthony, and as boys are wont to do, Anthony's first instinct was to put a pillow between them. As Anthony fell asleep to the sound of the parents talking on the deck, he did not realize that his head slid past the pillow wall he had created, and he and his best friend slept peacefully for a good forty-five minutes before their parents came in.

Mindy and Dan went to their room first to make sure that the pull out bed was ready before they came back to walk their sleep drunk son to the adjacent room. When Sammy moved away from Anthony, he slid bonelessly down on the couch.

Danni and Army took off his shoes and socks, but when they got to his hoodie, he woke up enough to mumble *"No."*

"Just relax honey, its bed time."

"No," he said again, starting to sit up.

Anthony was moving away from his parents, putting his hand on the front of his hoodie. Even in his sleep, he knew the importance of the medallion he wore.

"No, I'll get ready for bed myself," he mumbled.

"Let him go," said Army to Danni who was still trying to help him off with his shirt. "Let him go. He's not a baby any more honey."

"I don't know how to do that Army, do you?" Danni said looking up at her husband.

"No, not really, I guess we have to learn though, don't we?"

They continued to look at each other for a moment, than Danni laid her son's head down on the small pillow and covered him with an afghan.

"Leave the fireplace on?" she asked.

"Leave it on. You know he loves it, and it will be a nice way to sleep won't it?"

Danni and Army made their way to the big comfortable four-poster bed. They laid in each other arms with all the other lights off, only the flicker of the fire illuminating the room.

Anthony slept soundly, peacefully in the room where his parents loved.

It was paradise.

Tuesday the boys and dads had gone to a survival course that had included learning how to build a lean-to, start a fire, and gather clean water and some horseback riding and hiking. Later, they had a lunch of corn bread, baked beans and steaks. The steaks were cooked over each fire that the teams had been able to start. Some of the steaks were smoky and tough; others were charcoal on the outside raw on the inside. Sammy and Anthony however, were bright stars. They had spent the summer honing their cooking skills over their fire pit outside the barn. Days and nights of burnt potatoes, hamburgers and hotdogs had taught them the way to move the meat to the hot spots for searing and then to the cooler spots to finish cooking. Their steaks were succulent and had a crisp caramelized exterior. The smell was so tantalizing that others wandered over to their fire for tips. The dads and sons had a good time, and for the boys, they could forget for a while what was on their mind regarding Ax-Man.

Danni and Mindy on the other hand, had spent a quiet day doing the 'spa' thing.' First was a forty-five minute stone massage with their choice of sandalwood oil, hot towels and quiet meditation. Next followed a manicure and pedicure that made their feet and hands feel somehow lighter and so very, very clean. Many Oooohs and Ahhhs later, hot tea and scones welcomed them while they sat wrapped in thick cotton robes and soft spongy slippers. Somehow, in their languid state, they made it back to their rooms, put on comfortable sweat pants and staggered back to the fireplace to relax. Danni sat on the left end of one long couch, Mindy on the other, and they read for a few minutes. As they flipped the pages, each page made a soft *swoosh* in the silence, until at last they drifted off into peaceful, Zen like sleep.

The day had been a very good day for everyone. The guys came back smoky, sleepy, and full. The mothers were relaxed, pampered and content. All had spent a day of bliss in their own way.

That evening they enjoyed another wonderful meal. Their waiter Dustin, was a very talented, experienced young man and was able to point out the finer items on the menu and offer wine choices. Since the boys were not able to drink any cocktails, he made them feel special by serving 'cocktails' of ice cold ginger ale in frosted glasses with a twist of lemon. Anthony and Sammy felt both responsible and grown up when they clinked glasses with their parents and made a pledge to come back as soon as possible.

The boys were able to put the impending confrontation out of their minds. They needed this time to be happy and carefree, and it worked. That evening after dinner, they had all made their way to the Great Room, and the ever-magical fireplace. It seemed all of the people who stayed at the Gateway Lodge wanted the same thing; quiet and solitude; a place away from the madness for a brief moment in time, and that was what they all shared on that wonderful evening.

When Anthony went to bed that night he tried not to think about what he and Sammy had read then night before, but his mind would not be still and he started laying out a plan. He had an outline in his head about what might work, but he would have to run it past Sammy during their trip back tomorrow. He finally fell asleep with a picture of the *Devil's Trap* in his head, sure he would be drawing it soon enough.

On Wednesday morning, their last at Gateway Lodge, they were getting their suitcases together after breakfast which had been a spectacular array of scrambled eggs with cream cheese and chives, chocolate chip pancakes with real maple syrup, crisp smoky bacon, fresh fruit and juice and crusty toast slathered with sweet butter. Mercifully, it had been uneventful meal with no flying food or other mishaps.

Checkout was not until 11 a.m., but they wanted to walk outside and walk for a while before leaving and enjoy another beautiful autumn day. The boys had decided to sit in the swing on the porch while their parents walked around the grounds.

The boys sat in silence for a couple of minutes until Sammy said, "What do you think we should do when we get home?"

Anthony seemed lost in thought as the swing moved back and forth, Sammy never looked at him, and they both just stared out across the trees.

The seconds moved by until finally Anthony said, "I think the first thing we should do is check that mask. I want to make sure of what I saw, that the symbol is really there. We have to watch it Sammy, we have to find out if it is really moving and walking."

They were both quite for several minutes, the swing creaking as it moved back and forth, the light from the autumn sun peeking in and out between branches, dappled light and shadow.

"I've been thinking Sam, have you heard on the news lately the reports about cats and dogs that are missing?"

"I've heard mom and dad talking about it I guess, but I never listen to the news," replied Sam, "but now that you mention it, what about the chickens?"

Anthony thought a moment, and then said, "Well, the chickens were before Dad bought the mask, but maybe some evil spirit or something, maybe before it got into the mask it did that to the chickens? Weird stuff has been happening but we just didn't see a pattern. If you really think about it, things have been happening since dad got the mask from that house sale; and Sammy, think about the way Ebony reacted to Ax-Man. She could sense something bad in it; she wanted to keep the kids away. Maybe she could smell the evil or something."

Sammy let his feet drag on the wooden floor of the porch slowing them down and turned his head slowly to look at

Anthony. "I'm positive it was Ax-Man that hit our car and ran into the woods Saturday Anth, I'm really sure," he said quietly. "Now that I let myself think about it, the way we were heading and the direction it came from Anth, it came from the direction of your house, I'm positive! I know now why I was so scared when it happened because deep down, somehow I knew it was him. He moves Anth, he moves and he runs and he jumps and he's hiding out at your house as a stuffed mannequin to scare kids at Halloween, but really he's prowling around at night killing things . . . ," the two boys looked at each other a long moment until Sammy finished the sentence. ". . . and maybe people too."

The quite between them was broken a moment later when they heard their parents voices coming toward the porch, sounds of happy conversation and laughter. As the parents came up the steps onto the porch, both of the mothers saw their sons sitting quietly on the still swing.

"Hey guys," said Danni, "want to stretch your legs a little before we start home? Enjoy a couple of minutes of fresh air while we check out and pack the car?"

When the boys did not immediately reply but turned and looked at each other, Danni and Mindy said almost in unison, "What's wrong?"

"Nothing," said Sammy

"Nope, nothing is wrong," chimed in Anthony.

"We'll help you pack the car," volunteered Anthony.

"Huh?" Sammy replied confused why they were offering to pack the car, a chore he hated. Then the light bulb went off in his head. "Oh, yeah, right, we'll start to bring the suitcases down."

Both jumped up from the swing, which caused it to sway away from them. Anthony had taken two steps forward, around the table. Sammy though, had stayed in place for just a second too long before the swing hit him just behind the knees causing him to fall backwards onto the rocking wicker swing. His feet flew up, he let out a yelp, and the whole thing was so very 'Sammy like' and unexpected that everyone broke out in laughter.

Sammy made a jump from the swing and took off after Anthony down the steps.

"Here we go again," said Danni.

"Wonder who will come back with the biggest bruise this time?" asked Mindy.

"Let's make a final look around in the rooms to make sure we haven't missed anything. By that time the boys will be back and they can start carrying out the suitcases while we pay the bill," said Danni to Mindy.

The flickering sunshine through the canopy of leaves bathed each of them in a golden glow as they made their way into the lodge, and got ready for what would be their final journey to home, as they knew it.

CHAPTER 19

Jon Wendels and Scott Champion slept until after 11:30 a.m. on Tuesday morning. Scott woke up to the sound of the recycling truck rumbling down his street as it began emptying the blue bins people had left at the end of their driveways. The bins held everything from plastic bottles that had contained and array of soda, dish soap, shampoo and ketchup; newspapers filled plastic bags bearing the logo of the local grocery store and glass wine bottles, whiskey and beer bottles overflowed some of the bins as they did every week.

Scott got up and pulled on his gray sweatpants and a Steeler t-shirt. He padded barefoot down the hall to the bathroom and emptied his bladder, full from the long sleep, and washed his hands with cool water and vanilla scented soap from a dispenser on the sink. He let the cool water run on his wrists, cooling him down and then ran his wet hands through his hair several times. It felt wonderful. He looked fully into the mirror for the first time. *I look like shit,* he thought, *but I guess anyone looks like shit after fighting the devil . . . wonder how Jon looks this morning?*

As he finished that thought, he heard the other bedroom door open. He turned and poked his head out of the bathroom and there in the doorway stood Jon, who actually looked rested and surprisingly good, considering.

"Good morning, how are you feeling?" asked Scott.

"Actually, I feel great, hungry, but great. I don't know that I've actually slept that soundly before. You ok. You look . . . a little worn out."

"I was just telling myself that I look like shit to be honest with you. Between chugging Jim Beam, battling Satan and breaking bread and wine with the Padre, I think my body is pulling on the reins and hollering 'whoa'. Oh and there was that little incident with you out at Jigs house and the hospital," he added.

"How about if I cook breakfast this morning. I promise to keep it down," said Jon in a jocular tone.

"Well, that would be just great but we ate all the eggs yesterday and except for dry toast, the cupboard is bare."

"Ok, then let's get dressed and go to Denny's for a Grand Slam. Then we can stop by Giant Eagle and I'll replenish the pantry."

"Do I have to get dressed up?"

"Nope, you look fine to me. I think they require shoes though," said Jon looking at Scott's bare feet.

"And underwear?" Scott interjected.

"Oh man, you don't have underwear on?" said Jon in a well-acted put on horrified voice. "Yep, you'd better, I don't think they allow swingers," laughed Jon.

"Get washed up then and I'll meet you in the kitchen," said Scott as he pushed his way around Jon. "And take that happy-go-lucky look off your face. It makes me look worse."

"You got it brother," said Jon as he went into the bathroom. "You need a shave," he tossed back to Scott.

"Not going do it, I'm a free swinger, remember?" He heard Jon laugh as the door clicked shut. Scott went to find his shoes. *I'm living right on the edge today. I'm boycotting underwear and shaving.*

He grabbed his car keys and went out onto the front porch to sit in the unusually warm sunshine on that fine autumn day. A gust of wind swept down the street giving birth to a small dust tornado and all around orange, brown, yellow and red leaves filled the air restlessly tumbling across the lawn. His stomach growled, he wanted coffee, and boy oh boy did they have a lot of planning to do.

The brunch crowd was just finishing up, which meant the next home fries and bacon would be very fresh. Jon asked Scott to go to his bank drive-thru where he made a withdrawal of $120.00 from his checking account.

"How much are you planning on eating?" asked Scott?

"More than you obviously. Man alive, I am so frickin' hungry I can't wait."

"Yeah, well, you were hungry Monday morning and whooped up in one swell swoop all those gooey eggs and cheese I slaved over," said Scott with a definite note of sarcasm.

"They were old eggs."

"Old eggs, are you kidding me? You are so full of bull-shit your eyes are brown," shot back Scott.

"Look for a close parking place. I don't want too many people to notice you don't wear skivvies," said Jon.

"There," pointed Scott.

"It says for 'Expectant Mothers.'"

"I'm pretty sure you gave birth in the bathroom before we left."

"Shut up and pull in you twit."

"Twit? What the hell's a twit?"

"You are. There, see those two little old ladies? They are on their way out. Follow them."

"Wow, wonderful. You're talking like the dirt-bags you arrest."

Two silver-haired women, each with purses that looked like suitcases packed for Vegas were leaving Denny's. Thick-soled rubber shoes, one pair tan, one pair brown, housed ankle hose that were supposed to ride just above their calves. Instead, they had rolled doughnut-like just above the top of their shoes revealing white, freckled ankles.

Jon squinted his eyes looking at the two, and as recognition crossed his face he said, "Pull up there, by the one with the red purse."

"You-have-got-to-be-kidding," said Scott.

"Pull up. Just put up, will you?"

Scott positioned his car slowly to the right of the two limping, knee-replacement candidates in front of him.

Jon pressed the button for the window, and as it rolled smoothly down, he called out, "Aunt Maureen! Aunt Maureen! It's me Jon!"

Both women stopped; the one with the red purse turned and pulled the left side of her top down over her ample hips.

"Jonnie? Jonnie! What do you think you are doing stalking us? What in the name of God is the matter with you? I was ready to push the red button my Attack-Alert necklace. Shame on you! Get out of that car right now!"

"Scott, pull up by that hunk-of-junk, right there," said Jon as he pointed to an old Dodge Dart.

Scott pulled parallel to the car as the two elderly women opened the trunk and put in their huge handbags, and as it turned out, several plastic bags of what appeared to be leftovers.

Jon opened the door before the car had come to a complete stop, and as Scott hit the brakes, he heard the souls of Jon's shoes skidding on the asphalt.

"Hey Aunt Maureen!" he threw his arms around the rotund woman who had just admonished him, and now that her hands were free, she swatted his rear-end with an open hand that made a low *whack*!

"Ooow! What was that for?" said Jon in feigned innocence.

"Because I haven't heard from you in . . . ? How long is it since you called or came over?"

"I cooked the burgers on Memorial Day."

"Memorial Day, shame on you Jon Wendels, I could have had a stroke and been laying on the living room floor all this time and you wouldn't have known the difference."

"Yes I would. My Denny's stock would have gone into the toilet," he said as the left corner of his mouth turned up in a mischievous grin. He saw the hand coming and arched his body out of the way, spinning behind Aunt Dee and hugging her from behind.

"Scott," said Jon happily, "this is my Aunt Maureen, and this . . ." he gestured to the other woman standing to his left who hadn't yet uttered a word, ". . . is my Aunt Dee."

Scott, who up until then was watching this scene unfold looking through the passenger window, nodded his head once, put the car in park and then got out. A he slammed the door and started to move around the car he remembered he had no underwear on and stopped dead in his tracks.

"Nice to meet you ladies," he said, placing both his hands on top of the car, the metal roof feeling very warm in the morning sun.

Jon had pulled Aunt Dee to him with his left arm and had just planted a kiss on her head. As Scott styed by the car, Jon looked at his questioningly.

"Come here so I can properly introduce you or Aunt Maureen will go into combat mode and let me have it again for bad manners," said Jon.

Scott stood his ground.

After a puzzled moment, it dawned on Jon why Scott was using the car as his backdrop. His laughter caused both Aunts' to look up at him.

"What?" Aunt Dee asked looking between the two men.

"He's a freebee this morning," said Jon as Scott closed his eyes and felt the blush run up his neck and start to burn on his cheeks.

"Oh," they both said in unison.

"Not to worry," said Aunt Dee a note of restrained humor creeping into her voice, "Jonnie spent many a night at our house in his shorts and pj bottoms in his younger days and I can assure you he was a freebee and proud of it.

"Thanks Aunt Dee," said Jon. "Scott here knows just about everyone on the force and I'm sure he won't hesitate to share that information with them."

"That's right, and don't you forget it," said Scott as he made his way around the car, the color leaving his face and a grin making an appearance. He put out his hand and said, "Miss Dee, Miss Maureen, it is a pleasure to meet you."

Both women shook his hand and Aunt Dee said, "So you work for our Jon?"

"No madam, I am the County Coroner."

Aunt Maureen and Aunt Dee looked at each other and then back at Scott.

"Dead people . . . you . . . deal with dead people? Aunt Maureen had paled slightly.

"That's my job, yes."

"Dead people that have been murdered?"

"Well, yes; and individuals who have died under unknown or unusual circumstances. It's my job, and that of my staff, to uncover any evidence that may show anything other than a natural death. In addition, at times families will request an autopsy to answer any questions they may have about a loved one's death. And then again, there . . ." Aunt Maureen put up her hand in a gesture of *stop*. Dee had blanched noticeably.

"Scott, I'm sure you find your job quite interesting, for I doubt there is no other reason you would have gone into that line. But I'd rather not get any details this close to the end of my breakfast."

Jon burst out laughing as Scott shifted his eyes between the three in embarrassment.

"Now you boys go on in and get something to eat. Jon you look like you've lost some weight. I expect you to come see us in the next few days," Aunt Maureen said as she looked up at him with steady eyes for a long moment.

"I promise," Jon replied as he bent over and gently kissed both Dee and Maureen on their respective cheeks and both women kissed him back. He and Scott walked them to the patina rusted but very clean Dodge Dart. Scott opened the passenger door for Dee and Jon opened the driver's side for Maureen. As they settled in their seats and snapped their seatbelts in place, the Dart roared into life, startling Scott who looked up at a still grinning Jon.

"I rebuilt the engine last summer and upgraded them to glass-packs," he said happily. Aunt Maureen gunned the engine several times obviously enjoying the healthy rumble and roar coming from her ugly duckling of a car.

"Nice pipes, don't you think Scott?" she said looking up at him through the open window.

"I'd say those are bitchin' pipes madam, absolutely bitchin'," he said, caught up in the joy of it all.

Aunt Maureen put the car in reverse, Aunt Dee put on her wrap-around sunglasses and they roared out of the parking lot, each with a hand out a window, waving goodbye to both Jon and Scott.

"Those two have been together for at least thirty years now," said Jon as he watched the car pull out onto the highway. "I used to spend every weekend I could at their house, talking, laughing, swimming, cooking and reading. Aunt Maureen loves to read and I guess because of her I got the reading bug myself. We had wonderful times together. She wants to write a book someday," he looked over at Scott.

"Oh? About what?"

"A horror story of some sort I think. Maybe she needs to talk to us," said Jon.

"Can it wait until after we eat? You have all that money and I want to spend some of it and I really need a cup of coffee."

"Me moola es su moola."

"Wow, you just butchered that saying," laughed Scott.

"Now you're talking about cows and butchering which makes me think of steak and eggs. Let's go."

As they opened the door to Denny's, a cool wave of air rolled out the door carrying the scent of onions, meat, toast and coffee. Both men sniffed the air like bloodhounds and Scott heard Jon's stomach growl in anticipation.

"I wonder if they can do something like a double meat lovers Grand Slam with extra corned beef hash," Jon wondered aloud.

"After yesterday, I believe in anything," said Scott as the door swished closed behind them.

Both men had sincerely expected to make serious plans for Friday and Saturday while eating their breakfast, and Denny's had indeed made a double meat Double Slam for Jon with extra rye toast. Scott had pancakes and eggs, a fruit dish and at least three hot mugs of coffee. Scott had become quite and strangely absent from the conversation. When Jon was about to make a smart-ass remark about being ignored, it hit him that this was the day that Scott's murdered brother was to be cremated. The two men finished their meals in silence, only the tap and click of the fork and knife on their plates penetrating the noise the patrons unknowingly laid down. After breakfast, they headed back to Scott's house, the silence enveloping them like a balloon, not full enough to burst, just full enough to keep the silence static.

When Scott put his key into the door and they entered the hallway he said to Jon, "I think I'll lay down a while. Is it ok if we maybe make our plans later? I just need to rest and be alone a while I think."

"Yeah man, sure. I'm tired myself. I think I'll sit on the porch and take a snooze or something. We'll talk later."

Scott's eyes said all the thanks Jon needed.

Later, as Jon sat on the front porch in the sunshine that pulled longer and leaner lines of shadow from the trees as the days got shorter and as he tried to outline a plan they could review and agree upon, he heard quite sobbing from the open window above him.

CHAPTER 20

All the bags were packed, the rooms double-checked and the boys were again lying in the back of the Envoy. Mindy and Danni were again drifting in and out of peaceful slumber as the sunshine moved shutter like through the trees and darted in and out of the car windows. The only change this time was that Dan was driving to get the feel of the Envoy. He had told Army he and Mindy were thinking of buying a larger car and were considering an SUV even though the greenie weenies made them out as the death of planet Earth.

While the men discussed the pros and cons of anti skid vs. pumping the brakes the old fashioned way, the mom's slumbered away peacefully, their pact secure that if one snored the other would wake her up.

It was a perfect time for the boys to plan before they got home.

Home meant Ax-Man. It meant Supernatural.

"What're we going do when we get to your house Anth?" asked Sammy quietly.

"I think we have to come up with a way to stop at your house first, unload your stuff and then you have to come to our house with me."

"Mom and Dad are going want me to stay home because of the whole *tomorrow is a school day* thing, ya know?" said Sammy.

"We can use the homework thing on them."

"What homework?"

"I dunno, can't you come up with something?"

"English, I have English homework. I just got a C on that poetry junk.

"I got a B+"

"That figures. Ok don't you have some notes I need?"

"I do?" he looked at Sammy's face and on came the light bulb, "yeah, I do, in my bedroom. And of course I won't remember anything until we are about to leave and you say you have to have it for tomorrow."

"That'll probably work although my Mom will be pissed after that whole school thing recently. What're we going do when we get to your house?"

Anthony thought for a moment and said, "We'll get the notes and tell my mom I'm going to walk halfway home with you, that I need to stretch my legs or something. Then on our way down I think we should just go up to *it* with our medallions on and see what happens."

"What if something happens?"

"I don't know. How should I know? I guess we'll figure it out."

"I hope you're a better figurer than I am, buddy," said Sammy worriedly.

"Sammy, I think we need to say something like, *let's take Ax-Man apart. Let's take him apart and make something different. I don't like that mask, let's get rid of this old thing,"* Anthony said in a hushed voice.

"Why?" Sammy asked sounding confused.

"We need to call it out; we need to make *it* think we are going to take it apart or something so we can watch and see if it moves. We need to see it."

"I don't think I want to."

"I know, I don't want to either, but you know we need to."

"Anth, if we call it out today you're going be the only one of the two of us at your house tonight," said Sammy the tone of his voice held a quality of fear to it now.

Anthony was quiet, thinking about that. It had not occurred to him that Sammy would not be by his side. He was always by his side.

"Shit," he said quietly.

"Let's wait Anth, let's wait to call it out until Saturday afternoon. You know I can probably sleep over then."

Anthony's jaw muscle worked as he clenched and unclenched his jaw several times.

"Ok," he finally said, "we won't call it out until Saturday, but let's still go up to it when we get home with our medallions on. I want to see if anything happens."

Both boys unconsciously put their hands on their chests where the Olive Wood of Bethlehem, carved into *The Fifth Pentacle of Mars* medallion rested. It felt warm on their chests, warm under their hands.

"What are we going say?" asked Sammy a few minute later.

"Today? Nothing. We're going get close to it, first with our medallions under our shirts, and then if nothing happens, we'll pull them out and see if we get a reaction. I'm going try and see if I can lift up a corner of the mask to see if that symbol is there."

"Ok," Sammy said with some uncertainty, "I'm with you on that. What about Saturday? I was thinking maybe we could talk like, you know, like we aren't happy with how Ax-Man turned out and don't like the mask and make it sound like after Halloween we're going get rid of it."

"That sounds like a good plan, we'll have to figure out exactly what we're going say and rehearse it so we're on the same page." Anthony glanced up at their parents. Danni and Kelley were napping; Army and Dan were talking about cars. Perfect.

"Sammy," he said very quietly.

"What?" Sammy answered just as quietly back.

"Open that side compartment next to you, the carving of the *Devil's Trap* is there. Let's take a good look at it while we have some time together."

Sammy reached back, pulled open the two latches at the top of the small hatch, and pulled it open. Inside was the *Devil's Trap.* They both stared at it unblinking for several seconds.

"I've got to memorize this Sammy, this is what I'm going have to draw with the holy charcoal," said Anthony.

"Where are you going draw it, and what are you going draw it on?" asked Sammy a 'V' forming between his eyes.

"I don't know yet. It's another one of those things we'll have to figure out."

"We sure have a lot of figuring to do, don't we?" Sammy said worriedly.

"Yeah, so I guess we'd better get started. See that crumpled up paper over there?"

"Where?"

"Behind your head . . . yeah, right there. Smooth that out the best you can. I can start to practice drawing the *Devil's Trap* while we're riding."

As Sammy un-crumpled the piece of paper, Anthony found a pen in the front of his Mom's purse.

"Lay it down between us," Anthony said still speaking quietly, "and put that little pillow in front of it. If they look back we can just lay the pillow over it and they won't know anything."

Sammy laid the *Devil's Trap* medallion between them and Anthony had the piece of paper next to it. He started to try to draw the circle with absolutely no luck due to not only the impossibility of drawing a circle freehand, but also the movement of the car.

"Crap, this isn't going to work!"

"Let me see it," said Sam. He took the piece of paper and put it over the wooden medallion between them, and pressed his hand down around the edge of wood under the paper, which creased the shape into it enough to give the outline substance.

"Sweet," said Anthony.

"I can press in some of the picture if it will help you draw it the first time," said Sammy.

"Do it Sam."

As Sammy carefully pressed the paper around the sigil to incorporate the shapes onto the paper, Anthony felt that something very profound was taking place. This was not a game, it was not a boy's fantasy it was real and it could be life or death. He silently prayed that both he and Sammy had the strength and courage to go through with this.

"There," said Sammy, "that looks like a pretty good shadow line for you to follow."

Anthony put his index finger to his lips and moved his eyes up to where their mothers were napping peacefully. Sammy nodded his head once indicating he understood to be quite. He pushed the sigil and the paper over to Anthony.

"Can you reach that magazine in the bag behind you?" whispered Anthony.

Sammy twisted around and quietly pulled out Danni's latest copy of *Better Homes and Gardens* and handed it to his friend. Anthony put the paper on the hard surface and lightly began to trace around the image embossed on the paper. As he finished a section, he would run his hand around that same section on the wooden *Devil's Trap* that lay between them.

The tires of the Envoy sang on the warm road, their fathers spoke about a Shelby with a Cleveland block, modified cam and four-barrel carburetor that would go from zero to sixty in the blink of an eye. The mothers napped in deep peacefulness and the sun flickered and fluttered in and out of the windows painting beautiful light and shadows on their serene faces.

They were oblivious to the fact that in the back, their young sons were formulating a plan to kill a monster.

Scott had been in and out of sleep since they had returned from Denny's, and around 2:45 p.m., the phone ringing interrupted the stillness at Scott Champion's house.

He rolled over and picked up the receiver of his landline phone. "Hello?" he listened without responding and finally said, "Thanks for everything. Would you put that file on my desk? Yes, that will be good. I'll be down before five to pick everything up. Bye."

He slowly returned the receiver to the cradle and scrubbed his hands up and down on his face. He sat up and slipped on the skipper shoes he had worn earlier in the day. He felt drained, emotionally and physically as he made his way down the hall. He checked the kitchen and living room and did not see Jon in either place. As he made it to the open front door, he saw Jon was sitting in one Scott's wicker chairs, looking up at the door as Scott opened the screen and went out onto the porch. As he leaned against the railing, the sun to his back, the warmth felt good on his shirt compared to the coldness he felt inside of him.

"I heard the phone ring," said Jon simply.

"It was my office. Phyllis called to give me the results of the autopsy." Silence hung in the air for a moment, Jon giving him the space and time he needed. When he finally spoke again, his voice was quite and somber. "My brother's death has been ruled a homicide. Because of the strange circumstances, they are for now, coding it as some type of ritualistic murder. Phyllis said there were no drugs or alcohol that showed up in any of the toxicology findings. Because of . . ." his voice began to falter, and he waited a moment to regain his composure. ". . . because most of his internal organs were missing along with his brain many of the usual tests could not be completed so lots of questions remain. The report has been sent to homicide."

"Devon Haskell will probably be given the case," said Jon.

"I suppose, yes, and I'm sure he'll be calling me sometime very soon. Phyllis said the funeral home would call today. The cremation should be complete and I can probably pick up his ashes tomorrow."

"Why don't you let Father Kaylan take care of that for you Scott? That way they will be at the church for the service and he can give them to you in private before we leave."

"Yes, that sounds good. I need to call him and find out what time he will be able to serve mass," his voice was shaking again and he moved away from the railing to sit in the other wicker chair next to Jon. He sat down heavily and sighed wearily.

"I'll call Father Kaylan for you Scott. Why don't you just sit here for a while and I'll call and come right back?"

Scott nodded his head in agreement, leaned his back against the clapboard siding of his house, and closed his eyes.

Jon got up, rolling his shoulders to loosen the stiffness that had settled in as he had sat in the warm autumn sunshine, dozing lightly while Scott had been in his room. He went into the house to Scott's small office area and found the church's phone number on the corkboard above the alcove desk. He programmed the number into his cell phone and hit the *send* button. Father Kaylan answered the phone himself after four rings. Jon relayed the recent information regarding the autopsy findings.

"Mother of God Jon, what vile fiend has been cast upon us?" Father Kaylan said in a hushed voice.

"I don't know Father, but I intend to get some answers on Friday when we go back to Jigs house with the cadaver dog."

"Tell Scott the memorial service will be at 10 a.m. I'll call the funeral home and make arrangements to pickup William's remains," he hesitated a moment and then continued, "have you made any plans on what you're going to do when you find the portal?"

Jon took a long breath, then said, "First we have to find it Father, then we'll destroy it. I think I'll spend some more time this afternoon on the internet. Is everything ready at your end?"

"I've already blessed the candles and salt; the two Aspergillums are prepared along with two flasks of holy water. When you pick everything up I will impart a special blessing on you and then I plan to spend the remainder of the time you are at the portal in prayer. Yes, I believe everything is ready on my end."

"I think after the service tomorrow I'll drop Scott off and take a quick tour of the shed at Jigs house," said Jon.

"Don't go there alone Jon. Don't. You have already been used by an evil parasite and we can't afford to have it happen again. Your strength is in your friendship, what you have endured and overcome so far. I repeat Jon, do not go there alone."

"I hear you Father. Ok, maybe I'll swing around to the station and see if anything unusual has happened that we haven't heard about on the news. I guess I need to turn on my radio and see if I can pick-up any chatter and find out the latest. I'm getting anxious. I want to get this done."

It was quite for several heartbeats until Father Kaylan continued, "I assume I'll see you both tomorrow?"

"I'll be there. We've come this far together; I'm not going to let him down now."

CHAPTER 21

Sammy was in the back seat of the Brogan car, all the bags separated, the last goodbyes exchanged and Dan had put the car into reverse.

Suddenly Sammy piped up, “Oh, hey Anth, do you have that poetry assignment? I forgot and left mine at school.” A collective groan came from both his parents.

Mindy turned around in the seat fixing a laser gaze on her son and said, “You’re just now remembering you had homework?”

The two friends worked it so smoothly, so slick as Anthony replied, “Oh yeah Sammy, I forgot about that too, come up and I’ll get it for you,” Sammy already had the door open and was sliding smoothly off the seat onto the gravel driveway.

“Samuel Brogan, wait just one minute!” demanded Mindy.

“It’s ok Mrs. Brogan, I’ll get it for him and walk halfway back to you house, I need to stretch my legs,” he turned his head to look at his mother.

“You have unfinished homework too?” questioned Danni who had an eyebrow raised in an angry arch.

“Well, mine is mostly done and Sammy and I were going to finish it together.”

“This homework is due when?” Mindy asked with a definite edge in her voice.

“Tomorrow,” said both boys.

The silence ran out for a few seconds, until Mindy finally said, “If it’s all right with Danni, you have one hour, and after that hour two things had better happen,” she held her index finger, “you’d better be home with your English book open and,” she held up two fingers, “you’d better ace the test; do you understand?”

"Gotcha," said Sammy as he caught up to Anthony.

The boys made it up the front steps as their parents had final words, most probably about their sons, before the Brogan car pulled out of the driveway.

They raced to Anthony's room and grabbed some school papers to make it look like they actually had the homework they used as an excuse.

They looked at each other and Anthony said, "Wait until mom and dad get in the house, I don't want them to see us going to Ax-Man. As soon as they get in they will probably go to the back of the house to unpack and dad will want to look at the mail. We should be ok then."

"I just got this weird cold feeling in my stomach," said Sammy.

Anthony reached up to his shirt and felt the pendant. "What do you think, should we wait and take the pendants out when we get in front of him, or have them out once we get past the house?" asked Anthony.

"Let's wait until we get up to it. We'll check it out and see if anything looks different. Then we should turn away and pull out the pendants and turn back to it, what do ya think?"

"It sounds like a good idea to me," said Anthony.

They both heard the front door open and close, and the sound of Danni and Army talking downstairs. As Anthony had anticipated, they went toward the back of the house.

"Are you ready?" Anthony asked Sammy.

"No. Are you?"

"I don't think so."

"Let's go then," said Sammy with what sounded like a great deal of confidence though the look on his face said otherwise.

As they started down the stairs Anthony's heart began to hammer in his chest, and as he looked over at his friend, he saw a bead of sweat run down the side of his face. He knew they had to get out of the house fast before either parent saw them or they would know that something was up.

"Mom, Dad, I'll be back in just a little bit!" Anthony yelled back through the door just before it closed.

As they started down the front steps and across the yard, they both felt a deep foreboding.

Sammy glanced over at Anthony, "Do you feel it?" he asked very quietly.

"Yeah, it's like we're getting close to something bad," replied Anthony in a hushed voice.

As they continued across the yard, the first thing they noticed was how the grass appeared trampled around the backdrop concentrated around Ax-Man. Anthony nudged Sammy with his elbow and nodded his head towards the area. Sammy acknowledged he saw it too, and then they were there, in front of it . . . in front of Ax-Man.

The stench was incredible. It hit them both at the same moment causing them to stop about ten feet from Ax-Man and put their faces in the crook of their arms. It made Anthony think of the butchered chickens in the chicken coop on that seemingly far away hot day of summer, but this was more loathsome and foul. His eyes darted around the area and he noticed that Ax-Man's coveralls were filthy and stained with something dark, and the positioning was very different from when they left. In fact, it gave Anthony the impression that it did not care if they knew, and maybe wanted them to be aware that it was moving. The mask was facing the plywood and Anthony's original intention to check the inside became a non-issue; he was not going to touch *anything* on it. The old work boots appeared covered in mud and something that looked like pieces of rotted hamburger. He realized the mass was moving; *Maggots, it's full of maggots*, he thought. Sammy pointed with his other arm at the boots also, but he was pointing behind where there looked to be a pale gooey substance . . . it appeared to be a piece of scalp.

"Oh my God," Anthony said into his arm. His eyes locked with Sammy's and he knew at this moment that they were both scared beyond words.

Sammy laid his other hand on his chest against *The Fifth Pentacle of Mars* medallion. Anthony lifted his head in understanding, and they both reached inside and pulled out their medallions, laying them against their shirts.

The reaction was immediate and violent.

Ax-Man's arms started flailing about, chitterling against the plywood, its legs jigging up and down like a marionette, a macabre dance, gruesome and ghastly to see. The face of the beast was horrific and grisly as the eyes narrowed on the two young boys, its nostrils flaring, mouth opening and closing in an nightmarish yaw of snapping teeth made more horrible by the low guttural noise coming from within it.

Both boys stumbled backwards away from the awful abomination, falling clumsily onto the grass, each struggling to put the medallion back under their shirt.

Then, just as quickly as it had started, it stopped. The boys looked at each other for a moment dumfounded, then back at Ax-Man, and slipped as they jumped up off the cold grass and ran quickly away from it.

That was when they realized the only thing moving now, was its eyes; the feline shaped, yellow, blood shot eyes narrowed and moved ever so slowly to rest their malevolent gaze on them.

The boys scrambled down the hill, getting well away from Ax-Man, away from the nauseating smell, away from the eyes that had turned their blood cold with fear. The school papers they had carried as their cover story lay scattered across the bottom portion of the yard, a light breeze sweeping them toward the road.

Anthony dragged Sammy along with him, his voice hollow and scared, "We can't let mom and dad see us, Sammy, come on!" They ran to the road to pluck up pieces of notebook paper before either of his parents happened to look out the front window towards the road.

As Anthony picked up the last piece of paper, he heard something moving through the dry grass across from him. He could see something, an animal of some sort, crouching, watching him from the grass. It all felt so unreal, the sun shining golden through the few wispy clouds in the blue crisp sky, the beautiful leaves against the remaining browns and greens. How then, on this beautiful day, could waves of evil roll down the soft green grass of their lawn . . . and feel like death?

The boys hurried down the country road towards Sammy's house each of them looking left and right at the tall grass and the brown dry corn, watching to see if anything was following, occasionally turning around to look behind them. They walked silently, each in their own way replaying the scene that had transpired only minutes earlier.

Finally about two hundred yards from his house Sammy turned to Anthony and said, "Anth, do you think it will come after you tonight, you know, now that we saw it, I mean really saw it move?"

"I don't know Sammy," Anthony looked solemnly at his friend, "There's nothing keeping it from coming to your house either, I guess." Sammy's eyes were large and round and he swallowed a lump of fear in his throat.

They were both quiet for another couple of steps until Sammy said, "Where do you want to practice the *Devil's Trap* tomorrow?"

"Practice is over," Anthony replied. "I have to start drawing tomorrow on the barn floor. We can cover it over with some straw or something to hide it. I don't think dad will be going in there before Halloween."

"Ok, I'll come over after school if mom will let me," Sammy said.

"Why don't you get off the bus with me? That will give us more time."

"That should work. I'll ask my mom after dinner tonight," he thought for a moment, "No, I'd better wait 'til tomorrow when I leave for the bus, she'll probably say yes then."

The sun was just starting to set, the horizon shimmering in the last rays of the day.

Anthony stopped and said, "Sammy, you can make it the rest of the way home? I want to start back before it gets dark."

"Yeah, you'd better," said Sammy looking at the sky.

Without another word, Anthony turned on his heel and started back toward home at a fast walk. As Sammy's house got smaller and smaller behind him, he broke into a run and never let up until he turned the knob on the front door of his own house, so focused on getting home he did not see the moving grass following behind him like a wave.

Later that night, when the house was closed up, snug, and after everyone had taken a shower, Army made a big bowl of popcorn with garlic butter and they all sat and watched a movie until Anthony started drifting off to sleep, and Danni got him into bed. He slept deeply that night. He had been afraid of nightmares, but instead he dreamed of a beautiful young woman whose stunning aura had enveloped their home in a protective cocoon of red, blue and green light.

Feather soft lips had kissed his forehead and a woman's voice had gently said, *sleep in peace dear one, you are safe tonight.*

Later that same evening . . .

Mary Bigfoot was a product of the 1960's. Her long frizzy hair looked exactly as it had for her 1968 senior picture. She had changed her last name to Bigfoot after an eighteen-month stay at a commune outside Los Angeles where she moved after graduation, much to her mother's lament and to the echo of her father's final *go ahead, you won't amount to a pile of shit anyhow!*

One of her partners, and she had had many while living in the progressive commune, had said Mary's habit to never shave her legs and her unusually amount of body hair reminded him of what it might be like to have sex with bigfoot. In a haze of hash and possibly with a halo of smoke around her head at the time, she had made a legal petition to change her last name to Bigfoot in order to please her man. The liberal judge, who also was in a hash haze a good deal of the time, swiftly granted the petition and Mary Bigfoot was born. She left the commune after the property they had been living on sold to a developer and communes lost their appeal after the 1970 conviction of Charlie Manson and several of his infamous family members.

Mary drifted from job to job and moved from place to place somehow migrating from sunny California to the cold of Pennsylvania. She ended up in a homeless shelter when she was out of work, out of money and out of a place to live because of the previous two events. The shelter's original supervisor thought Mary to be a nice woman, but never expected her to become a permanent fixture, much less take his job.

Her residency there seemed to bring out one of Mary's better traits; she was extremely talented at developing story lines a.k.a., telling lies to present to city council in order to bilk tax money supposedly to run the shelter. It was all so easy really, no one checked. The forms she had to fill out for the state and federal grants were a breeze for someone like Mary, and she was able to maintain a very nice apartment in the shelter; not too nice though, she did not want to set off any bells or whistles if someone managed to get a good look at her digs.

The bulk of the money she funneled off she used for a far darker vehicle to amass her wealth; smuggling young girls into the country for porno and snuff films. From their suffering and sometimes death, she had made an absolute fortune, a fortune, which she currently housed in several accounts throughout Europe and offshore investments.

Mary Bigfoot was thinking through her planned retirement in 2014 as she made her nightly rounds through the facility checking that lights were out (the increasing electric bill was eating into her cut of city, state and federal funds don't you know), the doors were locked and the security system was on.

She always carried a mini baseball bat with her, a purchase she made several years ago when the Pittsburgh Pirates hosted the baseball All Star game. Her trip to the game was a ploy to cover a money drop for a beautiful Brazilian child newly arrived the day before.

On the second floor were all of the existing inhabitants in the shelter and they had explicit instructions not to leave their areas after lights out. She did not want anyone trying to depart in the middle of the night leaving the place open to vandals. That too, would cut into her take if she had to replace anything, hence her nightly tour.

That was when she noticed the basement door, the last one she always checked, had a blinking red access light. Blinking red meant the door was unlocked. Almost simultaneously, she noticed with her peripheral vision, what seemed to be stealthy movement outside the door.

What the fuck? Her right hand, that a moment ago held the mini bat loosely, now gripped it tightly in a closed fist. The back yard was enclosed by an eight-foot high link fence surrounded by climbing roses she had planted many years ago and left to grow unchecked and wild, in effect forming kind of razor wire at the top. Her planning had been specifically to make access to the back yard extremely difficult, therefore in her mind, anyone out there now, was up to no good. Mary was not afraid. She thought she was the toughest broad in the city and no young punk was going to intimidate her much less vandalize her property.

She waited a long moment to see if she witnessed the movement again, and when she did not, she surmised the kid, or kids whatever the case may be, could possibly be casing the backside of the building to see a better place to gain entry.

The little bastards don't know that red means GO in my house, she thought smugly. She pushed the door open slowly, just enough for her to wedge her thin body through and show as little of her profile as possible. She saw a large shadow to her immediate left behind the huge rhododendron and thought gleefully, *Oh good a fat one, he won't be able to run while I beat the shit out of him.* She stepped slowly down the cement step and took four more quiet steps, gripping the mini bat tightly, anxious, excited even, to pummel and punish the dirt bag invading her space.

With inhuman speed, two hands, each seemingly the size of dinner plates, shot through the foliage of the bush; one grabbed her by the back of her head, entangling her long, frizzy 60's hair in a death grip that shred several huge portions of scalp from her skull and yanked her through the bush, tearing clothes and ripping skin. The other snatched the bat from her hand and in one fluid motion, stuffed it down her throat up to the rounded handle. The only sound was a quite gurgle escaping briefly around the head of the bat. Unfortunately, for Mary Bigfoot it took her a full forty-five seconds to die.

The creature above her, its eyes gleaming yellow with evil delight, slid its jaw forward its teeth unfolding and buried its face into her steaming guts.

CHAPTER 22

Scott looked at himself in the mirror as he pulled the collar down around his tie, and tried to remember if he looked much like his brother Will. Funny, he could not recall, but then he really had not seen Will out of costume for years.

Growing up, William Champion, the elder of the two Champion boys, had been Scott's hero. His sense of humor was infectious, and he had a way of making grown-ups like him when he talked to them. Those same people, their neighbors, or the owner of Kaller's Hardware, or Lou Bates (Will called him Master Bates) who owned the local five and dime store would always give them some type of gift. Al Kaller would slip them fifty cents for ice cream; Master Bates would give them a bag of penny candy. The neighbor women always had a treat for them that could range from popcorn balls, to pulled pork. The best, the very best, was the black walnut pie that Mrs. Neil made for them every autumn.

Mrs. Neil was the sweetest of women. At seventy-three, she was still attractive, though slightly plump with gray hair, and she usually wore a simple, straight dress that at that time was called a shift. She had a wonderful, endearing, soft Southern accent, and their mother always said she sounded like a refined Southern lady. Mr. and Mrs. Neil had no children and seemed to enjoy the visits of the nine and eleven year old Scott and Will, and Mr. Neil would always have the small rowboat ready if the boys wanted to go out on their lake and fish. Once, when Scott had managed to drop their father's favorite fishing pole and reel into the lake, Mr. Neil had come to the rescue. He attached to the rowboat two rakes nailed to two eight foot 2' x 4's and rowed ever so slowly back and forth across the lake where the rod had fallen in until just before dark, when he snagged it—and with a *Yahoooo!* dragged it to the surface and saved the day. Mrs. Neil had dished up some warm peach cobbler with homemade whipped cream and sent the boys home with an admonition to tell their dad the truth.

Later on, after Mr. Neil had died and Mrs. Neil had had to sell the house to help pay for the extended care facility where she lived, the two brothers, now 15 and 17, had gone to visit their longtime friend.

After their hellos and hugs and her kiss on their cheeks, they chatted about the 'old' neighborhood. While Will and Mrs. Neil were engaged in conversation, Scott had spied a picture on the dresser. It was a black and white picture of a stunningly beautiful woman, her head looking to the left and up, and for some reason, that picture captured Scott, and out of curiosity, he had picked it up for a closer look.

"Is this someone in your family?" he asked her innocently.

Mrs. Neil hesitated a moment and then said in her soft southern drawl, "You could say that Scotty."

The look on her face had caused the two boys to glance at each other, Will with the *why did you have to ask that?* look and Scott, his eyes wide, was horrified that he had possibly asked this sweet woman a question that may have upset her.

She tilted her head, much the same way as the young woman in the picture and said, "That's me, when I was 18 years old."

She looked up at both young men, seemingly to gauge her next words. "You see, at that time jobs were hard to come by and my mamma had died when I was sixteen. Papa, now he had four children to try to feed and care for. He was a good man mind you, he loved us, but he was hooked on the liquor and he couldn't keep the few jobs he was able to find," she sighed and leaned her head back for a moment, then straightened herself and looked at Will and Scott. "He turned to making the white lightening that was killing him and he built a still, deep in the woods behind our house. He made some money at that for a short while. Then someone, I never knew who for sure, turned him into the revenuers and when they came to destroy the still, Papa pulled a gun. He was drunk on the very same whisky and could hardly hold the gun much less aim it, so they shot him dead and burned the still and left us to fend for ourselves. They just left us."

She stopped speaking looking ahead, her eyes lost in a painful memory. Will and Scott stood still as statues, mute, until finally, Mrs. Neil took a long breath, her eyes fluttering, and she came back to present time.

"Well boys, I had to do something to take care of my sisters and brother. And that *something* was called show stripping," she looked up at both boys, her eyes slowly traversing between the two, gauging their reaction.

"I worked only the finer establishments mind you, and we did not unclothe completely. Men in fine suits, gentlemen, as they thought they should to be called, would come for dinner and entertainment and often times bring their young sons with them, and I, and a number of other young, women would dance to music and remove particular articles of clothing. I was able to earn enough money that my siblings did not go hungry or unclothed and I was able to give money to the sheriff to keep them out of the county home. It was not work that I wanted, but it was available to me to take care of my family. I had that employment for almost three years, up until the time I met Mr. Neil." A ghost of a smile touched her lips, slightly turning up the corners of her mouth, and her eyes softened the memory seemingly very sweet.

"One evening after a performance in Memphis, Dornetta, a sweet girl who danced with our group, was walking back with me to the room where we were staying. It was a hot, sultry night as I remember, the cicadas' chirruping in the background, the fireflies just starting to rise from the grass and even after the sun had set the heat was still like a blanket around us as the dark settled in. When we got back to our room, I turned on the ceiling fan and took off my hat and gloves. I sat down on the edge of the bed and looked up at the wobbly fan, as it spun in its sorry attempt to spread a breeze, when suddenly a man came to the screen door. Dornetta saw him first and it startled her so that the poor girl let out a small scream. Now, this *gentlemen* was of the opinion that because we were employed in our particular profession that we were also ladies available to service his individual needs," she stopped here and looked at the boys and said, "I do assume you all are old enough to understand what I mean?"

Will and Scott both felt they faces grow hot with understanding at what she was implying. They both nodded as they stared wide-eyed at the elderly woman before them, the woman who had tousled their hair, laughed at their stories and served them wondrous food. A different life, a different time, and it was difficult to comprehend.

As Mrs. Neil continued to look at them, a slight twinkle seemed to light her eyes. "This man, who was no gentlemen, looked at the paltry screen door with the wire latch at the top, and decided to come in uninvited. As he pulled that door open, I reached over the side of the bed and pulled up a revolver I had acquired from a kindly man some time back. As I brought that revolver up, intending mind you, to simply demonstrate to this individual that his intentions were unwelcome, I somehow managed to shoot myself through the knee. Well! Between the sound of the gunshot and my scream of pain, a brave man came to our rescue. That man was my Mr. Neil. He came into the room and saw what was going on and he grabbed that gentlemen and began pummeling him. He threw him like so much garbage out into the street. Then he bandaged up my leg enough to take me to the local doctor, where he pounded on that good doctor's door telling him to wake up he had an emergency. Dornetta had come with us and poor thing, she just could not quit sobbing, but Mr. Neil calmed her down in such a caring way that I fell in love with him at that very moment. That's how we met, Mr. Neil and me, and we were together ever after that."

Will and Scott continued to stare at Mrs. Neil, not knowing what to say, until she broke the silence with her laughter.

"Now, don't let my reminiscing spoil our visit, sit boys." She pointed to two straight back chairs that were in her small room; they looked to be the dining room chairs from the old house. "Please sit."

The two brothers took the seats she had indicated, and suddenly Will blurted out, "Mrs. Neil, where you dressed up in a costume when you would perform?"

Scott was horrified that his brother could think such things much less ask, and with eyes bulging in shock, he turned to look at his brother. What he saw he never forgot.

Will was enthralled. His face was animated and he had leaned slightly forward, eager not to miss a word of what she might say to say.

"Yes Will, I guess you could say we had costumes of a sort. Ladies fine dresses and hats. Layers of clothes don't you know, so that we had items to take off but still ended up with some coverings—and gloves, always gloves." Mrs. Neil gave Will the warmest smile and leaned toward him, laying her hand on his and in a hushed voice said, "You do like women's clothing, is that right Will?"

"Yes," he breathed quietly, "how did you know?"

"Mr. Neil and I had a very dear friend that I had met while traveling, that was much the same as you, a sweet man, so kind of heart and well spoken. He would sometimes ask to borrow some of my clothes in the beginning; he toured also, although with a different type of clientele. Sometimes I would go shopping with him, as though I was making the purchases myself, but they were for him. After a while, when his tours and his life took him further and further from us we lost touch, only to receive a holiday card, and perhaps a time or two a brief note. When we bought our home up here, we eventually lost all touch with him. I often thought of our friend, and wondered how and where he was."

Will looked frozen in time, his eyes unblinking. Scott's eyes though, were darting between the two, trying to figure out what was going on between them.

"There is nothing wrong with you Will; you just see life through a different color of a prism we all share. Do you understand what I am saying?"

Will nodded his head and sat back, the strangest smile on his face, and suddenly, they began talking about everything. To Mrs. Neil, Will opened as a book unfolds to an eager reader, spilling forth thoughts and feelings that Scott was, for the most part, unable to comprehend.

Their initial short visit turned into hours and finally when they said their goodbyes Will hugged Mrs. Neil and held her close. Scott saw tears in his eyes and heard him say, "Thank you Mrs. Neil, thank you for helping me get that all out. I can't tell you how much better I feel."

She took him by both his upper arms and said, "You must always remember that this is your life, you only get one chance at it, and you must do what makes you happy, you must *be* what makes you happy Will," and as he bent his head down, she kissed his forehead.

After that day, Will went every week to see Mrs. Neil. Sometimes Scott would tag along just to see her, but he realized that his brother needed this time with her, that he was working through something very difficult; he seemed changed.

One Saturday afternoon several months later, while their dad was at work and their mom was out shopping, Scott came home early from playing soccer with of his friends. He galloped up the steps to change clothes, as they had decided to go to the movies to check out the girls. Earlier that morning he left his wallet in Wills room, when they divvied up their earnings from chores they did for several of their neighbors. Mowing, raking, washing a car here and there, and he knew he had enough for a movie, a hot dog and a Pepsi. In one fluid motion, he turned the knob to the bedroom and went through the door when he stopped dead in his tracks. It felt as if he had hit a brick wall and for a moment, he felt all the blood drain from his head to his feet. There was a woman in Will's room, her back to Scott, facing the small mirror that hung on the inside of the closet door. His first thought was, *Mom is gonna kill Will if she finds out he has a girl in his room* . . . and then she turned around.

Scott's brain tried to process the form fitting green dress, the cream-colored hose and the tan heels his brother was wearing. He thought the wig a little cheap looking, and watched as his brother took his hands and ran them down the sides of the dress, smoothing out the material. It appeared that Will had been in the process of applying makeup, or at least practicing to apply it. Will did not say a word, his eyes searching Scott's for some type of understanding and acceptance. Scott heard the grandfather clock down stairs, tick, tick, ticking and suddenly one loud *gooooonng* for the half-hour. He saw that he was moving his hand in what looked like slow motion toward his wallet sitting on Will's dresser. Tick, tock, tick, tock.

"I'm going to the movies with Randy," the house was quiet except for the ticking. "Mom's coming back from the store soon," he kept looking at what was, and was not, his brother's face. "Is this the color you see in your prism Will?"

"Yes Scotty, it is," Will's voice low and somehow different.

"Well, you look good in green. Ok then, I'll see you later."

From that moment forward, he never told anyone about what he had seen. They never spoke of it. Scott just accepted his big brother, his hero, his best friend . . .

For the color in the prism that made him Will.

CHAPTER 23

The inside of St. Mary Di Rosa Church was cool and shadowed. Vigil candles flickered in alcoves on each side of the pews when Scott Champion and Jon Wendels arrived. The only bright point of light was at the altar. They made their way toward the front of the church slowly, their steps hushed against the carpet down the center aisle. Scott genuflected before he sat in the front pew, and Jon, not knowing whether he should or not, decided to follow, bending to one knee and crossing himself. *It can't hurt.* They were about twenty-five minutes early for the service and as they waited, an altar server came out and lit candles on both sides of the altar and by the ambo; that's when Jon saw the canister which contained what remained of Scott's brother William. Several other people came in, there was in total, possibly fifteen people attending.

Phyllis Johnson from the coroner's office was there; otherwise, it seemed that the few people who showed up must be friends of Will, or in this case, Fancy Mei. Each came up and said something to Scott, such as, *my condolences,* or *I'm sorry for your loss*, but each individual who expressed their sorrow seemed sincere.

Finally, the same alter server who lit the candles came down the aisle with a cross, followed quietly by Father Kaylan. They stopped in front of the altar, bowed, and preceded up the steps, Father Kaylan to the ambo, the altar server to a chair on the other side. Father Kaylan's eulogy was brief, focusing on Will's good deeds and not his lifestyle and the whole time Scott sat stock still, hardly blinking, never taking his eyes off the small canister that sat on the altar.

Father Kaylan was saying, "Each of us is put here with a purpose. Some find that purpose quickly, others slowly; some may think they never find their purpose but the whole time they are searching, they are completing God's plan. Will's purpose, I believe, was to help open a window so that others could look in and find understanding where before there had been none, to shine a light into places of darkness. Each of you carries within your soul something precious, something poignant and meaningful, and as you have been given, you must serve," Father paused, sweeping his gaze across the few people in the pews, his eyes stopping on each for a brief moment. "If you share with just one other person some point of light that Will shared with you, then his life had meaning," Father Kaylan paused a moment to let his words sink in, "let us pray."

Communion followed the prayer, and though Jon was not Catholic, he stepped before Father Kaylan with confidence.

"The body of Christ," said Father Kaylan, his gaze penetrating, unwavering.

"Amen," responded Jon.

As he took the wafer out of his cupped hand and put it on his tongue, a feeling of purpose flowed through him. He went around the pew and settled onto the kneeling bench next to Scott. After the final prayer, Father Kaylan came down the three steps and presented the urn with the ashes of William Champion to Scott. As Scott cradled the urn against his chest, he shook the priest's hand.

"Thank you Father. It was the kind of service that Will would have wanted."

Jon had stood with Scott and noticed the other few people who had come to the service were leaving silently, making their way towards the doors at the back of the church.

"I'm glad I could be part of his transition into God's protection," Father Kaylan said solemnly. "He was a good person and a true friend to my family."

Jon noticed a woman who had been sitting in the front pew on the other side of them during the service coming toward the three men. She came up and stood beside Father Kaylan, tentatively putting out her hand toward Scott.

"I'm sorry to interrupt, but I have to leave and I wanted to say goodbye."

Scott took her hand in both of his and held it for a long moment, his head slightly forward, his eyes intent on the woman before him.

"Thank you for coming, it means a lot to me and I'm sure Will is grateful," Scott's voice was low and quiet, almost intimate.

"Have there been any new developments in who did this to Fancy, or why?" she asked, sadness heavy in her voice.

Scott continued to hold the hand offered him and squeezed it gratefully. "No Nichole, not yet, but we think something will break soon. We have some leads but nothing solid. Tomorrow may bring some of what has happened into better perspective," he looked at Father Kaylan, then back to Nichole, and said simply, "I gave the notebook to Ralph."

Nichole, aka Nicholas Kaylan, looked at his brother, Father Ralph then back to Scott, and nodded in thanks.

"Come to my rooms later Nick . . . Nichole and I'll give it to you," Father Ralph said in a calm voice.

"Thank you Ralph, but I commend it into your safe keeping for now," said Nichole to her brother. She turned and made her way with silent, graceful steps to the church door, then turned briefly, the light shining through one of the high stained glass windows spilling a lovely ray of color across her left shoulder, illuminating the graceful cut of her jaw and the soft material of her dress. When she turned, her blue eyes swept the three men standing in the quiet recesses of shadow at the front of the church. Her smile was slightly sad, her beauty riveting. Then she turned and was gone.

The three men stood silently, looking at the spot where Nichole had just been, until Jon said, "I'm going to go pull the car up. I'll be out front when you're ready, there's no hurry," he put his hand on Scott's shoulder, "there's no hurry Scott, take all the time you need."

"Thanks, I think I'll just have a word with Father Kaylan before I come out."

Jon nodded while looking at Father Kaylan and said, "I'll see you tomorrow."

"Yes, tomorrow Jon. Don't forget to pray."

"Father, I've prayed more in the last week than I've prayed in my entire life, and I've meant every word of it." He turned and walked toward the door at the back of the church; very aware again of the hushed sound his leather-soled shoes made on the carpet. As he opened the door to go out, he saw the two men deep in conversation and thought, *if it's something important, Scott will tell me.* As the door closed behind him it puffed out a breath of air smelling of hot wax from the burning candles in alcoves around the interior of the church; $1.00 to light a candle, send a prayer to heaven and save a soul.

He felt warm in the sun with his suit on, and as he walked toward his car fishing through the change in his pants pocket for his car keys, he experienced that sensation that most cops have honed to perfection, the feeling that someone was behind him. The key to his car slid smoothly between his index and middle finger, his thumb locked in behind them as his hand turned into a fist with a lethal weapon able to gouge out an eye or puncture some other portion of soft tissue. He suddenly spun around on the balls of his feet, the smooth leather on the soles of his dress shoes a perfect conveyor of speed; his hand came out of his pocket with the knife like key, his knees slightly bent and his eyes narrowed and deadly.

"Whoa, wait a minute Jon! I just wanted to talk to you away from Scott!" said a startled Phyllis Johnson as she put her hands up in a surrender position and took several quick steps backwards, the heels of her shoes making a rapid click, click, clicking sound on the warm pavement.

Jon took in a few lungful of air and blew it out between parted lips, and let his hand fall to his side, "Jesus Phyllis I'm sorry, but you startled me."

"We're in the same boat then, you just scared the living shit out of me. Are you ok?"

"Yea, I'm ok, just a little skittish I guess."

"Just a little, to put it mildly; look, I wanted to tell you something away from Scott then you can make the determination as to what you want to do."

"Ok. So what's up?"

Phyllis looked into his eyes for a long moment, and then continued. "We had another murder victim, a woman, brought to the morgue early this morning. Initial identification marks her as the manager of a homeless shelter on the east side. The condition of the body is practically identical to Will's," she hesitated just long enough for Jon to prompt her.

"And . . . what else is there Phyllis?"

"The police in River Ridge got a call from a man last night. The prelims in the report say that he was calling about a stench from somewhere in the house next door saying it smelled like something dead and someone needed to come take care of it. What the officers found inside the house is in the morgue too."

"What did they find Phyllis?" Jon asked, his voice low, each word carefully and slowly enunciated.

"We haven't made a positive ID yet; the body is in very bad shape. Time of death appears to be five to six days ago and not all the parts were together . . . ,"

The look on Jon's face was slowing her down, and all she wanted was to get it out. She kept thinking if she said it aloud, it would get the picture out of her head.

"Go on," Jon said, still speaking slowly.

". . . what was left of the body of a badly decomposed elderly white male. It was headless when found. Another patrol car was called for backup and during the search, they found what was left of his head stuffed in the toilet. The brain was gone as were all of the soft tissue organs."

Jon felt his stomach tighten and his testicles draw up, but his voice remained steady and eerily calm. "Do you think they are related?"

"Jon, in all my years as a coroner I have *never* seen anything remotely like this. Do I think they are related? I'm positive they are related. Whoever, *whatever* killed Will is also responsible for what is left of the two victims in the hold room at the morgue."

It was surreal standing in the autumn sun, the birds chirruping their final good-byes as they prepared to leave for the winter yet to come. So surreal to listen to the description of more murders unlike any murders they had ever heard of before. In their midst was an entity, a creature able to sneak up on people so quickly no scream was heard by another human ear.

Some dark menacing, pernicious thing is eating human organs like so much foie gras and sucking out their brains like sweet liquor from a chocolate covered cherry, Jon thought on that day of bright sun, chirping birds and sadness.

So very, very surreal.

CHAPTER 24

Thursday, when Sammy and Anthony had gone back to school they had had little time to recount their mini vacation to their school friends. Some teachers disliked the fact that Anthony and Sammy had been granted leave to take the few days off, and so the boys ended up with several unexpected tests. The day had gone by in a haze of books and papers, sharpened pencils and much erasing.

When the two friends met for lunch, Sammy grabbed a tray and got in line with Anthony.

"I'm gettin' killed, how about you?" he said eying the fish sticks, mac'n cheese and coleslaw that was on the menu. He picked up milk and put it on his tray as he anxiously waited for the other kids in line to move it along so he could get some lunch.

"I want to go back to the lodge," said Anthony rising up on his toes to look at the front of the line, "What the heck is the hold up?"

Sammy leaned out of the lunch line sideways trying to see what was happening. "Hey, I think there is something going on with Jus Russelton," he said to Anthony as he straightened up.

"So what's the deal?" said Anthony impatiently.

They heard a racket at the front of the line, saw a tray hit the floor and heard Justin say, "Get off me I said!" his voice tense and sharp. Everyone in line was leaning out now, or standing on their toes trying to see what was happening at the front of the line.

One on the lunch ladies shouted, "Stop it right now, both of you or your next stop will be the principal's office!"

The ruckus at the front of the line appeared to stop, and they started to move again.

"What the hell do you think that was about? Jus never gets in fights," said Anthony.

Sammy shrugged his shoulders, "Dunno, Anth. Why don't we go sit with him and ask what happened? I don't think he's too crazy about the fish sticks so maybe he'll give me his."

"You are unbelievable."

"Yea I know, and unforgettable too," smiled Sammy.

They watched were Justin was sitting, and because no one else wanted to sit next to him, it was no problem to pick a seat at the same table.

Their trays rattled for a second and the chairs scraped on the green linoleum.

"Hey Jus, how are you?" asked Anthony as Sammy started eating fish sticks and mixing his coleslaw with his mac'n and cheese.

"Ok I guess," was his brusque reply. It was so unlike Justin that Sammy looked up, his eyes traveling to Anthony whose brows had drawn together as if to say, *what is going on?*

They ate in silence for several minutes, and then Justin laid his fork down and sighed. Suddenly he said, "Heard you guys were away for a couple of days."

"Yea, we went to a lodge in Cooks Forest, had a great time, didn't we Sammy?"

Sammy bobbed his head yes and his Adams apple moved up and down as he swallowed and eyed Justin's plate and the unfinished fish sticks, and just as he was about to say something Anthony kicked him hard under the table.

"Owwwh!" he cried. He was about to make a smart remark when he looked at Anthony who had narrowed his eyes and shook his head.

"Did you do anything over the weekend?" Anthony asked Justin, watching his reaction closely. The silence stretched out so long that Sammy quit eating and looked up again.

"Jus, what's up, what's wrong?" asked Anthony.

Justin looked up his eyes bright with tears as he worked to control his trembling chin. "Ebony's missing . . . she's gone."

"What do you mean she's *gone?*" Anthony voice was hushed.

"Gone. Mom left her out Sunday night and she never came back. Mom thinks she heard her yelp or something. We called the police Monday. Mom and Dad looked all over for her but couldn't find her. Then the police came out and they looked around the house and stuff, and well . . . ," he stopped again struggling to control his emotions, both Anthony and Sammy waited in silence.

". . . they didn't find her . . . just . . . just a part of her." A single tear ran down his left cheek, and he raised his shoulder to rub the tear away on his t-shirt.

Sammy put his fork down.

"What the hell . . . ," said Anthony in disbelief.

"A *part* of her? A *part?* What *part*?" Sammy had gone pale, his freckles standing out starkly on his face now.

"Her tail Sammy, just her tail," Justin's voice was quivering, full of sadness and pain. Another tear rolled slowly down his cheek, but this time he did not try to wipe it away. The agony in his voice made both boys want to cover their ears, make it stop; Justin continued telling them what had happened.

"It looked like it was ripped off of her," he folded his arms on the table and laid his face in them and sobbed, as all around them other students laughed and shouted, trays banged, the chairs scooted and scraped.

Only the lunch lady, who had admonished him in line, saw both boys put their hands on each of his shoulders. She saw one of the boys put his hand over his mouth; the other put his hand up to his forehead and rubbed his temples. Something in their behavior sent a chill down her spine, and something deep inside told her that when she got home she would lock the doors.

Later, on the bus on their way home both had laid their heads against the hard seat backs and listened to the bus brakes squeal at each stop and the *whoosh* of the door as it opened depositing each child at their designated drop off point.

"Are you coming to my house?" Anthony asked as he continued to look straight ahead.

"Yep, I'll get off at your house and call mom. We'll have maybe two hours to work on the drawing," he used his foot to pull up his backpack that was on the floor. He leaned over and pulled out a piece of notebook paper. It contained a pencil sketch of the barn floor layout with a circle. "I think I figured out how to make the circle perfectly round. We'll need to clear the floor in the middle first. Then we can try it in pencil and if it works, we can go over it with the olive-wood charcoal."

"Ok, I'll help you sweep up the floor and then while you are doing the circle I'll practice on the *Devil's Trap.* After we eat dinner I'll hurry up and get my homework done and I can have some more time to practice it freehand."

"You're going to need a good feel for it Anth to draw it so much bigger."

"How big do you think we should make it?"

"I don't know exactly, I guess we'll figure that out when we get the floor swept and see how much room we really have," Sammy hesitated a moment then continued, "what we don't know yet is how we are going to . . . well, get rid of Ax Man."

"We'll have to kill it somehow Sammy."

"How do you kill something that's not alive?"

"I guess that goes in with that big pile of stuff we have to do."

"What do you mean? What pile of stuff?"

"The 'figure it out' pile; it keeps getting bigger."

The bus came to a stop again and they heard a couple of kids running up the aisle between the seats, one of the kids' back-pack hit Sammy on the back of the head bringing a loud *hey!* as the child ray by.

"Stop running!" yelled the bus driver watching the back of the bus in the long mirror above his head as the children for that stop piled off the bus and the door *whooshed* closed again.

"That sounds like a pretty good idea," said Anthony.

"What sounds like a good idea?" replied Sammy rubbing the back of his head.

"Running."

The bus whined up as the driver shifted through the gears, turning onto Metz Road towards his next stop, and the trees became denser as they drove further out into the rural area closer to Anthony's house.

"I never really thought before about how far we are from town. Not until now," Anthony said.

"It's weird you said that, I was thinking last night we are kinda isolated out here, none of us have any really close neighbors, no one who can run across the street and help if we need it."

The bus bounced along getting closer to Sammy's house. Sammy piped up and said to the bus driver, "Mr. Bosco, I'm getting off at Anthony's house."

"Do your parents know?"

"Yeah," lied Sammy.

"Ok. You practically live here anyhow," replied Mr. Bosco, not thinking it was anything out of the ordinary with the two friends.

"You know how we said we would talk to our dads after we had some proof?" Sammy asked turning toward Anthony.

"Yep."

"I don't think we can. I'm afraid if we try to explain what we know is going on they'll keep us in the house as if we're crazy or something. We'd better just keep it to ourselves if we wanna get this thing done," said Sammy, deadly earnest.

Anthony sighed deeply and nodded his head. "You're right Sammy, we have to be able to be at the barn the next two evenings and as long as it takes on Saturday," he started digging through his book bag. "We still have to get through tonight though. You know that first night I told you I found the web link about *Devil's Traps.* There was also information I printed off about *Blessed Salt.*"

"What's that?' asked Sammy curiously.

"Here," said Anthony opening his school notebook and removing folded pages from a back pocket. He opened the sheets and looked for a moment. "Here it is. '*Blessed salt is an instrument of grace to preserve one from the corruption of evil occurring as sin, sickness, demonic influence, etc.*'"

"I think we might qualify under the demonic part. But what do we do?" questioned Sammy,

"Well, there is a prayer here that a priest is supposed to say, but I don't think we have any way of getting to church before Saturday night. My mom has a couple of boxes of salt in the cupboard in the garage with spices and stuff for canning. I don't think she'll miss one, a least for now. I was thinkin' maybe we could say the prayer in the barn before we start the *Devil's Trap*." Sammy looked at him without saying a word, the moments seeming to drag on forever.

"You think I'm nuts, don't you?" he looked hard at Sammy, who this time, was quick to reply.

"Nope, I think if we believe that Ax-Man is some possessed thing, and we do, then we sure as heck believe in God. I don't think there can be evil without God."

"No funny-farm for me then?"

"Bro, if you're going to the funny-farm then I'm sharing the same room with you."

The bus driver, Mr. Bosco yelled back, "Hey you two! Come on, let's go!"

They grabbed their bags, made a hasty retreat off the bus, and heard the final *whoosh* as the bus doors closed for the last time that day. As they started up through the yard they looked at each other and made a wide detour around the Halloween Extravaganza, that such a short time ago had brought them so much excitement. Now it brought only a portent of cataclysm yet unknown.

CHAPTER 25

Army had the rest of the week off as vacation, and because the weather was so unexpectedly nice he decided to go up to the barn and do some excavation along the north side and take some measurements in advance of a decorative fence installation they planned in the spring. Danni meanwhile had opted to go to the grocery store with her envelope of coupons surmising it might be a good idea to have some real food in the house. In addition, she always made a big pot of Sloppy Joes for Halloween night as friends and parents usually ended up in the house while the kids were whooping it up running outside in Army's most excellent decorations. She also planned to stop at a local craft store that was having a 50% off sale on fall decorations to see what she could find in the form of a wreath for the front door.

Army went to the garage and collected a wheelbarrow, a pick, shovel, two stakes, a line, a line level and a pair of work gloves. He made his way up to the barn and visually surveyed the area. The split rail fence they planned would give a finishing touch to the barn, and it was such a beautiful red barn, it deserved that final change. He stood with his back to the door facing west, deciding where to place the stakes. First, he measured twenty feet from the southwest corner and placed a stake at that point; then he measured thirty feet from that point west and placed a second stake. Next, he tied a line taunt between each stake, placed a line level along the span, and spot-checked it down the length. There were high spots in the ground that Army decided to cut down so he could get a better visual idea of the view that the actual height would allow. He spent the next thirty minutes working along his string line, moving dirt and raking out different areas. After fifteen feet or so, he hit something hard with the shovel, *probably a rock*, he thought. However, after several minutes of digging around he realized it seemed to be very square and much larger than he originally surmised, the shape indicating to him that it probably was not a natural occurring rock. *Maybe its buried treasure* he thought with a chuckle. After loosening as much of the dirt as possible, he got down on his hands and knees and began to brush away the loose soil. That was when he noticed that the stone appeared to have decorative chiseled scallops around three sides. Intrigued, he took the edge of the shovel and wedged it under one corner to use a fulcrum. He was able to lift it far enough to slide the shovel and pushing the handle down, he gained enough room to get his hands under it. He struggled to lift the stone but was finally able to stand it up. That was when he noticed there appeared to be an inscription carved into the slab. He carefully laid the stone down on the opposite side and began brushing the caked dirt. When he realized he would be unable to clean it off adequately enough to read with just his gloves, he headed back to the garage where he filled a bucket with water and grabbed a soft scrub brush. He walked back up to the barn, sloshing some water on the ground in his eagerness to discover what was on the stone. He dry-brushed it first to clean off as much of the dirt as possible, then he slowly poured water on the stone starting from the middle and working his way out so that the resulting mud ran off the edges. He used the brush again, gently scrubbing the stone. The words began to appear almost magically as the water hydrated the porous stone and caused the inscription to pop out. He could not believe what he was seeing.

Annaleah Grimmer
And
Devin Grimmer
Died
October 31 1875
Beloved wife and son
Of Brandon Grimmer

A grave . . . it must be a grave. He remembered then that when they originally found the property, the realtor on several occasions called it the Grimmer Property. He made another hasty trip back to the garage and finally found a piece of paper and a carpenter's pencil. The stone had dried significantly during the brief time it had taken him to go back to the garage. Again, he poured water on stone and carefully copied the spelling of the names and the date. He folded the paper and put it in his shirt pocket. Army had decided that he had enough time left today to make a quick trip to the local library and see if they had any old newspapers on microfilm. He hastily picked up all his tools, put them into the wheelbarrow, and hurriedly pushed them back to the garage. He brushed off his pants and shirt, made a brief trip to the small bathroom by the garage to wash his hands, run his fingers through his hair and grab his keys. As he backed out the driveway, his mind was tumbling over all the different questions. Who were they? How did they die and why had they been buried on his property? How would he go about getting the graves moved? He checked his watch and saw it was just past noon, so he was good on time. He realized then, he had not brought a pen, pencil or any paper. Since there was an office supply store in close proximity, he decided to make a pit stop to pick up a notebook and a couple of pens. The cashier asked if he found everything he needed. Would he like a thirty pack of Memorex 700mb CDs for 25% off? Do you have a Staples card? Finally, he was on his way to the library hoping he did not need a library card to use their microfilm files.

As he turned into the parking lot he noticed there were only two cars there, and he felt relieved. Why? Did he think there was going to be a line to get to the microfilm library? Parking in the first slot he came to, he took his spiral notebook and pens from the bag, stepped from his car, and headed up the four steps to the front door. He pulled the door open, and heard a soft *ping* probably alerting the on-duty librarian that someone was coming in.

The aroma of books enveloped him. Old books full of history, lore and art; love and hate, wars and wonder. New books fat with the knowledge of science, the revolution of $E=MC^2$ the wonder of a DNA chain. Leather and paper, ink and glue, hundreds of millions of words that could change men's minds and enlighten the world with knowledge and information. At this moment, Army needed information.

In the middle of the library was a large oval counter, and behind that counter stood a very attractive woman, not at all the stereo type of the bi-spectacled liberian of the past, but rather she had long, glossy black hair and hauntingly green eyes.

"May I help you find something?" she asked, as a warm smile moved across her face.

"Yes, thank you. Do you have records of news papers in this area from around 1875?"

"We do. They are on old media however, microfilm, which can be time consuming to search through. Do you have a specific item or event you are searching for or possibly a person?"

"Actually, all of the above. I'm interested in finding as much information as possible on a woman's death in 1875 and the way in which she and her son died.

"At that time the only newspaper in this area was the Pittsburgh Dispatch. In fact, it was the only newspaper in the western part of the state from 1847 through 1900. If who you are looking for died in this area, then you will find it in the obituary section. Let me take you to the microfilm corner and we'll get you set up, ok?"

"Thanks so much. I came across this by accident and I'm kind of anxious to find some info about it."

The librarian walked to a large table on which sat the microfilm reader that looked incredibly antiquated compared to today's computers and laptops. It consisted of a huge screen with two reels onto which the film was spooled. It had knobs to go forward or backward enabling a person to scan multiple documents quickly.

"Have you ever used a microfilm reader before?"

"No, I haven't. Is it hard?"

"No, not at all. First let's see if we can find the reel for that time period."

Behind the microfilm reader was a huge wall containing ten vertical and four horizontal drawers creating a sizeable wooden cabinet. Each drawer had typed at the top MICROFILM and below that two ascending years. Working together, they were able to identify what Army was looking for: Jan-Dec. 1874 and Jan-Dec. 1875.

"Here it is," she said opening the drawer and removing an envelope.

They turned back to the microfilm reader and she took from the envelope a small reel laying the envelope on the table. It took only a minute to explain how the reel containing the data fit onto the spindle on the right ran through the feeder and attached to the empty spool on the left. Army quickly understood the procedure and was eager to get started.

"Thank you for all your help," he said sincerely.

"You're very welcome. I'll be over at the desk; if you need anything, don't hesitate to ask."

Army laid his spiral notebook and pen on the desk and began slowly going through newspapers, getting a feel for the best way to scan and locate information. Because he had a date, he was able to navigate through the microfilm quickly, locating October 31. In less than fifteen minutes, he found the obituary for Annaleah Grimmer and her unborn son, Devin. It was quite extensive not only because of the manner of death, but because her husband was a prominent and successful businessman in this part of the state. When Army realized that their house was located at approximately the same location, he felt a shiver run through him. He decided when he got home he would walk the property and see if he could come across any of the old foundation. Out of curiosity, he scanned several days forward and came across another obituary that caused him to whisper under his breath, *Oh dear God.* Annaleah's husband, Brandon, died four days later, the same day of the funeral, apparently of a broken heart. His best friend and foreman, Shawn O'Farrell found him in the doorway of the barn. Army read and re-read the two accounts until he was satisfied that he understood everything. He jotted down notes and any information he considered pertinent and then re-wound the microfilm and put it back into the envelope. He went to the file containing the 1874 film, took it out and spooled it onto the reader. After another thirty minutes, he found what he was looking for—an article about raising the barn that was on his property. The article clarified some things for Army regarding the exceptional craftsmanship of the barn. It also explained the small room type alcove at the back that faced west and afforded a wonderful view of sunsets. He wondered where Brandon had been buried and suspected somewhere close to his beloved wife and son. He would do some more exploratory digging when he got home, and, he told himself, he would have to find out what the procedure was, if any, to have the coffins or remains moved to a more suitable location. He decided immediately that he would not mention it to Danni or Anthony yet. He would go home and put the grave marker back in the hole, put a piece of plastic on top of it and some loose soil, until he discovered what he could, or couldn't do.

After he had rewound the reel, he placed it back in the special envelope and then back in the appropriate file drawer location.

On his way out, he stopped at the counter and thanked the librarian.

"So did you find what you were looking for?" she asked with the same warm smile on her lips.

"I did, and more," he replied, "I really appreciate your help."

"You're so very welcome. The history of Brandon and Annaleah Grimmer is a very touching story of love and broken hearts. I've often thought it would make a wonderful book," she said quietly.

"Well, yes, I guess it might at that," Army replied, as he got ready to go. "Have a great day and thanks again."

"You also Mr. Petrucci."

Army was keen on getting back quickly now. He wanted to replace the stone and cover it before anyone else got home. As he looked at his watch, he wasn't sure if he would arrive before Danni since he wasn't entirely certain how long she would be gone, but he would be cutting it close, very close to Anthony getting off the bus from school. It did not occur to him to ask the very nice young woman at the library how she knew what he had read, or his name.

Thursday—4:15 p.m.

As Anthony and Sammy climbed down the steps of the bus and started across the yard toward the house, they both noticed Army walking toward house pushing a wheelbarrow in front of him.

"What's dad's doing?" Anthony wondered aloud.

"Dunno, maybe working out back someplace?" Sammy responded.

Since the garage door was open, the boys headed that way to drop off their book bags inside the door.

When they got into the garage, Army looked up. "Hey guys, how was school?"

"It was ok I guess, we sure had a lot of tests," said Anthony.

"Lots," added Sammy.

The boys dropped their book bags beside the two steps leading into the kitchen.

"Dad, we're going to take a couple of brooms up to the barn, ok?"

After what Army had discovered today, his hackles were up immediately, "What for?" he asked suspiciously.

"We just want to sweep up some of the old straw and hay that's in the middle of the floor and put it in the loose pile on the right side, that's all."

"Yeah, just clean it," Sammy echoed, "for Halloween," he finish lamely.

They all heard gravel crunching and turned to see Danni pulling up. She lightly beeped the horn twice and Army and the two boys stepped to the side allowing her to pull in. As she came to a stop and put the car in park, Anthony took the opportunity to pick up one regular corn broom and a push broom.

"Um, Sammy you take these to the barn and I'll be there in just a minute," Anthony said as he nodded his head slightly towards the barn.

"Why, what are you doing?"

"Just go on to the barn," he tipped his head a second time.

"It's ok, I'll wait," replied Sammy in complete innocence.

Army and Danni were carrying groceries up the steps into the kitchen and in that brief moment Anthony turned quickly to Sammy and said in an urgent whisper, "Grab a box of salt out of the cabinet and go before they can ask any more questions, I'm going up for the charcoal!"

"Oh crap, I get it," Sammy whispered back, "grab a hammer, a long nail and some string and bring it. I'll need those to draw a circle."

"Ok, I'll get what I can while mom and dad are in the house. I might have to wait until they carry in all of the stuff from the car."

"I'll start to sweep."

"See you in a couple of minutes."

Anthony went up the steps into the kitchen and started for his bedroom.

"Hold up kiddo," said Danni smiling at her son. "How was your first day back, and how about a hug?" She held open her arms, and despite being anxious and in a hurry, his desire for a hug was stronger. As he stepped into her embrace, he put his arms around his mom's waist and laid his head against her. She ruffled his hair and kissed his forehead. "So did they go easy on you and Sammy?"

"Not a chance. We had a couple of pop quizzes but we both did ok on them; I got A—and a B and Sammy got two B's and one was in English."

"I'm sure Mindy and Dan will be glad to hear that."

Anthony almost told his mom about what had happened with Justin, about Ebby, but he held back not wanting to give either his mom or dad, any reason to delay him going to the barn.

He released his hold on his mom and said, "Gotta go!"

"Go where honey?" Danni asked as she started putting groceries away.

"Sammy's up at the barn. We're gonna sweep some of the old hay off the floor and put some fresh down in case any of the guys from school stop over on Saturday before Trick or Treat to swing on the rope. We just want to clean up and make it look nice." *Oh crap, that sounded so lame* he thought sure his mom would be onto that misdirection.

However, much to his amazement his mom just asked, "Is Sammy staying for dinner? We're having grilled hot dogs, corn on the cob and some chips."

"Yeah, he'll stay I'm sure. We want to do as much as we can today and tomorrow because it gets dark early. I'm gonna change my shirt."

He made a beeline for his bedroom, pulled off his good shirt and grabbed a sweatshirt from a hook on the back of his door, then headed for the three-foot papier-mâché Mickey Mouse in one corner of his room. He and his mom had made several

Disney characters a year ago for a school play. After the play was over, they got two of the characters. Anthony had cut out a hole in the back and the front of each and then tunneled out the paper between the two holes. Next, he took two small four-inch speakers his dad had picked up at a yard sale and wired it to a turntable his parents had from the 80's. It had been the best place he could come up with to hide the cloth sack with the Bethlehem olive wood charcoal and the *Devil's Trap* when they had arrived home yesterday. He took them out of the hiding place, put the charcoal in his front pocket, the *Devil's Trap* in the front of his jeans, and pulled his shirt down as far as he could. He remembered Sammy saying he might need a regular pencil so he grabbed a short one off his desk. Fortunately, his parents had gone to the other end of the house giving him time to duck out the back door, grab a hammer, a ball of twine and a spike from a jar full of miscellaneous items on his dad's workbench, and he at last was able to make a dash for the barn.

On his way up, he realized how the light from the sun was different and that it was getting much cooler earlier in the afternoon now. Normally, he loved this time of year, but now the coming dark made his heart beat faster and fear was blooming like an ill-omened flower in his soul. He looked up and saw Sammy waving with his arm to hurry. When he got inside the door, he could see that Sammy had been busy in the last fifteen minutes; about halfway inside the main doors a large area was cleared of loose straw and hay showing the worn bleached looking floorboards.

"Wow," Anthony said looking around, "that was quick."

"I just have this feeling we have to get this done fast, I don't know why, I just do," said Sammy quietly.

"Me too bro. So where do you want this stuff?"

Sammy came over, took the hammer, spike and string from Anthony and set them down.

"Do you know how to pray for the salt?" Sammy asked.

"Not really," he thought for a moment, "maybe we could just say the Our Father and add something at the end about the salt?"

"Ok, let's do it now," Sammy stepped back, reached behind an empty five-gallon bucket, and grabbed the carton of salt. He and Anthony stepped into the area, which Sammy had worked so hard to get clean, and Sammy set the salt down on the newly swept floorboards.

"I think it's supposed to be in a bowl or something," said Anthony.

They both looked around and Sammy spied an old metal tin at the front corner where the door opened. It said *Borax* on the side and was rusty, but it was all they had right now.

"Hold on a sec," he said as he scampered to get the tin. When he got back to the circle, Anthony already had the carton open and began to pour the salt into the metal tin. He did not think it would all fit, but it did.

"Ok, I know this sounds weird, but I think we should hold hands."

"How about if we just put our hands on each other's shoulders," Sammy replied.

"That works."

It was quiet for a moment, and each unknowingly closed their eyes and Anthony's voice began.

"Our Father, who art in heaven, hallowed be thy name. Thy Kingdom come, thy will be done, on earth as it is in heaven. Give us this day our daily bread, and forgive our trespasses, as we forgive those who trespass against us. And lead us not into temptation, but deliver us from evil. For thine is the kingdom, and the power and the glory, forever and ever. And God, Sammy and I want to ask you to please bless the salt we have here. We want to use it to put around our houses to protect our families from whatever the evil thing is that we know is in Ax-Man. Please give us the courage to do this God. Amen."

"Amen too," repeated Sammy quietly.

There was a feeling of something rumbling, vibrating, a deep resonance of thunder with no sound rolling through them like a wave.

They dropped their arms from each other's shoulders and the boys looked at one another.

"What *was* that?" Anthony said wide eyed to Sammy.

"I don't know, but it didn't feel bad, just weird," replied Sammy looking around the barn.

Anthony looked down at their bowl of salt, and noticed that it looked . . . sparklie.

"How are we going to split this up and get it home?"

Sammy thought for a moment and said, "Let's cut the salt box in half, you can carry half down to the house and I can stick the other half in my book bag with my hat on top so it won't spill out too much."

"Ok, that sounds good."

They used the tip of the nail to go around the cardboard a couple of times until they were able to get it in two slightly ragged pieces. They pinched shut the spout end and folded it over as best they could and with the hammer tapped it flat. Then with cupped hands, each carefully put the salt in their half.

When they finished and stood, Sammy looked at Anthony and said, "Come and see what you think about where I cleaned."

He already had the hammer in his hand and moved quickly over to retrieve the nail and string going back to the approximate center of the swept area; he wrapped the string around the hammer head a couple of times and laid it down. Next, he played out a couple of feet of the string and said to Anthony, "See what you think this will look like." Keeping the string as taunt as he could without moving the hammer, he started to walk in a circle. As Anthony watched him, it looked like the circle was going to be about six feet in diameter.

"That looks ok to me. If it's any bigger I think I'll have a lot of trouble drawing the picture."

"Ok," said Sammy, "let's lay out the circle, I'll do it first with the pencil to see how it looks, and then if we think it's ok,

I'll go over it with the charcoal. Why don't you practice drawing the *Devil's Trap*?"

"Crap! I forgot to bring paper!" Anthony hit his fist on his leg in frustration.

"There's a pad and pencil in my book bag Anth, and I drew a couple of circles on different pages you can work on."

He glanced up, saw Anthony looking at him in bewilderment of his preparedness, and shrugged his shoulders. "I was bored in study hall. Be careful and don't spill my salt."

Anthony took out the pad of paper and pencil from the book bag, then sat down on a bale of hay and laid the *Devil's Trap* to his left. He stared long and hard at the symbol, ingraining the picture in his head, then set to work drawing in the first circle.

He drew for several minutes, glancing only occasionally at the woodcarving, until he heard Sammy say, "You wanna take a look at this?"

Anthony set the pad and pencil down and went to stand next to his friend. Sammy had pounded the nail in the floorboard where the hammer handle had been and then tied the string tightly to the pencil. Keeping the string taunt, he bent over and walked the diameter of the string making a light marking of pencil in a perfect circle. As they both stood staring at it for a moment, the reality of what they were about to do hit them both.

Sammy looked up and said, "We'd better hurry," nodding his head up toward the open barn door that faced west; "the sun is starting to set."

The sun was indeed low in the sky, the outside shimmering nuclear orange, rimmed in red just above the horizon. The long shadows cast through the trees seemed to be creeping slowly along the ground. They both felt a new urgency surrounding all that they needed to do. Anthony pulled the pouch of charcoal out of his pocket, wiggled open the top and pulled out a small piece handing it over to Sammy who quickly untied the pencil replacing it with the charcoal, and making sure to match the pencil marks, redrew the circle with the holy charcoal. They worked in silence, Anthony picking up Sammy's pad of paper and tearing out the three sheets with circles, one with his partially finished drawing, putting the pouch back in his pocket and the carving in the waist of his jeans. He watched his friend finish the circle, the line dark and perfect, then as Sammy stepped carefully into the circle, wiggling the spike from the center and stepping back out to stand next to Anthony.

"I think we should cover it with something, don't you?" asked Sammy. Anthony nodded his head in agreement and started toward the back of the barn where a dark blue tarp lay folded. He brought it back and the two of them unfolded it and laid it carefully on the circle. Sammy motioned over to the pile of fresh straw they had planned to put down. They both scooped up big bunches of straw pulling it to their chests and then proceeded to spread it randomly across the tarp obscuring it from any sharp eyes that may look in the barn. At the last moment, they decided to front it with bales of hay.

"Do ya think your dad will come in?"

"No, I don't think so."

They heard Danni's voice calling them for supper and they hurriedly closed the doors firmly before starting toward the house, only a small sliver of sun remaining above the lip of the earth's horizon.

"Would it be ok if I ask your mom or dad to drive me home?" Sammy asked anxiously.

"Yep, they will. I'll ride along."

"That's ok, you don't have to."

"I know. I want to."

The hot dogs were brown and sizzling, the sweet corn slathered in butter with lime-juice and the chips salty and crisp. Danni noticed the boys, who were usually so animated, seemed quiet tonight but just put it down to them both being tired.

Later, after dinner and taking Sammy home, as the moon began its nightly trip from east to west, Anthony told his parents he was going to take a shower. It was Thursday night and Danni and Army always watched *TV Land* to catch some of the classic shows from their younger days and share a laugh. It was a perfect time for Anthony to quickly and quietly slip outside and sprinkle a line of salt around the perimeter of his house by the light of the waxing moon. As he worked, he wondered if his friend was doing the same, and imagined that he was.

An unexpected shiver caused him to quicken his pace and look anxiously over his shoulder toward the front of the yard where in the shadows he knew *it* was probably watching him. In his haste to get back inside the relative safety of his home, he did not hear the low malicious growl emanating from the malignant dark form whose eyes watched feverishly as the young boy marked his territory with pious salt.

The fiendish puppet master held tight to the strings of its reeking creation, choosing instead another night to send it out to reap madness.

It was still early on Thursday, just after 12:30 p.m. The funeral for Scott's brother was over and Jon sat in his car waiting for Scott to finish talking with Father Kaylan and come outside. He was replaying the tape in his head of his conversation with Phyllis Johnson, considering all that had happened in such a short time and wondering whether he should tell Scott about the most recent new additions to the corners office. The motion of the church door opening and closing caught his attention and he watched as Scott walked down the sidewalk towards the car carefully carrying the urn containing the remains of his brother. Sunlight glinted off the polished surface casting almost a halo of light around it, continuing the surreal sense he had experienced earlier. The car door opened, Scott got in, sat down, and closed the door resting the urn on his left knee. He stared straight ahead taking a deep breath and letting out a long sigh.

"How're you doing?" He started the car, checked the mirrors and seeing no cars, started to pull onto the street.

"I'm not sure. My emotions are raw, but my mind feels numb; I've never felt this way before." He continued to stare ahead as Jon continued to wrestle with the information he was withholding.

"What did Phyllis want?" asked Scott bluntly.

"So much for me deciding whether or not to tell you."

"So, just tell me."

Jon spent the next few minutes relaying to Scott with as much detail as possible, what Phyllis had told him.

When he finished, silence hung between them for a moment until Scott said, "Swing by the morgue. I want to check something."

"Come on . . . no Scott," Wendels looked over and saw him clenching and unclenching his jaw, the muscles throbbing up and down, "please, let's just go back to your place and make sure we're ready for the dog tomorrow."

"It's important; I only need a couple of minutes."

"You're in a suit for God's sake!" Wendels said grabbing for any straw that would keep him away from the morgue.

"I'm usually in a suit when I go to work."

"Damn it Scott, we just buried your brother."

"I know that!" Scott shouted, anger washing through him. He took a deep breath, looking at Jon and continued. "I'm sorry Jon, that wasn't directed at you, but can't you see that's why it's even more important to me that I go."

As Jon looked over at him, he could read the pain in Scott's eyes . . . and something else. Determination.

Gripping the urn with his brother's ashes, Scott turned in the seat looking directly at Jon.

"You and I both know, Father Kaylan knows, there is something evil going on here. We need as much information as possible if we are to stop this . . . *thing* . . . and stop innocent people from being murdered; we have to do this, and you know it. I feel we're being pushed along some timeline that *it* wants.

We need to establish our own timeline, *we* need to run the show, and for us to do that we have to have all the information possible. I want to see if the death of the old man corresponds with anything we know about, or ties in with something we might suspect."

John was already making a wide birth to start the standard Pennsylvania 'U' turn. He was renowned for being able to pull it off in downtown Pittsburgh traffic at rush hour.

"Umm, the light is red. Just thought I'd mention it," said Scott as he looked around for a police cruiser.

"Yeah, I know, but this is official police business," the tires squealed on the pavement and a horn blared as he gunned the car toward the morgue.

"Where's the Vicks?" Jon asked his stomach already becoming a little queasy.

"Right inside my office, first shelf on the left, but . . . well, if this man has been dead as long as Phyllis thinks, I don't know how much that will help. Maybe you'd better stay in the car."

He glanced over at Jon and noticed he swallowed hard, his eyes straight ahead.

"Why don't you wait in the car and go over everything you think we'll need for tomorrow so we don't waste any time?"

"I think that sounds like a plan. That is, if you're sure you won't need me?"

"I'm sure. I just need a few minutes to read over some reports and if necessary take a cursorily view of the bodies."

They drove the next few minutes in silence, the early afternoon sun splashing in and out of the windows, occasionally rolling off the bright urn resting on Scott's left knee, his right hand holding the base. The parking lot of the coroner's office came into view and they saw four other cars were there.

"Oops," said Jon when he saw the cars, "that car looks like Jess Givens, buddy."

"Crap. I don't want to be stuck with her. She'll nag me for an hour," Scott said vehemently. "Why the hell is she here?"

"Well, let's see," Jon said, "being the intuitive detective that I am, I would hazard a guess that maybe because there are two more bodies in there that appear to be following a bizarre and unexplained murder pattern, well, hey, call me crazy but I'll bet she's investigating it."

"Shut up smart ass, I know that, just why does it have to be now?"

"I'm still in that wild and crazy mode so I can't help it, but she's probably hoping you'll stop by?"

"Drive past, just drive past," Scott said irritably as he took the urn and put it between his legs and reached inside his suit to his inside pocket and pulled out a cell phone. He pushed the *start* button and waited for it to turn on. When it was ready, he hit the speed dial for his office, put it on hands free and waited for an answer.

After four rings one of the assistants, Colleen, picked up and said, "Orange County Corners office."

"Colleen, this is Scott, don't say anything yet please, just answer my questions."

"Yes?"

"Has Jess Givens been there long?

"Yes."

"Is she asking about the two new bodies?"

"That's right," the tone in her voice made them both sure that Jess was close by.

"Is she leaving soon, do you know?"

"That will be taking place immediately."

"Gotcha kiddo. I'll drive around the block then."

"Ok, thanks, goodbye."

Scott hit the disconnect button on his cell and looked up smiling.

"Such intrigue," said Jon.

"Worthy of an Oscar don't you think?

"Coleen was magnificent."

"Not Colleen, me!" laughed Scott.

Both men started laughing; it was a wonderful feeling and an even better sound. They laughed all the way around the block and by the time they got back to the coroners' parking lot, Jess's car was gone.

As Jon put the car in park, Scott extended the urn. "Do you mind holding this until I get back?"

Jon put out his hand hesitantly at first, then took possession of the urn. "See you in a couple then?"

"Yep, go through what you think we should take with us tomorrow."

"I will. Leave me your phone and I'll call and get a firm time on when Dave will show up at Jigs house. Since we only have the dog for an hour, I want to take advantage of every minute."

Scott handed over his phone and nodded his head, "He's in my contact list." He got out and closed the car door, and walking across the parking, lot disappeared into the black hole that appeared when he opened the door to the Coroner's office.

Colleen was peering through the side door glass waiting for Scott with a concerned look on her face.

"Dr. Champion, are you ok?"

"Yes, I am. Thanks for covering for me."

"No problem. But what was I covering?"

Scott chuckled, then said, "The fact that I didn't want to see Jess Givens. Is Phyllis in the autopsy room?"

"I think she just finished up and is starting her reports, do you want me to check?"

"No, I'll just head back. I understand the elderly gentleman was pretty bad?"

"Not pretty bad, just plain bad with a capital B," Coleen replied seriously.

Scott headed down the hall toward his office and took off his suite jacket, removed his tie and went into the outer room of the autopsy area. He donned a white impervagown and shoe covers and pressed the enter button to the examination room. The two bodies were on different sides of the room to prevent any cross contamination of evidence during autopsies. Coleen was right . . . it was bad. Over the years, Scott had become immune to the smell of decomposing bodies, but there was something worse about these, something beyond rotting putrid flesh; the stench of everything dark and vile, the reek of adulterated corruption seemed to have permeated every inch of them and it was unsettling. He viewed both bodies, noticing the large section of skull torn away in each head and the missing brains. Next to the woman was a mini baseball bat, next to the man a handgun. Both bodies were missing soft tissue organs. He heard the door open and turned to see Phyllis looking at him.

"Scott, can I help you, do you need anything?" she asked tentatively.

He met her eyes and they looked at each other wordlessly for several seconds. "Do you have the reports done on these two individuals?" His voice was level and calm.

"I'm not completely through with the woman yet, I still have the summation to finish. Do you want to view the bodies?"

"No, but I would like to see what you have reported so far." He looked around the room and said, "In all your years, have you ever encountered that smell?"

"No, never. I wondered if it was just me because of the unusual circumstances," she replied.

"Let me change and I'll meet you in your office," said Scott.

He showed up in her office several minutes later with his tie and coat back on and sat down in the chair across from her desk.

"So, how are you holding up?" Phyllis asked.

"I'm tired, but ok. Thanks for coming today, I mean that."

"You're welcome Scott. So . . . I guess Jon decided to tell you about my visit. I wasn't sure if he should, today of all days."

"Actually, he didn't. I saw you through the door as I was thanking Father Kaylan. Don't be too hard on Jon, I caught him off guard."

"I won't, I was just worried about you, that's all. Well, what is it exactly you are looking for here? Do you have an idea what or who the link is?" She leaned back in her chair, throwing her pen on the stack of folders, frustration and exhaustion plainly evident on her face. "The MO is the same, but there is no tangible evidence except for the condition of the bodies. I swabbed the soft tissue areas for DNA samples, but honestly, there was really nothing to focus on. The woman was the only one with any hair actually, and I went through what was left of it with a pair of tweezers and magnifying goggles. Nothing but twigs and material from the bush she apparently was pulled through."

"What was the baseball bat used for?" asked Scott.

"It was shoved down her throat so violently that it was easier to remove from the stem of her esophagus than try and remove it from the same direction it was put in. I've never seen *anything* even close to that before Scott."

He reached forward and picked up a folder in front of Phyllis. "Is this her file?"

"That's it, yes."

He opened the folder and began paging through it, stopping several times to study a particular paragraph, then asked her, "Time of death; you've determined eighteen to twenty-four hours?"

"Yes, and that is really an approximation because of the condition of the body. The body temperature was inconclusive because of the missing internal organs. It could be as little as twelve hours."

Scott closed that folder and looked over the desk. "Where is the report on the elderly man from *River Ridge*?" As she handed it to him he asked, "What is your best determination on his time of death?"

She sighed and leaned her head back against the chair, then sat up stretching her shoulders and placing her hands on the desk.

"That is even harder. Age is one factor, but again lack of much of what we depend on for investigation. This particular victim had what was left of his head stuffed in a toilet, the water washing away any evidence, and he was found in an abandoned house in a part of town only drug users frequent. Part of his torso was also eaten by rats."

"So your best determination of death is?"

"Five to seven days."

Scott quickly calculated and realized it had been Saturday, the same day of the attack on Jon at the shed on Jigs Seederly's property. It could be connected, but what had been done to the victims who were now in the autopsy room, what had torn his brother apart had been some *thing* with claws and teeth, something tangible, powerful and cruel. He suddenly realized that Phyllis was watching him oddly.

"You ok? Scott?"

He realized he must have sat there unblinking for a minute, staring straight ahead, as he tried to put the pieces together. He blinked his eyes rapidly several times, saying, "Yes . . . yes I'm fine. Just thinking that's all." He stood up laying the folder back on Phyllis's desk. "Call me if you come up anything significant."

"You know I will. Just go home and take it easy for a few days. You've had a lot to deal with this week."

"You have no idea," he murmured turning to leave the office. He heard Phyllis sigh again as she turned back to her computer to complete the latest report.

When he got to the main office area, he could hear Colleen say, "Oh Jesus, you've got to be kidding!"

Then the voice of the other coroner's assistant on duty, Brian Lescome replied, "Swear to God. His dad and mine work together. He said it was really hard had to tell their kids what they found, or I guess what they didn't find."

"Did it really look like it was ripped off?"

"That's what he told dad. Said there was a lot of blood around the area but they never found what might have been left of Ebony."

Scott decided to make his presence known and moved the rest of the way around the corner his interest peaked.

"Oh hello Dr. Champion I didn't know you were there. Can I get you anything?" asked Colleen a nervous note in her voice.

"No, nothing at all, thank you for asking though." He turned to Brian and said, "How have you been Brian?"

"I'm fine Dr. Champion. I'm very sorry about your brother."

"Thank you, I appreciate it. What was it I heard you saying about your father's friend having someone missing?"

"Oh no, not someone Dr. Champion, it was their dog Ebony. I guess his kids had been over to the neighbors who have a bunch of Halloween decorations. Ebony, that's their dog, just barked and barked at one of the decorations.

"One of the decorations . . . I don't understand what you mean," said Scott trying to assemble the pieces of this story together in his mind.

"Yeah, like mannequins' dressed up from horror movies, you know? I think he said Wolfman, Dracula, and Jason, and one the dad came up with himself, Ax-Man or something. Anyhow, their dog just went nuts over that one. Later that night Mrs. Russelton let Ebony outside and I guess she heard the dog yelp, and then the dog never came back. They all are really attached to the dog, so the next day they called the police. They came out and looked around and I think dad said they followed some footprints, that lead to a clearing and that's when they found the dog's tail; just her tail and a big bloody spot." Brian shrugged his shoulders and said, "That's all I know. Something or somebody ripped off their dog's tail and probably killed it."

"Where do the people with the Halloween decorations live Brian? Do you know?"

"Sure, I'll write it down for you." He reached across for a pad of paper on Coleen's desk and wrote for a minute handing the paper to Scott.

"Thanks Brian," he looked around the office and said, "Ok you two, get back to work. You're on the tax payer's time and you know how I feel about that."

He made his way to the door and pushed it open; taking in deep lungs full of fresh air, he walked toward the car where he saw Jon on the phone. He made his way around to the passenger side and got in at the same time Jon snapped the flip phone closed.

"So, how'd it go?"

Scott unfolded the paper and said, "I have a lead, let's go. You can fill me in on tomorrow while we drive. I think we just caught a break."

Jon and Scott could not miss the Petrucci's house; Brian was right when he said they had a lot of decorations.

"Wow, I bet this is something at night when it all lit up," Jon said in wonder. He pulled in the driveway and turned to Scott, "So why are we going to tell these people we're here?"

"I don't know yet, I guess we'll wing it."

"You wing it; I'm not good at wingin' unless it's with hot sauce and a side of blue cheese dressing," Jon had a lopsided grin on his face; and a break in the tension was welcome.

"Ha ha, what a career you'll have in comedy when you retire from detective work. When's that going to be again?"

"You should know you're going be my manager. You know, doctor, lawyer, Indian chief? That's me, the Indian chief."

"Who's the lawyer?" asked Scott as they both got out of the car.

"I wanted to be one, that's about as close as we're gonna get, and besides instead of cutting the profits three ways we can keep it at two."

"Yeah, that sounds like a lawyer, double spiff yourself," Scott replied smiling as they walked up the sidewalk to the front door.

"Seems kind of quiet doesn't it?" said Jon.

They reached the front door and Scott pushed the bell. They both could hear the *dinggg-donggg* inside. After a minute when no one answered, he rang it again with the same result.

"Let me go see if there is a car in the garage," said Jon. As he trotted over to the garage door, Scott rang the bell for a third and final time. By the time he turned to go back down the steps, Jon was back.

"No car in the garage," he glanced up the hill at the barn, "I didn't see any vehicles up there and it looks like the door is closed."

"Well, let's go take a look at this Halloween shabang while we're here," Scott said.

"Shabang? What the hell is a shabang?" Jon asked with a grin on his face.

"I have no idea, except my pop would say it in situations like this. I think this is a shabang."

They walked toward the back of the biggest display that had three four foot by eight foot sheets of plywood with the two end pieces at twenty-five degree angels; the back was painted black along with the wood braces holding the whole thing up. As they made their way toward the large display, where they assumed the figures were, they looked at the other decorations; the cemetery with styrofoam headstones, what appeared to be an old lard kettle transformed into a witch's caldron complete with a witch stirring her noxious brew. A huge spider web strung between two poles camouflaged with vines and twigs looked as though each section of the web had been hand tied. They also spotted two fog machines, torches secured in the ground ready to provide eerie flickering light and a whole host of Halloween favorites, jack-o'-lanterns, bats and ghosts suspended from trees with almost invisible fishing line, and, what appeared to be a sound system with two speakers hidden in hay bales scattered around the area.

"Wow, these people take Halloween seriously," said Jon as he took in all the details, "this had to take a while to put up."

"I had a med school buddy who considered Halloween a hobby and was constantly looking for weird or unusual stuff. I would guess this guy is the same, it's a hobby," responded Scott as he looked around taking in the whole scene.

They came to the front of the plywood, and both stopped short looking over what must be the main attraction to the Halloween theater in which they found themselves.

"Are you kidding me?" breathed Jon looking at Scott, "this is incredible. This guy is a real aficionado for all things Halloween. Look, there at the end," he said pointing in the opposite direction. They were standing about six feet away from Dracula and began making their way down towards the two end figures.

Suddenly it hit them stopping both in their tracks.

"Jesus, what the hell is that stench!" Jon asked, repulsed looking around. "Where's that coming from?" he said covering his nose and mouth with his hand. When Scott did not immediately answer Jon looked to his left and saw Scott backing up a tangible look of fear taking over his features. "What's wrong?" he said stepping back next to Scott.

"I just experienced that *exact* same smell in the autopsy room where the two bodies are; they didn't have the normal smell of decomposing human flesh," his eyes were moving rapidly over both figures, taking in all the details, and he stepped sideways down the line closer to the figure in the blue-black coveralls. The stench was much stronger there, overpowering and cloying. Jon could see Scott was concentrating his attention on the last figure.

"What is this? What's going on?" he sounded unnerved. Scott had begun to lean in, examining the figure.

"See, here . . . ," he had taken out a pen from his pocket and was pointing at several very large dark spots on the blue coveralls, ". . . here and here. I am positive those are bloodstains. Look on that sleeve; it's possible that's hair along the side, and something that looks like tissue. Do you see it?" As his gaze worked its way up the figure, he sucked in his breath in alarm. "Jon," he whispered, "look at the mouth, look . . . ,"

They easily identified the other figures as so much plastic and rubber, faux monsters. This one though, was different. The hands and face appeared supple with none of the rigid lines and staged expressions of the factory formed faces. The mouth was open, the head tilted back as though it was baying at the moon. The teeth appeared sold, shiny and very, very sharp. On the chin was a substance that seemed to have run out of that awful mouth and down the neck disappearing under the dark blue coveralls. It had the look of real blood. Not costume blood, but rather the glossy reddish-brown color of freshly dried blood that had not been long under the influence of sunlight and weather. They stared, unable to process all that they were seeing when suddenly a piercing, knife like pain struck them both in the form of a cacophony of noise. Wailing, howling, moaning and weeping. Screams of ungodly terror and pain. Both men grasped their head on either side, hands over their ears trying to stop the agonizing sound. It was then when they saw the fiend in front of them blink, and settle its cold, dead gaze on them. Both men staggered backwards and Scott fell to his knees, unable to bear the excruciating acid like stabbing in his brain. He crawled several feet, and then fell on his side rolling away and as he rolled, the pain lessened then finally stopped. He gingerly pulled his hands away from his ears expecting to see blood on them. Turning his head in the damp grass, he saw to his left, Jon, on his knees, his head down in front of him as if in prayer, as he looked up, they made eye contact and Scott struggled to his feet taking the several steps to Jon's side, putting a hand on his back.

"Are you all right?" he said in a trembling voice. Jon slowly dropped his shaking hands from his head and laid them flat on the ground on either side of his head keeping his forehead in the soft cool grass.

"Look at me Jon. Are you all right?"

Jon looked up ever so slowly, "We have to end this."

"We will, you know we will. But we need to leave this place, we need to leave now," Scott's voice became quiet, secretive, "I think we've stumbled on the trigger, I think *this* . . . ," he used his thumb to point back over his shoulder, ". . . is the trigger. We need to get away from here; it knows . . . *IT* knows we are aware of it. Get up now, we need to hurry," Jon struggled to his feet, grasping Scott's forearm to steady himself. As he began to turn toward it again, Scott jerked him back, "No, don't look over there, *it* wants you to. Start walking to the car, let's go."

Together they made their way back across the yard toward the car. No other vehicles had gone up or down the road, and everything seemed eerily quiet.

"Are you ok to drive?" asked Scott.

"Yeah, I can drive," Jon reached in his pocket and clumsily pulled out the keys.

By the time he got the key in the ignition, Scott was next to him slamming the door, "Let's roll then.

Jon jerked the car into reverse throwing up gravel, and with a quick look left and right over his shoulder, backed onto the dusty road. As they drove away, both remained mute for several minutes until finally Jon broke the silence. "We're looking for the portal and instead it seems like we found the trigger, is that what you think?"

"Yes, I do. It makes it even more important for us to find and destroy the portal. What's going on tomorrow? When are they able to bring the dog out to the shed?"

"Jerry said hopefully by noon, he'll call in the morning and give us an exact time. We can use the morning preparing ourselves and getting the holy items from Father Kaylan. We'll make it work Scott. We have to."

"Let's get back to the house then, and go over what our next move is," Scott said wearily. He thought a moment and continued, "It just occurred to me, do you think those people at that house are ok?"

"I don't know. I was just thinking about that too. I'm sure I can get a patrol car to go by later and see if there are lights, any activity.

"Maybe no one knows they're missing?"

"I'll Bing the address when we get home and see what I can find."

They did not know that they passed Army on their way back into town, and they had no way of knowing that even he was avoiding looking at the Ax-Man display. He could no longer convince himself that the constant movement of Ax-Man or the stench around it was something kids were doing. He remembered too well the same stench coming from his trunk the day he bought the mask on that bright Saturday not so very long ago. How odd it was that the song playing on his radio at that very moment made him suck in his breath and grip the wheel with a sense of unknown dread. He listened, his eyes unblinking, staring straight ahead, as the song rolled out of the speakers causing them to thrum with the beat of the base, the words unnerving him, making the hairs on the back of his neck bristle in fear.

You never listen to the voices inside
They fill your ears as you run to a place to hide
You're never sure if the illusion is real
You pinch yourself but the mem'ries are all you feel
Can you face the fire when you see me there
Can you feel the fire will you love me in the dark . . .
In the dark
Ah ah ah ah
In the dark."

CHAPTER 26

Anthony's alarm went off as it did every morning, eight minutes before his official get-out-of-bed time. Usually, he used that time to slowly wake and get ready for the day and wait for his radio to come on. Not today though, today he was immediately alert when his alarm woke him. He listened for the normal morning activity in the house; sounds of his mom getting breakfast ready for his dad. The clink of the lid on the coffee jar, the click of the cupboard door, the ring of a cast iron skillet being removed from its resting place, the rattle of the drawer that contained the spatulas, spoons, tongs and other utensils of cooking. What would follow was the intoxicating perfume of fresh brewed coffee, the mouth-watering smell of bacon cooking and the aroma of toasting bread. In the background, the radio would be playing the news and there would be the rustle of his dad shuffling the newspaper as he turned to the editorial page. All those sounds and smells that made it cozy, made it safe and made it home.

As the seconds passed, he realized that he was not experiencing any of those sensations and his brow furrowed in concern. He sat up in bed looking at the clock again, and though he did not realize it, his ears rose in the primeval pose of listening. Just as he was about to get out of bed and head downstairs it hit him; his dad was still on vacation and therefore must still be sleeping so Danni would not be fixing Army breakfast, she was probably just pouring herself a cup of tea and had orange juice over ice for Anthony. It was at that moment he heard the radio and realized he had been holding his breath; he let it out through parted lips and drew in a fresh air. In record time, he was out of bed, dressed and on his way down the steps and hallway to the kitchen. There on the kitchen counter was his OJ on ice and the toaster was just offering up his favorite toaster strudel, and yes, there was his mom drinking a cup of tea and leafing through *Better Homes and Gardens.*

"Hey," he said as Danni looked up.

"Morning honey, did you sleep ok?"

"Yeah I did," he picked up the juice and took a long swallow, "thanks mom that tastes good," he said putting the glass back on the counter.

He went to the toaster and put his pastry on a plate then went back and sat across the table from his mom.

As Danni sipped her tea, she looked up at her son and said, "Is Sammy coming over tonight? If he is I think I'll make tacos for dinner, I thought you guys would like that."

"Oh yeah, I forgot to ask you if it's ok. We want to . . . umm . . . make sure everything is ready for Halloween, you know, help dad?"

Danni chuckled quietly as she set her tea down, "Honey, I think everything is all set. Your dad really hasn't been out there the last couple of days, so I guess everything is ready," she closed the magazine and took another sip of her tea, "actually Anthony, now that I think about it, this is the first year that your father isn't running around with his last minute finishing touches. You and Sammy must have done everything to his satisfaction when you guys did the set up!" A buzzer went off in the laundry room and Danni rose from her chair. "Wait a second while I put the clothes in the dryer."

As Danni went to the laundry room off the kitchen, Anthony took the last bite of his strudel and stood to finish off the final two swallows of orange juice.

On the radio, the local news anchor voice brought everything to a standstill: *"And finally, last night local police responded to a 911 call from a city bus driver who spotted two bodies laying beside a fence on West Moreland Ave. A representative for the Officers who responded said that two males, known to be leaders in one of the city's most violent Hispanic gangs called La Raza, were found near an abandon building. A cause of death is under investigation, but one of the officers who responded to the call stated on condition of anonymity, that the bodies appeared to have been mauled. This follows a spate of disturbing occurrences in the last three weeks here in the city and in surrounding areas. The Chief of Detectives confirmed that no new information is available concerning the unexplained murders, but will release a statement when the corners office submits their reports. One reporter asked if they suspected any connection with the rash of murders that has plagued the area, but he declined to comment stating they had no reason to suspect a link."*

Danni heard what sounded like glass breaking on the kitchen floor, and rushed back into the kitchen where she found her son looking out the window with glass scattered around him.

"Anth! Are you Ok? Stand still honey, just wait," he turned to look at his mother, and what she saw on his face caused a knot of fear to tighten in her stomach. "What happened? Did something happen?" When he did not reply, she said with real concern, "Anthony, what *happened?*"

His voice sounded tight and shiny, "I . . . I guess, it must have slipped out of my hand," he started to bend down, but Danni stopped him.

"Just wait a sec, let me sweep up around you," she grabbed the broom and dustpan from behind the door and swept around her son's feet as he stood still staring out the window. From the kitchen window, he could see down the yard to the where Ax-Man was, he could see it looked different. He knew *it* had been out stalking last night and had killed those two men, he was positive. He gazed back at his mom sweeping up the glass around him and felt afraid for her, afraid for his dad.

"Mom, let me sweep that up, it's my fault."

"No, I'm almost done. You're going to miss the bus, go brush your teeth," she looked up at him and smiled, "and you forgot to comb your hair, it looks like a scarecrow kiddo. Go on now."

He stepped out of the circle where he had been standing, and started toward the bathroom. When he came back, his mom had put the broom away and she had the damp mop out picking up any small pieces.

"Hurry Anth, I can hear the bus," Danni said bending over looking closely at the floor as she mopped.

"Sorry about the mess mom," he said picking up his book bag from the counter

"It's ok honey, as long as you didn't get cut. Just be more careful next time."

"I will," he leaned over and kissed his mother on the cheek.

Since he had gotten older Danni usually had to kiss her son first to get one back, so his kiss caught her off guard and as she glanced up to ask what the occasion was, she noticed what appeared to be a small round amulet on a silver chain that had fallen out of the front of his shirt. "Where did you get that Anthony?" she asked curiously, "I haven't seen it before," he had not realized it had come out from under his shirt and quickly reached up to tuck it back in. "What is that Anthony? It looks so unusual, let me see it again."

"Sammy and I both got one at the school fair. I think it's some kind of astrological sign or something," just then he heard the squeal of the bus brakes and the horn. "Gotta go mom, there's the bus!" He turned to go out the back door and as he left, he made sure he turned the latch to the lock position when he pulled it shut. As he ran toward the bus, he could see Sammy's anxious face pressed up against one of the small windows, because Anthony had not been at the end of the driveway. The doors creaked open and as Anthony disappeared inside the bus, Sammy's face disappeared from the bus window.

Back in the yard, yellow eyes shifted slowly, like a camera panning a scene. They stopped briefly at the bus, but as it pulled away, the narrow, deadly yellow eyes set their sights on the house bathed in early morning light.

Jon had slept until nearly eight-fifteen on Friday morning and had awakened to a quiet house. When he came out of his room, he realized that Scott was still sleeping so he made an executive decision to run cold water into the antique steel coffee pot and bring it to a boil. The pot had to come to a boil so that the water would be forced up an aluminum tube, spill over the top and cascade down into the small basket full of fresh coffee grounds to percolate. Antique or not, it made great coffee. He sat at the kitchen table with an empty mug in front of him thinking about the day to come, anxious to get started with the cadaver dog over at Jigs' shed.

In addition, last night he had called in a favor with an old friend who scheduled the patrol cars, and he had been able to arrange for a unit to go out by the Petrucci residence several times. He had received a phone call by eight-thirty that evening telling him that there were indeed people, a family of three, and the boy apparently had a friend over for dinner because they had taken him home by seven o'clock. Jon had relayed this information to Scott and they both felt a sense of relief, at least temporarily. Jon could not help but think that this family was unknowingly living on the same property with some unnamed, inconceivable evil entity that somehow had been summoned through the gates of Hell into this time continuum. All that had happened, flashed strobe like behind his eyes like the old trick of drawing progressive pictures on cards and thumbing through them rapidly to make them move, making them come to life. That information rolled around his brain wanting to make sense; he wanted to put all the pieces in the correct location but there were so many pieces and the edges kept morphing and blurring just enough to prevent him from pressing them into place and make a complete picture.

The toilet flushed, the sound startling him in the silence of the house, and he pushed his chair back rising to get another mug and fill them both strong hot coffee from the antique pot. The soft padding of slippered feet came down the hallway as Jon finished filling the mugs.

"Hey, that coffee smells good," said Scott in a sleep raspy voice, scrubbing his face with his hands, which made a scratching noise as he rubbed over the stubble of beard on his face.

"Yep it does," Jon quipped, "and just so you know, whatever happens today, when this is over this coffee pot goes where ever I go."

Scott chuckled as he sat down in the chair next to where Jon had set a cup of steaming coffee on the table. He blew over the rim on the hot liquid cooling it just enough to take a quick sip. Jon settled in the chair also taking a careful swallow of the steaming coffee, and then sat with his hands around the hot ceramic of the mug. Silence surrounded them, the only sound was the click, click, click of the round, large faced battery powered clock that hung above the sink.

Scott was looking out the window to his left as a slight breeze stirred up leaves in the yard. "Cooled off quite a bit last night," he said.

"Yeah, I looked at that over sized thermometer you have on the porch and it said forty-five degrees. I read in the paper it's supposed to be a cool weekend." The silence drew out between them, each lost in their own thoughts of what the next two days might bring.

As Scott continued to sip from his cup, Jon broke the silence. "I need to stop over at my house and get some warmer clothes. You know, it occurred to me when I woke up this morning that I haven't been home in almost a week."

"Has it really been a week?" Scott responded, "so much has happened that I hadn't thought about that." He sipped his coffee again, setting it down then and looking at Jon. "I'm glad you've been here Jon, really glad."

"Me too. I think it might be divine intervention that we go through this together. If you hadn't come across me outside Jigs' shed . . . ," his eyes became vacant for a moment, his mind traveling to another place, and then he blinked and came back to the present. ". . . God only knows what would have happened to me, or what I might be by now."

Scott drew a deep breath in and blew it out slowly through is slightly parted lips, all the time running his left index finger in a small circle on the side of his mug. His eyes fixed straight ahead, lost in thought, until at last he said, "How odd it all seems while we sit here in our sweat pants, drinking coffee from my twenty-five year old percolator at the start of what appears to be a beautiful fall day. If I had not found you, what would I have made of the bodies that would have inevitably turned up at the morgue? How would I have handled the murder of my brother? There is a hand guiding us, of that I am sure, and I can't help but wonder, are there others out there? Counterparts so to speak, that *are* also being lead down a path to an ultimate destination that will stop this madness? Will we meet them? Or do we already know them and not realize it?" Scott leaned back in his chair, pushing up the sleeves on his sweater to his elbows and crossing his arms.

Jon's eyes were fixed, focused; there but not there, lost in thought. His mind was busily sorting and reevaluating events, moving quickly over each piece of information they had discovered, quickly putting odds and ends of their experiences together like a Rubik's Cube master trying to beat a record.

Suddenly he said, "Scott, the trigger; we found the trigger yesterday do you agree?"

"Yes, I do."

"Our counterparts then, could they be the husband and wife—the Petrucci's. They must suspect something, they must. Whoever put all the work into the elaborate Halloween decorations, and let's assume it is the husband, must realize there is something very wrong with one of his props."

"I follow your line of thought Jon, but how do we prove that? We can't just saunter up to the front door, knock and say, *Hi, we've found a portal to Hell and we think you have the trigger right over there in your front yard. Can we come in and talk?* Kook-A-Doodle-Do, where are the strait jackets, that's what they'll be thinking."

"I know that Scott, we've just gotta think it though, that's all."

"We don't have time now, we just don't," said Scott as his phone began to ring. He got up and answered it and Jon heard him say, "That should work for us fine, yep, ok. We'll see you then." As he came back around the corner from the small alcove where his phone sat, Jon had a *so what is going on* look on his face. "That was Jerry. We're on for this afternoon at one-thirty."

"Why so late? That won't give us enough time," Jon complained.

"It is what it is Jon. Let's figure out a way to maximize the time we have. We need to call Father Kaylan and tell him we'll be over soon."

"Ok, you do that and I'll get the gym bag and the lighters."

"Do you have your cross on?"

"Does the Pope wear a pointy hat?"

"That is such an old cliché. Can't you do better than that?"

Jon thought for just a moment, and then said, "Does the devil have a pointy tail?"

"I see what you're getting at. Let's stick with the Pope's hat," he looked up at the clock. "By the time we get dressed and get out the door it will be eleven. We really should eat some breakfast. Do you want to just do a Mickey D's drive through?"

"Yep, let's do that. If something unexpected happens today and we get attacked by some gut ripping blue faced monstrosity, I want to have lots and lots of gooey cheese, butter, bacon, greasy hash browns and salt in my bloodstream, maybe the devil doesn't like his meals with too much salt and grease. Just a thought."

Scott threw his head back and laughed aloud, a belly whopping, table-thumping laugh until he wiped the tears from his eyes. "Buddy, between what we've eaten and the booze we've soaked ourselves in the last few days, we're probably both one big, bad gas bomb just waiting to be set off and destroy this part of the state! Mickey D's it is, double cheese and salt, and don't spare the grease. Let's go."

They got up from the table taking their cups to the sink. Scott reached over, turned the burner with the coffee pot completely off, and moved the pot over to one of the other burners so that it would cool enough to take out the grounds before they left.

"Can we heat that back up later?" Jon asked.

"We can. It will probably be strong enough to stand a spoon straight up in, but then again, we may need it."

"Hey, we'll just thin it with some Jack. That will dilute the caffeine so it won't keep us up tonight."

"You are most brilliant my friend."

"I know. I try to be humble but, well, it just spills out before I can stop it."

"Humanity will miss you if we screw this up. Let's get ready to go."

They took turns in the bathroom, both men opting for jeans. Scott had hiking boots that would keep his feet warm and offered Jon a pair of boots. He declined telling Scott he was choosing instead his tennis shoes for a quicker get away. Scott grabbed the gym bag with the two stick lighters, picked up his keys and as a last thought turned on a small light in the living room. He did not want to come home to a dark house. Go figure.

৯০ ৯০ ৯০ ৯০ ৯০ ৯০ ৯০ ৯০ ৯০ ৯০ ৯০ ৯০

The two men were laughing as they pulled away from the Mickey D's drive through. The girl who took their order was breathless after repeating it back: Six bacon egg and cheese biscuits; six hash browns, two cinnamon melts, one McSkillet Burrito w/sausage and two McCafe' Mocha's. The gangly young man who passed bag after bag of food to them and one cardboard coffee cup cutouts kept looking into the rear of Scott's car expecting the front line of an area football team to be sitting in the back seat. As Scott put his bank debit card

284

back into his wallet he imagined he would be getting a call any minute from the fraud division of the bank, checking to see if his card had been stolen. That was when he and Jon started laughing.

By the time they pulled into the church parking lot everything was gone but their coffee. Jon gathered up all the food wrappings and bags and balled them into one bulging mass.

"I'm stuffed," moaned Scott rubbing his stomach after he had put the car in park.

"Me too, really, really full. I guess instead of ghost busters we're gut busters."

"Well if I bust a gut it ain't gonna be pretty boyoh. Grab the bag and let's go."

As they got out of the car and Scott slammed his door shut, Jon passed gas loud, long and robust. He met Scott's startled look by raising his eyebrows in mock surprise and shrugged his shoulders.

"May God forgive you," Scott said.

"Buddy, I know God will forgive me, I just hope you will after being stuck with me all day."

The front door of the church opened and from the dim interior stepped Father Kaylan. Scott waved in recognition as they started up the sidewalk, Father Ralph waiting patiently until they reached him. The vicar then turned and they followed him into the dimly lit church. Candles flickered on sconces along the wall and two large pillar candles burned on carved three-foot holders on the dais. It was very quiet, only the sound of their footfalls on the carpet, and somewhere in the background the hiss of one of the candle wicks.

"Wait here," Father Kaylan said in a quiet voice.

He continued to the sacristy that was to the right of the altar and the door opened silently on well-oiled hinges. He reappeared in a moment with two jackets draped over his left arm and a tray covered in a white cloth. As he reached the two men, he continued in the same quiet voice, "I need you both to stand on my right, please, and follow me up the steps."

They nodded, and followed Father Ralph up the three steps to the altar table covered in white linen. He laid the jackets on his left, and the tray in the middle, folded his hands in supplication and leaned forward touching his head to the altar. After a moment, he stood back up and turned to face the two men whose faces had taken on a solemn expression as they realized and understood the importance of what was taking place. Father picked up the jackets and handed one to each man.

"Please put these on now."

The soft tonal sound of his voice was mesmerizing somehow to both Scott and Jon, and they obeyed without question. The jackets were light, made of nylon and as Father Kaylan had promised, he had sewn pockets on the inside left of each jacket. Scott set down the small gym bag by his feet, and after they put on the jackets, Father bent to pick up the bag. He made the sign of the cross before the small bag then set it on the altar and removed the pristine white cloth covering the tray. There, laid out neatly, reverently, were twelve white tapered candles, which looked to be eight inches long. Next to them were two quart sized square containers, much like a milk carton because they had what appeared to be sealed spouts. One contained holy salt and the other holy water. Finally, the two aspersoriums filled with holy water seemed to shimmer in the light cast by the candles.

Father Kaylan turned to the men, made the sign on the cross, and said, "In the name of The Father, The Son and The Holy Spirit."

"Amen," responded both Jon and Scott.

In a quiet voice filled with love, Father began to pray, "We ask you Lord, to protect these men in their quest to purge the evil that is in our midst. We humbly ask you Lord, to bless the items we offer to you on the altar. Empower them with your white light so that the evil one will flee from their sight. Show these men, your servants, the way to the light through the truth of your word and protect them with your love. In the name of Jesus Christ our Lord, Amen."

From the altar, Father Kaylan picked up a small, round gold container two inches in diameter by two inches high with the initials CHR on the top; it looked like a thimble of sorts, and what it contained was Holy Chrism oil.

He dipped his right thumb in the oil and then on Jon's forehead he made the sign of the cross and said softly, "In the name of the Father, Son and Holy Spirit." He repeated the blessing on Scott and looked each directly in their eyes, seeing into their souls. Finally, he put the items from the tray into the gym bag and zipped it shut.

In the still quiet of St. Mary Di Rosa Church with the smell of balsam and olive oil and the faint sound of hissing candles surrounding them, they moved toward their destiny.

CHAPTER 27

The day at school had seemed endless because of the anticipation and apprehension coursing through their blood streams like fire and ice. Lunch was a Halloween smorgasbord; Ghost burgers, witches brew milk, skeleton bone French fries and goblin sugar cookies. All the children were loud and rambunctious, but not rowdy. A number of friends came to the lunch table where Sammy and Anthony sat and said they were looking forward to coming over to the Petrucci house for Trick or Treat. Both boys put on their best faces, nodded and smiled and said things like, *ok brother, see you then* or *yea, we're excited too.* When the bell finally rang, they were the first out the door and onto the bus.

Each boy swung a book bag on his shoulder as the bus pulled away with a rumble. It was a beautiful October day with cobalt blue skies and a sun that was more orange than white. As Sammy started up the gravel driveway, he realized that Anthony was standing still.

"What's wrong?"

"Do you see it? Across the road there, see the grass moving?" Anthony said his voice almost a whisper.

Before looking across the road, he shot a quick glance up toward the Halloween decorations. He could see the dark coveralls of Ax-Man. Looking back in the direction where Anthony was staring he concentrated hard to what Anthony was staring at.

"I don't see anything bro. What did you see?"

Anthony hesitated, scanning the field across the road then turned back to Sammy. "I can't really explain it Sammy. I have a feeling we're being watched by something. I've noticed it before, like there's something across the road in the weeds . . . just watching."

"I've had that feeling too," said Sammy, speaking quietly, "but it's not what I see, it's what I feel. Sometimes at home, even if I just look out the window I *feel* like something is watching our house. I try not to look out 'cause it creeps me out.

He looked across the road for a moment and turned to Anthony, "It's probably just a raccoon or something. There's lots around my dad says."

"Yeah, you're probably right, just a raccoon," Anthony turned away from the road. "Come on; let's get up to the house.

The house was empty when they walked in, and Anthony began calling, "Mom, dad! We're home!" When there was no immediate reply, he felt a sharp bite of worry but spied a note on the message board. He quickly moved over to the board and pulled the note from between the pushpin and the cork.

Anthony

We went to Walmart. Be back by five.
Call on the cell if you need us. Love Mom

Anthony turned and said to Sammy, "Mom and dad won't be home 'til five. Let's get to the barn and get as much done as we can before they come back."

Both boys raced to Anthony's room, Sammy throwing his bag on the bed, stripping off his shirt and digging for a hoodie from his bag. He stuffed his school shirt in a ball back into his bag. Anthony grabbed a hoodie from his closet as he tossed his shirt into a hamper, and then retrieved the charcoal and the *Devil's Trap* from the hiding place making a beeline for the barn.

As they slid back the left side of the door, the squeaking wheels echoing in the barn, Sammy noticed something odd outside of the barn and said, "Hey, what's the hole over there?"

Anthony glanced back over his shoulder and replied, "Nothing really. I think dad is getting ready to put up a fence or something."

"Oh. It looks kinda big," Sammy remarked, and with that, they dismissed the hole that was a grave.

The late afternoon sun spilling in the door cast a blush of light into the barn. The boys quickly moved the bales out of the way; each took a corner of the tarp, pulled it toward the other end, and folded it into thirds. The dark ring stared back at them as Anthony pulled out the charcoal and the *Devil's Trap.*

He nodded at the ring and said, "I need to get started."

"I'll be right here bro," Sammy assured him.

As Anthony stared at the *Devil's Trap* ingraining the first strokes in his mind, Sammy moved off towards the back of the barn, looking around and up, thinking . . . thinking.

The only sound in the barn was the soft tap . . . tap . . . ssheee of Anthony drawing on the old floorboards and the hushed drawn out squeak of the running horse weather vane on the peak of the roof.

Sammy walked along the back wall of the barn until he came to the tack room. There he saw an old wringer washer in the corner with the name *Satonia* etched on one of the wooden slats. There were also various tools, saws, screwdrivers, hammers, a scythe a spool of nylon rope a . . . .

Wait a minute, wait just a stinkin' minute. He went over, picked up the spool of rope, and read what it said on the side, black twisted nylon rope—then glanced back over at the ringer washer. *Maybe, just maybe it will work* he thought rapidly. In his mind, he could see how it *could* work. He went over to the old ringer washer and inspected it. The tub was rusted in spots, but when he rapped it with his knuckles, it seemed sound. He ran his hands around the wood frame that held the two heavy solid rubber rollers. The wood was very dirty but it was solid, and though the rollers were cracked, it was only superficial. *I'll have to take out one of the rollers,* he reasoned, *but it could work . . .*

On the other end of the barn, Anthony was not aware of time passing, or of the fading light. It was with single-minded determination that he continued with the drawing, which now seemed seared in his brain. His lines were no longer tentative, but sure and strong, the corners sharp, the symbols accurate. He did not hurry or rush but continued steadily without pause. In the background he could hear Sammy moving something, could hear him grunting with effort and then the sound of hammering. He started to come back to the *now* when heard a voice.

"Anth, I think your mom and dad just pulled in. We have to get everything covered before they come up," exclaimed Sammy excitedly; his comment was met with stony silence, and he said again, "Anthony!"

Anthony came up then, up and out of the place he had gone to and he saw that it was nearly dark outside, and he heard the car doors close and the sound of his mother's voice.

"Anthony! Sammy! We're home. Boys are you at the barn?" called Danni.

Anthony stood up blinking his eyes and shaking his head to clear his mind. Sammy stood on the far side of the circle looking towards Anthony, and then made an executive decision.

"Go to the door and tell them we'll be right down," Sammy said quietly, "you've gotta buy us some time."

Anthony ran to the door skidding to a stop, his hand over his head waving, "Hey, we're up here! Do you need help carrying anything?

"No honey, we're ok," his mother called back, "we'll be eating in about thirty minutes so come down and get cleaned up."

"Ok mom, we'll be right there," replied Anthony and he felt relief flood through his body as he saw his dad go through the garage, his arms full of bags.

He turned to Sammy and said, "Ok, we've got a couple minutes, let's get this covered up."

Sammy stood on the other side of the circle where he was staring at down at what Anthony had been working on, the *Devil's Trap.*

"Geez," Sammy said astonishment in his voice; he looked up at Anthony, his eyes wide, "Anth, how'd you do that?"

It was then that Anthony really looked at the drawing, stunned by what he saw, by what he had drawn.

"I don't know Sammy. It just came out of me," the boys stayed like that for a moment, and then moved in unison, each grabbing a corner of the blue tarp and pulling it over the drawing. Once again, they scattered hay over everything and wrestled the bales into place. As Anthony straightened up, he noticed something sitting in the middle of the back wall.

"What's that?" he asked turning toward his friend.

Sammy shrugged and replied, "I'll explain later. If your dad comes up, will he notice it?

"I dunno. I'm pretty sure he won't come up though."

Just then, the lights outside the garage came on and they heard Army's voice calling them both to dinner.

They made a dash for the door, sliding it closed and flipping the latch into place. Sammy took the lead on their race toward the kitchen, his nose in the air sniffing dinner.

"Tacos!" he yelled over his shoulder, "I smell tacos!" It brought a huge smile to Anthony's face as he raced behind his friend.

Tacos and cheese. That is what two best friends should be worried about on a Friday night sleep over. Tacos and cheese.

It was 1:30 p.m. on Friday afternoon, November 30 and Scott and Jon were the only two people at the Seederly residence.

Scott had walked to the shed and tentatively unlatched the doors and propped them open. He then walked to his car, sat with the door open, and used his cell to try to reach Jerry DelTorro, the trainer of the cadaver dog. Jon came over to the car and stood with his arms resting along the top of the door.

"Anything?" he asked irritably.

"No, and I've already left two messages so don't ask again. Just be patient, if something else has come up he has to do that first. It's a civilian team Jon, you know that."

"I know, I know. I'm just anxious to get started." He was silent for several long moments. "If there are bodies here and we both believe that to be true, do you think the dog can find them?"

Scott stood up from the car seat, arching his back, stretching out, and then rolled his shoulders. He snapped his phone shut and slipped it into his jeans pocket, and then looked at Jon choosing his words carefully.

"It depends on the dog," said Scott, "that's why they pair them up with permanent handlers. The scent of decomposing human bodies remains for a long time, and the dogs are trained to react only to that smell. Slipping into his Medical Examiner voice, he continued to explain. You see, because they appear nowhere in nature, the odors, the gases, given off by decomposing human remains are like," he stopped for a moment, looking up at the sky, trying to think of the best way to explain the process, "let's say ribbons of color. Imagine all human scent is blue, but all various shades of blue. When the dog picks up a shade of blue it will follow it to the source. Again, the dog is trained to pick up that scent only, and ignore all others. I know Jerry has been with his dog for six years or more, so I feel confident that if there's something here, we'll find it."

Just then, a black Jeep turned into the driveway, the gravel crunching and popping underneath the wheels. Scott stepped away from his car door and Jon pushed it shut as they started toward the Jeep. The driver's door swung open, and Jerry DelTorro stepped out nodding towards Jon and Scott, and then moved to open the back door. Out jumped a beautiful bright-eyed Golden Retriever that eagerly loped onto the grass running in a circle, then stopped and sat looking up at Jerry.

Scott put his hand out and as the two men shook, he said with total sincerity, "Thanks for coming Jerry," he turned toward the dog and said, "and you too, Strider." Strider responded by thumping his tail vigorously on the ground as his ears perked up and he panting happily. "Jerry, this is Jon Wendels."

After handshakes all around, Jon squatted down in front of Strider. "Well buddy, are you ready to help us today?" Strider thumped his tail all the harder.

"Sorry I'm late Scott," Jerry apologized, "I had a phone call and learned that after I leave here we have to drive to Creighton. They have a child who has been missing for six days and rescue hasn't come up with anything so we're going to take a run at it for them. So, I read the file on this site and my understanding is we are going to concentrate on the shed over there?" he motioned with his head to his left towards the shed.

"That's it, Scott confirmed, "what do you need us to do?"

"You can come over, but I need you to stay near me and remain quiet while Strider does his job, ok?" Jon and Scott nodded. "Good. Then let's go."

Jerry walked forward and motioned with his hand in a sweeping motion, "Strider come. Heel."

Strider ran to catch up to Jerry then trotted obediently along at his right side. As they approached the shed, Jerry signaled with his left hand to Jon and Scott to hold their position. Jerry stopped and surveyed the area as Strider stood attentively beside him, his ears up and alert, eyes unblinking, nose twitching unceasingly.

Jerry swept his arm forward and said in a deep authoritative voice, "Go out—track"

The dog immediately responded, nose to the ground, running the area. Jon and Scott realized quickly that the dog, much as forensic personnel do, was running what they call a *grid*, which simply meant breaking down an area into quadrants, and working one entire quadrant from side to side.

As Strider approached the open doors to the shed, he came to a complete stop.

"Go inside," commanded Jerry.

Instead of going inside to investigate, which would have been normal, the dog stood for a moment with his ears turned forward then backed several steps away and began working the grid again; the grid minus the shed. They watched in silence as the minutes ticked by, Strider spending more and more time in the right two quadrants finally settling on the area directly around the shed. Oddly, Strider ignored the back; he focused on small two-foot sections on each end and about four feet in the front.

"Strider, come."

The dog obediently trotted over to Jerry and sat down, panting heavily, his tongue hanging out of his mouth like a piece of liver.

"Scott, that's going to have to be a wrap for us, we need to leave so we can make it to Creighton."

Jon looked at his watch and realized it was 2:45 p.m. He and Scott walked over to where Jerry and Strider waited, as Jerry gave Strider a treat.

"I can't say with complete certainty that Strider had any direct hits," he said, "but I can tell you *something* is going on around the perimeter of that shed. I have never seen him refuse to canvas an area . . . never. I would concentrate on the shed."

"Thanks Jerry," said Scott, "we at least know where we can focus now, and I agree with you, I believe our answers are here too, we just have to find them."

The men shook hands all around and Jon squatted down and looked Strider in the eyes and said more to himself than the dog, "What scared you about the shed buddy?" he reached out and rubbed the dog between his ears, "What scared you?"

Jerry walked to his Jeep and opened the back door so Strider could jump in and both men watched until he had pulled away before they spoke.

"Should we go look inside the shed?" Jon asked.

"Do you feel up to it?"

"Would it matter if I didn't? We have to go inside and take a look around; we have to find out what made Strider afraid."

Scott nodded his head, "We better get started then, we don't have that much light left."

They both slowed as they approached the shed, not stopping and then walked through the open double doors.

The place was full of junk and because of Jon's demand of an ongoing investigation, none of it had gone to the estate sale. To the left along the side wall was a workbench with tools all over the top; behind the workbench was a pegboard loaded with pliers, hammers, brushes, wire, screwdrivers and many other hand tools. The back wall was shelves full of still more junk. A joiner/planer, a radial arm saw and a bike that hung on the wall. The opposite side wall had an old mower still more shelves and, oddly out of place, a neatly folded stack of black plastic tarps. Jon walked to the center where a chain dangled from a four-foot fluorescent light. He pulled the chain and one of the two bulbs struggled to emit a weak light in the dim interior.

"Let's each take a side so we can canvas it more thoroughly," suggested Jon.

Scott nodded his head and moved left to the workbench, while Jon took the opposite end. They each pulled from their back pocket, a small halogen flashlight and switched them on. The beams flickered eerily on the walls, as the interior grew rapidly darker. They looked carefully, slowly, making mental notes on what would need more attention tomorrow in better light. The sun had dipped much lower in the sky, and Scott had moved away from the workbench to the back wall flashing his light into the corner noticing what appeared to be a 6 inch round black plastic pipe running from the floor through the ceiling; he focused his beam on the opposite corner and saw an identical pipe there. As he leaned in closer to the wall, he accidentally pushed against a garden hose causing part of it to begin falling off the hanger. As he turned trying to stop the garden hose from completely unraveling, he noticed that the 2x4 seemed loose. As he ran his light to the left towards the post, he saw a coil of rope on it, and stepped over to pull it down. Something about it did not look right, and then his light caught the glint of the pulley hanging underneath the top 2x4. He ran his hand along it, curling his fingers in behind the wood and pulling it forward. The post began to rotate out along with one of the 2x4s the motion causing Jon to turn and focus his beam on the area. Both men stared as the unit moved silently, smoothly out.

"What the hell is it?" Jon wondered aloud.

Scott hesitated a moment, then put the end of the flashlight in his teeth and ran the rope in his hand through the pulley "It looks like a crane of some kind." His eyes followed the rope to the floor where he noticed the material used was not plywood, but strangely, poplar boards.

"To lift . . . what?"

"Maybe not to lift, but to lower," Scott said his eyes widening in understanding as he took a step closer.

Suddenly the overhead light went out and they were plunged into darkness.

CHAPTER 28

Dee pushed the button on the slot machine to play her thirty lines of pennies, or ninety cents, and Maureen sat further down the row playing Treasure Island on her penny machine. Maureen had hit for four-hundred and fifty dollars, and Dee for only seventy-five dollars so she was pumping her winnings into the Treasure Island machine hoping to hit big.

Like many senior citizens, they liked to gamble and at least twice a month made the seventy-mile trip to Wheeling Downs to spend the afternoon and evening joyfully playing their 'fun' money on the penny machines and occasionally hitting a nickel slot if they felt lucky. Usually around five o'clock they would take a dinner break and decide how much longer they would 'stay and play.' It was almost five now and Dee was getting hungry, so with high anticipation, she ran her next three lines of thirty and when there was no payout, she stood up and stretched. The casino was beginning to get busy and if they left these machines now it was a certainty that someone else would jump on them immediately. She looked down the row at Maureen who glanced up and smiled rubbing her stomach in a circle, their signal for dinnertime. Maureen stood taking her point's card from the machine.

"Are you ready then?" asked Dee.

"I am. I hate to leave this machine though, I have that feeling that it's about to hit."

"You always have that feeling," laughed Dee.

"True. But never more so than when you hit and I don't," Maureen answered moving away from the Treasure Island machine.

"Buffet or menu tonight?" Dee said raising an eyebrow.

"Hummm, menu I think. The salmon is calling my name."

"Salmon it is. Then let's swim on over there girl."

With a final fleeting glance at the uncooperative Treasure Island mega bucks machine, they moved away with the ease of a couple who had been together most of their adult lives, never for a moment knowing that a dark force was moving ever closer.

CHAPTER 29

Anthony, stuffed to the gills with tacos, fired up his computer. God only knew what was happening with Sammy, he had been in the bathroom a *long* time and the fan was running. Unconsciously Anthony kept touching the carved medallion beneath his t-shirt, the exact same medallion Sammy wore, *King Solomon's Silver Seal, The Fifth Pentacle of Mars.*

He heard the toilet flush and the sound of water running in the sink, and then the door opened and out came Sammy in his sweat pants and t-shirt, which was the boys' normal garb for sleeping.

"You ok?" Anthony asked his eyes wide.

"I think that little bit of cheese I ate is working on me."

"Little bit! Are you kidding me Sammy? I think you ate a whole pack!"

"Did not!"

"Did too! Now shut it, we have some stuff I want to look up again."

He keyed in some strokes on the Bing toolbar and within a minute was at the site they had seen before about *The Fifth Pentacle of Mars.*

"Here it is. Listen to this. *The seal protects its bearer from demons and dark forces, and submits them to do as he may command. It is associated with courage.*"

Sammy was standing behind Anthony now, reading along with him. "I could use some courage I think, how 'bout you?"

"Yeah, me too," Anthony said looking up at Sammy. "We're still going to call it out tomorrow right? Like we talked about?"

The silence drew out long, neither boy saying anything, until finally Sammy's voice filled the quiet. "We have to. You know we do. I hope this courage thing works 'cause when I think about that thing in the yard, I feel like I could pee my pants. I told you I put an extra line of salt around my house didn't I?"

"Twice."

"I heard my mom and dad talking last night. I guess your mom and dad are going over to our house for drinks after Trick or Treat."

"Ok, and?"

"It could be our chance. One of the things that we could say tomorrow when we call him out is we will be alone at the barn around ten. What do you think?"

Anthony was lost in thought for a moment, tapping his thumb absently on the corner of the computer keyboard. "It might work. It we say it right, it just might work. Dad usually wants to get everything set to go in the morning. Then he and mom spend the afternoon making the sloppy Joes, punch and chips and stuff. While he's doing that I can finish the *Devil's Trap* and then we can call him out."

"Ok. That will give me time to finish my thing."

"What is your 'thing' Sammy?"

"You'll see if it works."

The clock downstairs rang ten and the boys heard Army on his nightly rounds making sure doors and windows were locked while Danni called up stairs.

"Do you boys need anything before we go to bed?

"No," they both called in unison.

"Lights out in thirty minutes!" When they did not immediately answer, she called out again, "Got it boys?"

"Got it," their combined reply floated down the steps.

"G'nite then, love you."

A few minutes later Anthony logged off the computer turned off the light and went to sit next to Sammy on the bottom bunk bed by the window. After their vision adjusted to the dark, they watched out across the yard, their eyes searching for any movement. The moon was full tonight and the light it cast was eerie and pale making things appear silver and gray.

Then suddenly, *it* was standing underneath the bedroom window, standing away from the line of blessed salt surrounding the house, standing there looking up with its yellow eyes burning brightly; evil orbs, vile and insidious, eyes adrift in a sea of blood.

The boys sat frozen, unblinking, hearts pounding . . . pounding. Suddenly *it* turned and with inhuman speed loped across the yard in a weird unnatural gate that was profoundly unnerving to witness, and they watched, wild eyed, as the darkness swallowed the abomination.

They sat together for a long time, afraid to move, afraid somehow, it could still see them.

They prayed for courage.

The glass-packs Jon had installed rumbled like low thunder as the old Dodge Dart pulled into the rest stop on Interstate 79. It was after 11:30 pm and the Dart was the only car in the lot as they swung around back, away from the lights. They left the car running and the heater turned up to keep the chill away. A ball of light erupted from the end of a small lighter, and then went out leaving a faint glow in its stead.

Out of the darkness like a flash of lightening, a grotesque face strobed for a nanosecond across the windshield as glass exploded into the driver's side door.

In the space of time between heartbeats, both people were yanked through the broken glass, their skin peeled off in chunks like an overripe banana. Small bits and pieces left behind on the glass and grass joined the sticky trail of blood. The low thunder of the glass packs rumbled on straining in the end to maintain their throaty dominance in that dark place.

At last, they too died and finally, mercifully, the night became still.

CHAPTER 30

The sudden darkness caught both men off guard and they both yelled, "Hey! Hey!" into the sinister gloom that enclosed them. The beams from their pocket flashlights flickered from wall to wall, roof to floor in a staccato dance.

"Jon! Are you ok? Are-you-ok?" Scott's voice sounded jagged with alarm.

"I'm fine!" Jon's voice came from the left.

Scott shined the light onto Jon's face, which was ashen.

"Let's get out of here now!" he rasped.

As they made a run for the door, Scott cracked his hip against the corner of the workbench; a white-hot pain flashed down his leg. Jon was out the door first, turning back toward Scott and backpedaling.

"Hurry . . . hurry!" He pin-wheeled his arm toward the car as Scott limped toward him. Jon ran back, grabbed Scott's arm and pulled it around his shoulder. They staggered toward the car realizing that the sun had set, the moon was low in the east, and that somehow they had been in the shed so much longer than they imagined.

"Keys . . . get the keys out of your pocket!" Jon said his voice tight with fear.

Scott slipped his hand into his front jeans pocket and pulled out the keys handing them over to Jon. He leaned against the door, the pain in his hip throbbing as Jon fumbled with the keys, his hands shaking badly.

"Just push the button," he said his voice no more than a croak.

With a *click-click* the doors unlocked, Jon grabbed the passenger door and pulled it open sliding Scott inside. He rounded the front of the car and made a dive for the driver's seat and in one fluid motion had the key in the ignition, the car started, pulled into gear with a dust cloud following them down the road.

"You ok?" Jon asked glancing over at Scott.

"I think so. I just cracked my hip on the damn corner of that work bench and gave myself a hip pointer."

"In less than seven days we're running away from that place again like scared kids."

"Well, I may not be a kid, but I am scared," Scott turned in the seat and looked at Jon. "I got into this because I wanted to write a paper for the coroner's Newsmax page. How I got from there to here, I'll never know.

"We have to regroup and get out there early tomorrow. What the hell were we thinking about not taking our bag in with us?"

"I guess we just got caught up in the moment."

"Yeah, and it could have got us killed. Let's just get home. I need a drink, how about you."

"Me, I think I need a couple."

They had each taken a shower at Scott's house and changed back into sweatpants and sweatshirts. Scott had examined his hip looking at the huge dark purple bruise. It caused him to wince as he stepped into the shower. *I'd better get some ice on this tonight or it will hurt like a bitch tomorrow,* he thought.

Later, they had sat talking and discussing every scenario they could think of for their return trip tomorrow. Scott kept an ice bag on his hip and ice in both their glasses as they took turns pouring the bottle, keeping their glasses full. Now it was late, after 1:30 a.m. The edge was long off them and they were just tipping back the last of the bourbon on the rocks when Jon's cell phone began to ring. He set down his glass, ice clinking in the bottom and reached toward his phone on the counter.

He glanced at the caller ID on the front and with a puzzled expression flipped it open.

"Detective Wendels here. Doing good Greg, thanks. Yeah, me too. No, I was awake, I couldn't sleep and a friend and I were having a couple of drinks. So what's up? My Aunt Maureen? She has an old Dodge Dart, why?"

The silence in the room for a moment felt more frightening than the darkness in the shed. Scott looked over at him in alarm and sat his own glass down ever so slowly.

"Wha . . . What? Wait, just wait a second, say that again," seconds ticked by in agonizing slowness. "Are you sure?" his voice was terrible to hear, raw and full of pain. "Read it to me again dammit!" he swallowed once, his eyes fixed on some lost point far away. "That's her car . . . it's hers. Stay right there, I'm on my way." He snapped his phone shut and it slid out of his hand clattering on the kitchen table as he fell into a chair.

"Jon," Scott said, "tell me, what is it?"

He looked over at Scott, his eyes glistening with tears, his voice breaking. "Aunt Maureen, Aunt Dee. Their . . . their car was found at a rest stop outside of town. It's full of blood and they're both missing."

Silence. Long and suffering silence.

"God, no, please no!" his voice was a whisper.

He dropped his head into his hands; his body wracked with trembling emotion . . . pain without a sound.

Pain unimaginable.

In the hours between two and four a.m., the dark is deepest and nothing moves, and the haunting wail of a train whistle in the distance can cause you unconsciously to burrow deep under the imagined safety of your covers. Then is the time a stealthy sound can wake you, and an unknown shadow can cause a thread of hot fear to run like molten lava through every nerve in your body; bad dreams can come and bad things can happen, in that dark, deep, still time.

It had returned to the house and stood well back in the tree shadows looking up at the room where the boys slumbered. It knew it could not reach them, for yet again the house lay sheltered by the protective red, blue and green aura that floated like mist around it. With impotent fury, the creature pounded, beat, whipped and tore at the thing that it had dragged so far. *Soon my pet,* a guttural voice whispered to the creature, *Soon they will be yours. You will bathe in their blood and deliver their souls to me! Go now, return to your place and wait until I call you forth again.* With inconceivable strength, it threw the object it held, high and far into the trees, safely away to where it never would be found, where it could rot and putrefy in obscurity.

Off to the left in the grass, low and quiet, another set of eyes watched the fiendish sight, and trembled.

CHAPTER 31

The morning of October 31 had dawned bright and clear. The sky was indigo blue and the weatherman had predicted a high of 69 degrees for the day. It was slightly past eight o'clock and the boys were just beginning to awaken to the sounds of the house and the smell of frying bacon.

After seeing Ax-Man outside the bedroom window, they had sat at the end of the bed for quite a while until finally they knew they had better get some sleep. Neither boy wanted to sleep alone so they had ended up in the same single bottom bunk, Anthony's head at one end, Sammy's at the other. It had taken both a while to get to sleep, for Sammy it was hardest because he was worried about his mom and dad.

He had said to Anthony, "I'm sure glad I put that double ring of salt around my house. I think mom and dad will be ok. Don't you think so Anth?" His voice had been thick with worry.

"I'm sure they're ok. For one thing, it us he wants 'cause we're onto him, and for another, there is only a single line around our house and he wouldn't pass that. They're ok buddy."

They had drifted off to sleep, unaware of the aura of safety that surrounded and protected the Petrucci's house. No bad dreams had visited them and considering the circumstances, once asleep they had rested well.

Anthony, who was at the foot of the bed, blinked his eyes open and realized that one Sammy's feet was shoved under his left armpit. He untangled himself from the covers and Sammy's foot and half fell out of the bed.

"Hey, you awake?" said Sammy, his voice gravely with sleep.

"I am now. You sleep like a tornado. I held on to the covers so you couldn't pull 'em off of me. Come on, let's go down stairs and see what dad has planned for this morning."

Sammy sat up in bed and clunked his head on the underside of the bed frame letting out a loud *Ouch* and then stumbled out of bed as Anthony laughed at the rooster like appearance of his friend's hair.

They heard the kitchen door close as they reached the bottom of the steps and as they arrived in the kitchen Danni was standing at the kitchen counter.

"Morning guys," she said looking up, "Nice hair Sammy, did you do it special for me?" she laughed.

He reached up and attempted to smooth down his bed-head hair and it stood straight back up like a spring, causing everyone to laugh.

"I just cooked some bacon, do you want eggs?" Danni asked as she picked up the coupons she had been cutting from the newspaper.

"I'll take an egg sandwich," Sammy said eagerly.

"I'll take one too mom, but don't put any cheese on Sam's ok?" Sam knocked him with his arm and went to get some orange juice from the refrigerator.

"Where's dad?"

"He wanted to get an early start on his final set up on your decorations. I'm assuming you'll be giving him a hand?"

"Yeah, then we want to get a fire ready in the pit. We thought it would look kinda cool tonight with the torches and stuff."

"You'd better ask your father about that first," Danni warned as she cracked eggs into a bowl.

"We're gonna play in the barn for a while. I'll ask dad when we go down."

The eggs sizzled as they hit the foaming butter, the edges quickly forming a dam for the rest of the whites. Once they were set, Danni gently flipped them for a moment to make them the over-easy type the boys liked. A piece of buttered toast went down; the cheese went on, a layer of bacon and a top piece of toast slathered with real butter.

As the boys sat at the table eating their breakfast sandwiches and drinking orange juice, they watched out the window as Army put the dry ice container in the caldron for Brunhilda the Witch, and they exchanged looks as Army made a deliberate wide loop away from Ax-Man.

"Dad knows something is up Sammy," Anthony said softly, "I hope it doesn't make it hard for him to leave us alone, that could screw up our plans."

They finished their breakfast in silence, picked up their plates and glasses and took them to the sink

When they finally went out the garage door, they saw Army pumping up his gallon sprayer at the edge of the driveway.

"What are you doing?" Anthony asked curiously.

"I need to spray Ax-Man. God-all-mighty that thing *stinks* and I can't have it smelling like that with kids and their parents coming later."

"What are you spraying it with?"

"Just water and that Fabreeze stuff your mother uses. Hopefully that and some sunshine will take the stink off of it," Army replied, his voice irritable. "How about if you guys get the pumpkins set up over there," he motioned down to the front of the yard, "and put the candles in them. Then get the other candles set up around the graveyard, put the tike lights up and fill them, ok?" He stopped pumping and looked at the boys, an odd expression on his face.

"Sure," Anthony said as Sammy nodded his head.

"Thanks," said Army. "I want to give your mom a hand with the cooking and decorating at the house so you guys can really help me out."

As he turned to go down toward Ax-Man, Anthony asked, "Dad, can we have a fire in the pit later? We thought it would look kinda cool for Halloween night."

Army thought for a minute then smiled at the boys and said, "I don't see why not and it would look kind of spooky coming up the drive. You'll have to keep an eye on it though."

"We know," they said together.

"Go get the pumpkins and candles then, let's get this show on the road."

The boys scampered back toward the garage while Army took a deep breath and started to walk toward Ax-Man. When he reached the mannequin that he had so enjoyed putting together not so very long ago, he stared at it and felt . . . fear. *That's irrational*, he thought, *it's a mannequin, a dummy for Christ's sake.*

He held up the sprayer, depressed the lever and began to douse it from top to bottom with the concoction of Fabreeze and water. "I think I'm looking forward to taking you apart this year," he said aloud.

Just then, Sammy hollered something from the garage that Army could not quite hear and he turned his head toward the boy.

"What?" he yelled back. "Hold your horses, I'm on my way!"

Army lowered the sprayer and began walking up toward the house; he did not see Ax-Man's lip rise ever so slightly in a sinister snarl, or the baleful eyes following his movement.

Army, father to Anthony, husband to Danni well liked neighbor and co-worker had unknowingly set in motion a fate that no sane person would wish on his worst enemy.

After giving the boys some additional instructions on pumpkins, lights and getting the cooler out for the dry ice, Army made a pit stop in the bathroom, then went to the small island counter in the kitchen, and turned on the laptop to check email. He made a quick stop at his AOL site to see which college games were on today; Michigan State vs. Ohio State, a classic that he was looking forward to seeing. After logging onto his email, he saw a response to his query to the County Recorders' Office, which was surprising considering he had just sent the email, and it was after all, a Government entity, which meant it was incredibly inefficient. He double clicked the link and opened the email.

Dear Mr. Petrucci

In response to your inquiry regarding the possible grave you have identified on your property, please note, once a body is interred, it is extremely difficult to have it moved. You must first gain permission from the family and have it notarized by County Recorder's Office. There have been a few instances where natural disasters disinter graves or an inactive cemetery becomes a nuisance subject to abatement. The dead cannot defend themselves; therefore, the fate of their remains is in the hands of the living. We suggest you exhaust all avenues of locating and contacting family members if you feel it is imperative that the grave eventually be relocated. Please do not hesitate to contact our office if we can be of any further help.

Best regards

Bob Dinninger, Clerk of County Records

He closed the email and dragged it to his 'Army' folder for safekeeping. He knew he should tell Danni, but he decided to wait until after tonight. Once the Halloween decorations were down and stored away she always seemed to relax. Then somehow, he would have to find the words to tell her that on their property was the grave of a young woman and a baby, a wife and son who in 1875 burned to death in a tragic fire, almost exactly where their house was sitting right now. Finding the right words, that would be the challenge. He checked the time, it was noon now, and he and Danni needed to get the Sloppy Joes, macaroni salad and dips ready. Maybe while they browned ground beef, chopped celery, onions, garlic and carrots, mixed, stirred, tasted and possibly had a couple of cold beers, they could put the football game on and hopefully listen to Michigan State beat the tar out of Ohio State. Their Halloween extravaganza had always been one of his favorite days, and he intended to make sure that this day was no different.

Halloween day—1:30 p.m.

The boys had finished helping Army with the final preparations of the Halloween decorations. Because they had all stayed away from Ax-Man, and for a time put it out of their minds, it had seemed like the old days and had been great fun. They worked together setting up the pumpkin family, positioning the tike lights and filling them with lamp oil. Next, they put the dollar store candles in strategic locations to cast eerie fingers of shadow and light after dark and finally they hid the containers that would be filled with dry ice just before everyone arrived. For a while at least, the boys had forgotten about what they were planning to do that afternoon.

The boys found Danni in the kitchen with a large wooden spoon stirring an enormous pot containing a goodly amount of garlic and onions. The boys had decided on the direct approach.

"Hey mom, I forgot to tell you we're going to sleep out tonight," said Anthony making his voice sound confident.

"It's going to be too cold Anthony," Danni responded.

"But mom," he pleaded, "this is the last time we'll be able to sleep out this year!"

"Uh-huh. Then you and Sam get colds and miss school. I don't think so."

"The weather guy said it's supposed to be seventy degrees!" Anthony implored.

"Yeah seventy degrees," Sammy offered up lamely.

"Oh really, seventy. And Samuel, have you talked to your mom or dad to see if you can sleep out too?" Danni's asked as her left eyebrow rose, which meant possible trouble for the boys.

"Well, no. Not yet that is. It'll be fine with them though," Sammy stated positively.

Danni removed the towel from her shoulder and wiped her hands. The aroma of sautéing onions and garlic was wafting up from the pot on the stove, and like a magnet Sammy leaned over and took a deep breath.

"I'll give your mom a call right now, how about that Sammy? Then we can get this settled early and you two won't be after me all day," she picked up her cell phone and pushed the speed dial number for Mindy, "wait here," she instructed the boys in a voice that was not a request but a command, "I'll be back in a minute."

While this conversation was transpiring, Army, on the other side of the kitchen, had remained mute.

"Dad? Please?" Anthony pleaded.

"Don't pull me into it Anth; you know your mom will make that decision. I'm just trying to stay out of the dog-house for Halloween," he looked up at the boys and shrugged, smiling, "you guys know how it works."

The boys both nodded and stood waiting. They could hear Danni's voice in the other room, but could not hear what she was saying.

After what seemed like an eternity, she returned to the kitchen. "Here's what we've decided. We will see how cold it gets this evening. I will decide what is too cold. But understand, this is the last time this year, got it?" Danni said sternly.

"Got it!" Anthony and Sammy said collectively.

"Thanks mom," Anthony planted a kiss on her cheek.

"Yeah, thanks Mrs. P!" Sammy said, dipping his hand into the pot and trying to snag a pinch of the hot onions. Danni smacked his arm away.

"Get out of there Sam you'll burn yourself! Out, both of you, out!" she was smiling as she swatted both as they dashed out the door.

Confident that Army and Danni would be pre-occupied for the remainder of the afternoon, the boys knew that they had to get the barn ready. Anthony had to finish the *Devil's Trap* and Sammy had to build . . . well, whatever it was that he had in his mind.

They brushed straw off the tarp, removed it and then folded it into thirds. Anthony took the picture of the *Devil's Trap* from his back pocket and unfolded it. From his front pocket, he removed the leather pouch and took a piece of the holy charcoal. He stared hard at the drawing, again ingraining each symbol and stroke into his head. As the moments ticked by, it felt as though he moved into another plane where he was at a calm center, then he knelt and began to draw; not tentatively but with knowledge and authority. Time slipped away and for him it became the drawing, nothing but the drawing. He drew each line carefully, perfectly; as he knew somewhere, deep inside that it must be in order to work. He did not realize he took measured breaths or that hay dust billowed softly around him. Several times, he stopped and drew from the picture in his mind, and at those moments, it was almost as though someone was beside him, a comforting hand on his shoulder, a whispering presence at his side and he was able to shake off his indecision and continue.

Meanwhile, Sammy had gone to the old ringer washer and stood looking at it. When he decided on what he would do, he eagerly set to work. First, he went back to the tack room and picked up tools he thought he would need; a hammer, screwdriver, pliers, a crescent wrench, pipe clamps and duct tape. He began by first taking off the top horizontal support bolted on each side. Next, he removed the top rubber roller since his plan only required one. That left the bottom roller next to the handle. The handle had been hard to turn at first, but after cleaning and a good lubing with some silicone spray he found, everything was now moving smoothly. He tied the nylon rope tightly along each end of the roller and then he used thin strips of furnace tape to wrap around the rope at the front to hold it tightly in place. He slid a sliver pipe clamp on each vertical upright and then moved the horizontal support back, but this time he placed the top bolt hole in the bottom position and the two vertical pieces that had previously been flush together now overlapped in the front. This left approximately three inches of space between the roller and the horizontal support that would be the guide for the rope. He tightened the pipe clamps, ran one bolt through each hole and pulled out the rope on each side.

Sammy took first one and then the other piece of rope to the blue tarp they had folded in thirds. He put the end through silver grommets located at each corner, tied them off and again wrapped it with a thin strip of furnace tape. Next he walked back to stand behind the ringer-washer and inspected what he had done, analyzing it in his mind to decide if it would really work. He moved to the left side, grabbed the handle and quickly cranked it three times. The result was immediate and impressive. The blue tarp jerked away so quickly that it startled Anthony and as he yelped, he fell backward out of the drawing.

"Shit! Sammy what the hell *is* that?" he got up dusting off his jeans as Sammy laughed gleefully. He laughed because the contraption worked, he laughed because he had sat Anthony on his ass and he laughed just because it just felt good to laugh.

Anthony came to stand beside him studying the revamped ringer-washer. After several moments, he looked at Sammy curiously and said, “Ok, I give up, what’s it for. What does it do?”

Sammy, his voice full of pride at his accomplishment, began to explain. “We’re going to have to keep the trap covered until we get Ax-Man inside; if he sees it, I doubt we’ll be able to get him to step into it. I figure if we stand at this end with our faces lit by a couple of flashlights, he’s gonna want to come after us. That’ll make him walk across the *Devil’s Trap* since the bales are on the left and the loose hay is on the right. We need to have some way of yanking the tarp off without being too close or it’ll get us. I figured we can each stand on one side of the washer; I’ll be on the side with the crank and when he goes to step on the tarp, I can yank it off.”

Anthony just stood staring at his friend as the seconds ticked by.

Sammy said finally, “So you think it’s pretty lame I guess.”

“No,” said Anthony, it’s brilliant.”

Sammy beamed.

Saturday—2:15 p.m.

Jon looked haggard, his face was drawn, and he had dark circles under eyes that were bloodshot. He had spent the night at the rest stop where his Aunt Maureen’s car was found. Scott had come with him and worked the scene for the forensic end of the investigation. Jon watched everyone to make sure that evidence was properly collected and all bases were covered. He stood looking at the car; one moment his mind worked the area like any other crime scene, the next moment the emotional pain was numbing his thought process and threatening to buckle his knees.

The shattered glass in the driver’s side door was smeared with gore; two heavy trails of blood went across the parking lot and into the woods behind the rest stop. What appeared to be human entrails were at the edge of the blacktop along with a huge pool of blood. The detectives had followed the blood trail as far as they could in the dark; the area was then yellow taped and several officers were posted in key locations.

The place reeked beyond the blood and guts, flesh and sinew that splattered the area; it was a landscape of fiendish depravity. It had officers looking over their shoulders into the darkness, making sure their firearm was available, searching the perimeters around them for any movement.

Just before dawn, Jon had gone to the station to make a statement about the car and give a detailed description of both Aunt Maureen and Aunt Dee; that was the hardest part of all. He could describe what they looked like on the outside, but he kept thinking about how beautiful they both were on the inside. He could not explain that, he could not put it into words.

After all the statements were completed, he called Scott at the coroner's office. The phone rang several times before Scott answered.

"County coroner's office, Scott Champion speaking," his voice sounded fatigued.

"Hey, it's Jon. Got anything yet?"

"No, it'll take a couple of hours and I don't know if we recovered enough blood for any good toxicology. I was just blood typing. How're you doing?"

"I feel like a hole was punched through my chest. We just finished up with the statements and descriptions," he was quiet a moment then continued, "when you're done there I want to take a ride out by the Petrucci house; I want to see if that thing's still there. Then I want to meet those people and look in their eyes and see if they have any idea what is going on."

"Do you still want to go back to the shed today?" Scott asked.

"We have to. If we can find the portal, maybe we can put a stop to this madness. I know in my gut that this is all connected. Jig's was some kind of sinister lightening rod in all of this."

"Ok then, come pick me up. I'm so tired right now I'm not even thinking straight and I don't want to make a mistake."

"On my way," he snapped his cell phone shut and started to his car, unbearable sadness with him every step of the way.

It was just after two when Jon turned into the Petrucci's driveway and immediately Scott said, "It looks like they have put other things around the yard, wonder what that is about?"

"Don't know," said Jon pulling up to the garage while looking down across the yard, "but I see *its* still over there. Let's go ask."

He put the car into park and they both got out and walked up the steps to the long front porch. As they rang the doorbell, they looked up the hill to the right where the barn sat and saw two boys come out the front sliding door.

Just then, the front door opened and the wonderful perfume of food greeted them as a tall dark haired man said, "Hello. Can I help you?"

"Sorry to bother you sir," Jon held up his badge with his picture, "my name is Jon Wendels and this is Scott Champion," he motioned toward Scott. "We're with the Lamont police department. Are you Mr. Petrucci?"

"Yes. Is something wrong?"

"I'm sure you're aware of the animal mutilations' and other disappearances over the last few months." Army nodded his head, his eyes going back and forth between the two men. "We're just canvassing neighborhoods for any possible new information. Do you have a few minutes?"

"Why sure, I guess so. Come on in." He called over his shoulder, "Danni, would you please come here a minute?"

"Just a second hon," they heard the voice of a woman in the background.

"Something smells mighty good," said Jon.

"That's for sure," Scott agreed.

"Oh, we have a big Halloween party every year. My wife and I are getting the food ready for later."

In the background, they could hear cheering from a TV somewhere.

"And watching Michigan St. cream OSU," he said happily. Just then, Danni arrived wiping her hands on the towel that still hung on her shoulder.

"Hello," she said tentatively looking from Jon to Scott to Army. "Is something wrong?"

"I just asked them that too," said Army.

"No, not specifically," Jon replied, and then introduced himself and Scott to Danni. "We're just canvassing neighborhoods regarding the animal mutilations' and missing persons' over the last few months. Have either of you seen anything or anyone out of the ordinary?"

Danni and Army exchanged a look that did not go unnoticed by the two men.

"I take that as a yes?" Jon asked.

Army proceeded to explain what had happened late in the summer regarding the chickens' and that the police had been out at that time. "I'm surprised you don't have that report," Army finished.

"Actually, I am too. I'll have to find out who was here and follow up," he took out a small notepad from his jacket pocket along with a pen and wrote something in it. "Other than that, anything else?"

Army and Danni looked at each other again and shook their heads. "No, nothing I can think of right now," Army said. "Oh, wait, our neighbor's dog Ebony, came up missing. I don't know all the details though," he finished.

"Ok then. I'll note that and we can check on a report for that too."

Scott had remained quiet throughout most of the conversation. Suddenly he said, "Those are pretty elaborate Halloween decorations, your kids must love it."

"Well," said Danni looking at Army, "It's the mad scientist in my husband. He has bought and added on and collected forever, right honey? "There was no mistaking the slight edge in her voice. Army shrugged his shoulders and smiled, accepting the little dig from his wife.

"Yep, she's right. I've collected stuff over the years, I watch for yard sales, things like that. My son and I have a good time building everything each year."

"Oh, are those the boys we saw up at the barn when we pulled in?" Scott inquired

"The dark haired one is our son, Anthony; the redhead is Sammy, his best friend. I'm afraid I've infected him too," he gave a quick look at his wife, "I'm not sure if his mom is crazy about it, but his dad is like me," said Army laughing.

"Could we talk to them?" Jon asked.

Once again, Danni and Army looked at each other. Danni was the one to speak up this time, "I suppose so. We just don't want them upset. What type of questions are you going to ask them?"

"The very same we've just asked you," Jon replied.

"I'm ok with it then, if Army agrees."

"I don't see a problem. Let me go call them," replied Army. He went out the front door and to the far end of the porch and called, "Anthony! Sammy! Hey guys, come down to the house for a minute!" When there was no immediate response, he called again. "Boys! Come down here a minute."

In the background a young man's voice responded back, "Be right there dad!"

Army went back inside to the sound of cheering coming again from the TV. "I wonder who just scored?" he said anxiously. "Hey, you guys want a sloppy Joe and a cold beer?"

"Well," said Scott, "I'll definitely take you up on the sloppy Joe but I'll have to pass on the beer, though it sounds really good."

"Same here," said Jon.

"I can see the boys coming now," said Army. "Let's go to the kitchen, we can watch the TV from there and I can guarantee you it's where the boys will show up."

All the adults laughed and as they moved towards the kitchen area, for a moment, just a moment, everything seemed so normal, so Saturday, so October, so football.

As always, the two boys were just *STARVING*, so soft buns, porous to all the good tomato sauce, came out of a plastic sleeve; fresh chopped onions, along with cheese and sour cream were piled high, and a bag of golden crisp, salty chips filled a bowl. The officers and boys all had soda, Danni opted for water and Army pulled another beer from an ice-filled cooler in the corner.

"Please, help yourselves," Danni invited.

"Wow, what a spread," Scott said in wonderment as he surveyed the bountiful feast taking shape on the counter.

"Whooooohoo!" shouted Army, "Michigan scored again. Nananana Nananana, Heyy Heyyyyy, gooooodbye! You're goin' down OSU!"

The boys cheered, Danni cheered, Scott and Jon cheered as the OSU coach shook his head in disgust on the sidelines.

Jon was wiping his mouth several minutes later, the growling in his stomach abated for the time being, when he suddenly said, "So boys, have you seen anything unusual around here lately?"

Their reaction was immediate and palatable. They looked at each other, at Army and Danni and back to each other again, their eyes round and wide.

"So, have you seen anything unusual, or what you would consider weird around here lately?" Jon asked again watching them closely.

"Like what?" asked Anthony trying to buy some time while his brain processed what to say.

"Anyone you don't know. Any*thing* not usual or normal to the area," said Jon slowly continuing to watching the two friends. Another first down by Michigan ramped up the sound from the TV.

"No, not really, Sammy you see anything?"

"Umm, no, I don't think so, nope," his answer sounded lame and made up.

Scott watched each person around him very closely, choosing to let Jon do the questioning, while he did the observing. Each person here seemed to be hiding something; Danni the least, Army was preoccupied, but he definitely knew *something* was not right, though Scott surmised he had not put all the pieces together yet. The boys though, they knew a lot more than what they had thus far revealed.

Jon spoke up again, wanting to break the obvious tension that had invaded the room. "Hey boys, will you show us your Halloween decorations? They look impressive from the road and I'd like to see them up close. Scott, how about you?"

"Yeah, me too. I would really like to see that whole horror show in the front. Who is that? Freddy and Dracula? What else is down there?"

The silence that followed could not have been more pronounced.

Danni spoke up looking between her husband and the boys. "Wow, what's the matter with you guys? You've spent weeks working on everything, now you don't want to show it off. What's up with that?" her laughter did nothing to dispel the unease in the room, and as it died out, she looked around her in surprise. "Army? Anthony? Ok now, come on Sammy, not you too?"

Army took the awkward pause to wipe his chin and say, "Sure, of course. Come on you guys, let's show them our work."

Something had changed. The fact they were going down to the front had set an odd hush on the father and two boys, which sent up red flags to Jon and Scott.

"Ok then, let's go take a look and let you folks get back to your festivities," Scott wiped off his hands and set the napkin on his empty paper plate.

"Thank you Mrs. Petrucci," Jon said as he took a final swallow of soda.

"You're welcome. Just leave the plates there; I have a system for picking everything up," she said smiling. "Enjoy the horror show, hope it doesn't give you nightmares'!"

Army began the Halloween tour at the far end, commenting on how they hand tied the string to make the giant spider web and how he and Anthony had carved the gravestones from construction grade styrofoam insulation. The boys chatted away showing how they had strung fishing line on the bats. When activated, the bats flew in a fashion, spinning in large circles. There were blow up ghosts and skeletons, cardboard cutout goblins and the like, that had been attached to wood and carefully cut out and made waterproof. It was actually quite an amazing collection. Yet, they still had not made it to the biggest most elaborate portion of decorations, the one containing what Jon was coming to refer to in his mind as the *beast.*

"This is amazing you guys," Jon commented. "Now I'm really anxious to see that," and as he pointed to where Ax-Man was, again the mood became different, somber, and pensive.

"Yes, let's walk over there," Scott remarked, "lead the way."

As Army and the boys went ahead of them, Scott noticed that both boys put their hands up to their shirts and appeared to grab something. Army made a wide birth and stayed well away telling them they 'would get a better overall view from here.'

There was silence all around for a moment, then Army began to explain how they planned the backdrop, the staging and why each monster came to be in a particular location; then he made a comment that stunned both Jon and Scott.

". . . and actually this year I went to an estate sale not too far from here, Seederly was the name. I ended up buying more tools than anything, but I did get a good mask there, that one on the end. We call him Ax-Man."

Jon struggled to keep his composure and he could sense the tenseness in Scott, as they stood transfixed. *The beast has a name,* thought Jon. He saw Scott clenching his hands into fists.

"I'll bet you get a lot of kids here," Jon remarked trying to make small talk.

"Well, this is our first Halloween at this house, but if it's anything like previous years, then yeah, we'll have a ton."

"No trouble with vandals or trespassers then?"

"Well, we have had some problems. I haven't directly seen anyone, but Ax-Man seems to draw the attention.

"How do you mean?"

"Oh, I think they've been messing around moving it just to tweak us, and lately it smells like someone smeared it with road kill. I just finished spraying it down a while ago with the wife's Fabreeze it smelled so bad.

"Just this one, not any of the others?"

"Yep, just Ax-Man, they've left the other stuff alone," he paused a moment, then continued. "I never thought of it that way but they haven't bothered one other thing. Huh, isn't that odd."

During this exchange, Scott had been watching the two boys who had stayed off to the left, the furthest away. They had been whispering to each other, and their conversation seemed quite animated.

"So what do you boys think?" Scott interrupted. They were so deep into their private conversation that they did not immediately respond.

"Boys," Army said, "the officer asked you a question."

They looked up and Scott repeated his question.

Anthony was the first to answer, "I don't know who it is. I don't know anyone from my school that would do anything like that;" he turned to Sammy, "do you?"

"Nope, me neither," Sammy replied, looking past Jon and Scott towards Ax-Man.

Scott watched as Anthony's hand went to his shirt again, touching the unknown thing he carried out of sight.

He then said the strangest thing in a loud clear voice.

"After tonight though, I think we'll just take that one," he pointed at Ax-Man, "apart and get rid of it, start fresh. What do you think Sammy, take him apart and get rid of it right? Especially that old mask, we need something new for next year."

There was a subtle change in the air, a feeling almost like static as they all looked across the quiet deadly space between them and Ax-Man.

Seconds ticked by until Army broke the silence, "Funny you said that son; I just voiced that opinion when I was spraying him down earlier."

"What?" Anthony gasped obviously taken aback; his face was getting a doughy, pale look to it. "No, you can't do that! You leave it alone Dad! Sammy and I will take care of him!" his voice was now near hysterical.

"Calm down Anth, don't worry about it now. We'll deal with it after tonight," Army said carefully, surprised by the passion in his son's voice.

"Well then," Jon remarked carefully, still watching the scene unfold, "we'll let you guys get back to the game and your party prep. Thanks a lot for showing us around and taking the time to answer our questions. If anything comes up, or you remember something else, call me, any time day or night." He handed a card to Army who looked at it and nodded.

As they turned to walk away the boys let the men get several steps ahead, and then Anthony said, "We'll take care of this one," using his thumb to point at Ax-Man, "tomorrow. We might as well get it thrown in the trash before they pick up the garbage Monday."

Like a wave of thunder with no sound, some form of energy moved through the boys rocking them back on their feet. The men apparently did not feel it as they continued across the yard toward their car.

Anthony and Sammy took off at a run, wasting no time getting away from Ax-Man, looking once over their shoulders. Anthony's horrific sense of fear a few minutes earlier was like a cold white knife in his belly. His dad had called it out, how could that happen? He could now only hope that what he had said changed the events so that their plan would work.

Suddenly he looked at Sammy and said with an edge of panic in his voice, “Oh crap, I just realized we left the drawing uncovered. Let’s go!” They took off at a hard run, waved good bye to the two men who watched them in their mad dash back to the barn.

Scott and Jon shook hands with Army thanking him again for taking the time to talk to them.

“Don’t hesitate to call us with anything,” Jon said keeping his eyes on Army, watching for any inkling that he may be hiding any nugget of information, “and thanks again for the soda and sandwich.”

“Yes, thank you,” added Scott.

“Hey, you’re more than welcome. You do know it’s a full moon tonight?”

“Oh? I’d forgotten,” said Jon, “all the loonies come out on Halloween anyhow and now a full moon. Priceless.”

He opened the car door and slid into the seat as Scott settled into the passenger side. With a last wave, Army disappeared back inside his house ostensibly to finish watching the game.

Jon started the car and looked at Scott, who in turn was gazing up at the barn. “What do you think that was all about?” he mused.

“I’m not sure, but I’ll bet they know a whole lot more about their Ax-Man than they said. Did you see the look on the son’s face when he heard his dad had said he was going to take it all apart after Halloween?”

“Yeah, he looked scared.”

“Not just scared Jon, but scared shitless. He was falling all over himself to say they would be the ones to take it apart and trash it. I wonder what their up to at that barn?”

“You want to go up?”

“No, it’s getting late and we have to get to shed,” Jon looked at the dashboard clock. “Damn! It’s after four!”

"Damn is right. We have to go back to the house, get extra lights and the gym bag, so let's hall ass."

The shadows stole ghost like along the ground, not pausing to linger now in the waning light, anxious for the night to come.

CHAPTER 32

It was done. The *Devil's Trap* was complete. Anthony and Sammy stood at the bottom of the drawing looking at it, and it looked exactly like the picture Anthony held in his hand.

"That's amazing Anth. I didn't know you could draw like that," said Sammy, admiration in his voice.

"Me neither. Sometimes it felt like someone was standing next to me, helping."

"What do you mean? Who was helping you?"

"I don't know how to explain it, maybe like my mom calls my guardian angel or something. It was like when I got stuck, she helped me."

"She? It was a lady?"

Anthony eyes seemed distant for a moment before he replied. "Yeah, it *was* a lady. I guess it doesn't matter, as long as the drawing is right," he turned toward Sammy and said, "so, show me what you made."

They walked around the right side of the trap where the loose hay was and made their way to the back of the barn where Sammy's invention waited.

He explained to Anthony again how it should work and Anthony said, "Let's try it then."

"You sure? It won't mess up the drawing will it?"

"Well, if it doesn't work I'd rather know now than when that thing steps in."

They walked back to the tarp and pulled it over the trap carefully shaking loose hay over it. Then they walked back to the ringer washer and rehearsed pretending to hold flashlights on their faces so it would see them.

Sammy kept his right hand on the handle of the ringer washer as Anthony said quietly "Now!" Two hard cranks brought it to the top of the drawing, and the third took it completely off. The boys rushed over to the drawing to look at it. Very little of the hay had come off the tarp onto the trap, and Anthony carefully looked at the drawing.

Finally, Sammy could stand it no longer and said, "So how does it look? I don't see any messed up parts, do you?"

"Me neither. You're gonna have to give it three hard cranks bro."

"I know. Can we try it one more time?"

"Yeah, let's set it up again."

They pulled the tarp back over the drawing, moved back to the washer, took their positions and again Anthony said quietly, "Now!"

One-two-three cranks and the blue tarp was completely off the drawing. This time, because he had cranked as hard as he could, it had literally blown the hay off the drawing.

"Perfect," said Anthony.

"Pretty cool," breathed Sammy.

"Ok, let's get it set then. We need to have it all ready then get the fire going."

They looked out the door at the same time and realized the sun was very low in the sky.

"What time does Trick-or-Treat start?" asked Sammy anxiously.

"Six to seven-thirty. Did you bring your costume?"

"I'm gonna be a hobo 'cause it seemed easy. What about you?"

"I guess we're bums together then. I figured the same thing."

They carefully pulled the blue tarp over the *Devil's Trap*, scattered hay over the whole thing and made sure the ropes to the tarp were set.

"Let's start the fire, that way it will be hot and easy to keep going," Anthony suggested.

Working quickly they gathered tinder from the pile they kept inside the door of the barn. They piled small sticks on the tinder, lit it watching as the fire hungrily licked at the wood, and then put the longs on in a hatch pattern. By the time they had a good hot fire going it was getting dark and time for them to change into their hobo outfits.

Closer to the house they could smell the sloppy Joes mingling with the aroma of wood smoke from their fire. It smelled like fun, it smelled like home. Army waved up at the boys as he went around lighting the tike lights and candles, putting dry ice in the containers and watching the mist it created flow slowly across the leaves and grass. The sun was just a small thin orange line on the horizon. It was here, Halloween night, All Hallows Eve, the time when the veil between the two worlds becomes thin, a time when the living and the dead mix and meld; and there, on the other side of the veil, the shimmering, thinning veil, the Dark One waited, panting as though involved in some insidious copulation.

By the time Jon and Scott returned to Jigs Seederly's property, it was well past five. The dark was coming down fast and both men were lost in thought as Scott turned into the driveway. Jon had spoken with the detective in charge of his missing Aunt Maureen and Aunt Dee; there was no new information and no toxicology results were available. Waiting was all he could do now. He could not allow himself to think about it, it was just too painful and he could not afford to be distracted, there could be no mistakes.

As he turned the car key off, they both hesitated for just a moment in the near dark. Then without a word, each got out of their side of the car, Jon reaching in the back to pick up the small gym bag, Scott grabbed the trouble light he had brought from his garage and the two large flashlights. They each had on the jackets into which Father Kaylan had sewn a pocket; each having an aspergillum filled with holy water. The bag contained twelve holy candles, two lighters and two containers with the remainder of the holy water and salt. As Scott closed the back door, he bumped his hip and let out a groan of pain.

"You ok?" Jon asked, concerned.

"Yeah, I just bumped my hip again. The way I wacked that workbench yesterday it's probably in pieces."

"I guess we're about to find out."

"Did you check the lighters?"

"Twice."

"Let's go then."

Every step they took closer to the shed seemed to bring a shroud of doom around them. The unknown was a fearsome enemy; the unknown could suck the resolve out of the strongest person without them knowing it. What your mind could imagine was often far, far worse than reality. However, this might be one of the rare times when ignorance was bliss. It was quiet and still—eerily still. As they turned on their flashlights, both men realized just how secluded it was back here; in the near darkness you could not see any other houses at all.

"Wait," said Jon before Scott went in the door. "Let's walk around the perimeter together. We can start at this end and make our way to the back."

"Ok, but why?"

"We never checked out this foundation. I want to see if we can look under it."

"Let's go then."

Starting on the far end, they ran the beams of their lights along the ground. Pressure treated 4x12s were along the length, flush to the ground with no gap between them and the floor of the shed. They made their way to the back, where they noticed for the first time, two pipes; each was set approximately two feet in from each corner, going up through the roof.

"What do you think those are for?" Jon wondered aloud.

"It reminds me of a sewer stack," Scott said more to himself than to Jon.

"Or," mused Jon, "breather tubes."

"We should concentrate on the back wall and floor inside," said Scott.

It was so still around them, and in the stillness, they could almost feel a sinister presence that felt thick and cloying.

Making their way again to the open doors, they hesitated only a moment then quickly entered the shed and immediately plugged in the work light hanging by its hook over the florescent fixture. There were tools scattered all over the floor that had fallen off the bench when Scott had rammed into it yesterday in his haste to get out. They bent and pick up the tools and laid them on the bench to avoid tripping over them.

"Jon, I noticed this yesterday but in all the commotion I forgot to tell you. Look at the floor," Scott said motioning with his flashlight.

Jon looked down and then said, "Ok, so what am I looking at?"

"Have you ever seen a shed floor made from individual boards and not plywood?"

Jon's eyes shot back to the floor, staring hard, and turning slowly around looking with fresh eyes at the dirty floor of the shed.

"No, I've never seen that before," his eyes continued searching the floor and finally he said, "look how perfectly the boards fit; why would he put so much effort into that?" Above him the 4x4 post loomed with its makeshift pulley system. "Do you think we can we pull up the whole floor tonight?"

"No," said Scott, "we have to go with our gut instinct. I say we concentrate right underneath that bastard," he pointed at the post with his thumb, "that winch has to be here for a reason."

They looked closely for several minutes, searching for something that lifted up or made sense.

"There's no break in the boards that I can see, can you?" Jon said in expiration, trying to ascertain an opening or a hatch of some sort. Scott stood up, walked to the workbench, and picked up a screwdriver. He returned to the back wall and bent to several areas putting the tip of the screwdriver between several boards to see if he could find any loose ones. The tip of the screwdriver was too large so he went back to the bench to select a slimmer one. That was when noticed that one of the screwdrivers had several screws stuck to the bottom of its *handle*. He pulled the screws away then slid the handle towards them again and watched as the screws attached to the bottom of the handle.

"Jon, look at this. Don't you find it odd that the base is magnetized and not the tip?"

He took it over to show Jon and just then, his cell phone rang. He laid the screwdriver on the floor and dug his cell phone out of his pocket, looked at the screen and flipped it open.

"Champion here," he listened intently for a moment then said, "Are you sure? Ok then, we'll be right over, bye."

Jon was looking at him quizzically, "What's up?"

Scott snapped his phone closed and slipped it back into his pocket and said, "I knew it would be problematic that the blood samples we had were mixed with dirt and debris, so last night I called in a favor on those samples to our forensic serologist who just happens to have been my roommate in college. He just called. The tox screen is complete. He thinks I should come and take a look at it and bring you."

"How long will it take? We've got to get this placed searched. Maybe I should stay here and you go, split up the time."

"No," said Scott, "we don't split up, that would be a mistake. It won't take us more than an hour. That will put us back here sometime after seven. We should be ok."

Jon hesitated, wanting to continue the search but seeing the wisdom in what Scott said. "Ok then. Let's leave the trouble light on and the flashlights here. We'll take the gym bag with us."

Scott bent to shut off his flashlight and pickup the screwdriver. When he did, he noticed that it pulled a nail partially out of the floor. “Jon, check this out,” he did it again and the nail pulled about ¼ of the way out.

“What’s up with that?” Jon bent and squinted at the place on the floor.

“Don’t know, but it’s the first thing we’re going to check when we get back. I’m leaving this screwdriver on the floor so we don’t get it mixed up with the others. Let’s go so we can get back here ASAP.”

They hurried out the door and to the car making quick work of jumping in and heading down the road.

Truths were about to become known and secretes revealed.

It had begun.

CHAPTER 33

The boys had donned their hobo outfits and the stage was set for Trick-or-Treat to begin. The house was alight, the table inside set up buffet style with all the food Danni and Army had prepared earlier. The boys had just returned from the barn, this time taking the two flashlights with them. They had put them back near the ringer-washer, checked everything again and stacked four more pieces of wood on the glowing fire. It was just past 6:30 p.m. and as the boys started down the hill, two cars pulled in the driveway. One was the Russelton's and they watched as Freddy was the first one out of the car; Justin was right behind him and Christine was along for the ride as she now considered herself too grown up to wear a costume.

It was fun as everyone began to arrive. Many of their school friends came and cars started to line up along the road as the night settled in around them and all the lights, candles, and pumpkins cast a magical luminosity around everything, washing the house and yard in a soft orange-golden glow. The turnout was large for two reasons. First, this was their initial year at their new house for Halloween and second, it was Saturday night and most people did not have to get up early the next morning. Army had the original *Frankenstein* movie playing on the big screen with *Wolf Man* and *Dracula* to follow depending how long everyone stayed. Kids laughing and giggling in the background and shrieking as boys tried to scare girls and then each other. The night was warm and the moon full, the silvery light it cast causing deeper shadows at the edge of the yard like a curtain. Everyone noticed the fire when approaching the house and commented on how it lent itself to the eerie surroundings. The two boys, as all young people their age are able to do, put away their troubles for the time being and lived in the moment. They only thing they were both aware of, was the fact that their medallions, hidden beneath their hobo shirts, seemed to get warmer. Neither boy said anything to the other, letting that knowledge slip away for now. Army was calling the kids to the front porch; it was time to bob for apples. There was a piñata yet to be broken open to gain entry to the treasures hidden within, and the bouquet of fresh popcorn soaking up warm butter was in the air as Danni set more baskets around for everyone to enjoy. It was all wonderful, joyful and fun.

And oh, it felt so marvelous to laugh.

The parking lot at the coroner's office had two bright lights outside, but essentially, the office was dark. The loading/unloading dock, always illuminated with blue lights, served only to cast an eerie hue over all they touched.

As they pulled into a reserved spot, they both had on their minds what the serologists report was going to reveal. Neither said a word as they got out and made their way to the door and, once inside, to Scott's office. On his desk, they found a manila folder that had the crime scene pictures of Aunt Maureen's car and a post-it-note that said, *Scott, read immediately.*

Scott went around his desk and sat down, opening the folder as Jon sat in the chair directly across from him. The minutes ticked by as Jon sat quietly, allowing Scott to review the report and digest all the information it contained.

Finally when he could stand it no longer Jon spoke up, "Ok then, what does it say?"

Scott looked curiously up at Jon and said, "First, the blood types don't match what we received from hospital records for Maureen and Dee. Second, unless your Aunt Maureen and Aunt Dee were into heavy-duty crack cocaine, this absolutely was not them. Have a look," he passed the folder to Jon and rested his arms on the desk.

Blood was found at the site of an abandoned car on 10/31/09 at approx. 08:00; there were no bodies for autopsy. Toxically from blood samples are as follows: Blood: Ethanol, 0.261%, Cocaine 0.043 mg/L, Cocaethylene 0.092 mg/L, Benzoylecgonine 2.422 mg/L and Acetaminophen 43.38 mg/L; Urine: Ethanol, 0.241%, Cocaine 7.549 mg/L, Cocaethylene 7.749 mg/L, Benzoylecgonine 66.501 mg/L and Acetaminophen 20.30 mg/L and Oxycodone 7.222 mg/L. Bile had Ethanol 0.270 and Nasal Swab Analysis EME, PTROPINE, COC; Microscopic."

Jon scanned the report for a moment and then said, "I don't know what all that shit means, just give it to me in layman terms."

"It means that the individuals that were pulled out of that car window were trashed on cocaine, and, by the way, two different blood types came back. Neither matched Maureen or Dee; *both* samples were nearly the same for drugs."

"So it's not them?" Jon's voice was barely a whisper.

"No Jon, not them." Jon's face started to light up and Scott hurried on. "That doesn't mean your Aunt and her friend are ok. They're still missing."

Jon's face for just a moment been hopeful, but the reality of the situation reared its ugly head and his years on the police force brought him back down with a thud.

"Is there anyone else you can think to call who might know where they could be?" Scott asked gently, seeing the stark pain again on his friends face.

"I don't think so, but I don't know all their friends."

Scott let the silence linger knowing that Jon needed the time. Finally he said, "Jon, its 7:30, we've got to get back to the shed. I'm sorry buddy, we've gotta go."

Jon looked up at the clock startled, and stood up quickly. "Shit, let's go, let's go."

He started for the door as Scott gathered up the paperwork and put it back in the folder and into the top metal bin on his desk.

The moon was bright and full, still close enough to the horizon to appear at its biggest but, on this night as they drove to the location of a serial killer, it also seemed somehow sinister. They drove in silence, each man lost in his own thoughts and private fears, and it seemed the closer they came to their destination the more the night seemed to close in around them. When they pulled in the driveway, they could see into the back yard and it was oddly comforting that the light was still on inside the shed.

Walking across the cool damp grass they stepped back into the shed, and immediately each reached for the large flashlights on the floor.

They walked directly to the other side, where the screwdriver still laid exactly where they left it; they fell to their knees, and began a frantic search for the truth.

Halloween night—7:45 p.m.

The laughter of children doing their best to scare the bejeebers out of each other had subsided as friends and neighbors had come and gone oohhing and aahhhing at the decorations, the children especially intrigued by how the mist of dry ice spread across the grass adding a spooky ambiance to the festivities. Only a few servings of sloppy Joes remained the bottles of orange drink consumed and the last bag of nacho chips opened. Mindy and Danni were busy cleaning up the kitchen and discussing if the boys would be allowed to sleep out. Dan and Army had gone to the garage to empty the cooler of beer and were going to begin extinguishing the tike lights. Sammy and Anthony had gone up to the barn to add more wood to the fire and, in anticipation of getting a yes to the sleep out, they carried their sleeping bags with them. Away from the security of the house and lights, they found themselves glancing anxiously over their shoulders.

Once inside the barn, they unrolled their sleeping bags on the built in chests in the alcove and Anthony took the wooden *Devil's Trap* from his pocket and put it down inside his bag.

Both boys had a sense of urgency to make it back to the house before their dads' were done, the timing had to be right, and everything could hinge on the next few minutes.

As they hurried back the yard, they noticed something off to their left just at the edge of the flickering firelight, right at the point where darkness and light merged.

Glowing eyes low to the ground.

The shining pearlescent eyes were there and gone in an instant, but those eyes caused the boys to stumble, their legs to move jerkily and their resolve to waver.

"What was that?" whispered Sammy, his voice tight and strained.

"I . . . I . . . think it was a raccoon or something," Anthony said uncertainly. "Come on, we gotta go!" Anthony said as he grabbed Sammy by the arm and they ran headlong down towards the remaining burning tike lights and the comforting sound of their fathers voices.

Watching the boys closely, it crept closer, secluding itself behind a large clump of weeds in the shadow of the barn, certain they would be back.

CHAPTER 34

The first thing Scott inspected upon their return to the shed was the screwdriver left on the floor. After a minute or two he realized that a small piece had been sliced off the end, and then replaced with surgical precision; he wiggled it a moment until it came loose. The inside had been hollowed out and a cylindrical piece of metal inserted. He stretched up on his knees, grabbed a screw from the workbench, and placed the end of the screwdriver against it. It stuck. It was a magnet deliberately hidden inside the handle.

Methodically, he began to put the end against the nails in surrounding floorboards and a pattern began to emerge, as certain nails would come partially out of the floor. Jon was placing an 'x' by the ones that were loose and it finally revealed to them two floorboards approximately forty inches apart. Each had three nails spaced the same distance. Only those two floorboards had that peculiar pattern of nails. Scott held the screwdriver against the nail closest to him and lifted it. He and Jon both leaned in looking for anything special about the nail. Jon noticed it first. The hole was drilled and a small slot went down and out of sight. He pointed at it with the pen he was using to mark the floor.

"Why do you think . . . ?" he mused.

"Ah, I see what you mean," Scott replied. He tugged on the nail, which made it fall away from the magnet. Placing the end against it once again, he slightly turned the handle as he lifted, and incredibly, it came out.

"What the hell?" wondered Jon aloud.

That was when he noticed the end of the nail was bent like a L

"A puzzle . . . it's like a puzzle box," Scott said as it dawned on him what this could be.

"What's a puzzle box?" Jon asked.

"It's a box that will have pieces or pins or magnets that have to be taken out in a specific way or order to be opened. They usually are used to store small valuables," he again studied the planks and nails they had identified and marked. "I would venture a guess something here has to be taken out in some particular order to lift the boards. Let's get the others pulled."

They bent to the task, and as Scott was able to rotate each nail carefully with the magnet, he found the corresponding slot and removed the nails. When all six were removed Scott attempted to lift one of the boards with the tip of the screwdriver but had no luck doing so, and after several attempts, he sat back on his haunches to rest his back and again study the boards.

Jon had been watching him carefully and after a moment said, "Try the board on your left, try to lift the *right* side of it first."

Scott did and miraculously the board came up. They both noticed that the end of the board was cut to have a type of fin, or hinge on it.

Scott looked up at him and said, "And the next one?"

"That must be the right board, so try lifting if from *left* to right."

Scott's hand trembled slightly, but within a moment, the board lifted out. That was when they could see that underneath each was the outside wall of a box and at the bottom of each open plank was a metal silver handle.

"Mother of God," breathed Scott, "it's a hatch of some kind."

He looked up above them at the lifting device so cleverly hidden into the 4x4.

"And that," he said, "was what was used to lower women into whatever is below us."

Army and Dan were ready to put out the last four tike lights that illuminated the Halloween backdrop as Anthony and Sammy reached the yard. The moon was high now, almost directly overhead, and the boys caught up to their fathers as they snuffed out the first, second and third light; the only one left was closest to Ax-Man, and Dan went over to place the bamboo cap over the last flame. The medallions around the boys' necks began to grow very hot, and the silver-gray light of the moon cast ghostly shadows all around them.

It was time.

They both knew it was time.

Strangely, Sammy was the first to speak, his voice sounding confident. "Dad, are you and mom still having some friends over to our house later?"

"Yep we are son why?"

"Well, we want to sleep out and we want to be sure it's still ok even if Mr. and Mrs. Petrucci aren't here and we're alone for a while. It's ok then?"

"Are you ok with that Army? Do you think it'll be a problem?"

Army seemed lost in thought for a moment, then replied, "You two have to promise to keep an eye on that fire until we get back and absolutely no running around the neighborhood, got it?"

"We won't," promised Anthony.

"Nah, we won't, we'll just stay up at the barn," added Sammy.

"Ok, everybody," Army said, "let's go up to the house and make sure your moms agree."

As they turned to go, Dan, who was nearest to Ax-Man, said, "Good Lord, what is that smell?"

"It's *that*," Sammy spoke up using his thumb to point over at Ax-Man. "We're taking it apart tomorrow and getting rid of it, right Anth?"

"Yeah, gettin' rid of it."

Army was already halfway to the house when he turned around and waved his hand toward them, "Come on you guys, hustle!"

The boys passed too close to Ax-Man and pain flared white hot through the medallions hidden beneath their sweatshirts. They both sucked in a quick painful breath. In an earlier conversation, they had discussed that something like this could happen, and they had indeed anticipated it. They did not show on the outside the fear that was doing its best to plant a dark destructive seed within them, but instead continued going at a normal pace to the house, as cold sweat ran down the small of their backs.

It was just after 9:30 p.m. when both cars pulled out of the driveway going up the road toward the Brogan house. Mindy and Danni had individually issued marching orders to their sons. They were to travel only between the house and the barn, they were not to stuff themselves on a bunch of junk, no soda after ten and each was given an extra blanket to take to the barn. In addition, when Danni came home, if it seemed too cold they would have to come to the house.

Army and Dan stood in the background trying, but unsuccessfully, to keep the smiles off their faces. Multiple kisses and hugs later the boys stood by the fire watching the taillights go up the road, and when out of sight, they made a dash inside the barn. Grabbing the flashlight's they pulled *The Fifth Pentacle of Mars* medallions out from beneath their shirts. Next, they made a beeline back outside and quickly stacked four more big logs onto the fire wanting a large blaze to illuminate the door to the barn as much as possible, knowing it would give them the advantage of looking out from the dark into the light. Hopefully, they should see *it* before *it* saw them. That was the theory at least.

Again they looked down to the Halloween backdrop, but because all the lights that had earlier illuminated the area were now out, it was impossible to be completely positive what was there and what was not. They moved back inside the barn with great urgency and got into place. It was very quiet for the first several minutes as they listened intently as they had never listened before; they listened with their heart, they listened with their soul.

Finally, Sammy whispered ever so quietly in the darkness, “How long do you think ’til it gets here?”

“I dunno bro, we just have to wait.”

“It’s the hardest part Anth, this waiting.”

“Yeah, it is. That thing out there is hoping we’ll let our guard down, and if we do, that’s when it’ll get us, so stay alert. Can you see anything out the window?”

“No nothing,” Sammy sand as he turned to his left and looked out the small window

They were lost in their thoughts in that space and time, looking out of the windows and the main door, watching. The fire outside flickered, waxing and waning. It became mesmerizing; the glimmer of light, the perfume of smoke; radiant red coals, yellow and blue flames. Sammy yawned and Anthony’s eyes felt grainy and tired. Their tense bodies were relaxing, lulled into a false sense of security. Sammy’s flashlight slipped from his grip and rolled toward Anthony who bent over to retrieve it. As they straightened up and he handed it back to his friend, their eyes caught the change in the firelight.

Shadows suddenly seemed to dance in wicked, depraved movement, the beginnings of a ritual sacrifice. Sammy’s hand fumbled with the flashlight as he struggled to get it to his chin and his thumb on the switch.

“The handle Sammy, grab the handle!” Anthony hissed his voice choked in absolute fear.

Then suddenly, in that awful, unnerving, inhuman movement, Ax-Man filled the doorway. Its eyes were yellow and feline, insidious beyond anything the human psyche could truly comprehend.

Anthony’s legs trembled as adrenaline coursed through his body and his heart hammered like a piston in his chest.

"Anth! Anth!" Sammy croaked, terror, deep and chilling taking over.

"Go!" was Anthony's urgent reply and they both committed simultaneously to fate and illuminated their faces with the flashlights.

Ax-Man remained in the doorway; the campfire behind him looked as though it had become a raging inferno, or the entrance to the gates of hell. A hot coil of air gushed in around him filling the barn with a revolting stench that caused both boys to gag.

Its hands flexed into fists, opened and closed, claws scraping against leathery, hard palms. The thing before them opened its jaws showing double canine teeth on each side, the incisors both top and bottom were pointed, like the teeth of a panther. It closed its mouth slightly and those awful, nightmarish teeth began to chatter together faster and faster making an un-earthly loathsome sound.

Sammy was breathing hard through his mouth, his flashlight wavering, his hand on the handle of the washer trembling enough to cause just the slightest movement of the tarp.

Anthony could see it at the same time Ax-Man took two steps into the barn turning its head left and right, eyes glowing, the hideous sound of those teeth chattering, "Come on! Come on!" Anthony suddenly shouted at it, the sound of his voice breaking the lasso of fear threatening to pull Sammy into an abyss.

The tarp continued to jiggle, the straw dancing ever so slightly.

The beast began to look down.

Both boys started to wave their flashlights yelling, "Here! We're here!" It looked back up at them, and began to move to its right, just outside of the tarp . . . toward the loose hay.

"Nooooo," moaned Sammy, "Nooooo," the horror in his voice was chilling.

Chattering, chattering, sharp teeth, chattering as it moved *around* the *Devil's Trap* and towards the boys.

Suddenly, from out of the darkness, something large and dark launched through the fetid air toward the form of evil incarnate, and in that moment, Anthony began to scream.

Still on their knees, Jon and Scott looked at each other from across the hatch they had just discovered.

A feeling passed between them, one of resolve and acceptance, and then Jon said, "I'll get the bag."

He stood quickly, grazing his head on the 4x4, causing it to bang against the wall; the loud noise made them both jump.

"Take it easy Jon. Get the bag and let's double check everything before we open this thing."

He rushed to the door where he had set the bag, picked it up and began unzipping the top. It was all there, two lighters, twelve candles, a container each of holy salt and water.

"Check your aspergillum, make sure it's still full," Scott told Jon.

Both men reached inside their jackets pulling out the microphone shaped instrument used to sprinkle holy water on a congregation during religious ceremonies. The head, or bulb and shaft were reservoirs for the holy water.

"Mine's full."

"Me too," said Scott. "Grab the flashlights. When we pull this door up, shine one down to get an idea what's down there." When Jon did not move, Scott looked at him and said, "Jon, you ok?"

Jon looked up, his face ashen.

With dread in his voice, he said, "It seems like a lifetime ago you found me outside that door," he lifted his head motioning toward the doors on the shed. "I've been pushing for this, to stop whatever it was that attacked me and invaded my body but Jesus, Scott, I'm so scared . . . I've never been so friggin scared." Putting his fear into words seemed to bring the darkness in around them as though a force was listening, an iniquitous voyeur, feeding off their emotions.

Scott realized what was happening, saw Jon withdrawing into himself and felt the tide changing. He reached across the space between them and slapped Jon hard in the face. Jon's eyes cleared and for a moment flared in anger.

"Stop it right now!" yelled Scott "pick up those flashlights and let's go!"

Jon blinked; understanding how forces surrounding them were manipulating him, he slightly nodded his head, his eyes clearing and pulled both flashlights next to him.

"I'm set, go on, open it."

Scott grabbed both handles and immediately lifted, not wanting to allow either of them to have second thoughts. The door fit so perfectly that he had to strain to open it, and then it pulled loose and Scott swung to his left laying the hatch door out of the way.

Immediately Jon shined a light down into darkness that looked like a deep well of black water. All they could see was a ladder down to a dirt floor. He handed the other flashlight to Scott, put the strap of the gym bag over his shoulder and without hesitation he lowered his leg to the first step and started down. Scott was right behind him and as soon as both stepped off the ladder, their flashlights darted hurriedly around, on the walls the floor the ceiling and into corners. Like flashes of lightening, they swept from side to side and up and down, illuminating everything in a ghost like manner. Even with flashlights, the dark seemed to envelope them in a hostile and intimidating cocoon.

The walls appeared to be of black plastic attached to a wood substructure. Everywhere on the walls were demonic symbols painted in white; and in the dim flickering light, they seemed to be undulating in anticipation. Directly to their left was a filthy mattress on the floor, and on the right was what appeared to be a medical examination table with a stand next to it.

Scott turned in that direction and played his light on the table looking at the instruments and tools. In a hushed voice he said, "Jon, he built this to work as an autopsy table . . . medical tools," he swept his light along one side then then the other and said, "and dental too."

Across from them, they could see shackles along the wall, and an area that appeared to have been to force someone to kneel and be tied down. All had dark heavy stains around them. Nearby was a toilet, which had a shelf above it that held several different size hoses and bottles. Next to that was a wooden chair with wide arms and foot restraints. As Jon played his flashlight along it, he saw what appeared to be electrodes attached in different spots. He followed the wires up across the ceiling, also covered in black plastic and saw above them a cone-shaped light.

"Scott, up there, look," he said stepping forward and reaching up to pull the small chain next to the fixture.

A weak light splayed-out in a small area around them, as the fixture swayed slightly from side to side, causing shadows to ebb and flow around them, motes of dust from the dirt floor flowing up like mist

That was when they saw it, saw what was carved into the mostly clay dirt at the end, saw what unbridled evil and depravity could truly do.

The undulating walls seemed filled with voices now, murmuring in eagerness. Both men stood completely still, their flashlights at their sides, dreading to see in detail what that weak light had revealed.

The heavy clay earth was dug and carved into small niches. The entire wall was full of niches, and each niche held the head of a woman. It looked as though the face and scalp of each had been stripped off, the flesh beneath removed, and the face replaced like some garish, dry mask. Each one had been done differently, all to accentuate their moment of absolute horror. Some had eyes squinted shut, brows furrowed, mouths open in a silent, unheard scream of pain. Great care had been taken to stage those pitiful, tortured faces. One mouth had been twisted to somehow end up almost under the cheekbone; another had precise stitches between top and bottom lips, sealing them for all eternity. Yet another had lips that had been peeled back much like a twist open can, revealing teeth that had been filed to small, sharp points. They saw also, that every one of the mouths' was carefully painted in deep red lipstick. Here and there, eyes were open revealing dark sockets that stared back at them from the depths of utter, total madness. Several had disheveled hair hanging down, lank and greasy, and then there were those whose hair seemed to have been brushed away from their faces very carefully to display Jigs handiwork. Each had a small dark candle next to them, the whole display was in the shape of a pyramid and every possible space on the wall was filled.

It was macabre, grisly and horrific beyond description.

"Oh dear God," breathed Scott.

The murmuring seemed to get louder in their heads, and both men took a step back, Jon turned to Scott, his face pallid, and said, "Can you feel it? All around us like static. That portal is here, can you feel it Scott?"

They turned together, again playing their lights toward the other end still shrouded mostly in darkness. It revealed more black plastic covered with white symbols. Jon began to walk toward the opposite wall and Scott stepped carefully with him.

"We're being watched," said Scott, "and not by those poor tortured souls behind us."

"I've been here before," said Jon in a voice just above a whisper. "This is my nightmare, this is the lair. But there's no portal . . . where is the portal!" His voice almost hissed.

It was not the voice of a man looking for a portal to destroy, but a portal to worship.

It was the fiendish hiss in Jon's voice that scared Scott, and the way his face seemed to slightly contort and become misshapen. Frightened, he sensed that Jon was being pulled back by the parasite that had desecrated his body just a few days ago and tried again to gain a foothold on him just minutes before in the shed.

The bag fell off his shoulder and hit the dirt floor as Jon looked at Scott with eyes that were not entirely his; Scott dropped quickly to the bag, unzipped it, fumbled for a candle and lighter, and with trembling hands lit the wick. It caught immediately, the glow bright and steady, and as Scott stood to hold it up, the light cast a conical luminosity around them. In relief, he saw the beastly glint leave his friends eyes and his face relaxed.

For a moment, Jon looked disoriented, and then his eyes came back into complete focus and opened wide as he realized what had almost happened. It seemed to harden his resolve, and he began with renewed vigor to turn his flashlight into dark recesses of the hellish place.

"Look there Scott, see both those pipes? That's what's going up inside the body of the shed, and there are the small intake fans. They *are* breathing tubes; they're used to bring fresh air down here."

The light danced along the wall that had the hatch door and landed on a shelf that had what appeared to be dozens of DVDs in clear plastic cases. He stepped over and picked up several, looking at the writing on the front.

"What's written on them?"

"The word *Invisible* and then numbers, 1, 2, 3 and so on."

He turned away from the shelf back towards the end wall and his light hit on something that did not make sense. The end piece of black plastic did not appear fixed to the wooden substructure, as were the other walls; instead at the top was what appeared to be a one-inch piece of black PVC pipe attached by a bracket to each long sidewall. There were black grommets punched into the plastic through which black rings of some sort were fitted, essentially turning it into a huge plastic curtain. Jon turned and looked at Scott, signaling with a circle like movement of his light toward the top of the pipe. They stood for several moments looking at it, feeling the static's powerful force more intense closer to this end; each could feel the hairs on their neck and arms standing up.

The noise was becoming louder, unnerving, sounding more like some ghastly chant.

They both bent quickly to the bag between them, Jon removing the candles and Scott the salt. They began with the salt first, Scott pouring a large ring around them. They were alarmed when they watched the rock hard ground within that salt ring soften like sand, until Jon realized what they would now be able to do. He worked quickly to place the twelve candles within the circle, in the now loose, sandy soil.

With the lit candle he still held, Scott began lighting the wicks as Jon clicked on the lighter and did the same on his side of the circle. There was a change in the air, and both men were further unnerved when they realized that the darkness had closed in around them. Utter, total, complete blackness. Their circle of light was like a beacon that contained them, unwavering and nova like, but the light did not blind them, but rather gave them clear vision directly ahead. Jon reached out from the circle with the end of his flashlight toward the black plastic curtain, and immediately the darkness closed around his hand and arm, coldness painfully compressing his flesh. In shock, he jerked it back into the protective light and looked in alarm at Scott, lines of fear etched in his face.

"We have to get that opened," he said, a sharp edge of alarm in his voice.

When Scott questioned what it had felt like, the only word Jon could use to explain was *repulsive.* Scott thought for a moment, then reached down and picked up the other lighter. Each was about eight inches long. The metal ends had notches stamped into them, and he took those two ends and forced them together, twisting them a half turn so they became, essentially, one piece, which then made the whole thing approximately fifteen inches long. Holding the lighter contraption in his right hand, he reached inside his jacket with his left, pulled out the aspergillum, and sprinkled holy water from his elbow to the end of the two entwined lighters.

Jon watched him, eyes wide and he nodded slowly. "It should work. You ready?"

Scott nodded his head and plunged his hand and arm forward out of their protective circle toward the plastic curtain. The reaction was immediate and unexpected. The darkness pulled back, away from his arm and the lighters as though in agony, and in that brief moment of surprise Scott was able to use the end of the lighter to find the edge of the plastic and in one fluid motion, he swept the plastic back like a curtain along the PVC pipe revealing the wall behind.

It was Sheol. It was Acheron. It was Gehenna. It was Tophet.

What they saw was beyond words.

It was the abyss of eternal damnation.

CHAPTER 35

As the sound of Anthony's scream echoed across the barn, Ax-Man was hit hard on its right side by the dark form that had come from out of nowhere, causing it to stumble awkwardly sideways to the left . . . towards the *Devil's Trap.*

Anthony realized what was about to happen and screamed at Sammy, "TURN IT SAM! TURN IT! TURN IT!" his voice pleading and commanding at the same time.

Fear flooded Sammy's body with adrenalin and he cranked the handle on the washer so hard that the blue tarp came away with a snapping *whoooosshh,* the straw being pulled along with it leaving the drawing miraculously clean of any debris. The creature recoiled at the sight of the trap, but nonetheless, was drawn into it as a magnet draws steel, pulling it across the perimeter to the center of Solomon's seal where it laid motionless.

Sammy and Anthony looked at each other, slack-jawed, eyes large and round in shock and astonishment. On their right, the dark form remained in the shadows lying near the bales of hay. They could hear panting, and saw eerily glowing eyes, and yet in the depths of their fear, they turned their flashlights towards the unknown entity just as it rushed them.

Anthony backpedaled away from the lunging creature, dropping his flashlight, which spun in a circle of bizarre flashes of light and dark. Anthony threw his arms up crossing them in front of his face without thinking, covering his throat as he was hit hard in the chest. He heard Sammy yelling something, but could not understand what he was saying; that was when he felt something wet on his face. He wondered for a moment if it was blood when suddenly Sammy was beside him pulling his hands away, pushing the weight from his chest. As he opened his eyes, he heard Sammy's voice again and this time he heard clearly.

"Ebony! Ebony! Come here girl! Come here!"

In astonishment, Anthony realized it was the Russelton's missing dog, which everyone thought, was dead. Her coat was matted and dirty, she smelled horrible and was shockingly thin, but it was Ebony. Her body wagged back and forth wildly, and it was then that they realized her tail was missing.

"Jesus God, look at that, it looks like her tail was just ripped off," said Sammy, sorrow and disgust in his voice.

Then sudden movement caught their attention and they looked up just in time to see the beast charge at them from across the *Devil's Trap* . . .

Is e Dia fhèin as buachaill dhomh, cha bhi mi ann an dìth

. . . Scott and Jon looked into a maelstrom hideous beyond belief and saw a vortex of black, blue and red, whirling and spinning sickeningly, it was violently shot through with what looked like bolts of thin lightening. Through those powerful currents of evil moved faces ghastly and macabre. Faces white and deformed, horrid eyes sunken and black. Lipless mouths dripping blood and black death, grotesque heads with elongated noses, lumpy nostrils flaring above fat flabby lips that looked to be sucking the flesh from a human hanging out of that hellish mouth, blood sprayed like so much juice from an over ripe piece of fruit. Being eaten alive, those poor souls raised their hands in a final plea.

Into the whirlpool of insanity the men stared, transfixed by the bulging insidious eyes, forked tongues, and squirming serpents. Through that portal, they saw into the nightmarish core of hell and it was unimaginable suffering; what they heard was every sound, and no sound. It was crying, moaning and shrieking. It was whimpering, screaming and sobbing. Voices that were pleading, begging and praying to the Dark One for mercy that would never in all eternity be given.

Suddenly all those faces and all those eyes turned their way. The portal bulged towards them and the candles glowed brighter, the ring of holy salt gleamed white as the sun.

No words were spoken between the two men. Jon reached in his jacket and removed the other aspergillum. He held it in his left hand and shook holy water onto his right arm and hand, the water refreshing and cool on his flesh.

The portal swelled and throbbed like a putrid boil ready to burst and spew its corruption. Jon trembled slightly and looked at Scott with eyes full of resolve. Scott nodded his head once, and together they plunged their hands and arms into the void of hell . . .

. . . . Ebony jumped in front of the boys, her jaws snapping as Ax-Man rushed toward them. They scrabbled backwards on all fours trying to get away from it, Sammy ramming his head into the washer. Incredibly, when it got to the edge of the *Devil's Trap,* Ax-Man was pulled violently back, as though it had run into an invisible wall. The force threw it across to the other side, and as it slid on the floor its boots stuttering across the boards. With blurring, unearthly speed, it was up again running at them, and again it hit the invisible force that seemed to surround the *Devil's Trap.* They could see shimmering ripples, like waves of heat rising in the dead of summer, or like the plane of a still lake when a fly barely touches the surface to drink, making small, thin, perfect ripples cascade across the water. Repeatedly it ran at them only to be stopped as the boys watched mesmerized, not knowing what they should do.

Sammy noticed it first. The shimmering was more pronounced now, the ripples less perfect, deeper. When it hit the next time, the creature seemed closer.

That was when Sam realized what was happening.

"Anthony, it's scraping the drawing off the floor . . . look."

He pointed with a ghostly finger toward the *Devil's Trap;* Anthony saw it then too. The drawing was becoming defaced, damaged, and blurred, and as it did, it was becoming weaker.

Ebony was still snapping and barking at the creature, and Anthony called her back to them and looked at Sammy.

"What can we do? I can't fix it, and once it scrapes enough off, the trap will fail!" his voice had an edge of hysteria to it.

It stopped.

It looked at them and then at the floor.

It understood.

It dropped to its knees and began feverishly sweeping at the floor . . .

Is e Dia fhèin as buachaill dhomh, cha bhi mi ann an dith

. . . and as their arms left the haven of light and entered the dark, the portal pulsed like a laboring heart. They reached as far as they could and began to flick their aspergillums scattering holy water across the engorged surface. The result was instantaneous and violent. The earthen floor around them began to heave and boil making their circle of light an island. Jon, in his frenzied attempt to close the portal, had quickly emptied his aspergillum. He pulled his arm in from the darkness that encircled them and grabbed for the gym bag, quickly refilling the reservoir with holy water. Again, he sprinkled his arm and hand, thrust it back into the darkness, and began anew to douse the portal.

Suddenly a high-pitched keening began. The intensity of the sound caused Jon and Scott both to flinch. The piercing sound felt as though it burrowed deep within their brains and burned molten hot. Scott began to falter, his arm lowering as he grabbed his head with his free hand within their safe wall of light and tried to push the pain away.

"Don't stop Scott!" yelled Jon, "don't stop!"

Scott pulled his arm back within their dome, bent to the gym bag, and grabbed the jar of holy salt.

"What are you doing?" yelled Jon, his voice jagged and hoarse.

Scott stood with the jar and poured his right hand full of holy salt, pushed his arm again into the darkness, and with strength he did not know he possessed, cast the salt into portal.

No verbiage known to man could ever explain the sound that erupted from that mass, nor the reeking, fetid smell, nor the visions that rolled past at a furious speed, a whirlwind of sickening sights that caused both men to gag.

It was then that the throbbing portal began to split open and something dark and demonic began working its way through the split, the birth canal of all that is evil, depraved and fiendish. What they saw caused them to recoil towards the back wall of their sanctuary in abject terror, for out of the split emerged a ghastly giant hand. Gray and red mottled, it appeared covered with scales; the palm was black and leathery, with thick bristling, stiff hairs that might be found on the abdomen of some monstrous bloated spider. All of the long fingers had ghastly gnarled, sharp looking protrusions from each knuckle and ended in black pointed claws. Beneath the skin, some*thing's* seemed to writhe repulsively. The horrific appendage of Satan rolled slightly to its right and then curled into a fist rising above them and the glow of their sacred candles.

Helplessly they watched as the oncoming strike from the fist of Belial rushed down toward them and they felt despair grip their souls in the nova of light that exploded around them . . .

. . . and the Beast they had in innocence named Ax-Man, rushed the edge of the circle again, and to their horror, part of its arm and leg broke through. Enraged, it jerked and pulled until it was back within the trap, and again fell to its knees and with a sleeve of the coveralls, began once more to try to wipe away the drawing that was the *Devil's Trap.* Anthony and Sammy remained immobilized by terror as they watched powerlessly; Ebony remained at their side, her lips drawn back in a snarl, eyes slits of hatred, her ears high on each side of her head, a low growl rumbling from deep inside her.

It charged again, ferociously trying to tear its way through whatever the invisible wall was, struggling until again it freed itself and returned to the drawing, this time scrubbing another part of the *Devil's Trap*. It moved impossibly fast, and this time when it charged, the latest erasure resulted in over half of its body coming through. The Beast tilted its head back and roared with an unearthly sound that made their blood run cold in unbound terror. It thrashed violently to release itself upon the two boys who stood helplessly transfixed, panic etched in their faces.

They were backed up now, almost against the wall, except for Ebony who held her ground. It was coming through, they knew it was coming through and they realized there was nothing they could do to stop it.

Strangely, calmness washed over each boy, and they found themselves thinking of wonderful happy times with each other and their families, their minds picking out scenes to view. Anthony closed his eyes in those last moments, his mind choosing to relive those flashes of happiness; he felt the swirling movement of air and sensed a prickling sensation on his skin, he was ready.

Ebony began barking again, though differently now, almost like her old self, as if she were bounding through piles of leaves and joyfully romping with the kids. Somewhere within the calmness, Anthony realized that the prickling sensation was not unpleasant, and he realized the howling from the Beast was no longer triumphant.

As his eyes snapped back open, he saw before him the form of a beautiful woman with long dark hair, her arms out stretched, the palms of her hands focusing towards the Beast. All about her was a flowing aura, beautiful and breathtaking; colors of red, blue and green, glimmering, shining, emitting wave upon wave of inconceivable power.

Incredibly, she was somehow holding the creature at bay, pitting the strength of her will, of her aura against the embodied evil before them.

Sammy stumbled next to Anthony, his voice sounding small against the horrendous noises all around them. "Who is she? What . . . what is she?"

"I don't know Sammy. I don't know who she is or what is going on and I don't know how long she can hold it back," Anthony responded as the beast thrashed madly back and forth, jerking, pulling and kicking, to try and lose itself upon the woman. Her arms, now thrust stiffly forward, were straining against the force of the Beast

"Look," said Anthony, as he felt sweat running down his back, soaking the top of his jeans, "her light isn't as bright. I think she's getting weaker Sammy, I don't think she can hold out much longer . . . ,"

Is e Dia fhèin as buachaill dhomh, cha bhi mi ann an dith

. . . it materialized from nowhere, bright beyond imagining, bright as a super nova, and their skin burned with a million pinpoints of light, light flowing into every corner of the hellish hole. They turned their faces up towards the radiance in veneration, and felt more than heard a thud as The Hand of God slipped under Satan's Fist, abruptly stopping its decent, delivering to Scott and Jon, a new providence.

The battle began then, and the light . . .

. . . . shot down through the barn, into the circle that was the Devil's Trap, and into the Beast, jerking it back, away from the woman. The creature's arms stiffened straight down its sides, it legs appeared to lock, and the vile Beast began to rock and buck as though it was secured in an executioner's electric chair, a deadly current coursing through its body. The head began to turn back and forth, faster and faster until it was a blur of uncontrollable movement and the floor began to smoke. The woman pressed forward, her aura becoming again bright, now blazing; she lifted her hands higher . . .

. . . and The Hand of God forced Satan's Fist back, back towards the putrid rip in the portal, back to the nightmare vision of Dante's inferno, back, all the while Satan's Fist squirmed and twisted and clawed. The Hand of God drove Satan's Fist through the tear in the portal then suddenly the abomination retreated, darting spider-like back into its hole.

The bright, searing light from The Hand of God blazed on the portal and the portal began to shrink as if a healing wound purged of corruption, and as it became smaller, the sounds waned and the wailing became distant until at last they were no more.

Then The Hand of God turned its palm toward the men as if in benediction, banishing the evil from that cursed place and returning to both men their souls. The Hand began to dissipate then, becoming mist like, the tendrils spread out around them and met again on the opposite end, seeming to caress the dozens of decapitated heads stored on the clay shelves, releasing them from their prison of darkness.

It brightened for just a moment, and then winked out leaving Jon and Scott within the circle of light and it was then they both realized they had fallen to their knees, in awe of the miracle they had just witnessed . . .

. . . from the Beast's head, a tar black shadow began to twirl and twist. Corkscrew like, it rose up toward the roof of the barn like a rope of smoke, escaping out through the area where the weather vane was located. As it spiraled up, Ax-Man's convulsions became more violent and its clothes took on a sagging appearance. The woman's aura radiated now all around the *Devil's Trap* and the tar like smoke spun faster and faster until suddenly it pulled straight and jerked powerfully upwards pulling with it a nightmarish lump studded with root-like appendages that squirmed like the serpents of Medusa head. As it hit the roof of the barn, wood exploded, raining pieces around them causing the boys to throw their arms over their heads in protection.

The form that was once Ax-Man lay crumpled in the center of the *Devil's Trap.* The boots turned out away from one another, the dirty, stained coveralls were in a heap along with the clawed gloves that had been its hands. The mask, the bane of all the evil that had transpired, was several feet away with the face turned up toward the ceiling of the barn.

The aura of the woman receded until it surrounded only her and she turned to face Anthony and Sammy. Though her form was not solid but more mist like, she possessed a head of gleaming shoulder length black hair that framed emerald green eyes. She wore an exquisite flowing white gown that brushed against the floor with long sleeves that came to points just above her slim lovely hands. She began to move toward them, her slippered feet and gown disturbing not a single piece of straw, until she stood no more than an arm's length away. Her gaze, tranquil and calm, and her lovely, slightly sad smile entranced the boys. She leaned in, first toward Anthony, then Sammy taking each face between her beautiful loving hands and gently bestowed a feather soft kiss on each forehead, drawing each in turn into her aura. They both felt a warm glow flow through them, calm and clean, and within the aura of their guardian, they knew . . . rapture.

She turned and moved back across the barn passing over the drawing of the *Devil's Trap*, and where she passed it became as though the drawing had never existed. When she reached the doorway, she looked back at the boys and gestured with her right hand, first toward the clothes and mask, then toward the fire outside that was blazing brightly. She stepped away from the door and was gone.

The boys stood silently for a moment, then without a word, set about the task given them, the last request of their Guardian Angel.

CHAPTER 36

What had once been the *Hell Hole* was now bright with lights as was the shed above. Before calling the station for a forensics crew and backup, Scott and Jon began picking up all the candles, noticing as they pulled them out of the sandy soil, how each one went out. Quietly they packed the gym bag with the holy candles, water and salt along with the aspergillums and took everything to the car packing it away from anyone who may look in the back. In the quiet darkness, they had gone back to the underground room to take a closer look at the women's heads set into the wall. There were thirty-two. The same amount of purses they had found stuffed into cupboards in Jigs house when the investigation had begun in what now seemed like a lifetime ago. They stood quietly for several minutes giving each victim the dignity they deserved.

They intended to have their own look around before the place was crawling with police and news reporters; they wanted to have the first chance at putting all the pieces together.

Part of the puzzle remained at the Petrucci residence and Jon said to Scott, "Do you think we should take a ride out there now?"

"No. I think we should get a team out here first and get the ball rolling. Then we can leave here knowing we have the scene under control and a perimeter staked out. We don't want anyone coming by because they saw lights or the car and start poking around where they shouldn't be."

They split up, each taking a half of the space, looking closely and taking notes and pictures on their cell phones. Finally satisfied that they could make the call to the station, they went back up the ladder to the shed area to get a clear signal for their cell phones. Just as Jon was ready to flip his phone open to call, it began to ring.

He looked quickly up at Scott and said, "Its Brian Shockley, he's handling Aunt Maureen's case," he tapped his phone and said, "Hello? I'm fine Brian, what's up?"

Jon listened intently, and when Scott saw the shocked look that came over his face, he moved next to him ready to support his friend in whatever way he needed.

Anthony and Sammy went to the tack room where Sammy picked up an old pitchfork and Anthony a long handled shovel. They made their way back to where the pile of clothes, shoes, the mask and hands lay on the floor, where the *Devil's Trap* had been just minutes ago.

Sammy slid the pitchfork under the pile of clothes while Anthony scoped up the shoes and they walked silently outside to the fire-pit. Though it felt as though a lifetime had gone by, the fire looked as though only minutes since they had put on the last logs, but the position of the moon in the sky told them it was much later.

Sammy walked without hesitation to the fire and threw the clothes on first. The flames roared up, and he quickly step back from the intense heat. Anthony was right behind him with the shoes, and when he tossed them onto the fire, it again flared high and burned very hot. They stood for a moment only, and went immediately back into the barn. Sammy was able to get the rubber hands on his pitchfork while Anthony walked up to the mask and stood looking down at it. He noticed the symbol that he had seen weeks ago on that first night his dad had brought it into their house. He pointed it out to Sammy with the tip of the shovel.

Sammy nodded and said, "Let's go."

They walked with deliberation to the fire, which had amazingly already completely consumed the clothes and boots.

Together, they threw the clawed hands and stained face into the inferno, the result, astonishing. A huge flair of flames climbed at least twenty feet into the night air, and the fire roared loudly. The lower jaw of the mask seemed to drop open showing one last time that hideous maw. The hands merely melted; the mask seemed to burn away like layers of diseased flesh, horrible to see, yet they were unable to look away. They watched until even the ash was gone, and once it was, the fire instantly retreated to normal; still the boys remained standing next to each other, staring at the pious flames, each lost in his own thoughts.

Sammy spoke first. “I’m ready to lie down, are you?”

“Yeah, I’m tired. You ok sleeping out here?”

“I’m ok with it.”

“Me too. We’d better pick up the rest of the stuff in the barn in case mom and dad check on us when they come home.”

They each put an arm around the other’s shoulder and went back into the barn. They unhooked the tarp from the ringer washer and folded it up then rolled the nylon rope up around itself and together they were able to move the washer back to its original location. When they looked up at the hole in the roof they realized there was nothing they could do to repair it and decided they would have to deal with it tomorrow in the light, when they could see.

After they climbed into their sleeping bags, they laid for a long time watching the moon, each lost to the memory of the euphoria they had felt within the aura of their Guardian Angel. They fell asleep as the luminescence from the full harvest moon spilled into the barn, bathing them in silvery light that lulled them both into peaceful slumber.

Sometime after midnight, Danni and Army pulled in the driveway. They drove slowly by the barn and could see that the fire had burned down to red coals. The night was cool but not cold and Danni and Kelley had decided earlier that the boys could remain in the barn for this, their final sleep out of the year.

“Do you want to go up?” Army starting to brake.

"No honey, I'm sure they're sound asleep and just as tired as we are," said Danni turning toward her husband. She reached over and rubbed the back of his neck, "Let's just go to bed and get some rest, everything else can wait 'til tomorrow."

As he leaned over and kissed his wife on the cheek, he missed the shadow lurking by the grave he had discovered near the barn.

It was something he would regret the next morning.

Jon stood stock still listening unblinking to the voice on the other end of his cell phone until at last he said, "Thanks for calling Brian. I'll get back to you in just a bit," he listened again for a moment then responded, "ok, I'll wait then bye."

He slipped his phone into his pocket, and scrubbed his hands over his face, his eyes bright with tears.

"What did they find?" Scott asked quietly.

Jon looked up, his eyes glistening, and with a quavering voice, he said softly, "Aunt Maureen and Aunt Dee. Brian found them at the Casino hotel in Wheeling. Apparently, they went there to gamble, and the car was stolen from a security parking lot that they paid extra to park in. The hotel management put them up until they could get them a rental car and file a police report. They're both fine, celebrating at the hotel. The hotel gave them $100.00 worth of free coins to play . . . Aunt Dee hit for $500,000.00."

How mysterious that tears can be shed in the depths of despair or the pinnacle of joy. Scott stood looking at Jon, stunned. They began to laugh, and laugh so hard that they bent over when their stomach muscles began to hurt.

They laughed so hard they cried.

CHAPTER 37

It was several minutes past eight, and Anthony and Sammy had not yet come down from the barn. Danni had started breakfast, positive that the aroma of frying bacon wafting out the partially open kitchen window would soon have the boys at the house. She peered out the window thinking they must have been more tired than she had originally thought.

Army had decided to go outside for a while and begin taking down decorations with a plan to focus on the big items first since they took up the most space in the garage and basement.

As he got closer to the main display, with a jolt he immediately noticed that Ax-Man was gone. He stopped and looked around the yard to see if any of the parts were strewn about the yard but saw nothing at first, and then what he thought he saw didn't make sense. As he walked closer he realized what he was looking at and fear ran its cold zinging blade painfully down his spine, causing him to suck in his breath as his eyes became round in disbelief.

Four prints in the soft dirt of the thinning grass.

Boot prints.

Ax-Man's boot prints.

Heading toward the barn.

Army took off at a run, his heart pounding like a freight train as he saw several other areas where the grass was laid down from those easily recognizable prints. He was trying to put together all the thoughts and emotions that were pummeling his brain when suddenly the barn door opened and Anthony and Sammy stepped out rubbing sleep from their eyes; the sight of Army sprinting towards them like a lunatic caused both to stumble backwards.

"Dad! What's wrong?" Anthony almost shouted in a voice filled with dread.

Army came to an abrupt stop, taking deep gulping breaths; he bent over resting his hands on his knees, looking back and forth between the two boys.

"Oh . . . Hi guys . . . I was . . . just coming up to . . . get you . . . for breakfast. Are you hungry?"

"I smell bacon," Sammy piped up looking toward the house.

"Nope Dad, we're not hungry. We're . . . STARVED!" he shoved Sammy aside and took off like a gazelle with a loud, "Whooooo!" along the way.

"You rat! Wait til' I catch you!" yelled Sammy galloping after him.

A smile broke out on Army's sweating face as he watched them race off, but as be began to straighten up, he felt something cold and wet on his hand. Quickly looking back down, he was astonished to see two chestnut brown eyes looking up at him from a raggedy coated, tail-less black dog.

"Dear God, Ebony," he whispered.

As she began to bark happily and dance around him, living in that moment, all was right with the world.

CHAPTER 38

Legions of police, detectives, forensics and reporters deluged on the Seederly residence in the weeks and months following the destruction of the portal.

Everyone who saw it left stunned and saddened by what had transpired in that hidden underground room. The FBI requested by the Chief of Police at the behest of the Governor to assure that no stone was left unturned, interviewed hundreds of people, poured over the contents of the purses and began collecting DNA samples. All the major networks had deemed the *Hell Hole* the largest serial/mass murder grave ever identified in the eastern United States, not something that Lamont Mayor Bret Knowles was pleased to have broadcast around the world via TV and the internet. FBI agents, homicide detectives, two profilers, Jon Wendels and Scott Champion, had viewed the DVDs. They were so ghastly, so gruesome that they were immediately sealed. The mummified heads were carefully and respectfully removed, and the long, arduous job of identification began. The purses that had been in Jigs Seederly's house appeared to belong to each of the victims and except for one head, which had had each tooth pulled out prior to the victim's death, they were hopeful the dental records would help shorten the process. When identified it was still going to take a long time to bring to these women and their families, the closure they deserved.

Neither Jon nor Scott ever revealed the existence of the portal. It would serve no purpose and further complicate and already complicated situation. They had gone to the Petrucci house, several days after Halloween when they felt confident no one was home, and the first thing they noticed was that Ax-Man was gone. They went to the barn and found the doors unlocked.

Jon was first to point out the perfectly clean, perfectly round spot in the middle of the floor.

"It looks the same size as the portal doesn't it?" Jon commented.

"Maybe this was their last stand," replied Scott his eyebrow raised in question.

As the weeks and months went by, both men found that they had lost the passion they once had for their respective professions. Instead, they had begun to surf the net, searching out stories of unsolved or unusual missing persons or murders, those that struck them as supernatural. Finally, they decided to each take a leave of absence from their jobs to follow up on a case in a small W. Virginia town that had caught their eye. They took the little gym bag back to Father Kaylan and got re-equipped with holy candles, salt and water and politely listened as the vicar had cautioned them about the dangers inherent in what they were about to do and promptly gave them some reading materials for the trip.

On their way out of town, they planned to stop by Aunt Maureen and Dee's house.

"Did you finish revamping their new car?" Scott inquired as he turned off the main highway onto the sleepy street where the two women lived.

"Oh my, yes, that baby is sweet. 1972 banana yellow mustang fastback, four barrel, modified cam, a Cleveland block and throaty glass-packs. Oh God, I love watching the two of them drive down the street with their wrap around shades! The motor heads look at them with their tongues hanging out," the two men shared a good laugh and Jon continued, "Isn't it amazing that ever since they hit that $500,000.00 they've been incredibly lucky?"

"Yeah, especially for us too, since they fronted the seed money for this expedition," Scott replied as a huge smile played across his face.

"In the last six months between the two of them they've won, I think another $60,000.00, and they're having the time of their lives."

"God bless 'em. I love it when deserving people come out on top," said Scott as he shook his head and laughed.

An odd ringing filled the inside of the car.

"What the hell is that?" Scott asked, as Jon began digging in his jacket pocket.

"A new Droid with all the bells and whistles." I had it programmed to alert me when stories regarding possible supernatural occurrences appear on news feeds," he began to feverishly push buttons, paused for a moment then said, "whoa, listen to this!"

With that they began the next phase of their new careers, having no idea the wild ride on which they were about to embark.

ɕɤ ɕɤ ɕɤ ɕɤ ɕɤ ɕɤ ɕɤ ɕɤ ɕɤ ɕɤ ɕɤ ɕɤ ɕɤ ɕɤ

The Monday after Halloween was a parent/teacher conference at school and while Anthony's mom was attending the conference and his dad was at work, the boys had decided to go down to the barn to clean up the straw and the fire pit.

It was colder now, and they had on jackets, hats and gloves. Luckily, Army had shown no interest in going into the barn since that night. He had been busy cleaning up Halloween decorations and returning the yard to normal. Much to Anthony's surprise, he was throwing many things away. When the issue of Ax-Man came up, Army maintained that some high school kids must have come to the house late and taken it as a prank.

"We'll probably see it in somebody else's yard next year," he had said.

Anthony could tell by his lack of concern that Army was secretly glad it was gone. He wondered how much his dad knew, or at least suspected. Someday, maybe someday, they would talk about it.

The boys went into the barn first, and each grabbed a broom walking to where the *Devil's Trap* had been. A perfectly clean, perfectly round circle was still there, with no vestige of the drawing remaining; no sign that smoke had risen from the floor as if on fire. It was pristine.

They both looked up at the roof and could see the hole at the top by the old weathervane. It looked smaller than it had the other night, as though it was . . . . healing. They began to sweep the loose hay to the right half of the barn and then raked it into a neat pile. They restacked the bales on the left and made sure the alcove sleeping area in the middle was also picked up and clean.

Once they were satisfied that everything they could do was complete, they went out to the fire pit. The ashes lay cold and gray, a fine packed powder all that remained, yet it still had an ominous memory about it that unsettled both Anthony and Sammy.

"Where do you want to move it too?" Sammy asked.

"I don't know, let's look around," replied Anthony. They began to walk away from the barn, with the door to their backs along the left side where Army had placed stakes for the wall he planned to put in. As they walked along the line, they both noticed the rather wide hole around which Army had stacked some stone to keep anyone from falling in.

"What the heck is this?" Anthony murmured more to himself than to Sammy.

When they approached the hole, they saw there was a stone in the bottom covered with a piece of plastic and some loose dirt that had mostly washed away. Both boys squatted down looking at the marker.

"Pick up your corner and I'll pick up mine. Let's see if we can pull this off with the dirt in it," Anthony said to Sammy. They gently pulled the plastic off, capturing the dirt in the middle and put it off to the side. They could see printing in the sandstone. Sammy was the first to speak.

"I can't tell what it says, can you?"

"I'm not sure but I think it might be names . . . yeah, I think its names."

"What would names be doing on a stone out here?"

"I think it might be a grave stone Sam," Anthony said quietly, looking up at his friend.

"Tell me you're kidding, right?"

"I'm not sure that's what it is, but I'm not kidding. I think we should go ask my dad."

"Let's finish the fire pit first Anth. I want to get that done. Ok?"

"Yeah, you're right, let's get that done first before we get him up here in case there are any questions." Anthony looked around him at all the loose dirt. "Why don't we just cover up the fire pit with this dirt? We can get done sooner that way and find out what this about."

Sammy nodded his head, and they started back for shovels and buckets.

Before the first bucketful of dirt went into the pit, Sammy said to Anthony, "Wait . . . ," he dug into his front pocket and pulled out a small sandwich baggie partially filled with salt . . . holy salt.

"Good idea Sammy. I still have a little left too, wait a sec and I'll go get it,"

Anthony loped back to the house as Sammy stood and looked around the area of the barn, so serene and beautiful with the last autumn color still clinging to trees, the surrounding fields beige and brown, sunlight slipping in and out of the scattered clouds in a blue sky. It was easy to lose yourself to the beauty of this setting, and Sammy just let his mind wander. Oddly, he could picture in his mind what this must have looked like one-hundred years ago. He let his mind drift and somewhere in the 'between' times, he could hear voices, that of a man and a woman talking happily, quietly. His senses picked up the distinctive smell of a horse, warm from a ride, being curried with a soft brush and he could smell apples ripe on trees.

"Sam . . . Sammy?" the sound of his name being called brought him back, so very reluctantly to the task at hand.

"Hey bro, I've got a little more than you. Do you want to pour it all on?"

"All of it, let's put all of it on," said Sammy with sure conviction. Between the two of them, they poured the pure white blessed salt into the black ash that was the last vestige of the evil that for a short time had walked among them. The black ash changed, and seemed to shrink away from the salt, leaving a soft sandy soil behind.

They began then to methodically fill the buckets with dirt and carry them back to the fire pit and fill it in. After each bucket, they packed it down by hitting the top of the dirt with their shovels. They could have stamped on it but neither wanted to be in the pit that had held the remnants of Ax-Man. They packed and pounded until they felt confident everything was completely filled in, and then they started to scavenge rocks to stack on top. They even pounded the first of those into the dirt, stacked them around, and stacked some larger ones on top.

"What are we going to tell your folks about why we filled this in?" Sammy asked wiping his hands on his jeans.

"I don't know, I guess maybe we just want to be on the other side for a change? Hey, let's move our stack of wood over on the other side that might be more convincing."

They heard the crunch of gravel in the driveway and turned to see Army's car driving up toward the house.

"Ok. There he is, let's go see what he says about this stone.

Starting down the hill to the house, by the time they got there, Army was picking up his lunch bag, coat and the mail.

"Hey you two, did you enjoy your day off?"

"I enjoy any day off from school," replied Anthony.

"Me too, especially from English," Sammy offered up.

"So, did you do anything special?"

"Na, we just played some x-box games and then we went up to the barn to clean up and sweep, you know, clean up from the summer and our camp-outs."

"Good. I'll have to go up and take a look."

"Yeah, well, that would be good because we found that big hole along the line where you want to put up the fence and are wondering what the heck it is."

Army stopped halfway in and halfway out of the door between the mudroom and garage.

"The hole," the tone in his voice caused Anthony to look at Sammy then back at his dad.

"Yeah dad, the hole with the stone that some names on it."

Army stepped back holding the door open and said to both boys, "Come on in guys. I'll tell you about the hole . . . and what I found out."

Over the next forty minutes, Army recounted what he had found and what he had learned about the woman named Annaleah Grimmer, her husband and their unborn son. The boys sat in rapt attention, never interrupting, listening and putting pieces of a puzzle together in their own minds.

"And that's all I know," Army said simply when done. "I didn't want to scare you guys before Halloween or before I found out if we could move it. However, we can't move it, so I don't know quite how to settle this. I have to talk to your mom about what she wants to do. My God, I have to tell her too. I forgot to tell your mom," he was lost for a moment in thought, and then said to the boys, "do you have any questions?"

Sammy and Anthony just shook their heads slowly, so very slowly.

They looked at one another, each knowing exactly what the other was thinking without a word spoken.

Deep autumn set in and the last of the leaves had fallen to the ground, silently feeding Mother Earth for another year. By Thanksgiving, the trees had a barren look that made you wonder at the miracle of spring, but it was not ugly, it was simply a different perspective on beauty that God provides, a life lesson if you choose to accept it.

Time is like a soft fragrant breeze that moves past you causing you to turn in its wake and wonder where it had gone. Thanksgiving had turned into Christmas and Christmas in to New Year that quickly. Danni and Army, Mindy and Dan commented when they were together that the boys were growing up so fast. Sammy wanted to be called just 'Sam' now; Anthony, always the steady one seemed more quiet and reflective. That breeze of time had blown through and taken their age of innocence on its breath.

Both Sam and Anthony had been spending time at the library on research. Not research for school projects, but research on the family that had lived on the property where Anthony now lived.

Annaleah and Brandon Grimmer. They were convinced it was Annaleah, who had been their Guardian Angel, but they wanted, they needed, to see a picture of her. As had Army, the boys went to the library whenever they could get a ride to town and later they would hit a movie. They quickly mastered the Microfilm reader, and with the information they gleaned from there began a search on Ancestry.com to hunt records and for relatives, or anyone who could possibly provide a picture of the elusive Annaleah Grimmer. They had been able to learn that she was originally from Cambridge, Massachusetts and that she had met Brandon while he was on a business trip there, and that her maiden name was Tiernan, but for months, that was all they could find.

The first weekend of March found their parents off to the mall to an antique show being held in the concourse. Danni and Mindy planned to shop for summer shorts and shoes, Army, and Dan were going to hit the antique tools that were advertised as the biggest in the northeast. Anthony and Sam had asked to be dropped off in town to go to the movies. The theater was small compared to the ones at the mall, but the boys liked it because it was always less crowded and the snacks cheaper. It also would give them some time to go to the library.

While watching *Avatar*, each had eaten a chili cheese dog with onions, Pepsi and popcorn. After the movie, they walked over to the library, Anthony to go online and continue their search, Sam to look at some hot-rod books, which really meant he wanted to sit in one of the high back, comfortable leather chairs and take a nap in the sun as it streamed in the windows.

Anthony logged onto the public internet and decided to look at the Ellis Island website. He had been checking under the surname of Tiernan with no luck for some time so instead he changed tactics and typed in "Annaleah" when he had no luck, he moved on and retyped it, not realizing he had misspelled it until he tapped enter. He immediately had a hit and saw it was for Annaleaigh MacTiernan—not Annaleah Tiernan. *MacTiernan*, he thought, *an Irish name*. Excitement built within him as an idea began to come to fruition. A common misnomer about Ellis Island was that during its heyday sloppy or careless inspection agents changed names. However, that was not entirely true. Most of the agents were themselves immigrants and often times knew several languages. If any miscommunication occurred, a translator was requested to help.

Rather, names changed because families or individuals chose to change them to fit better into American culture, or occasionally because the written portion was misinterpreted. *Could it be? Could Annaleaigh MacTiernan and Annaleah Tiernan, be the same person?*

He keyed back to Cambridge records and finally found an Annaleaigh but her last name was MacTighearnain. Anthony sat thinking, trying to reason it out. Could this be the same person? If so, why three names? Suddenly he realized Sam was standing next to him.

"How's it going bro?"

Anthony explained what walls he was running into with the different names.

"Anth, that's the same name," Sam said with confidence."

"How can three different names be the same person hot shot?"

"They're the same. Here's how it used to work. My name is Brogan, it's Irish right?"

"Yeah, ok, so what?"

Sam picked up one of the pencils and a piece of lined paper that was on the table and began to write.

"My dad told me our name in Ireland was O Brogain, that's the Gaelic spelling," he wrote the name out for Anthony to see. "Then the King of England made it illegal for the Irish to use their Gaelic surnames, so they had to change them, so then it was O'Brogan," again, he wrote on the paper for Anthony. "See the difference in the spelling? On their way from Ireland to the US, my Great Grandfather decided to Americanize it even more and dropped the 'O' altogether before they got off the boat. So here I am, Samuel Brogan. I bet if you can find a way to check Gaelic, that's the spelling of Tiernan. And she could have decided to just change the spelling of her first name so it looked more American too," he put down the pencil and slid the paper in front of Anthony.

Anthony had not taken his eyes off Sam; he stared at him in disbelief.

Finally, he said, "Sam, you have moments of absolute brilliance."

Sam cuffed him playfully on his head and said, "Ok so start typing again."

Anthony turned around in his seat and began keying in a string in Bing search.

In a few minutes, he found the Cambridge courthouse records. Sam pulled up another chair, and together, they began their search again, armed with new information, and a resolute will to find the woman named Annaleaigh MacTighearnain Grimmer.

The mall was packed, but a lot of it seemed to be young people who tended to congregate at the food court. With a fixed time and place to meet and everyone with cell phones, Army and Dan waved goodbye to Danni and Mindy. The girls had spied a jewelry table and found some cute costume jewelry that they purchased. There were tables with silverware, tables with dishes, tables of lace, linens, scarves and figurines. Then they found the real collectables. Many of the vendors there specialized in one or two things and prided themselves on having some unique pieces.

One man had antique candleholders of every size shape and price; another, butter churns from not just around the country, but the world. Still another had lamps from the early 20th century with ornate and beautifully crafted glass bases and shades. While Mindy was engaged with the owner of the lamp booth bargaining over the price, Danni looked around and suddenly spied on the opposite side a booth that looked to carry clocks; she loved unusual clocks and it immediately caught her eye. She signaled to Mindy where she was going and started through the crowd.

It was not one of the bigger booths, but a clock filled every available space. Presently, she was the only one there, so she took her time looking at the faces on the clocks, the different carvings, feeling the satiny wood and listening to the diverse sounds made by the pendulums and clock works. Something about the sound was soothing, almost hypnotizing. She heard a clock chiming quietly from somewhere, cutting above the other noise, a chiming such as she had never heard before, musical, haunting, and it caused her to look up and around to find the source. In the back left corner was a floor clock so incredibly beautiful that she immediately walked towards it. The wood was polished to a high sheen and appeared to be a lustrous dark walnut. Three sides had thick beveled glass and beautifully carved columns on each corner. The top of the clock had a swan neck pediment with rosettes and a finial, yet it was the dial of the clock and the pendulum that captured her attention.

The dial was gleaming brass with raised numbers and delicate letters stamped adjacent to each number between eleven and two. In the dome, above the face, was what appeared to be moving moon phases that were captivating to look at, the detail intricate. The pendulum though, had a sunset painted on it, looking across a stream, with a field of golden waving grasses phasing into a sunset. The colors of the sunset went from dusky blue to burnished red and a pale pink that faded off to a ribbon of pale blush. It was a sunset that showed the rarest of sights, the moon rising as the sun was almost finished setting. Above the painting was a plate that carried a family crest of some sort. It was mesmerizing.

Danni was not sure how long she had been standing there when she heard a man clear his throat and say, “May I help you?”

She turned to see an elderly man standing next to her. He had a kindly, weathered face and traces of white wispy hair on his mostly baldhead. His lips were relaxed in an inviting half smile. His eyes though, were like nothing she had seen before, a most uncommon shade of blue.

“Oh, hello,” she said somewhat startled. “I was just admiring this clock. It is so unusual.”

“Ah yes,” replied the old man, “that actually is one of my favorite pieces. You have good taste in clocks.”

“Actually,” said Danni looking back at the clock, “I don’t know much about them, but I’ve always wanted a floor clock and while I was looking in your booth it chimed. I’ve never heard chimes like these; it’s almost like . . . like they say a name.”

“Mmmm, that is correct. Well, that is how they were designed. These are unique and so is the story of the clock. Would you have time to hear it?”

Danni had forgotten about Mindy, or Dan or Army; this man and his clock drew her in. She needed to hear, she needed to know.

"Yes," her voice sounded very far away.

He began to tell her the history, the story of the clock, and time slowed until she was traveling back to another era, a different yet familiar place.

It was his gift. He always knew what they needed.

Mindy had been looking for Danni for a while, browsing other booths, but when she was unable to find her, she decided to call her cell phone. It bounced right into voice mail, which was odd; they had all checked their phones before splitting up earlier. She looked up into the crowd, sudden concern making a crease between her eyes. Suddenly, she spotted Danni standing outside a booth and quickly started toward her.

"Danni! I'm over here!" said Mindy waving an arm above her to signal her location. Danni looked up, smiled and waved back.

As Mindy caught up to her, she said, "Hey girl, where have you been? I have been looking all over for you and even tried to call. Do you know your phone is off?"

"I was talking to a man . . ." she turned and looked into the booth at the ticking clocks, ". . . and I guess I lost track of time. How about that, in a tent full of clocks and I lost track of time. That sounds like something Anthony and Sam would tell us."

They began to laugh at the truth in that and Mindy said, "Well, I got the price I wanted on the lamp. They're going to package it up and I can get it after lunch. Did you find something here you want?" nodding her head toward the interior of the booth.

Danni looked slightly confused for a moment then said, "Yes, I . . . I did. A floor clock. I've always wanted a floor clock for the living room."

"Really. Where is it? Let's see," she started to go into the booth, then saw the *OUT TO LUNCH* sign hanging on the front.

"Are you supposed to come back later?"

"No. He's already taken it out of his booth I think. It's going to be delivered tomorrow."

Mindy looked at Danni closely. Danni, always so confident and sure seemed slightly confused and out of it. "Hey, are you ok?"

"Yeah, sure, I'm fine."

"So how much did you pay for this clock?"

"That's the weird thing Mindy. He gave it to me."

"He *gave* it to you? Why in the name of God would he give you a floor clock? What . . . is it stuffed with drugs or something he smuggled into the country?"

"No, don't be silly. He is an elderly gentleman who said he is going out of business and the particular clock that I fell in love with is his favorite. He said he's been trying to find someone who would love and take care of it as he has. I guess that was, or is me."

Mindy just stood and stared at her, then shook her head in wonder. "I can hardly wait to hear how you explain this to Army."

"I'm not. I'm just going to wait until they deliver it and let the clock speak for itself."

"Oh brother, this is going to be good. Come on, let's go find the boys and get something to eat, I'm starving."

Danni broke into laughter, sounding once again like herself, "Mindy, when you talk like that you sound *exactly* like Sammy!"

ঔ৽ ঔ৽ ঔ৽ ঔ৽ ঔ৽ ঔ৽ ঔ৽ ঔ৽ ঔ৽ ঔ৽ ঔ৽ ঔ৽

Anthony had called his dad in the afternoon and asked him to pick them up at the library on their way home. Army had said his timing was perfect they were just leaving the mall now. It was about twenty minutes until they pulled up by the library, and the boys jumped into the back seat.

"Where's my mom and dad?" asked Sam.

"They went on home. Your mom bought a lamp, had it packed, and she didn't want to take any chances of bouncing it around.

"Dad, can Sam stay for a while this afternoon?"

"Is that ok with you Danni?"

"It's fine with me, but you need to call your mom or dad and get the ok from them," Danni replied.

Within two minutes, he had confirmation from Mindy that he indeed, could stay for the afternoon. Everyone chatted about their day as the scenery lazily moved past the windows of the Envoy, and the warm, pre-spring sunshine flooded the interior, warming everyone up and making them all feel somewhat drowsy.

When they pulled in the driveway and up to the house, Army said, "I think I'm going to have to take a nap."

"Me too," said Danni. "Between the walking, the fresh air and sunshine I feel sleepy. How about you guys, a nap and then some dinner?"

"Na, I think we're going to play some computer games. If we get tired we'll just lie down in my room," replied Anthony. As they got out of the car, Army popped the trunk and reached inside pulling out a small, old looking leather case. "What's that?" asked Anthony.

"I found an old set of stone chisels at the antique show."

He and Sam huddled around his dad, and Anthony whispered, "Does mom know?"

"Yes," Danni called back, "mom knows."

Sam piped up, "I'm kinda hungry Anth."

You could hear Danni's laughter all the way into the house.

Anthony was putting paper into the printer as Sam was getting the computer booted up. They worked without talking; such was their excitement to get back online.

Sam's information had been right on point, and they had a hit on Ancestry.com. But just as they were about to open the file, one of the library assistants had informed them that their time was up on the computer and someone else was waiting to use it. They hurriedly copied down the link and that was when Anthony had called his dad.

Anthony closed the lid to the printer and said to Sam, "Paper's loaded. Are you on yet?"

"Not quite, that's a big site and you're computer is kinda slow."

Anthony stood beside him, and then pulled over a wooden stool he had in his room and sat down. Finally, the link opened. A family tree was just that; roots, a trunk and branches, each branch with leaves. They had been able to find out that Annaleah MacTighearain was the daughter of one Michael and Olivia MacTighearain who had immigrated to this country in 1855 when Annaleah was just two years old. Her father was a pattern maker and master carpenter who specialized in clocks, her mother, a talented musician who played harp and sang. Unfortunately, her mother died of typhoid when Annaleah was only six. That was when her father moved them to Cambridge, Massachusetts, where he had found work in a pattern shop, eventually opening his own fine furniture business. They had indeed, changed their name to MacTiernan, and eventually then to Tiernan; what caused real confusion were the times Michael would occasionally use his original moniker, which was no problem in Cambridge at that time in the small Irish district where each knew the other, but caused problems down the road into the future when trying to identify him.

That was when the boys struck gold; they uncovered that Brandon Grimmer was a business partner of Michael Tiernan. They had found the link.

Their excitement building, they continued to click and scan, click and scan. Suddenly they found it, a newspaper article of the May 23, 1875 marriage of Brandon Grimmer to Annaleah Tiernan. As they read it, the part that jumped out at them read:

Following came the bride and her father. The bridal gown was a white satin princess robe, which was enhanced by the brides flowing black hair and emerald green eyes, and was flounced and draped with old point lace, and with a white satin court train. The bride's point lace veil was caught with orange blossoms and a diamond crescent. She wore a pearl collar, the gift from her father, Mr. Michael MacTiernan and a diamond bowknot, the gift of Mrs. Warren Delano, Jr. Her bouquet was of lilies of the valley.

The boys looked at each other, and then back at the computer . . . there below the article, in black and white was a picture of the bride and groom. Both leaned close the screen,

"Save the site Sam, then enlarge it," Anthony's voice was a soft whisper.

He was afraid if he spoke to loud, if he did anything wrong, it would go away and be lost to them again forever. Sam saved it under favorites opened the photo software and enlarged the picture.

They both took an audible breath and Sam said in awe, "It's her, Anth, it's her."

The two turned to stare at each other for a moment.

"Yes, it is her," Anthony said, his voice trembling slightly, "give me a sec to put in a piece of photo paper, and then we'll print it. Can you print it enlarged?"

"Yep, I think so."

Anthony, ever so carefully, leaned down, pulled out a piece of photo grade paper, and slid into the printer hopper.

"Go, Sam, it's ready."

The printer engaged and they watched as slowly the picture came out the other side. Sam pushed the keyboard out of the way and laid the picture down between them.

The silence drew out as they sat staring at the picture, and then Anthony leaned forward and put his forehead on the desk in supplication.

Sam leaned forward and kissed the picture of the woman who had saved them, their Guardian Angel, Annaleah Grimmer.

They waited until after dinner, and then asked Army to come up to Anthony's room while Danni was doing some laundry. Anthony closed the door.

"So what are you two up to?"

Anthony went to the desk and picked up the photo and before handing it to his dad, he told him how he and Sam had been trying to find some information about the woman whose name is on the gravestone.

When he was done, Army looked between both boys, "I'm sorry if I upset you guys telling you about the grave."

"No dad, you didn't upset us, that's not what this is about. We wanted to find out what we could because, well, we thought it would be nice to fix up the gravesite, you know, maybe get the stone fixed and reset and plant some flowers. We, Sam and me, we wanted to do something about her considering how much time we spend at the barn and all, right Sam?"

Sam stood there, his eyes very round and big, trying to take in all that Anthony had said,

"Yea, that's right . . . what he said," Sam responded inanely.

"Dad," continued Anthony, "we found this online and wanted to show it to you."

First, he handed him the description they found of the wedding, when Army looked up from reading it, Anthony then handed him the picture.

"We thought you would want to know what she looked like. We did."

Army stared at the picture, the look on his face indescribable; shock, surprise, disbelief and oddly a shadow of fear crossed his features. He suddenly sat down heavily on the computer chair.

"Dad," Anthony said concerned, "are you ok?"

Army continued to stare at the picture. Finally, he looked up at the boys and said, "This is the woman who helped *me* with the microfilm at the library. It's her. It's . . . her," his eyes stared straight ahead but he was not looking at anything. "How can that be?" he whispered to himself, and then looked up at the boys. "How can that be?"

"I think we just need to accept that it *is* dad and fix the grave to honor her."

Army looked into Anthony's eyes, and understood the wisdom in those words, realizing his son was no longer a boy.

CHAPTER 39

On Monday morning at nine o'clock, a truck backed up the Petrucci driveway. Two men got out, and took into the house the clock that Danni had been told she needed. Later when thinking about it, it all seemed rather dream like. She had taken a soft cloth, cleaned the glass, and lovingly polished the wood.

She found on the back of the clock, inlaid in the wood a small brass plate that said:

Crafted by Michael MacTighearnain 1875

Danni looked at the plate and ran her fingers across the lettering wondering who Michael MacTighearnain had been. To think that in 1875, with no electric tools of any kind, such an extraordinary piece had been built and that its beauty had endured all these years was a marvel to her.

She moved around to the front and opened the glass door to the dial to wipe it off, and noticed again the letters on the dial. She studied them for a moment, and then went to get a pencil and paper. First, she wrote from two to eleven.

H-G-I-A-E-L-A-N-N-A

That makes no sense she thought looking at the letters like a puzzle. Then it hit her, and she reversed the order.

A-N-N-A-L-E-A-I-G-H

A name. It's a woman's name.

She made a mental note to show Army.

Then she remembered that Army did not know about the clock. *Well I guess we'll have a lot to talk about tonight, it should be interesting.*

She had no idea at that moment how incredibly accurate that fact was going to turn out to be.

Later that evening after Danni had talked to Army regarding the clock, he had told his wife they needed to bring Anthony into the conversation. Anthony brought with him the information he and Sam had uncovered, and they were stunned by how each had been touched in some way by Annaleah Grimmer.

Danni revealed that the man at the mall had told her the history of the clock, but not the person, Annaleah.

The clock was built as a gift to his daughter in celebration of her first child. His intention had been that the clock be delivered after the birth of the baby. When his daughter and her unborn child had died in the house fire, her father, heartbroken and despondent, had closed his shop and disappeared. Since he had owned the property and building, it could not be sold until seven years had passed and he could legally be declared dead. The clock for his daughter had been sold at auction, and in an ironic twist of fate, had been purchased by Rowena, the wife of Shawn O'Farrell the former farm manager for Brandon Grimmer. Rowena had cleaned the clock and wound it by pulling the chains inside the front next to the weights. She had started the pendulum swinging, set the time and then went out to the garden. Shawn had come home early that day, waived at his wife and went into the house as Rowena took off her apron, removed her gloves and went to the kitchen to see him. Their beautiful new clock was chiming as the door closed, the sound haunting . . . that was when she saw that Shawn's face had gone ashen, and the water glass he held, frozen in space half way to his mouth.

By Shawn's hand the clock was stilled, but it remained in the O'Farrell family. Eventually, the story goes, it again went to auction and was purchased by the elderly clock collector Danni had met at the mall.

"The clock vendor told me he knew what I needed," Danni told them.

Anthony put his hand to his chest where he still wore the medallion and asked his mother what the old man looked like. He listened quietly and simply nodded his head.

They talked for a long time, putting together the pieces that had somehow touched each of them. All the pieces that is, except the fact that the ghost of Annaleah Grimmer had saved Anthony and Sam from evil incarnate. He did not think he could bear what that might do to them.

CHAPTER 40

Spring had come early that year, and it was magnificent. The blooming trees had lasted for an unusually long time; their white and pink flowers dotted the landscape and woods, and the wind carried an intoxicating fragrance of apple and cherry blossoms. Tulips, hyacinths and daffodils were thick and even the bees had come out early, hungry to drink from the sweet nectar filled delicacies that had pushed through the sleeping soil.

The weather had been ideal to restore the grave of Annaleah Grimmer and her son Devin. Danni, Army, Anthony and Sam each had ideas of how to renovate the area. Army had removed the stone, and with the mason's chisels he had purchased, cleaned up the names and dates, taking special care to make them perfect. After some research, they decided it would be appropriate to carve a Dove on the head stone; it symbolized purity, love and the Holy Spirit. Army was no artist, but when he worked on the stone, a feeling of blessing came over him and hours seemed to pass in the blink of an eye. He had sealed the sandstone with a special product that made the names prominent and the grave marker look new. Anthony and Sam had helped Army dig and pour a footer and drive two pieces of rebar into the wet cement. Adjacent holes were drilled into the bottom of the headstone so it could be permanently mounted. On the top was fitted a bracket to hold a vigil candle.

As the days warmed, rich loamy soil was purchased from the local hardware store and raked into the soil surrounding the stone. A large semi circle in the front was prepared for flowers; deep red salvia, blue begonias, geraniums and miniature roses were interspersed with dusty miller with the remaining area planted in grass.

Finally, on Saturday, May 23rd, the same day of Annaleah and Brandon's wedding all those years ago, the white vinyl picket fence and gate were completed.

Just like Annaleah, it was beautiful and gentle, a place of serenity, grace and peacefulness.

That evening from the door of the barn, Sam and Anthony watched as the sky glowed brilliant amber, until at last the sun slipped past the edge of the world and the blue-black night sky filled with stars.

They drifted off to sleep in the alcove of the barn, and as feather, soft lips brushed their brows, through the open window of the house, the clock chimes sang, *Annaleah . . . Annaleah . . . Annaleah.*